Overhead the Sun

John Ashworth

Overhead the Sun
John Ashworth

Copyright © 2008 by Adrienne Ashworth

ISBN 10: 0-9771079-9-X
ISBN 13: 978-0-9771079-9-5

Published by Chapin House Books, a division of the Florida Historical Society Press

All rights reserved under International and Pan-American Copyright Conventions. No part of this book may be reproduced in any form or by any means, electronic or mechanical, including photocopying, recording, or by any information storage and retrieval system, without permission in writing from the publisher, except by a reviewer who may quote brief passages in a review.

Chapin House Books
A division of
The Florida Historical Society Press
435 Brevard Avenue
Cocoa, FL 32922
www.fhspress.org

PUBLISHER'S PREFACE

Overhead the Sun is a period novel that graphically captures the essence of race relations in the post-Civil War period. It is a novel about the changing relationships between whites and blacks in Florida in the aftermath of emancipation, a period when both races sought desperately to establish a new social equilibrium that would govern society for decades to come. It is also a novel that documents the triumph of the institution of Jim Crow in the Sunshine State during the latter part of the Nineteenth and early Twentieth Centuries.

The Jim Crow system of segregation was based on the belief by southern whites that their former slaves were inferior—and immoral—creatures. To reinforce this belief, words were used to drive home white superiority at every turn. With each use of such words—nigger, burr head, coon, pickaninny—by whites, they conjured up stereotypes of African-Americans as sub-humans, with no rights and no likelihood of gaining any. As much as anything else, the use of derogative terms was an attempt by dominant whites to convince themselves that they had the right to continue the oppression of African-Americans.

It has become the socially correct thing to do to purge the "N" word from conversations and writings. We heartily concur with this movement. There is no reason for any enlightened or educated person to use that word in any present context—even as a sometimes reference by African-Americans to others of the same race. So, too, are terms like "honky," "peckerwood," or "redneck" denigrating and offensive to whites. Similarly, the use of words like "kike" or "greaser" is offensive to other sections of our population. They, like the "N" word, should be eliminated from our vocabularies.

When writing history or historical fiction, however, the use of such words reflects the reality of the period and not the situation today. If any reader is offended by the use of the "N" word in *Overhead the Sun*, let me hastily assure you that this is not the intention of the author or the publisher. John Ashworth has used this word to complete the depiction of an oppressed race that faced not only physical hardships on a daily basis, but equally oppressive emotional and intellectual burdens.

While there are still extremists and racists who use words such as these, thankfully the majority of Americans have rejected the ideology of racism in favor of a multi-cultural society that recognizes the value of each ethnic group, each individual and each value system.

Nick Wynne
General Editor

Victory, union, faith, identity, time,

The indissoluble compacts, riches, mystery,

Eternal progress, the kosmos, and the modern reports.

This then is life,

Here is what has come to the surface after so many throes

    and convulsions.

How curious! how real!

Underfoot the divine soil, overhead the sun.

        —Walt Whitman

1

It was just after ten o'clock on New Year's Eve in St. Vincent, and there was a ball to celebrate the opening of the magnificent new Alhambra Hotel. For two-and-one-half hours men in full dress suits and ladies in sumptuous gowns had partaken of an extraordinarily elaborate dinner. Now, some of them were dancing in the ballroom to music provided by a Hungarian band, and some were strolling in the courtyards and gardens, which exuded heady scents. A few of the four hundred and twenty-four guests were from homes in St. Vincent or neighboring counties, but many more came from a distance—New York, Washington, even Europe. All were there free of charge at the personal invitation of the great oil, railroad and hotel magnate Arthur Wilkins and his wife Laura, the famous beauty.

The subtropical evening was balmy, sensual. The ladies could go outdoors without wraps over their décolletage. Seventy-four degrees—on the last night in December! Unbelievable!

Julia Richmond Clayton didn't like to think she was being small-minded or mean-spirited, but the fact was she had mixed feelings about being there. Most of the time she found it a matchless and exciting occasion, as she was supposed to. She had never been to such a grand affair and she was dazed by her own curiosity and admiration. *The St. Vincent Chronicle* said that the dedication of the Alhambra Hotel was a historic milestone, and a harbinger of boom through the 1890s and beyond. Florida would never be the same, and everybody with get-up-and-get was going to become very rich. If the *Chronicle* was right, being at this ball was a once-in-a-lifetime experience. So why shouldn't Julia bask in the unwonted luxury and stop thinking?

Unhappily, she couldn't put entirely out of her mind who she was, and consequently that she didn't fit in. Julia lived near the wilderness town of Olustee at Richmond Plantation, which she had inherited, where for twelve years, since her father's death, (two years before her marriage to Tom) she had successfully run and was still running her naval-stores business, as well as bringing up two children who frequently went barefoot. To Julia, this opulent hotel and ball suggested lives that could never know getting up before daybreak, lighting a lamp, having cornbread and milk, and gleaning something useful from timber, animals and soil. Also, Julia shared somewhat in the suspicions, fears and animosities of businessmen she dealt with, which were born of an impoverished frontier and a Civil War-ravaged deepest South. How had this Yankee multi-millionaire Arthur Wilkins raised the money to build this hotel? Just manipulation of commercial paper? Somehow it didn't seem honorable.

Furthermore, Julia didn't know her host and hostess. She had met them for the first time, before dinner, in a receiving line with hundreds of others. She had been invited here only because of Tom, who had become construction superintendent for building Arthur Wilkins's new railroad line. From St. Vincent to the Gulf. Important to both Tom and Mr. Wilkins. But not to Julia. Ever since her marriage, her husband had been away from home almost all the time, building railroads for Mr. Wilkins.

After three years of marriage to Tom, Julia had begun to realize that she was happiest when he *was* away. Then, after observing other marriages in both Olustee and St. Vincent, she concluded that her married life was natural. Now, having become as she thought so mature and sensible, why couldn't she feel just cheerful and complacent because, as Tom's wife, she had a *right* to be at this ball regardless of the limp hands and empty ceremonial smiles of both the Wilkinses, which clearly suggested she was a nobody. Actually, in spite of the many novelties and pleasures of the evening, she constantly felt somewhat demeaned—her marriage was giving her a fraudulent identity. No doubt she was being silly to feel this way but she couldn't help it—she *did* feel this way! She'd been a fool to sit up nights cutting up and stitching a new dress for the occasion, and she was being punished for being such a fool because it turned out that the dress wasn't right at all. Most of the other ladies were gowned in all sorts of fanciful and extravagant furbelows, and they flaunted half their bosoms! Julia's dress was made of very nice purple silk, but the pattern, which she had bought in Olustee's one store, was much too simple and was high in the neck. All right! I'm a country hick! Julia thought, defiantly. Like it or lump it!

Luckily, Julia had the company of her best friend and sister-in-law, Esther Clayton Rourke, whose understanding was a sure thing. Esther had been crippled in childhood by infantile paralysis, and Julia was pushing her wheelchair. For almost as far back as she could remember, she had helped Esther to get about. In their teens they'd been roommates at Aurora Academy for Young Ladies where they'd learned Latin and Deportment, had read forbidden novels, and had mused upon the cosmopolitan universe enough to become skeptical.

Now, they roved through plush corridors, golden and mysterious in the new electric lights—"What goes on behind all these doors?"...explored courtyards where nymphs and dolphins spouted sulphurous water into steamy clouds illuminated by rainbow tints—"Mighty pretty!" ...marveled at a carved ceiling looted from a Spanish monastery—"How do you suppose Mr. Wilkins got that?"...observed an appealing upholstery—"Is that thread really gold?—Where is it sold?—It must cost over a dollar a yard!" They were most enthusiastic about the bathrooms—tiles or marble easy to clean, hot and cold running water all the time, and flush toilets!

But like Julia, Esther not only admired but also had qualms. "This is all such a big show-off," she said.

Julia laughed—"Do you feel it puts down folks like us?"

Esther didn't reply, but their intimacy with each other was such that it was clear she did feel put down. Esther was a country woman too and shared with her husband Joseph Rourke the responsibilities for running Clayton Plantation—cotton mostly. After another minute of being wheeled she asked, "What was that meat they gave us for dinner? Venison? Rattlesnake?"

"It was so gussied up I couldn't tell."

"Well, it was interesting, but for every day I'd rather have hog meat and greens." Esther knew that Julia could appreciate being obstinately rural, old Florida family, as worthy as the next folks, especially rich Yankees.

They were at loose ends, having a good time whether they praised or damned. Their men were having brandy and cigars—Esther's husband Joseph with some local business and professional men in the billiard room, and in the exclusive Renaissance Room Julia's husband Tom with their host, the magnate Arthur Wilkins, and the guest of honor, the President of the United States.

Esther said that she hated to agree with *The St. Vincent Chronicle* about anything, but she had to admit that the ball *was* a historic milestone and harbinger of boom. But she also declared that historic milestones and harbingers of booms were exhausting and she would like to go to the room reserved for her and Joseph. She would have to rest if she was going to tolerate the President's address just before midnight, and if she expected to stay awake during the collation after midnight.

Well, why not rest up? Julia didn't need to rest, but she was agreeable.

The door to the room reserved for the Rourkes was locked, and Esther handed her key to Julia.

While Julia opened the door and groped inside for the ceramic cylinder with the knob for turning on the electric lights, and while she was beginning to comment on how wonderful it was not to need matches, she was aware of a rustle and thought she could see a movement of shadowy forms. "Oh!" she exclaimed. The rustle and movement made it like going into her own dark kitchen with a lamp and seeing a mouse, a coon, a snake.

With her left hand Julia pushed the wheelchair with Esther, and with her right hand she finally found the knob for the light. Then the room became yellow and dim, revealing a scene which brought a hot flush to Julia's face. A man and a woman were sitting up in the rumpled bed, and they held goblets of red wine at exactly the same angle as though they were about to sip. The white sheet was drawn up to their waists, above which they were naked.

The woman's long dark hair streamed over her smooth shoulders and her rosy nipples stood out. "My goodness!" she cried. She thrust her wine onto a small table beside the bed, spilling a little, and then slid under the sheet. Did Julia know the woman? Maybe—maybe not. There was no similarity between what she saw in that second and what she might have seen in the ballroom swathed in multiple fabrics, with hair primped and pinned and perhaps crowned with a hat like a bushel basket.

The man had long yellow hair and bushy yellow mustache, and the hair on his chest matched the hair on his head. He looked lanky and Norse. Julia thought she could smell him—he was like drying hay.

"Why, Thorstein Brach!" Esther exclaimed. "You *do* astonish me!"

Was Julia saying anything or just breathing hard? Was this reality or an unmentionable dream? It must be reality because Esther knew the man's name.

The man's hand holding the goblet of red wine remained at exactly the same angle. In his calm immobility there was a suggestion that in this room provided for the Rourkes, Esther and Julia were the intruders, not he and the woman. If Esther and Julia left, the woman would pop up from under the sheet, retrieve her wine, and both goblets would continue in upward motion to lips dry from much kissing and therefore thirsting for the tang of fermented grape. Julia could imagine it.

"Well, Esther, we are *both* astonished," he said—he had an accent, Northern and vaguely foreign. "The Wilkinses didn't give me a room, and our need for yours was urgent."

"Was it indeed?"

The dubious tone of Esther's "was-it-indeed" added to the confusion in Julia's mind and senses. Was Esther shaming him, expressing outrage, or just joking because of their mutual astonishment?

Whatever the intent of Esther's "was-it-indeed," the man didn't find it necessary to respond. "Can't you introduce me to your companion, Esther?" he requested. His large eyes were as placid and innocent as those of a cow being milked.

Esther made a choking sound. "Well, Thorstein—"

"In spite of the unusual circumstances," he added.

Unusual? Julia thought. Shocking, daft! And the madness was compounded by Esther's doing what he asked. "Oh very well," she said, in an irritated tone. "Julia, this is Professor Thorstein Brach, who teaches at Rowland College and often visits Joseph and me. Oh, I've told you about him."

Indeed she had and been very enthusiastic and complimentary about his ideas and his book, never saying anything about the kind of behavior now witnessed.

Esther concluded, "And Thorstein, this is Mrs. Julia Clayton."

"How do you do, Mrs. Clayton."

Julia couldn't speak.

"I can see you're very embarrassed, Mrs. Clayton, and I'm sorry about that," he said. "I've admired you from a distance. With all the conspicuous waste in this hotel, and especially in the clothes and gewgaws of the ladies, you stand out in your purple dress because it's simple and classical, sort of Greek—the color is right for your cornsilk hair and well, in short, it's beautiful on you." He wasn't smiling. He seemed sober, thoughtful, and completely unselfconscious about his exposed body, which was golden in the dim light. Complimenting her in this quiet way while another woman, naked and trembling beside him under the sheet, must be hearing what he was saying—well, what could be said?

"How can you—" Julia began and then couldn't go on.

Esther became brisk—"Look, Thorstein, I *do* mind that you're using my room, and my bed, but I also believe in live and let live. Julia and I can go to her room, which I hope won't be occupied."

"Thank you, Esther. You're the sole person in this benighted hole who could say that."

So Julia wheeled Esther to the room reserved for her and Tom, and on the way she recovered her power of speech—"The gall of the man! How could you be so nice to him?"

"Was I really nice? Well, I like the man—"

"Like?"

"Why not? Talking with Thorstein feeds my spirit, and he's Joseph's closest friend."

Julia respected the intelligence and judgment of Esther's husband Joseph Rourke, and if he liked the naked man who had borrowed his room and bed in this spectacular and pretentious hotel—well, who was she that she should pass judgment? For the moment she had nothing to say. When she reached her room—mercifully unoccupied—Esther heaved herself from her wheelchair and swung on her crutches so that she could sprawl on the white bedspread, and as Julia poured some cold water into the basin on the washstand so that she could wet a washcloth and soothe her flushed face, Esther went on about Thorstein Brach's belief that marriage was fatuous make-believe concealing men's coercive ownership of women.

Julia became sarcastic—"So he thinks up a clever excuse for going to bed with some other man's wife!" She didn't know that the unidentified woman under the sheet was another man's wife, but the assumption was strangely satisfying.

Esther changed the subject—"You should read his book, *The Tumefaction of Property*."

"Tumefaction?"

"Swelling up like a tumor, becoming diseased."

"Property becomes diseased?"

"Well, property can become like a tumor and make people diseased." Esther became testy. "Read his book, Julia. You always used to read *everything*!"

"I *still* read everything I can get my hands on—"

While Julia's thoughts and feelings sputtered like a brushfire, Esther continued about Thorstein Brach: "He's straightforward about what he believes, and I'm sure he was honest with that woman under the sheet, whoever she is. I imagine he can be very sweet to a woman."

"Sweet? Oh dear!"

"*Definitely* sweet!" Esther chuckled and then told how Thorstein had been dropped from the faculty at Yale University after scandals that could be hushed up until the wife of another professor dedicated to him a volume of poetry that exulted about flesh opening like a bud in sunlight. Cast out of the prestigious academic establishment, Thorstein was now reduced to a professorship at little Rowland College in St. Vincent, where in addition to teaching he had to live in a dormitory for young men and see to it that they behaved. "Imagine—Thorstein Brach telling young men how to behave!" Esther gave a throaty chortle.

A crust over Julia's deeper feelings crumbled: "Oh yes, Esther, I *can* imagine—him being cool and sure of himself and wide-eyed like my big old dog when I scold him, and in all seriousness telling young men to be in their dormitory rooms by nine o'clock and to stay away from colored women. Oh dear yes, I can imagine! And in your room, Esther, during this ever-so-grand ball—" and Julia broke down in uncontrollable laughter, collapsing in an easy chair, her tears running.

Esther laughed with her but said, "My land! Thorstein's not so funny as all that, is he? Goodness, Julia, why are you so wrought up?"

But Esther's bewilderment merely added to Julia's inability to control herself. Finally, she wiped her streaming eyes with the washcloth and was able to gasp, "This is even crazier than anything we ever saw or did when we were at the academy!" But she knew this did not explain why she couldn't control her laughter. The real reason was a puzzle.

Esther went to sleep on the white bedspread for more than an hour and awoke greatly refreshed. Julia slumped in the easy chair or silently paced the spongy carpet and remained all keyed up. Then they washed, redid their hair, smoothed their dresses, and, with Julia pushing the wheelchair again, went to the vast and exotic Eldorado Ballroom for the President's address.

They found their husbands in a noisy crowd.

Thomas Ewell Clayton said nothing but crooked his right arm, which Julia took. Formally correct, but how distant they'd become! She felt she was being worn for appearance like the gold stud in his starched and billowing shirt. That naked man and woman in Esther's hotel room were not so distant! Then she burned with guilt for having this thought — she really was proud of her distinguished husband! Yet, appearing suddenly in the swarm around her, he was like a stranger in a dream.

Joseph Rourke took over wheeling Esther and began a lively report on conversation among the men in the billiard room, which had to do with how sleepy St. Vincent was before the enterprising Arthur Wilkins came with his railroad and hotel, and how now there was a plenitude of money-making opportunities.

Tom made comments, cool and barely polite.

Joseph's dress suit was too large for him and he seemed more thin and stringy than ever. He had shaved but not well so that there was a little black growth on cheeks and chin. Once, Julia had strolled with him through the vegetable garden at Clayton Plantation and heard the story of his life. He'd come to America from Ireland when he was fifteen years old. His father had been killed in a fall from a scaffold and his mother had died from tuberculosis. He'd been a bricklayer, a carpenter, and a hobo. He'd appeared at Clayton Plantation looking for work, had done it so capably he'd been asked to stay, had become foreman and finally Esther's husband. The community summed it up — "Too bad Esther Clayton got hit with that polio — she's lucky to have any man at all and that Joseph Rourke do seem a gentle sort, but have to say he ain't what a Clayton woman would have got if she'd had her health." Any hint at such an opinion angered Julia.

Esther kept interrupting whatever Tom said. Most of the time she and Tom didn't get along.

Julia tried to butt in but wasn't good at it. It was always distressing to be with Esther and Tom at the same time. Esther had introduced Julia, her academy roommate, to Tom. After a romantic but efficient courtship and the wedding, it had turned out that Esther felt miserable and guilty for having brought them together.

So Julia was happy that the vexing conversation of Esther, Tom and Joseph was broken off by the entrance of the President, who was preceded by six bulky Secret Service men and followed by Arthur Wilkins and the two wives.

A pattering of applause swelled to a roar, with men shouting hoorahs. The Hungarian band struck up a military air. At a liturgical pace the President and magnate and their wives strolled across the glassy floor, through a furrow that opened before them between receding waves of chiffon and silk with garnitures of ribbons and flounces, into the fecund air of the subtropical night scented with perfume and sweat, to the foot of the dais occupied by the band. With the applause always mounting, with the band lingering on long brassy chords, they climbed steps first to the dais and then to an even higher platform on the dais.

The President was like a picture in Julia's *Stories from the Bible*—sobriety, dignity and resignation in his face, and his beard would have been right for Moses. His brow was exceptionally broad and high, and it swelled in a smooth curve which phrenologists regarded as an indication of exceptional intelligence.

The President's wife was a tiny gray-haired lady with a much-admired air of delicate gaiety.

The railroad, oil and hotel magnate Arthur Wilkins, was tall, very straight and distinguished looking. His bearing suggested control of aggression, and his face was red.

But Julia and almost everyone else gazed mainly at Mrs. Wilkins, their hostess. Her oval face with enormous blue eyes had a natural upward tilt as she turned slowly toward one side of the ballroom and then the other, a slight smile on her rather full lips, which even at a little distance were a remarkable violet-red. Her great crown of auburn hair was adorned with a tiara of pearls and diamonds.

With her figure, she should not stand up so high to be looked at, thought Julia. She was conscious of the contrast with her own slender body, which had made her so good at games with the young ladies at Aurora Academy, and which was healthy enough, thank goodness, so that she rarely thought about it. But she did think now that her figure would never mesmerize a whole ballroom as Mrs. Wilkins's did.

And Mrs. Wilkins's dress! A far cry from Julia's. *Not* simple, classical and sort of Greek, as Mr. Brach noticed even from his state *in flagrante delicto*. No, Mrs. Wilkins's gown was Babylonian—white satin with pleated panels of pale green silk edged with gold embroidery in which pearls were set. There was a collar of diamonds around her throat and drooping down her half-naked bosom, which was so white and lucent in contrast with her brilliant auburn hair as to take on complementary greenish tints. Every flicker of expression on her face, and the barely perceptible inclinations of her form in acknowledging applause, which she was assuming was for herself as well as the President, showed a pride that blazed beyond Julia's comprehension.

The band stopped playing, and Mrs. Wilkins made an indolent command with her fan, all the time smiling with the withdrawn and static superiority of a monarch.

Immediate silence.

"My dear friends," said Mrs. Wilkins, her voice was rich as a cello, "how happy I am that I can present to you the first lady of our land"

Thunderous applause.

The President's wife smiled daintily and bowed.

Mr. Wilkins spoke. For several seconds nobody heard him. Then—"... a few words. Ladies and gentlemen, the President of the United States!"

"Hoorah... hoorah... hoorah!"

The band played. Applause went on and on.

The President looked this way and that. "Thank you, my friends... thank you... thank you..." At last he held up his hand, quieting everybody, and with a schooled eloquence talked about inexhaustible resources, rural virtues, and how his heart was touched when he visited the land of the pine and live oak and palm.

Julia and Esther shared looks which expressed their contempt for this political guff. During the War Between the States, the President had been a brigadier general with Sherman, he was the honored guest of the Yankee magnate Arthur Wilkins, and he was obviously trying to establish common ground with former Confederates among the guests. But some of the President's words, Julia thought, might possibly come out of honest feeling. He said, "During the darkest days of the war, I was frequently comforted by the reflection that in nature there is no life except the seed be cast into the earth and die. From this I received assurance that in our national life the sad time of death would yield its fruits in a purer, higher and surer mode of existence." Julia thought of the modest prosperity of the plantation she had inherited, of its isolation, of the doubtful security of her children and the black people who worked and lived there, of the violence of the Klan in neighboring counties. Could she share the President's apparent confidence in a purer, higher and surer mode of existence?

Then she happened to notice that Mrs. Wilkins had the rapt look of a person listening to music and that Tom, along with almost everybody else, was looking at her, not at the President, who was now being humorous. "When, after peace came, and I resumed my law practice in Indianapolis, I was visited by a gentleman known, I expect, to all of you—" the President smiled, Mr. Wilkins grinned, and there was a patter of applause—"who came to me about a collection claim but was more interested in talking about Florida than anything else—"

A belch of laughter—"Hoorah!"

"What do you think of her?" Julia asked Tom.

He didn't reply.

"... I wish he'd paid my fee in St. Vincent town lots—"

"Haw haw haw..."

"... our host presented to me a young man, only about thirty I believe, the boss of some two thousand men working on the new railroad to Pay-hokee-on-the-Gulf, a gentleman who embodies the golden promise in this fairest of states—"

People looked at Tom and applauded. Julia felt a blush of pride in the President's accolade—along with more obscure sentiments—and then reasoned that she was *entitled* to feel pride as reparation for her cool and intermittent marriage. She *was* Tom's wife—he was hers just as she was his.

The queenly Mrs. Wilkins was looking at Tom with an extraordinary kind of interest. With contemptuous disregard for what her guests might think of her behavior, she gazed at him for minutes, her great eyes dawdling with sensual delight and unwavering arrogance as she took in his massive proportions. And while the President mentioned the eight billions of dollars that since the war had been received in the South for cotton, and the further billions that would flow for turpentine and oranges and beef and railroads, and while he singled out Mr. Thomas Clayton as representative of those who were destined to become new conquistadores of enterprise and progress, Laura Wilkins's lips parted with unrestrained pleasure.

Tom smiled back and bowed.

"Have you been talking to *Mrs.* Wilkins along with Mr. Wilkins and the President?" Julia asked.

Her husband patted her arm.

The President next launched into a peroration concerning the ladies he and Mrs. Harrison had had the great happiness to meet—goddesses of the household, angels of Florida's homes. During the cannonading cheers he waved his hand and then ignored the common guests to accept the congratulations of a selected or especially aggressive few.

Tom seized Julia's elbow in his huge hand and steered her up the steps to the platform.

As the President brushed her hand she said, "I'm glad you like it here in Florida."

He probably didn't hear her.

A wizened old man was assuring the President of his support. Apparently the President knew for what.

People on the floor of the ballroom were still clapping, and Arthur Wilkins gesticulated violently at a gilded clock. Its tinkling chimes could barely be heard. Midnight!

"Happy New Year!"

The guests shook hands, hugged each other—men, men and women, women—and bawled cheers. Servants distributed papier-mâché revolvers that rocketed streamers of colored paper in the air. These looped over invisible wires that crisscrossed the ballroom, and soon there was a forest of bright tissue which tore from time to time, held all persons in a bright and gay net, and made little drifts which they had to kick out of the way as they moved about.

The Hungarian band struck up *The Star Spangled Banner*. Everybody except three or four irreconcilable Confederates stood at attention, and some people sang. Then, in a more spritely mode, the band played *Dixie*.

In the group around the President, one gentleman proclaimed that it was the happiest New Year he'd ever seen or hoped to see, and so far forgot the polite society he was in, which provided special rooms for nasty male habits, that he lit a cigar.

Mrs. Wilkins made a face—"Oh pee-oo!"

Tom was prompt—"Sir, your weed is offending Mrs. Wilkins."

The man said, "Sorry, Mrs. Wilkins," and crushed the thing out in a potted palm.

Julia had a spiteful thought—Tom had defended Mrs. Wilkins, not her. But then, she hadn't made a face.

She spotted Esther and Joseph's friend Thorstein Brach, scarcely recognizable in a dress suit, standing at the edge of the crowd on the floor of the ballroom. He looked very bright, and Julia had to smile. He reminded her of a hunting dog that has discovered an intriguing scent.

Turmoil.

Most of the guests surged toward the hotel's main dining room for the collation. A select few headed for the relatively small Ponce de Leon

Room. Tom and Julia were among those few because Tom was such an important asset for Mr. Wilkins and because the President regarded him as a kind of symbol of the New South. But why were Esther and Joseph included?

Esther had an explanation—"Arthur Wilkins wants to buy our timber, and he wants to dazzle us before making a low offer."

Joseph joked. "Keep your best eye peeled, sister," he said to Julia. "You're among Yankees."

Julia laughed. This was Joseph's kind of irony. He regarded himself as a Yankee and jokingly just as unscrupulously shrewd as Arthur Wilkins! But she was surprised. Nobody—not Esther, Joseph or Tom—had told her about any Wilkins interest in Clayton Plantation timber.

"We have to talk about that, Joseph," Tom said.

Julia was annoyed. That timber was none of Tom's business. Clayton Plantation had been willed to Esther, not Tom. His persistent attempts to become involved in its management belittled both Esther and Joseph.

"It's this way," said Joseph—"any talk you have will be done with Esther as well as me."

"This is a matter for men."

"For men is it now, just for men!"

Esther spoke to Tom—"I know what you're going to say to Joe, and I can tell you right now we're not interested."

"What's this all about, Esther?" Julia demanded.

"Let's not talk about it now. It's painful."

They'd arrived in the Ponce de Leon Room. Joseph helped Esther into her chair at the table, and he stowed the wheelchair and her crutches against a wall.

With the imperious guidance of the radiant Mrs. Wilkins they were all seated: the President and his wife; the governor of Indiana and his wife; a visiting English viscountess, Mary Burleigh; the captain of Kaiser Wilhelm's cruiser *Moltke,* on a friendly visit in St. Vincent harbor; the Claytons; the Rourkes; and of course the host and hostess themselves—Mr. Arthur Wilkins and Mrs. Laura Wilkins. Twelve people—after the hullabaloo in the ballroom, very quiet and intimate.

Arthur Wilkins hailed his young construction boss—"Tom, why don't you go into the ice business in Payhokee? The fish are practically free. Just get a few niggers to dip them out of the Gulf. All a man needs to clean up is ice."

"Useful idea," the President commented.

"I suspect Mr. Clayton has more ambitious plans," said Mrs. Wilkins.

A strong white wine was served with the red snapper, and Arthur Wilkins, while drinking some, failed to notice his wife's remark. "There's nothing like trains," he said abruptly, his speech somewhat slurred. Was he just a little drunk?

The President chuckled.

Then the magnate repeated his statement belligerently, daring any fool who might have sneaked into the Ponce de Leon Room to contradict him. Since no fool showed himself, he repeated the words a third time, his voice clanging like a gong.

Now that the select few at the table were looking at him expectantly, he declared, "When I travel across the country, I sit on the observation platform of my train and I must say I don't believe there's a better way of seeing how the common people live." He paused, grimacing.

What's he so scared of? Julia wondered. Then she reflected that after all, as she had read in the *Chronicle*, Mr. Wilkins had been a poor boy.

He went on—"I look into the backyards—I look at a clothesline with a wash on it, and I can tell at a glance from the kind of wash I see on a line what kind of town it is I'm passing through. I think now there's a family with a good woman, and where you find a good woman you can find a good man. Of course sometimes you can find a good man where there *isn't* a good woman. But where there *is* a good woman there's almost *certain* to be a good man. If I were setting up a textile mill, or a foundry, or even a little plant to manufacture ice, and were out hiring help, I could go through the backyards on a Monday washday and get the *best* help. And if I had my say I'd go into the yards where the sheets *weren't* white and I'd say to the woman of the house I'd say, 'My good woman, your sloppiness, your slovenliness, your slipshoddiness has just lost your husband the golden opportunity of his life.' And I'd tell that woman straight out that she ought to take that wash in off the line and do it over. And if she wouldn't take it in, and if I had my say, I'd put her in a room with plenty of soap and water and by God she wouldn't come out until those sheets were *white!*" After a meaningful glance at his resplendent wife, he attacked the snapper.

"That is all ridiculous," Mrs. Wilkins said.

"Oh, there's something to it," said the President, laughing.

Mrs. Wilkins persisted—"Arthur has been seeing himself making everybody do exactly what he wants—yes, *exactly*—ever since Tom Clayton sent packing all those Swedes who went on strike somewhere out in some swamp—"

The President's wife tried to joke—"The way young wives talk today!"

Mrs. Wilkins became airy—"Oh, I don't object to what Arthur wants to do, but can he do it?"

"Mister-r-r Wilkins," said Joseph Rourke, with a lilt in his natural brogue, "you'll have to give folks jobs so those women hanging out washings in their backyards can make their sheets white. Then they can afford to use soap more liberally."

Who cared to listen? Who was Joseph Rourke anyway, and what was he doing in that select company? The President's wife was whispering to the President, and Viscountess Mary Burleigh was laughing at something the captain of the *Moltke* had said.

Then Tom spoke, and everybody listened to him. "That's right, Joseph," he said, "Don't sell."

"Sell? Sell what?" demanded the President.

"Three thousand acres of virgin yellow pine."

"Who wants to buy it?"

"I don't." Tom winked at Arthur Wilkins.

The magnate didn't respond. He was twirling the stem of his empty wineglass, gazing at it without blinking, his thoughts apparently elsewhere.

"This talk of buying and selling is neither here nor there," Joseph went on. "I'm speaking of washings. My mother did her own washings. Other people's too."

There was more than an undercurrent of hostility in his populism.

The viscountess said to the captain, "It is only in America we find this kind of boor—"

Perhaps the German captain didn't understand her. He responded in such a complicated and roundabout way that it was hard for Julia, listening, to know what he was getting at. It had to do with oil and beef from South America.

"Respectable people do their own washings," Joseph was declaring.

The governor of Indiana seemed to be the only one at the table more interested in Joseph than in the captain of the *Moltke*. Had he mistakenly judged Joseph to be a clever operator, a man who knew his way around in

Florida, a fellow who'd risen from the laboring class to become the owner of three thousand acres of virgin yellow pine? "Mr. Rourke," he asked, "what do *you* see as the best investment opportunities here in Florida?"

Joseph cocked his head on one upraised finger in clownish miming of profound thought.

Julia and Esther laughed. They shared a certain disenchantment. On coming into the Ponce de Leon Room, they had expected percipience, possibly enlightenment, at least wit. And at Aurora Academy they had learned in Deportment class that polite people don't interrupt, and that in a small group it's absolutely impermissible to have conversations about different subjects going on at once. How should one react to this rudeness, this fatuousness, this confusion? Perhaps Joseph, clowning, had the right idea!

The President was ignoring Joseph and staring at the captain of the *Moltke*. "Captain," he said, sternly, "perhaps in the spirit of this happy occasion you can perceive the determination of the rulers of this country to fill our markets with all that this great nation of sixty-five million people needs. Furthermore, we will reach out to other markets and enter into competition with the world for them."

Arthur Wilkins was aroused—"Splendid, Mr. President!"

The captain drank his wine.

Joseph was now irrepressible. Bypassing the President's pronouncement, and the rare respectful attention it commanded, he said, "Anyway, give credit where credit is due. Mr. Wilkins worked hard, saved his money, and got ahead—"

He apparently touched a nerve in Laura Wilkins, who had not contributed to the babel. "Let *me* tell you how my husband got ahead," she said. "It is quite different from what you believe, Mr. Rourke. He has oil wells in Oklahoma. He has never seen them. Did he work? Well, he talked with some men and signed some papers. Is that work?"

Julia wondered what she was getting at. Was she putting down Mr. Wilkins? But he just smiled indulgently.

Mrs. Wilkins took no notice of her husband. "The men who really did the work had a good drink after they finished the job and went somewhere else. Take his hotels. The thousands of carpenters, masons, plumbers, electricians—they did the work. And when they are living on the county or their children, or dying in some gutter, the hotels they built will still be paying for Arthur's private train and his bad taste in art. Work hard and save money indeed! Those men worked hard. The niggers working for Mr. Clayton on the new railroad line are working hard now. It's true none of them had or have much money to save. They go to their graves without saving money. The work of dead men pays my husband, who does *no* work! Oh my dear Mr. Rourke, you don't see the world as it is, at all!"

There was no longer any glint of amusement in Joseph's dark face. Laura Wilkins had been too dense to grasp his irony, but she had expressed what he believed. Julia understood him. And she knew that Esther shared her own surprise at what Laura Wilkins in these words had shown about herself. There had been no hint of this as she had exhibited herself in the ballroom. Julia recalled hearing that this empress, now glittering with diamonds, had once been a nurse in Boston, Massachusetts.

"Your economic doctrine is very harsh, Mrs. Wilkins," said the President.

Tom laughed.

Laura Wilkins smiled at him—"What are your ideas about getting ahead, Tom?"

To Julia, the use of her husband's first name seemed predatory.

"I'm a construction boss," rumbled Tom. "Main thing for me is to get folks to do what I want. There are people like mules and people like monkeys and people like oxen…"

Laura Wilkins gave a rapturous bellow—"Now we're getting somewhere!"

Tom joined her with a great roar that seemed to begin in the cage of his pelvis and roll out between his big teeth. Along with Mrs. Wilkins's howl, this made a startling animal cacophony—"Some people you have to give a whack, some you have to throw a banana, and with some you have to put an iron ring in their noses and give them a good yank whichever way you want them to git."

"Oh!" Laura cried in ecstasy, as though these homespun words were an imperishable paean to the spirit in her own heart. And with her cry, which was like the summons of a bugle, she rose to her feet. "To this great man—this wonderful man—this superb man with the God-given soul to rule…" She snatched her wineglass and raised it—"To the great builder of the mainline to the Gulf—to Tom Clayton: good health and happy days!" With her left arm flung out in a gesture that bade the guests to rise and at the same time bestowed a kind of blessing on the construction superintendent, she touched her glass to her lips.

The shock was general.

Julia thought: Even I, Tom's wife, would not have presumed to call him builder of the mainline to the Gulf. Surely, Arthur Wilkins, the president and chairman of the board of the Pamlico and Gulf Corporation, and the man who had hired Tom, must be credited with that. She herself would never have made such a mistaken claim for Tom, would never have flaunted such admiration. But she felt unsure of herself. After all, she was glimpsing the realm of power and great wealth for the first time. Was it due to her own ignorance that she found it muddleheaded and freakish? Yet, Mrs. Wilkins's toast did seem the ultimate madness of a mad night in a mad world.

In silence, the empress stood like an image for several seconds, draining her glass.

What was one to do?

The President coughed into his napkin.

Arthur Wilkins finally pushed back his chair and stood up. He smiled, intending without much success to appear magnanimous and generous. Raising his own glass, he muttered, "Good for you, Tom. I join in that."

John Ashworth

II

South and west from St. Vincent the workers toiled with mules and dragscrapers; with axes, pick-pointed plows and spades; with hammer, crowbar and wrench—lifting the ties and rails; in gangs, heaving the bridge timbers in place—twelve or more hours a day, from can't see to can't see, so that the railroad unrolled through the cut-over barrens, breaching dark walls of virgin timber, through wintry-gray cypress swamps and over black creeks, at the rate of seven miles a day.

Most of the workers were blacks, about half free labor and half chain gang, rented for the job from the sovereign state of Florida at $12.50 a month per head. Foremen and overseers were all white and all wore holsters with Colts or Smith & Wessons. Guards with rifles kept eye on the chain gangs, and of course they were paid by the state.

The majority of workers were graders who dug drainage ditches through wet country and piled up earth to form a bed for the track. Down the finished roadbed mules dragged a great pile driver and precut bridge timbers, which "bridge monkeys" raised and bolted.

Every morning, including Sundays, in the pitch dark before daybreak, the construction engine pushed to the end of the finished track flatcars loaded with the proper proportion of rails, half-pound spikes, angle irons, angle-bar splices, and tools. From more gondolas behind the engine the workers eased themselves to the ground and shuffled into gangs. Bosses dropped from three cabooses. One would squint at the pale eastern sky, note the amount of light on the roadbed, already covered with ties around the next bend, casually remark, "All right, men," and the day's work began.

Four ironmen seized a rail on each side, ran forward until the rear end could be placed between the loose angle-bar splices of the preceding rail, dropped it in place, and returned for another. These men were limited to thirty seconds a rail. Another gang aligned the steel, roughly set it to gauge by half-driving eight spikes, and placed bolts in the splices. A boss checked the alignment and if necessary ordered the rail forced into its exactly right position. Still another gang drove home the half-driven eight spikes and then put in the rest with an average of three blows of the sledge to each spike. If a man with a sledge often made more than three swings, the bosses had orders from Tom Clayton to yank him off the job and put him to work grading, at six dollars a week instead of ten. The grading was bossed by white men who happened to live along the right of way. It was widely believed by both black and white that some of these bosses were as ready to blow out a black man's brains as look at him. (Mr. Clayton didn't like talk to this effect and pointed out that it had happened only once.) Last came the surfacing gang, which spread ballast and tamped around the ties.

Some bosses kept watches in their hands most of the time. "Hump to it!... Shake a leg!... Get the lead out of your jeans!" Some cursed a lot. Others were pious men who never cursed, but without warning fired a worker if he wasn't quick enough.

At the end of the day the construction train backed up to camp in the dark, the workers lying exhausted, many asleep, on the bare planks of the flats. But the Pamlico and Gulf Railroad Corporation had pork-meat ready for them, which some bosses declared was a downright and shameful waste. Every man counted the days to the First of April, when the line was supposed to be completed in fulfillment of a contract between the Pamlico and Gulf and the state of Florida, when the workers themselves expected the line would be completed, when they would collect their last pay, and this particular spasm of terrible toil would come to an end.

Thomas Ewell Clayton, the marshal of this cataclysm, was then thirty-two years old, having been born two years before the War Between the States. His father, Captain Merion C. Clayton of the Confederate Army, owned a cotton plantation and thirty-six slaves. His mother, the daughter of a St. Vincent merchant, had died of fever following the birth of Esther just before the War. So Tom couldn't remember his mother.

His earliest memories had to do with helping the overseer left in charge of cotton production during Captain Clayton's absence. He recalled giving orders. He'd had a slight lisp until he was about seven and instead of saying "hump to it," he'd said "humth to it." But it didn't matter because a slave always did.

The year after the War, Tom was sent to school in St. Vincent. A big and sturdy boy, he rode the twenty-three miles on horseback and stayed in the teacher's house three nights a week. This teacher was the widow of a Confederate soldier killed in a skirmish with Sherman's men in Georgia. She had no children of her own, never scolded, and could bewitch a dozen pupils into doing their numbers accurately and into ascertaining the meaning of words on a printed page. Her talent was respected. At age ten Tom began to take over some of the teaching. By this time he was driving a buggy on weekly trips to St. Vincent, taking Esther along.

The year he turned fourteen, several events changed his life. Esther got polio and remained at home for more than a year in the care of a doctor and Piney, the black nurse who had cared for both Tom and Esther during their infancy. She was called Piney because she was very tall and possibly because of an awesome seriousness in her character. Tom wouldn't have anything to do with Piney after he was six, but Esther and Piney remained close.

After Esther became agile on crutches, she went away to Aurora Academy. So she no longer needed to be driven in the buggy to school in St. Vincent. Also, the respected teacher was urging Tom's advancement to higher learning, Latin and law. But Tom was not so inclined.

And that happened to be the year of the national economic depression. The wholesale price of cotton declined about fifty percent. Merion Clayton blamed the family's hardship on costs rather than price. It wasn't like the old days and he now had to pay black folks—men, women, and you might say even children—who crawled on hands and knees in the long rows, dragging bags into which they stuffed the bolls. Merion drank too much and became active in the Klan, beating or just scaring colored folks who tried to leave their duties or otherwise became "uppity." Tom occasionally rode with the Klan, too. He was respected and admired, but he secretly despised most of the men in the Klan. He saw hysterical cowardice in the epidemic of hatred. But he learned to be sociable and apparently outspoken while concealing his critical assessments, which he realized would not be understood anyway. He felt more and more that he was unique, special among humans—that he was alone in a world of warring irrationalities.

A few prostitutes in St. Vincent became routine, and he likened his relationship with them to the problems of cotton production on the Clayton Plantation. No wild physical gratification could obscure his conviction that cost and price were fundamental in human affairs.

At this time he was so tall, broad and muscular that strangers guessed he was about twenty. Leaving school and becoming free of his pathetic father, he got a job in Jackson County bossing a crew to improve a road between Olustee and St. Vincent. He knew this road better than anyone because of his trips to school. It was an important road. The products of a poor countryside had to move over it—sawed lumber, oranges, sweet potatoes, cotton from Clayton Plantation, and turpentine and pitch from Richmond Plantation. Wagons were miring in mud holes. A horse fell in a swamp and had to be shot. A road that was passable in all weathers was needed, and Tom was credited with providing it. He became known as the most up-and-coming young man in Jackson County.

When he was eighteen he became involved with an indiscreet wife of a St. Vincent commission merchant who threatened to shoot him. Tom's father was still able, in spite of his alcoholic haze, to appraise public opinion in such matters, and it was clear that this shooting, if it happened, would be condoned. Justice and morality must be served even at the sacrifice of a capable road builder. So Merion C. Clayton gave his son one hundred dollars as a birthday present and suggested he enjoy himself at the 1876 Centennial Exposition in Philadelphia.

Tom went. The experience crystallized a conviction in Tom that almost all people lived with dreams of what-should-be so that they couldn't see what-was. No wonder most people never got ahead! What-should-be was the singing "darkies" in the cotton exhibit. Tom knew what-was — the sullen blacks at Clayton Plantation still waiting for last year's wages and kept by the Klan's whips from departing for parts unknown. What-should-be was the picturesque Indian exhibit — neat wigwam, wax image of meek squaw with papoose and so on. Tom read in the papers about what-was — the killing of General George A. Custer and his troopers by Sioux warriors led by Crazy Horse and Sitting Bull. What-should-be was displayed in a power loom supervised by a genial but primly dressed lady. But further north, in a city called Fall River in the state of Massachusetts, textile workers had been on strike for some time. How could the owner of the mill be such a fool that he couldn't get together a Klan to teach workers what-was? The answer was obvious — he himself was thinking too much about what-should-be.

After a couple of days Tom was bored by the Exposition and found it more interesting to chat with Republican politicians in a saloon near the Philadelphia city hall. It was easy to be genial and appear to admire these men in order to gain their confidence. Their attitudes were even more fraught with meaning than their information. They appreciated the ambassador to England for the tidy little fortune he'd acquired by giving his name to a prospectus of a worked-out Utah mine in which English investors lost millions. They esteemed the Secretary of War for kickbacks from an Indian trader he'd appointed. They positively venerated the

Speaker of the House because he got a land grant for the railroad in which he owned stock. They debated feverishly the involvement of the President's personal secretary in a ring that managed to rob the government of millions in internal revenue. Just how was this done? Two men would have come to blows over the answer if Tom hadn't separated them and made them shake hands. The stories went on and on, with occasional convincing mastery of detail, with invariable enthusiasm for the enterprise under discussion and with much whiskey. Faces writhed and burned with envy. Laughter compensated for despair that ordinary political hacks, which they might or might not suspect they were, could never do so well.

Tom met one man who never laughed—Grotius Van Bibber, a Dutchman stopping in Philadelphia to recruit men for his industrial services organization. He had a contract with Arthur Wilkins, who was then in the petroleum business—wells, mills and refineries. Tom got a job breaking a strike at one of the Wilkins mills. He made good by shooting a leading striker.

So it came about that he got the attention of Arthur Wilkins, who hired him away from Van Bibber. For the next ten years Tom managed subdivisions of men, materials and equipment for building railroads. He broke three strikes. He gained a reputation for frightening calm. It was known that on a few occasions, without showing any temper at all, he had struck men in the face with a hand gloved in hard leather and had broken noses and jaws.

Wilkins thought highly of Tom's ability. He kept raising his salary, gave him overall supervision of building a short line in the Carolinas, and finally made him top boss for construction of the Pamlico and Gulf's main line across Florida.

Meanwhile, when Tom was twenty, his father had died. The obituary in *The St. Vincent Chronicle* attributed his "untimely passing to the Great Beyond" to a war wound. Tom knew he had drunk himself to death. Merion C. Clayton willed the plantation to Esther, explaining in an ingratiation from beyond the grave that his son Thomas didn't need it because he was eminently successful as a construction boss and his daughter Esther did need it because of her infirmity, which made it unlikely she'd ever have a husband to look after her. Merion's will was a sensation for a while. Who ever heard of willing a big property to a daughter instead of a son, no matter what the circumstances? Tom wouldn't talk about it.

The following year, when he was twenty-one, he'd married. He'd chosen Julia Richmond, who'd inherited Richmond Plantation, which was conveniently near the Clayton place. Its business in naval stores brought in a good cash income while the price of Clayton Plantation's cotton declined from over a dollar a pound to about twenty cents. And he kept a home base in Jackson County in spite of his father's will.

Tom saw that people regarded marriage even more than most other aspects of life in terms of what-should-be, with little or no heed to what-was. Women were especially stupid. But this stupidity itself was a fact to be recognized and dealt with. He figured out the sources of Julia's modest self-satisfactions and made the most of them—"You are one smart little lady, Julia, and I heard tell and I do believe they really appreciated you at Aurora Academy and they had to be blind, deaf and dumb if they didn't I swear!" He was delicate in referring to her skill and apparent gratification in running Richmond Plantation, now that both of her parents had passed away—"You'd enjoy your home even more if you had a loving husband." He found out from Esther that the girls at Aurora Academy had admired Julia's excellence in games—races, wheelbarrow, sack race, and horseshoes. "You're a lot more graceful than a deer—look, I'll race you to the bridge." When they finished in a tie, he kissed her for the first time, and she had to sit down on a log. That seemed a good moment for a romantic outburst, a histrionic indulgence in what-should-be—"I love you by God I do—everything about you—your bright blue eyes, your long wavy hair, your slender form prettier than I don't know what..."

All rivals stayed away from Richmond Plantation after Tom showed his interest. So he was the only man around anyway. Was she content? Or in the confusion of her virginity did she think about whether she was content or not? They were married just after her eighteenth birthday. A second cousin had to come all the way from North Carolina to give her away. On their wedding night she became more talkative with him than ever before and confessed she had terrifying dreams—the sun would become so scorching hot the trees would wither... the house would blaze up... she'd grow a shell like a turtle's and have to stay under it without ever poking out her head so that she wouldn't burn up. He was solicitous and tender. After all, she was just his and not some whore he shared with every Tom, Dick, and Harry.

During the first year or so of their marriage, he felt that he got genuine satisfaction and real profit out of Julia. Unlike other women he'd "had," she was smart and she was a virgin. But this state of mind soon passed. He had another kind of passion.

All in all, Thomas Ewell Clayton had the right experience, a brain as good as any adding machine, and a quality in his nature not only beyond comprehension by ordinary folks but preferably left that way. A man had to take off his hat to the sound business judgment of Arthur Wilkins in appointing him top boss for building the main line to the Gulf.

On February 20, a month and eight days before the line was supposed to be completed, in compliance with a contract between the Pamlico and Gulf and the state of Florida, the grading was almost completed, but track was still being laid almost a hundred miles from Payhokee-on-the-Gulf. It was a pleasant cool day, and Tom was observing the track laying. He wore a split-tailed fawn-colored riding coat with a velvet collar, English boots, and a broad-brimmed Stetson hat. His curly beard was auburn like his hair so that his face was framed in a tawny mane, like a lion's. His whole coloring—the coppery red-brown and auburn of his skin and hair, along with the tropical aquamarine of his eyes, in which there was a yellow glint—suggested some exotic jungle beast. His appearance beside the work gangs made men turn their heads, but they found it best not to take much time in looking at him.

He drew from his waistcoat pocket a large gold watch—an act which always stimulated record-breaking vim. This watch was famous. It had belonged to Merion C. Clayton, who acquired it on a raid early in the war. It was as large as the palm of a lady's hand, was adorned with figures in relief of near-naked women blowing horns, had a cover that sprang open when the stem was pressed and a second hand that moved with clicks. When Mr. Clayton was next to a crew and opened this watch, it was certain that he was checking the pace of the work with that second hand. Faces of bosses became taut, and some sweated. As for the black men toting rails, swinging sledges, holding spikes, dumping and spreading and tamping ballast—well, they either didn't notice or took some small pleasure in pretending not to notice.

On this particular morning of February 20, Mr. Clayton checked with his watch for only a few minutes before putting it back in his pocket. A horse was galloping toward the crews on the level path, only a foot or so wide, between the finished track and the embankment of the roadbed. It was reckless because a wrong step on the protruding end of a tie could have broken the horse's leg and possibly the horseman's neck, or a fall over the embankment could have landed both in the drainage ditch. But there was no wrong step. The rider was Sanford W. Payne, and Mr. Clayton called him his right-hand man even though all he seemed to do was go about in towns near the construction and listen to talk. He didn't talk much himself, and behind his back the bosses of the crews called him Gray Man. He was the only man around beside Mr. Clayton who dressed elegantly. He always wore clean and pressed gray suits, gray hat, gray boots, and a white shirt with a gray tie. The saddle on his fierce stallion and the scabbard for his rifle were made of gray leather, and even his smooth-shaven boyish face had a gray pallor.

As he rode next to Mr. Clayton, his stallion was steaming, but Sanford Payne himself was casual and gentlemanly and icy as he might have been hanging around in the billiard room of the Alhambra Hotel in St. Vincent, or in Amos Whitaker's saloon in Olustee. His report was brief and was delivered in a drawling mumble—"White trash shooting at niggers in Myrtle."

Myrtle meant a lot to the Pamlico and Gulf Corporation, to Thomas Clayton, and to almost everyone in that part of Florida. This community of black people, only about a mile-and-a-half from the center of Olustee, had been founded in 1865 when Joshua Washington Dale arrived with a squad of Sherman's troopers to enforce a field order giving land to former slaves. All through the years when the courts or the Klan had taken back land so given or taken, the blacks in Myrtle had retained possession, worked enough to keep body and soul together, and developed skills. Some were carpenters or blacksmiths. All grew some kind of crop.

Most of the best men in Pamlico and Gulf's crew came from Myrtle. Sanford Payne didn't have to waste words with Thomas Clayton explaining that the workers from Myrtle had to stay on the job in order to complete the line on schedule, that shooting in Myrtle could provoke an intolerable work stoppage. It could cost the Pamlico and Gulf a lot of money. It was insulting to Thomas Clayton.

And why was anybody shooting at Myrtle blacks at this particular time? Nobody had shot at Myrtle blacks for many years. Why now?

Mr. Clayton whistled and waved at a boy who was holding his horse. "We'll have to see about this, won't we, Sanford," he said.

It wasn't necessary to have more conversation.

He heaved his huge body into the saddle as though he didn't weigh anything at all, and they both galloped on the narrow path in the direction from which Sanford Payne had just come—toward Myrtle and Olustee. Now they both risked broken legs for their horses and being thrown. But they seemed to know just what they were doing.

*

The sun was low when nine riders thundered in front of the one store on the principal street in Olustee.

Joshua Washington Dale, the proprietor, went out on the front porch. A new road stretched from directly in front of his store to the Pamlico and Gulf's new cross-state main line to a half-finished loading platform, and to Myrtle on the other side of the newly-laid track. Dust was still settling on the road, hedged in by the tall bare trunks of pines that had died after being gouged too much for turpentine or pitch. The riders must have come from that direction.

Most of them were skinny and ragged, but they had guns which looked as though they could be used. One man was small, fat, and had a face almost as white as flour, with pink eyes. His jeans were filthy and his jacket was torn, but his broad-brimmed black hat was new. "You Joshua Washington Dale?" he shouted.

The man was a little drunk, and he spoke with the hint of a sneer. Almost everybody in that part of Florida knew about Joshua Washington Dale, and their attitudes differed.

Joshua bristled—"Yes, I am Joshua Washington Dale and this is my store and this is my town. Where you from?"

The man had his own question—"You know the whereabouts of a nigger named Charley, Charley Williams?"

"Don't know any nigger by that name."

"Got away from Wehadke Farm. We come from Hamilton County to take him back."

The Wehadke Farm was a prison, and a few of its inmates had been rented to the Pamlico and Gulf. One escaped black man should not require such a large posse, and Joshua was suspicious.

"Where'd you get them horses?" he demanded. Good, well-fed and curry-combed horses—not for this gang! He looked them over, and he felt certain he knew the meaning of the way they looked at him. Three or four had the kind of smiles that apologized for existence, while the rest showed the kind of torpor that precluded knowing enough to apologize for existence. Joshua made strong judgments. His own existence had sometimes depended upon strong judgments. As the fat man hesitated, Joshua went on with harsh sarcasm, "Them horses. Too good for you and your friends. Did you steal 'em?"

"You got no call to say that," said the fat man. "There's some can lend good horses for a good reason—"

Joshua said, "You want to take some man back to Wehadke Farm you better see Leroy McIlvey. He's marshal here." Joshua pointed—"Third house on the left."

Flour-face drew a bottle of store liquor from a pocket in his jacket. And how did he come by store liquor? He took a swig. It was a way of disregarding Joshua's recommendation.

Joshua tried again—"If I was you I'd see McIlvey."

"But I ain't you." The fat man threw the empty bottle on the sandy ground so that it bounced against the porch.

Some of the skinny ones laughed.

Flour-face gave a hoarse bellow—"I'm half rattlesnake, half catamount, and got a little bear in me. Hain't killed and skinned and et a nigger in more'n a week and I'm wastin' away! Look ou-ou-out for me!" He drew his revolver and fired in the air.

"Yee-ee-ow!"

Then they all rode sharing a jug, some firing in the air, toward the north side of the town. Calculating from the direction of their shouts and howls, Joshua figured they were stopping at Amos Whitaker's saloon.

In February, 1890, Joshua was fifty-six years old, a small hard man able to heave a hundredweight keg of nails to his shoulder in one motion, owner of a store that at prices generally conceded to be fair supplied almost everybody within ten miles. His store was appreciated, but his point of view often distressed people or made them wonder. It was a complicated point of view.

Could episodes in his life explain it?

He came from a family of early settlers in the Tennessee mountains, a restless young man who tried his hand at lumbering, carpentry, blacksmithing, and even at reading law for a few weeks. He married out of passionate love when he was nineteen and within a few months his wife Joanna bore a healthy son. Like most of the mountain people, the Dales were for the Union; and as some of the mountain people were *not*, they were against slavery. The Dale cabin was on the edge of rolling or flat country where there were large farms worked by slaves. So the Dales were located right at the great divide that brought on the War. When a neighbor was burned out by secessionists, Joshua was among those who shot two of the guilty party and hanged a third. Then the Dale place was attacked while Joshua, his wife and son were visiting in Asheville, North Carolina. His father and mother were shot, and a brother was hanged after being cut up.

When Abraham Lincoln called for volunteers, Joshua joined up. Joanna and the boy, then aged seven, went to stay with her parents in Torrington, Connecticut.

Probably because Joshua was then twenty-seven as well as quick and smart, he almost immediately became an officer, at first lieutenant and then captain. And since he was a mountain man with experience in dealing with diverse viewpoints toward the Union, slavery, and the value of human life, he was put in command of a cavalry detachment that scouted and skirmished. He went with Sherman on the March to the Sea, and when the main body of Sherman's army turned north toward the Carolinas, Joshua's troopers went south, taking emancipation with them. In a wild celebration the slaves at Clayton Plantation were freed.

So it was that Joshua found Olustee. In one way it was like the Tennessee country in which he'd grown up—it was located where slavery met the frontier, where there were both secessionists and Unionists. For Joshua, delivered from the years of bloodshed, the black river with its slow current insinuated peace, and the whirr in the tops of the lofty pines was like the intake of breath before a hymn.

He became the agent in Olustee of the Freedman's Bureau, the Federal agency charged—indecisively, ineffectively—with providing former slaves with protection, medical services, land, and schools. Joshua's work was not at all what he expected and hoped. His only lasting accomplishment was the schoolhouse in Myrtle. He himself nailed on the last siding after being fired from the Bureau over a difference of opinion with his supervisor.

Joanna came from Connecticut. Their son, now aged thirteen and in poor health, remained with grandparents and near a presumably competent physician. Joanna liked Olustee, too, and kept anticipating that their son would become well enough to join them. They opened the store, raised pigs and chickens, cultivated a garden, and planted orange trees which froze. The great cause in which Joshua had lost parents, brother, and many comrades-in-arms became a banked fire.

Behind the counter in the store, hanging on the wall between shelves of merchandise, was a large clock. Joshua was so accustomed to it that its brassy tick and gong on the hours and half-hours were like sounds from nature, the chittering of insects or calls of birds. He took pains to keep this clock in good running order and on correct time. It was a service to customers. A man could set his watch by this clock.

It was nine minutes after five when the gang from Hamilton County showed up. At five twenty-eight they rode past the store again, silently this time, taking the road out of town.

The rear door of the store opened on a back porch where Joshua could unlock stock after carting it from St. Vincent. Across this porch was their kitchen, where Joanna was peeling a turnip.

"Well, they've gone," he said.

"Who were they do you suppose?" she asked.

"All I know is their excuse for being here warn't believable and their horses was too good for them."

Joanna was deliberate and cheerful—"Good riddance then."

"One forty-six on the clock I heard six shots over near Myrtle. First I thought somebody hunting. Then I couldn't figure anybody shooting six times."

Joanna stopped peeling and gave him a direct look—"Something peculiar going on, no doubt about that."

"I locked up the store," he said. "I'm going to Amos Whitaker and see if he knows anything. I figure they stopped at his place while they were here."

Whitaker's saloon was like a small barn separate from the Whitaker house, where room and board could be had. There were three men inside.

"Good evening, Josh," said the proprietor. He had lighted his lamps, and his red face was rigid with controlled emotion, as though he were carved in cherrywood.

"Hello, Amos," said Joshua, and with slightly cool formality added, "Good evening to you, Mr. Clayton." During his first year in Olustee, Joshua had suspected but was never certain that Merion C. Clayton had once tried to bushwhack him. But whether he had or hadn't shouldn't determine his feeling about Merion's son, Thomas!

"Good evening, Mr. Dale," said Clayton, holding out his huge hand.

Joshua hesitated for the briefest of moments before taking this great paw, which had surprisingly soft skin and amazingly hard flesh. He'd read in *The St. Vincent Chronicle* about the President's praise for this young Florida man at the ball in the new Alhambra Hotel, and being thick with high muckety-mucks aroused Joshua's suspicion. Also, Clayton's clothes were offensive. The golden-brown, split-tailed riding coat asserted superiority to men who worked with their hands. But Joshua immediately reproached himself for his hesitation and suspicion. Tom Clayton had bossed bringing the railroad to Olustee—a good thing! And his wife Julia was Joshua's best customer. Anyway, he'd come to Whitaker's saloon to inquire about the trash from Hamilton County.

"I'm glad you happened to come by just now," rumbled Clayton in an unusually pleasant and melodious bass voice. "I hope you'll join us in a julep."

Julep! Nobody drank juleps. Did anybody who came into Whitaker's saloon drink juleps? Could Amos make a julep?

"Thank you kindly," said Joshua. He eyed the third man.

From a pitcher, Amos poured a julep for Joshua.

The third man was medium in height, slight, and beardless. The sallow face under the gray hat was expressionless, without movement, as though modeled in milky clay. His gray suit and white shirt with gray string tie were dandified.

"Mr. Sanford Payne, Mr. Joshua Dale," said Clayton, pleasant but formal.

Sanford Payne! Joshua had heard of him but had never seen him before. He'd be damned in Hell before he'd shake the hand of this gentleman! Wanted for murder in two Western states and the killer of three blacks since coming to Florida. Joshua thumped both hands on the bar and gave Payne a nod.

Gray Man gave no sign at all of greeting or recognition. He sipped his julep.

Clayton passed over the failure of his introduction. "Did you see those fellas just rode out of town?" he asked Joshua.

"Yes, they went right by my store."

"They come from Hamilton County, and their object was to stir trouble in Myrtle."

"I heard them talk. So this don't surprise me, Mr. Clayton."

"You saw them enough to know what kind of men they are?"

"Yes."

"Most of the grown-up nigger men in Myrtle work for the railroad."

"Earning ten silver dollars a week, I understand."

"That's only for them can help in laying track."

"Well, I'm happy to see the colored folks get ahead—" Joshua said this somewhat defiantly.

Clayton remained calm—did he share Joshua's sentiment? "For the time being," he said, "I'm responsible for the colored folks in Myrtle."

"Long as we don't let the niggers be responsible for themselves, we have to be responsible for them. Oughtn't to be that way but it is."

Clayton smiled. He wasn't going to discuss what-should-be. "You were a Union man, Mr. Dale."

"From the cradle."

"My father was Confederate. But I don't hold with keeping up old arguments."

"Neither do I, unless the reason for the argument persists."

"I hope we can agree the Myrtle niggers ought not to be bullied."

"We can."

"To keep that from happening, I fired a shot and sent that white trash back where they came from."

"You did?" Joshua grinned. Such behavior in a son of the old South, a militant act in support of what should have followed emancipation but generally did not, was for the former Sherman trooper and agent of the Freedmen's Bureau a regular hallelujah. "Mr. Clayton, by God Mr. Clayton, I sure am glad to hear this!"

"And I'm glad you feel this way, Mr. Dale. You're an influential man in this town—"

"I don't know about that—"

"I swear you are, Mr. Dale. Joseph Rourke speaks very highly of you, and my brother-in-law is a very principled man."

"Well, Joseph Rourke—" Joshua began.

"And my wife too. You know, sometimes I think it ain't right for me to work so much for the Pamlico and Gulf and be away from home so much, leaving too much responsibility for my naval-stores business in Julia's hands. It ain't what a lady ought to be doing, and I realize you and Mrs. Dale lighten it as much as you can."

"Always glad to help Mrs. Clayton."

"And I do appreciate it. You are more influential than you realize, Mr. Dale."

"No, my influence don't amount to much."

"I want folks here to understand I didn't shoot to disturb the peace. I did it to keep the peace."

"That ain't hard to understand."

"I can't prove that fella Bascomb Good from Hamilton County intended to break the peace. But he did. Sanford Payne and I have information—because of our connection with the railroad."

"Nobody's going to ask you to prove anything, Mr. Clayton."

"I'm right grateful to you for saying that because Sanford and me ain't in a position to say how we got this information." Clayton turned to the saloon keeper and continued without pause—"Amos, I hope you'll give my regards again to Mrs. Whitaker and tell her from me she serves the finest breakfast in Jackson County."

Joshua was puzzled. Had Clayton spent the previous night in the Whitakers' boarding house, even though his own home was only about five miles away?

Clayton was smiling—"Did I say *Jackson County*? Mrs. Whitaker serves the finest breakfast in the whole southeastern United States, from down in the black swamps to up where the red clay begins."

In the light of a lantern on the front porch of the saloon, Joshua saw that a colored man who worked for Amos Whitaker was holding a horse. This must have been arranged *before* Clayton fired his useful shot. He'd managed his encounter with the white trash on a schedule, expediently, as a natural part of a working day.

After glancing at the horse Clayton went on, "And Amos, I feel real bad about having to drive your customers away, even if they ain't the kind you want or ordinarily have. So I'll consider it a friendly favor if you let me pay for whatever they might have drunk up." In a ceremony of courtesy he stacked ten silver dollars on the bar.

"It ain't necessary, Mr. Clayton," Amos protested. "Seeing it my way, you did me a favor."

"Let's see it my way, Amos. Thank Mrs. Whitaker again for her hospitality. Tonight I'll go home. Seems it ought to be peaceful." He turned to Payne. "Sanford, I'd like a word with you—outside." Then he turned back to Joshua. "Goodbye, Mr. Dale." He held out his hand.

This time, Joshua took it without hesitation.

Sanford Payne said nothing, didn't look at either Joshua or Amos, and followed his boss out.

For a minute or so, Joshua and Amos were silent. Through a window and open door they could see the two Pamlico and Gulf men confer, until Clayton mounted and rode off, and Payne strolled toward Whitaker's house.

Amos said, "Payne is going back to his room. Probably tired. Last night they didn't come in till early morning."

"Where were they?" Joshua asked.

"I don't know."

"Of course it ain't none of my business."

The saloonkeeper went to the front door and closed it. "Won't be anybody else in here this evening."

"What happened here, Amos?"

"Those bullies from Hamilton County were shooting in the air and hollering for me to open up. So I did."

"When something like this comes along, you and me ought to send for the marshal."

"Another time I would."

"Let's hope there ain't another time."

"Clayton and Payne came in calm, dignified," Whitaker continued. "They used the back door. Before he said a word, Tom Clayton pulled out his gun and aimed at the drink that feller Bascomb Good was holding. It was only then he said, easy as you please, 'Good evening, Amos.' What was I supposed to do? 'Good evening, Mr. Clayton,' I said. Bascomb put his drink down like it was red- hot and Clayton fired through the place where it just was. The bullet went through the door and out in the road and didn't do no damage. 'I ain't wearing a gun!' Bascomb yelled. It's true he wasn't. There it is, over in the corner where he left it. Then Mr. Clayton said a few words. He said that Sanford Payne was a fastidious man and was hard put not to plant a bullet in Mr. Good's drooping guts, just because Mr. Good disgusted him. A lot of men would rather die than take what he said. What it amounted to was if Mr. Good said a single word or did the least thing except get on his borrowed horse and go back to Hamilton County, as sure as death comes to every man Sanford Payne would kill him. So Bascomb Good did exactly what he was told."

"How did Clayton know the name of this feller Bascomb Good?"

"I don't know but he did."

"What was Bascomb's gang doing while Clayton was dressing him down?"

"Nothing. When they was following Bascomb out, Mr. Clayton said, 'Hold it, men.' Then he said they might get jobs working for the Pamlico and Gulf if they showed up at the new freight office in Payhokee-on-the-Gulf the week after April First."

"I have to admit I'm astonished by all this."

"So am I, Joshua."

"I never expected to see a son of old Merion C. Clayton taking on the nigger-haters."

"Just because a man's father was a Confederate don't mean he's a nigger-hater."

"Well, it ain't right to prejudge a man."

"A man who pays niggers ten silver dollars a week is no nigger-hater, is he now?"

"Wouldn't seem so."

"But I want to give you my honest opinion, Joshua — a wage like that for niggers can ruin the South."

"You and me disagree about that, Amos. Anyway, I'm glad to see that Thomas Clayton is a reasonable man, and damned decisive too. Now, take Sanford Payne — *there's* a nigger-hater for you!"

"No doubt about that."

"What's he do?"

"I don't ask. He always has money."

"Why did that trash come here? The question keeps coming up in my head. It bothers me."

"There's nothing to worry about, Joshua. I better put away this gun Bascomb Good left behind. Mr. Clayton would want me to do that."

III

Julia knew that the night was going to be very cold. The sun set in vivid splashes of red and gold, and the cloudless pale blue sky directly overhead seemed to be higher than usual. No leaf stirred in the live oaks, and no bird sang. In the still thin air the voices of two women carried from far off beyond the shed for storing the barrels of rosin and turpentine. Even before the last red faded, Julia could see a bright star over the glassy black water of the Olustee River. She wrapped herself in a woolen shawl and went to question her oldest workman, who said, "That star say it going to freeze."

This meant an extra chore. Fat pine, sticky with pitch, had to be arranged among the nine orange trees her father had planted. Saving them became a festivity, a spree. At Richmond Plantation, turpentine, rosin and pitch meant labor, which one did without too much complaint because God told Adam he'd gain his bread by the sweat of his brow until he returned to the ground from which he came. But nobody labored for oranges. For years and years all that was carted away from Richmond Plantation was naval stores. No room on the carts for oranges. So everybody on the place ate the oranges from the few trees they had. Men, women and children ate them—especially the children. Who would take the time to pick oranges except to eat them?

Julia had only to repeat that it was going to freeze and lanterns swayed through the dark woods. Logs and stumps were dragged forth with much chatter, grunts and wheezes of effort. Next to the pigpen a tree dead but still sappy fell with a crash. Logs were crisscrossed, stumps piled up. A little kerosene was dashed over four heaps. Flames flickered, roared, and then a warming and protective smudge curled around the fruit.

Burning chunks of wood rolled out of the bonfires, and Julia used a shovel to toss them back. She gloried in saving the oranges. The time was too short when she could become more than just the boss lady who worked with the books and who went out two or three times a day to the sheds or the still to give this or that instruction. Now, a Richmond Plantation tradition took over. One man would feed the fires until midnight by the kitchen clock, another until dawn. While they were about it, they would also keep fires going in the kitchen and in the parlor stove, already glowing behind the mica in its door, so that heat could rise through grates to the bedrooms above, where Caroline and William were already asleep, or pretending to be asleep. Lucy, the young woman who had just begun to work as Julia's only house servant, would sleep on a cot in the kitchen instead of in the cabin with her parents and get up from time to time to provide the stokers with coffee, ham, eggs, and cornbread. Everyone was beginning to share in the first go-round of these victuals.

Even when Julia was a small girl, she knew she was especially favored, that her home was a singular and wondrous place, an Eden cherished by God, unlike other dwellings, forlorn and ramshackle among the endless pines, where people suffered during bad weather, didn't have enough to eat, and often feared violent neighbors. There was a happy loneliness in Richmond Plantation. Julia's father called it the world's secret diamond. It was fortunate even during the War, when naval stores were supplied first for Confederate blockade runners and then, after soldiers in blue occupied St. Vincent, far more profitably for the Union navy. The very land of Richmond Plantation was cut off from the rest of the world by its location in a sweeping oxbow of the Olustee River. Tom had appreciated this and when they were first married and he still had a little interest in selling naval stores, he had posted a sign next to the bridge over a swamp where the bends of the river nearly met—RICHMOND PLANTATION Go to Big House and State Business or KEEP OUT.

For three generations the Richmonds had gone out from their refuge in the oxbow to an alien world, and because of the steady profits in their business had brought back whatever heart, soul or body in all good conscience desired, either for themselves or for the three fortunate families of freedmen who worked for them. The carts that rolled to St. Vincent about once a month, heavy with barrels of naval stores, didn't have to bring back much. The plantation produced its own corn, pork, beef, fruits and vegetables. And every Sunday there was fishing in the river.

Julia hadn't seen her husband since New Year's Day. She'd gone to the railroad yard in St. Vincent to see him aboard the private train of Arthur

Wilkins, for a short trip to the end of the new track toward Payhokee-on-the-Gulf. A whole train just for Tom! It seemed as though the honors and privileges heaped on him were endless! Was having such a husband, and preening herself with pride on this account, a just compensation for giving him the Eden she'd inherited, along with her body, which had borne Caroline and William? A shabby question! She felt ashamed for thinking of it. Was marriage an occasion for barter, for dickering, for precise calculation of what one should get and what one had to give? She spent restless nights, not sleeping well, telling herself that she hadn't dickered — she'd given Tom her heart, too, along with her property and body. At the same time she found out for the first time in her life what a headache was. This matter of just compensation in her marriage kept coming to mind, willy-nilly, ever since that New Year's Eve ball in the Alhambra Hotel. She couldn't forget how Mrs. Wilkins had looked at Tom during the ceremony in the Eldorado Ballroom and how she'd toasted him in the Ponce de Leon Room, and she wished Arthur Wilkins had chosen to build his railroad in Alaska. She felt low. She was jealous of Laura Wilkins — no doubt about that! — and at the same time she was so obsequiously spellbound that her envy and bitterness turned to milk and water. Why couldn't she have risen from the table with a curse and thrown wine in the smug and hee-hawing faces of both this famous beauty and Tom — and if the President and the great magnate didn't like such behavior during their exclusive collation, let them lump it! An enjoyable fantasy for a moment but ultimately frustrating. Why couldn't she ever do such a thing? Must she live in a perpetual cringe?

Every Sunday after church, with Tom away, Julia went alone for dinner with Esther and Joseph. Esther had insisted on it. Thorstein Brach would come, too. He was a good horseman and rode out almost every weekend. Julia must put out of her mind any embarrassment she felt because of the way they met in Esther's hotel bedroom. She needed Thorstein's heresies to take her mind off the naval-stores business — to get some intellectual stimulation, fresh ideas.

In spite of Esther's behest about embarrassment, Julia felt herself blush on seeing him again, now dressed in warm jacket and pants of a cloth almost as stiff as canvas.

But Mr. Brach seemed relaxed. He inquired about her husband and children — "Yes, Esther's told me about Caroline and William — " and then, when she became evasive about Tom and tongue-tied about the children, he talked about himself—his childhood in Norway, his parents' farm in Illinois, how he'd become a professor because farm work required men with talent and capacity for hard work to which he could never aspire. He grinned with oversized teeth and smelled like his horse.

At the dinner table, a mixture of irony and seriousness baffled her. The others spoke very fast and invented little dramas:

Joseph: And now, Senator, how about that appropriations bill?

Thorstein: Yes yes, Governor, for dredging the Olustee River, I presume.

Joseph: That's what I am referring to.

Thorstein: It's in committee, old boy—

Joseph: Time is money, Senator.

Esther: Senator, I hope you do appreciate that folks living on the banks of the Olustee River are counting on you.

Thorstein: Rest assured, dear lady—

Joseph: Instead of bringing naval stores to the ships, it would be a convenience and good profit for one and all to bring the ships to the naval stores.

Esther: Isn't that so, Mrs. Clayton?

Julia (not yet wholly in the game): But the Olustee River could never be made deep and wide enough for ships.

Joseph: Who said that?

Thorstein: Do not put the lady out of this-here meeting. I see that she is a victim of that nattering negativism that erodes our national confidence and saps the energy of the purest society that God ever permitted.

Julia (catching on): Oh dear, I will never do such a thing as that, Senator! Dredge away!

After dinner, Esther required a nap, Joseph and Thorstein talked about national politics, and Julia mostly just listened.

On the third weekend, Esther gave up her nap, and as the afternoon was warm they all sat outdoors. Among the four of them, a feeling of lucky and precious intimacy had grown. A miracle of chance: two farm women on the Florida frontier with a man who had come from Ireland, and another who had come from Norway. What could one make of this? They talked about this a little, couldn't make anything of it, and gave up. Another bizarre happenstance: Julia's uncanny ability in Latin which, as Esther explained, had given her great distinction at Aurora Academy. So Julia had to tell how she'd fallen in love with Virgil—*The Georgics*, with an eye for rural life reminding her of home—and then *The Aeneid*, with its ordered fate for the hero, structured to inevitability in every polished line and syllable of imperious language, affirming that life was *not* puzzling, mixed-up, and bursting with agonies of indecision. Not a bit of it! Life was what Julia could recite, line after musical line, dancing among some oleander bushes next to the big house of Clayton Plantation, swishing her plain cotton skirt, chanting the sonorous Latin in ecstasy, drugged—then breaking off abruptly, aware that even the extraordinarily well-educated Thorstein Brach didn't understand a word of what she was saying. And dancing before him, just making unintelligible sounds, a silly pedant, showing off, freakish! "I don't know what's got into me," she apologized, sitting down. "It's just that I do find something very satisfying in my Latin, and I teach it to William."

Esther was clearly disconcerted by Julia's behavior and tried to explain it away—"Even when we were young and silly at the academy we realized there was something very odd about young ladies like us learning our Virgil while back near home the Klan were beating and shooting and hanging. And a lot of folks, white along with black, couldn't get enough to eat and some of the niggers were running away to live with the Seminoles or skattering north or west or God-knows-where."

"It *was* odd and it's *still* odd. I guess *I'm* odd," said Julia.

Thorstein laughed—"Your Latin is no great sin, Julia."

He was using her given name for the first time. She was moved and grateful but a little mistrustful. Was he trying to be particularly nice to her because he knew she felt she'd made a fool of herself?

Then—did he know what she was thinking?—he added, "I guess we four are odd. Why do we enjoy each other so much? Why do we talk as we do? Why are we pleased with going down roads that seem to lead nowhere?"

On another Sunday afternoon, Thorstein lured her into talking about Richmond Plantation's naval-stores business. Laughing, she explained that she really liked double-entry bookkeeping because it made everything seem very orderly whether it was or not. He caught her hands, which she was waving to underscore her point, and he gave them an encouraging squeeze.

And she rattled on like a wound-up music box. She had numbers for everything—the cost of a new copper worm and galvanized tank for distilling the turpentine, tools for the cooperage shed, nails per pound, salaries for the workers in the three families permanently employed, advances on loan to other people, single or in families out in the forest, who were willing to take work one season at a time bleeding anywhere from ten to fifty acres of trees. Losses had to be figured for people who took loans and then skipped out. The marshal in Olustee sometimes chased such runaways but never caught any, thank goodness! Nobody should get hurt, either the marshal or the runaway, just to save Richmond Plantation a little money! And what happened to Richmond Plantation's products? Tar and pitch were still real naval stores and were used in caulking boats. But more for roofing. Turpentine and rosin went for varnish and paint. And what about the money?

Thorstein did some calculating—he knew about other naval-stores operations. The factor in St. Vincent was rich—he had a big brick house, five servants, a stable with six horses, three carriages. Then Thorstein went into the profits of the paint and varnish business—he had figures for that! He summed up—"More and more of the money goes to people who spend a smaller and smaller number of hours to earn, say, a hundred dollars. Less and less of the money goes to people who produce the tar and pitch and turpentine and then have to work more and more hours to earn a hundred dollars. I surmise that our friend Julia works more and more hours."

He looked at her with a bright and expectant expression.

She stammered that perhaps she did and shrugged.

"Oh Julia," he said—he had a way of prolonging the pronunciation of her name which seemed affectionate, "you are very very wonderful!"

She had to turn away from Thorstein, from Esther and Joseph too, so that they wouldn't see her eyes moisten.

During weekdays she thought about Thorstein during intervals between this-or-that task, and especially before going to sleep in her bed. She had to define what he was to her—a true man friend, one who liked her anyway in spite of her being silly about her Latin and really appreciated her practical hard work in her naval-stores business. This sound definition of what Thorstein was to her made it possible for her to think of him even more, without feeling that she was doing what she oughtn't.

Was it merely coincidental that she began to think about Tom in a new way? She and Tom were so different in how they dealt with their own natures. He was perfectly satisfied with his own past, with himself, and she wasn't satisfied at all with her own past, or with herself as she was at present. She'd been foolish to think she should marry Tom to have a capable man look after Richmond Plantation and its dependent families. She was doing quite well by herself. Thorstein was sure she was! Worse, far worse, she'd lied to herself that the fire in her body was love. Was her soul crippled, like poor Esther's legs? And how about that fire in Tom? For years she hadn't permitted herself to think that Tom's overpowering lust was anything but love. Now she did not repress the certain knowledge of what went on during the long periods he was away—in the Carolinas, in St. Vincent, in New York, Philadelphia...Besides loose women were there special haughty and rich women like Laura Wilkins? From reading her Bible between the lines, she'd always suspected Abraham of being bad with women. Since she could think about Abraham this way, why not Tom? Her answer to this question was terrifying and degrading because it defined herself: was she a cow in heat, one among many, to moan and groan at the penetration of any old bull?

Saving the oranges was medicine for her mind. As she shoveled strewn embers back into the blaze, she could be at peace thinking about Thorstein, about Sunday dinners and conversations, about nebulous changes in herself since New Year's Eve, and about the element of good fortune in her life that Tom was away almost all the time. She stood close to one of the bonfires, opened her shawl to feel the warmth better, and gave in to end-of-the-day weariness and hope that she would sleep without becoming restless or worried. The light from the fires lit the front of the big house, the shed for the buggy, and a short stretch of the road toward Olustee and the outside. Beyond, fields and forest were dappled in moonlight.

It was Lucy who first saw the horseman. "There's a man coming, man on a horse," she said.

Thorstein Brach! It was her first thought. Then—he wouldn't come at night to be alone with her! He must know that her husband was away, at work on the railroad. Then again—perhaps he was coming. He certainly didn't care about being proper. She remembered him naked in the hotel bed, with his wineglass. Could she send for Joanna Dale to come at this hour and spend the night? She hadn't had a chaperon since her academy days, but a middle-aged and respectable white woman was needed—now!

But in just a few seconds the familiar tall white mare, plodding at a slow walk, came within the firelight. The rider was Tom.

Surprise and guilt kept her from speaking. However much she might deserve whatever peace and satisfaction she could get out of secret thoughts, she *had* been disloyal.

Tom had no words for greeting, either. He nodded in a way that might indicate approval or simply the necessity of recognition and said, "Noticed it was going to freeze, didn't you?"

"Oh yes, it probably will."

For such a big man he was very agile. He swung easily from his horse with no sign of being the least bit tired. Whatever he'd been doing all day, it didn't keep him from being fresh and vigorous now, about two hours after sundown. He seemed not to look at two men who were smiling at the rare presence of Richmond Plantation's master, but he tossed the reins to one of them—"Rub this critter real good before you feed her."

He drew off his gloves, put them in a pocket, and held his hands out toward the fire to warm them. For Julia, not seeing him since New Year's Day made him even more of a stranger than he had ever been after previous long absences. His ruddy face framed by his red hair and beard was startling in the flickers from the flames. Among the black women and men who worked with her every day, and in his elegant golden brown coat from another world, he was a phantasm.

"Have *you* eaten, Tom?" Her emphasis was supposed to suggest that she cared more about him than his horse.

"I had breakfast."

"Lucy!" Julia bawled.

The girl had already gone to the kitchen on the other side of the house, but she heard Julia. After a few seconds her voice came from the dark cave of the front door. "Yes'm?"

"Lucy, you got more ham from the one you been slicing up?"

"No ma'am—"

"Jeremiah—" to the man who was not leading away the horse—"you go to the smokehouse—take that lantern—get the biggest ham you see and take it to the kitchen."

"Yes ma'am."

"Lucy, you got more cornbread?"

"Cornbread all ate up."

"Oh dear. Lucy—"

"Yes ma'am?"

"You take hot water from the stove and fill the pitcher in my bedroom so Mr. Clayton can wash up. You hear me?"

"Oh yes ma'am—I hear you."

"*I* will make cornbread, Lucy. Is the stove real hot?"

"I put in another stick."

Hitching up her skirt, Julia ran to the house. It was lucky the stove was hot, unlucky that extra victuals for everybody who'd helped make the fires had used up the ham and cornbread. Lucky she'd had Lucy around the house for a few weeks so the girl knew what to do. Unlucky—something else had to be unlucky!

Certainly it had been and was unlucky that Richmond Plantation and Tom just didn't go together. He was truly at home in a place like the Alhambra Hotel where all the talk, clothes, furnishings, food, and envious people suggested leisure and the preoccupations of distinguished gentlemen with momentous enterprises. The phantasm lit by the fire came from a far more resplendent world. While Julia mixed a batter for cornbread as Tom liked it—with extra eggs, sugar and butter—she weighed the bitter thought that her Eden wasn't good enough for her ambitious and magnificent husband.

Richmond Plantation was a combination farm and factory. The big house had been built in 1848, unusually large for the frontier. It was almost square with four large rooms on each of the two floors, segmented by hallways and surrounded by wide verandahs, which were supported by square posts with simple moldings suggesting the Tuscan order of architecture. In the back, a separate cabin connected to the verandah contained the kitchen. The whole structure had been painted white at some optimistic moment in the past but had become a weathered gray. Cabins and sheds that had never been painted were scattered hit-or-miss within about a hundred yards of the big house on land that had never been completely cleared.

The surroundings showed both hope and a lack of time for amenities or aesthetic delight. No greensward swept down to the creeping black Olustee River. The natural, almost white, sandy woods earth extended up to and under the house, and was forever tracked inside so that it crunched underfoot in the cold hallways. Julia's grandfather had taken advantage of the climate to plant shrubs, fruits and flowers that could not live above the frostline, which seemed to be located more by debates in country stores than by shriveled orange blossoms. A bougainvillea vine that threatened to crush one corner of the verandah might have to be chopped down. Some ragged coconut palms, brown with winter chill, dropped beyond the little orange grove, where the smudge drifted.

The kitchen became so hot that Julia had to open the door to the verandah. The stove was growling with open drafts, the flames devouring dry oak until the lids over the firebox glowed, almost transparent. She poured the batter for the cornbread in thin layers in two buttered pans so that it would bake fast and crusty. Lucy cleared the big table in the center of the kitchen and covered it with a cloth. A thick ham steak was sizzling, eggs were waiting to be dropped, and coffee steamed. There was a dinner plate, cup and saucer and silverware for Tom—a cup and saucer and bread-and-butter plate for Julia. She'd have a little cornbread just to sit down with her husband the way a wife should.

This was not the Alhambra Hotel with its prettified victuals. And Tom would sit down in the kitchen, where it was warm, not in the cold and rarely-used dining room.

There were gravel-crushing steps on the verandah and he appeared. He had removed coat, jacket and heavy gun belt—his flannel shirt looked white and clean. His beard was dark where he'd splashed it.

"It smells good, Julia," he said. He looked at the table but did not sit.

Julia opened the oven door, then closed it. "You'll have fresh cornbread. It's almost done."

"That will be just fine."

"Will you have some coffee?"

Instead of replying, he opened a cupboard where he kept his liquor. "I recollect this bottle was almost full," he said. "Somebody been appropriating my whiskey." He took the bottle from the shelf and in the silence occasioned by his remark took a glass from another cupboard, poured it half-full of whiskey and then added water from an enameled pitcher. He wasn't going to have coffee.

"Who's this girl here?" he asked, nodding at Lucy.

"This is Lucy, the Johnsons' daughter. She's helping me here in the house."

"You keep an eye on that whiskey, Lucy. It ain't for passing around."

"Yessir, Mr. Clayton. I know it ain't for passing around and now you tell me I will keep *any body* from getting at it. Your ham ready, Mr. Clayton." Lucy was very cheerful.

"Drop three eggs and when they're done put them on the plate here with the ham."

"Yessir, Mr. Clayton."

"Seems smart enough," Tom commented to Julia.

"Lucy's doing just fine," said Julia.

Tom sat and sipped his whiskey.

Julia took the cornbread from the oven, cut a large square, put it on a bread-and-butter plate with a large scoop of butter, and set it on the table.

"Napkin," said Tom.

"Oh yes!" Julia darted out the door, went across the icy verandah to the dining room, opened the sideboard, took out two napkins, and hurried back to the kitchen.

She put a neatly folded napkin beside Tom's plate and another beside her own. "Lucy, you can bring me cornbread after you've finished serving Mr. Clayton."

"Yes ma'am."

Lucy held the frying pan with one hand and with a big spoon in her other hand ladled the eggs onto Tom's plate next to the ham. The yolk of one of the eggs streamed around the edges of the ham.

He's used to dining elegantly, thought Julia, not with putting up with a young girl like Lucy. It was incongruous and crackbrained that she liked Tom's manners even while her insides churned with far more powerful emotions. "Oh Lucy, hurry with that coffee!" she snapped. Immediately, she was sorry for her tone, but her head was beginning to ache.

Lucy hurried with the coffee. "A little cream, Miz Clayton?"

"Yes, Lucy, I'll take a little cream. Thank you."

Tom did not look at her. His gaze wandered around the kitchen, appraising, perhaps critical. Finally he nodded. Apparently everything was satisfactory.

Julia launched into a long narrative. Mr. Dale, the storekeeper in Olustee—yes, Tom knew who he was—had heard tell of a white man in St. Vincent who painted houses and had even done some work on the Alhambra Hotel. And it might be possible to put him up in the spare room for two or three weeks while he repaired and painted the big house. It would cost more than a hundred dollars but it ought to be done because a post on the corner toward the oranges was rotting, it should be replaced, and other parts of the house might rot too unless protected by paint.

She paused in her narrative from time to time to invite comment, wondering why she still tried to involve Tom in problems of Richmond Plantation. A stupid compulsion!

He did not comment but silently consumed his food.

Finally she demanded straight-out, "Do you think we should hire this man, Tom?"

"Can you pay for this painting out of what you get for your naval stores?" He seemed to suggest that naval stores was just a hobby like, say, needlepoint.

"Yes, we have enough in the big desk right now."

"Then paint the house." He was indifferent, even contemptuous—she couldn't know.

He finished the whiskey and water, tossed his napkin on the table, stood with a brisk air that suggested an obligation had been fulfilled, and strode out of the kitchen. He didn't take a lamp or lantern. The moonlight streamed into the halls enough so that one could see.

But Julia seized a lamp and hurried after him.

Upstairs, he walked past the bedrooms in which Caroline and William slept without even turning his head. He hadn't mentioned them, and Julia wondered at herself that she hadn't, either. Would mentioning the children somehow offend him?

She left the lamp on the dresser in the bedroom and then went to the small dressing room that contained the necessaries and lit another lamp. She saw that Tom was draping his tie over the back of a chair so that it wouldn't wrinkle. There was a precision and calm in his movements that insinuated he was perfectly satisfied with all his habits including those having to do with trivial matters. He was unbuttoning his shirt as she returned to the bedroom to remove her best nightgown from a drawer and go back again to the dressing room.

She sensed that he did not want to talk.

She had worn this nightgown on her wedding night more than ten years ago. It was elaborate, special. It was made of very fine white cotton and looked like a dress, with a full skirt and fitted bodice that laced up the front with five pink bows. With fingers that were stiff with cold she tied the little bows, undid and brushed her hair, and washed her face and hands and rinsed out her mouth with some of the hot water left over from what Lucy had brought upstairs for Tom. *Her* habits were fidgety when Tom was around. She was aware that his presence made her different, and she suffered from the awareness as well as the fact. But she didn't have enough will to change—her mind as well as her hands trembled.

She turned low the lamp in the dressing room and went to the bedroom.

Tom was under the covers. In the dim light she could make out that he was watching her—for the first time since he had come home. She went to the dresser, intending to blow out the lamp.

"Let the lamp be," he said. As she faced him, he went on, "Take off that nightie."

"Oh—oh—" she could barely speak—"it's very cold, Tom."

"You'll be warm soon enough."

She raised her hands toward the pink bows but did not immediately untie one.

"I want to look at my wife," he said. His tone was not unkind—it just indicated assurance he would not be denied.

"My fingers are like sticks it's so cold," she said. Her headache was worse.

As she fumbled, he watched in silence for a while and then said, "Goddamn, Julia, how long is it we've been married?" He was recognizing that her difficulty with the bows came from nervousness, not from cold.

"More than ten years, Tom."

He sat up a bit so that his bare massive shoulders humped up from beneath the quilt.

At last the bows were undone. She thrust the gown off overhead and tossed it on a chair. Facing him, she smoothed her disordered hair. She could feel her face become warm.

"You ought to eat more, put more flesh on your bones," he said.

Huddled over, she hurried to the bed, slid under the covers, and lay on her back.

Immediately he was over her. His penis was hard. He kissed her once, his coarse beard scratching her lips.

The bed was an old one with a network of ropes and an additional wire spring supporting a cotton mattress. Their weight made it sag so that her buttocks sank and his penetration, which was quick and only a little painful, was not deep.

"Put your legs over my back," he commanded.

She did so. She hoped she was responding to him but knew she was not. She couldn't know how long it was before there was a copious discharge of his semen and he rolled off her, saying nothing, taking a deep breath, and going to sleep.

Her headache was fierce. She crept as quietly as she could from the bed—she would break down and weep if he woke up—and went to the dressing room. She shivered from cold but remained naked until she had turned up the lamp and washed herself—there was still a little warm water in the pitcher. Then on silent bare feet she went back to the bedroom to take her warmest flannel nightgown from the dresser and put it on. She disregarded the wedding garment. Back in the dressing room she wrapped herself in an extra quilt and sat. The urine in the necessary's bucket smelled. She didn't want to go back to the bed, damp with semen on her side.

She thought of going to the kitchen and making some mint tea for her headache. It would be warm there, but she felt she couldn't face Lucy. Lucy would know there was something wrong as between man and woman—even Lucy would know that—and Julia felt she couldn't bear the shame. It was just unlucky that Lucy was staying in the kitchen on this night so that she could feed the men who were keeping the smudges going under the orange trees. Julia would have to do without her tea.

Wrapped in her extra quilt in the tiny cold dressing room that smelled of urine, she was condemned to sit. For how long? An hour? Two hours? Exhausted, she dozed, awoke, dozed again. Did she dream or just imagine things? The washstand, the pitcher, the basin, the lamp became mirages. And there was Thorstein Brach raising his wineglass. But the woman beside him did not cower under the sheet. She sat up too, boldly, raising her own wineglass, not ashamed of her breasts. But her hair! It had changed color. No longer dark! Now it was cornsilk blonde like Julia's.

IV

Whenever Joshua woke up, suddenly, during the night, there was always a reason. A change of weather. An animal. A ghost. Some presence close to the window where he and Joanna slept in the cabin attached to the store. It was the scamper of feet that had opened his eyes. He felt the same old chill around the face and neck that had followed quick alarms during the Freedom War. Would there ever be enough years in his life to rid himself of this terror? For a few seconds, the phantoms that were held in check by daytime sanity were let loose. There were sentries who whispered and reeked of goose-fleshed sweat. There were horses that shied at the smell of blood.

Then he regained the here-and-now. The fragrant February night of Olustee, sharp with chill, flooded around him. Using the brain that God had given him, he figured that the sound which woke him was bare feet padding in the dirt and pine needles outside. *Bare* feet! Anybody with bare feet was innocent.

Next, reasonably, there were raps on the door to the porch that led to the store—rapid, not loud—and a girl's voice, "Miz Dale!"

Close to his ear, Joanna's breathing was warm and slow. She had sat up late, two lamps turned up, mending. Let her sleep. "I'm coming," Joshua muttered, and reached for matches.

Before unlatching the door, he held the lamp higher than his own eyes and squinted through the screen.

"Can I see Miz Dale?" said a voice.

"Bina Peters?" he asked.

"Yessir."

Bina Peters was the granddaughter of Azri Peters, a farmer who had his own ten-or-so acres of ploughed land about a mile from the store. Her parents had left the locality about seven years before to look for a better living, leaving Bina and her younger brother and sister in the care of Grandpa Azri. Soon the parents had disappeared. It was believed they had died in the wreck of a ship headed for Savannah—no one knew for certain. Bina, aged fifteen, worked for Joanna around the store and in the garden, taking pay in stock. Sometimes her brother and sister tagged along. Joanna often talked about going to see their own three grandchildren in Torrington, Connecticut. Where could they find someone who could manage the store in their absence? When could they afford the trip? Bina and her brother and sister were a little like grandchildren.

The dog began to bark, and Joshua snapped, "You be quiet, Littlebit!"

The dog did as he was told.

"Fool dog!" Joshua observed. "Couldn't hear a thing until I woke him up!"

"Can I come in, Mr. Dale?" asked Bina.

"You know the store ain't open now, Bina, and Joanna's asleep."

"I don't want nothing from the store, Mr. Dale."

"Then what you doing out this time of night?"

"I have to ask Miz Dale for help."

Why can't she ask me? Joshua thought. Am I becoming so old and off-putting? He called toward the sleeping room, where another lamp now glowed, "Joanna!"

"What is it, Josh?"

"Bina Peters wants to see you."

Bina looked younger than fifteen, like just a child, even though she kept house for Grandfather Azri besides working for Joanna. She was very black, slender and graceful. Her thin bare neck and arms stuck through openings in a meal sack that she probably used for sleeping. Something unusual must have happened to make her go running around in that. Joshua bent to look at her in the dim light. "She's been through brush," he called to his wife. "Her legs are all scratched up."

Joanna came in her nightdress, pinning her gray hair in a bun. "What you done to yourself, child?"

"The Ku Kluck come and beat grandpa, Miz Dale."

"Ku Kluck, oh Lord!"

Joshua was startled, too. The Klan had been active around Withlacoochee City but hadn't been seen around Olustee for—well, it must have been about ten years. "They beat Azri?"

"Yessir."

Joshua felt his scalp prickle—"Is he hurt bad?"

"His back is cut. He's blooded. Can I have some lard, Miz Dale?"

"You can, honey."

"Ku Kluck—" Joshua didn't want to accept it.

"Yessir."

"I got some ointment for your legs," said Joanna.

The girl stood next to the stove, which was warm with a banked fire. She began to shiver.

"You must be froze," said Joshua. "You take that coat hanging there."

She did so and then held it open to catch the heat from the stove.

"Trash," he said. "Thought they was dead or paralyzed."

"Grandpa's moaning, Miz Dale," said Bina. "I would please like some lard quick."

"We'll come with you, child," said Joanna. "You'll go faster if we come with you and take a lantern. It'll take me a few seconds to put something on." She went back to the sleeping room.

"What's the Ku Kluck bothering your grandpa for?" Joshua asked.

"I don't rightly know."

"Look here, Bina Peters, while I'm putting some pants over this nightshirt, you light them two lanterns. Here's matches."

After he put on pants and shoes, and his best jacket since Bina had his old coat, he took his shotgun out of its cupboard and put ten shells in his pockets.

Joanna and Bina carried the lanterns. Joanna also carried lard and a sheet. "Go fast but don't run," she said to Bina. "At my age I couldn't keep up with you."

Joshua said to both of them, speaking softly and slower than usual, "If we meet anybody, anybody at all, set your lanterns down and move into the dark. I'll follow and keep out of sight all the time, with my shotgun ready." He'd never forgot lessons learned from years of war and bushwhackings. He'd learned to do his damndest to foresee whatever might happen, and to prepare accordingly. The lessons of his life couldn't guarantee staying alive, but he was sure that they had helped.

It was about a mile to the Peters farm, across the new railroad tracks and about a half-mile from Myrtle.

They walked fast, saying nothing. There was a freezing mist in all the swamps.

The Ku Klucks had torn the door of the Peters cabin off its hinges. Inside was an overturned pail of dried peas, which crunched under the boots of Joshua and Joanna. The cabin was dark until they entered with the lanterns, and there was no fire in the stove.

Joanna took her lantern to a bunk against the wall farthest from the stove, looked into the bunk for a few seconds, and then said, softly, "You're sweating, Grandpa Peters."

Azri's voice was husky and weak—"I sweating and cold at the same time—"

"Sweating's a good sign—"

"The Lord will bless you for helping me, Miz Dale."

Joshua thought of Azri Peters as a farmer, as one of the few black farmers with his own land. He'd put out of his mind that Azri was also a preacher. Joshua was a steward in the church for whites, but he didn't care much about going to church. He went because it was good for trade in the store, and going for this reason made him feel like a hypocrite. This miserable feeling kept him from thinking about church at all any more than he had to. Also, when Joshua had been an agent of the Freedmen's Bureau, he'd hoped that whites and blacks would go to the same church. It hadn't worked out that way. He himself had wondered about what church meant to blacks. He didn't feel right about shouting hallelujah or amen at any time during the sermon, about jumping up and down in ecstatic abandon before the pulpit, with the whole congregation swaying and stamping and shouting until the building shook. It all seemed heathenish. But he didn't like to pass judgment, and he feared that in some way he'd been wrong. If whites and blacks had gone to the same church, maybe there would have been no Klan. All *right*, praise the Lord! So Azri was a preacher on Sundays as well as a farmer on weekdays. Poor poor old feller! God *damn* the Ku Klucks!

"I put turpentine and water on him," said Bina.

"Can you turn just a bit, Grandpa Peters?" asked Joanna. "We want to put some lard on your back."

"Miz Dale, I don't believe I can stand any more fussing with my back."

"The lard will keep it from hurting so much."

"I bout scream when Bina put on the turpentine."

"Place here is blowed. You *need* a little more turpentine here."

"Miz Dale, please don't put more turpentine on me."

"You be still now. Bina and me is right to put on turpentine."

"It hurt most as much as the beating."

"This make it clean so it heal better."

"I's so whipped and blooded I don't care. If I don't heal up, I feel better in Kingdom Come."

"Your time ain't now, Grandpa Peters. You ain't even as old as I is."

"I's old enough so I was a growed man in slavery time."

"Well! I's old enough so I was raising my little boy while Josh was fighting the slavers."

"What year you born?"

"Eighteen Thirty-two. I is two years older than Josh."

"I's honest with you, Miz Dale. I don't know zactly when I was borned."

"If you stay quiet and still, I can put this lard on."

"I's quiet, Miz Dale."

"Put the sheet beside him, Bina."

"Yes, Miz Dale."

"I know it make you feel good to fix me up. The truth is—every day I plow I chop corn I chop cotton I say 'Sweet Jesus come and take me. I lived enough.'"

"Bina, you wet the corner of the sheet and wipe the blood off his beard."

"I's ready to see God, but I hope my old marse from slavery time ain't there to torment me."

Joshua found some dry moss and sticks, and he started a fire in the stove. "Look here, Grandpa Peters, why did the Ku Klucks beat you?"

"The devil was in them."

"No denying that."

Azri sat up, raised his eyes, and cried out, "Look, Amos, Ruth, look! See what them Ku Klucks did to your grandpa! Learn about them Ku Klucks!"

Joshua saw that two children were watching from an opening to the loft. "Yeah, listen to your grandpa," he murmured. Then he asked Azri, "Did you know any of these Ku Klucks?"

"There was big ones and little ones, old ones and young ones. One of the old ones was Colonel Lawrence Avery, I believe."

"I expect so."

"Mr. Dale, if I die, will you help Bina and the little ones?"

"You ain't going to die, Grandpa Peters. You might as well stop talking like that."

"I'd be comfortable if you was willing to help them just for a little while. In a few years they help theirselves as much as any poor niggers is ever able to help theirselves."

"I'll help them if it's necessary."

"God bless you, Mr. Dale."

One of the children in the loft began to cry.

"Don't you worry," said Joanna. "Your grandpa is going to be all right."

"I couldn't do nothing to stop the Ku Klucks." For the moment Azri seemed to overcome his pain. He rolled over and sat on the edge of the bunk. "I was weak and helpless like a little baby in his mother's arms. When the Ku Klucks come, Colonel Avery and some other property men too, every last-man-Jack of them with a gun, there ain't nothing a poor nigger can do. I's an old man now, and in all my years I never learned of nothing I can do when white men come with guns."

"You ought to lay on your belly, Grandpa," said Bina.

"I never had a gun!" cried Azri.

"You hush," Bina said to the child in the loft.

After a ten years' absence, why had the Klan beat Azri Peters? If Joshua knew why, he might be able to figure out what might be done to keep them from doing more, or worse. He thought of the Reverend Peters's sermons. He'd never heard Azri preach, but he'd discussed the contents of the sermons with Azri himself when he came to the store, and sometimes with Bina when she came to work for Joanna. The Reverend Peters spoke frequently about the divine right of black folks to land. Hadn't they been sold, with wives and children, over and over again so that white folks could get money to pay for land? Hadn't they raised the crops—the corn, cotton, rice, sugar? Wasn't white folks's property, all kinds of it, got from work black folks did? Didn't black folks have God's authorization to take what was justly theirs?

Moved by the Reverend Peters's sermons, one black man had taken a white man's pig. "Damn it, that's stealing!" Joshua had said, pointing out that this particular white man had never owned a slave. But he could see that Azri Peters hadn't felt the force of this observation. To Azri, no black person and no white person stood alone but was in the main part of a race, sharing in the behavior of the race and in all the consequences thereof.

Was Azri Peters beaten because of his sermons?

Also, Joshua speculated about the envy of poor white folks, trash especially, because of the wages paid to black workers by the Pamlico and Gulf

Railroad. Amos Whitaker had said what was generally believed when he said such wages would ruin the South. Whitaker wasn't a Klansman and would never condone beating Azri Peters. Apparently, Lawrence Avery wasn't so indulgent!

"Look here, Azri Peters," said Joshua. "I want to figure out what the Ku Klucks are up to. Did they give any reason why they beat you, or were they just drunk and mean?"

"They mean all right."

"They axed grandpa where Charley Williams is at," said Bina.

"So they did," said Azri.

Charley Williams! The fat man on the horse that was too good for him had mentioned a Charley Williams. Azri would tell him the truth. "Who's Charley Williams?"

"He a one-eyed man used to come to my church. Then he was sent to Wehadke State Farm. I heard the Farm hired him out to the railroad for digging."

"Why was Charley Williams sent to the Farm?"

"So he could be hired out to the railroad."

"Why did they ask *you* about him?"

"Charley Williams got away they say, and they axed me where he is at."

"I can't understand why they're so stirred up by one man like Charley Williams. You say some of the Ku Klucks were property men?"

"Yes sir, Mr. Dale, I saw their boots. Think to hide theirselves under sheets!"

"I ought to borrowed Martha Richardson's shotgun!" Bina exclaimed.

"By God, you're thinking along the same lines as me!" The surprising strength in this skinny little girl gave Joshua a kind of chill, as though a bugle had tooted while he and his troopers were galloping under fire. "You and me, girl, scouts for the Grand Army of the Republic! Put us in the dark with shotguns and there has to be six ready to die before they get us!"

Draped in his lardy sheet, Azri rose slowly and staggered to the opening where the door should have been but wasn't. He looked across moon-drenched fields where he had labored most of his life and addressed an indomitable congregation of the whole outdoors—"The niggers is down in the mucky swamp now. We down in deep shadow. We down in deep valley dark as death. But the moon shining on tall treetops—"

"It shining," said Bina.

"This bad road oh Lord it long. A million sloughs in this road—"

"A million sloughs!"

"You hear what I say, Bina. That the road we got to keep. There will be storms and worser storms. The weaker brother and sister will drop by the wayside. But we must keep our eye on the tall treetops—"

"Yeah, oh Lord!" said Joanna.

"A million panter-cats screeching all around. We must stretch they hides on Saint Peter's gate!"

The sheet dropped off Azri and Bina put it around him again. "You go on you belly, grandpa, like Miz Dale say. . ."

Joshua straightened the nails from the torn-off hinge with the heel of an ax, then nailed the hinge back on so that the door would close and heat from the stove could warm the cabin.

On the way back to the store and home, he and Joanna both shivered from the cold.

*

Wrapped in her quilt, in the dressing room, Julia woke from an agitated doze at some unknown hour during the night. Her spine was stiff from trying to sleep in a straight chair, and forgotten dreams made her brains burn. She took off the quilt, folded it, and put it back on its shelf. Her sex irritated her, not as though she wanted her husband but as though she would never want him again. She hiked up her flannel nightdress and bathed her crotch with a cold washcloth. Chilled, she turned down the wick in the lamp, leaving only a faint glow for the dressing room and the necessary, went back to the bedroom, and anxiously crawled back into bed.

Tom's breathing was slow and peaceful.

She woke again while it was still dark. Tom's breathing was quieter. She guessed that he'd gone without much sleep for some time. After doing this, he always made up by sleeping ten or twelve hours. It was his way.

She'd had plans for this day before Tom had appeared, a lion among lambs, while everybody made smudges to save the oranges. The bridge to Olustee and the rest of the great outside needed repair. Her men had measured and listed some heavy bolts that were needed, and Mr. Dale had promised to get them for her in St. Vincent. He'd assured her he'd have the bolts by this date, and Mr. Dale was dependable in such matters. So she'd go in the buggy to Olustee. Caroline and William wouldn't walk to school. She'd give them a ride on the way to the Dales' store. She'd have a kind of holiday. She'd gossip with Joanna Dale—Joanna always knew everything that was going on in Olustee and beyond. Then she'd drive the buggy back, pick up Caroline and William after school, and deliver the bolts to her men. She wouldn't accomplish much, but after her night with Tom this was what she needed.

Silently, so that she wouldn't disturb Tom, she slipped out of bed and took from drawers and pegs her clothes for the day—warm flannel underwear, a cotton house dress with floral pattern for going to Olustee, woolen stockings, high-button shoes, and heavy shawl. She went to Caroline's room to dress. It was warm there, with heat still rising from the parlor stove under the grate.

Caroline remained asleep, breathing like her father. Was she having dreams about him, of being admired, of being held in his lap? How did she feel about him, remembering his visit in December? Julia was unable to regret that she'd have to take Caroline to school before Tom was likely to get up. It would be cruel to encourage illusions about her father. She kissed her daughter awake.

William was already standing naked in his cold room and fumbling in the bedclothes for his britches. Teaching William Latin was eccentric, but Julia didn't care. She'd read that the Founding Fathers of the Republic had learned their Latin very young. And William found it fun, a shared secret with his mother. So Julia sat on the edge of William's rumpled bed and murmured some lines from Virgil—

"Tu modo nascenti puero, quo ferrea primum

"dsinet, ac toto surget gens aurea mundo,

"casta fave Lucina—"

William grinned and repeated, "Tu modo—I ain't had that yet. Translate, Ma."

"Upon this boy just born, in whose time the race of iron shall first cease, while a race of gold shall arise through the whole world, smile oh chaste goddess of births!"

They both laughed.

She felt that Latin was a charm which protected William, and also that she herself was toying with superstition.

Lucy stirred from her cot in the kitchen when Julia entered. "Give Mr. Clayton his breakfast when he comes down," she told the girl. Not she nor

Caroline nor William would see Tom that morning. They'd be off before he was up. He hadn't bothered to take a lamp and go into their bedrooms last night, so that he might have the pleasure of seeing their faces as they slept. Why should he see them now?

They chattered cheerfully as she gave them their grits and encouraged them to eat an orange. She had no satisfactory answers to their questions about the visitation. Caroline: "Do I have to go to school before Pa can see me?" William: "Did the dogs bark when Pa came? Did they know him?"

She left Caroline and William at the schoolhouse and headed for Olustee. The weather was brisk but sunny. She was expecting relief from thinking about herself in talking with Joanna Dale. She must *not* ask Joanna about how soon the Pamlico and Gulf would be ready to handle freight from Olustee, so that naval stores would no longer go to St. Vincent by wagon. It would be shameful to show that she herself hadn't got that information from her husband. She would ask Joanna about her son and grandchildren in Torrington, Connecticut, and about local news. Whose oranges had weathered the freeze? Had Joshua shot another deer and smoked the venison? Would Joanna joke again about the crazy dog who was hypnotized by his own voice and howled for hours under a tree from which a coon had long departed?

Were she and Joanna a bit like that dog, indulging each other with the presumptive music of their voices?

When Julia arrived at the Dales', the sun was well up and the day was warmer. She left her shawl on the buggy seat and hitched up at the rail. "Joanna! Where are you, Joanna?" she called. Often, the mistress of the store was in her garden so that customers had to shout for her.

There was no answer, and Julia walked through the open door.

Then she saw them, both of them, side by side behind the counter with the cash drawer. The fact that they were together there, not as usual busy with separate tasks, just looking at her without speaking for some seconds as though they were at a funeral, Joanna's round face unsoftened by a smile, Joshua's thin face grizzled with unshaven beard, shocked her into foreboding.

"Good morning, Mrs. Clayton," said Joshua.

"Good morning, Mr. Dale." Julia became solemn, matching their apparent mood. And rather formal, as always with Mr. Dale. There was a quality in his character she couldn't get used to.

"Oh, it's a bad bad morning, Julia," Joanna murmured, and wiped tears from her eyes with the backs of her hands.

"I expect you've come for your bolts," said Mr. Dale. He took from a shelf behind him a bundle of them, tied with twine, and dumped them with a heavy clangor on the counter.

"Something terrible has happened," Joanna whispered.

Julia waited, feeling a chill.

"The Ku Klucks whipped Azri Peters."

"Oh—" Julia couldn't speak. She knew Azri Peters but not well. They exchanged greetings, and once a few months ago he'd been very nice—"I seed you with you chilluns tother day, Miz Clayton. Glory be they grow up beautiful!" She knew more of him through conversations with Joanna—that he farmed and preached, that he brought up three grandchildren. She knew that Joanna hired the children to weed the garden and do other chores, and that she paid them with stock from the store. Joanna had many stories about the doings of the Peterses.

In trying to speak Joanna became choked up.

"We were up most of the night trying to heal him and make him comfortable," said Mr. Dale. The quality of his voice was frightening. No feeling was expressed. There were impulses so terrible that one couldn't even hint at them.

"This is monstrous," said Julia. "Oh Joanna, you've told me what a fine man he is." She stopped talking—whatever she might say would be inadequate.

Suddenly, Joanna became furious. She found her voice and growled not only about what happened but also about the kind of Christian souls that suffered from the Klan. Azri Peters was an inspired preacher, think what one might of his kind of Negro Baptist way of conducting services in that church over in Myrtle, which years ago Joshua had helped build. Bina was a jewel, the brightest sharpest girl Joanna had ever known, white or black. Amos was so full of high jinks there was no holding him. And Ruth—well, something beyond human understanding had happened to Ruth. Maybe it was connected with her folks going away and never coming back—right when Ruth was at a most tender age, just a little tot. Who knows? Whatever the explanation, there was a need in Ruth that made anybody with an ordinary heart want to cuddle her, feed her, care for her—

Mr. Dale's emotion seemed to become almost unbearable so that he could barely whisper, "Those bolts will be three dollars and fifty-four cents, Mrs. Clayton."

She took money from her reticule and counted out the precise amount.

Without checking, he swept it into the cash drawer.

Joanna went on talking about Ruth Peters—"What will it do to her, seeing her grandpa whipped by horrors in white sheets?"

Joshua turned away and fussed with stock on shelves or hanging from hooks or pegs. It wasn't necessary. Everything was orderly.

Joanna was still talking about Ruth when they heard from outside, in front of the store, a lot of shouting and stomping of horses.

Julia heard her own horse whinny, and she rushed out.

Her mare was trembling and yanking at the rein which tied her to the rail, her ears perked and her nostrils snuffling. As Julia patted her nose and soothed her—"There there there…" she was aware of several horsemen, all armed with a variety of guns.

From the direction of Myrtle and the new loading platform, more horsemen were trotting. Was there some kind of muster for the best-known spot in Olustee, before the store of Joshua Washington Dale?

Then she noticed Colonel Lawrence Avery in the first group. He was wearing his Confederate campaign hat, and in the slight breeze his tobacco-stained beard blew over his shoulder. Julia's father had always treated Avery with cool neutrality, and once when she was in her late teens and was beginning to take some responsibility in managing the business, he had explained—"for your ears only, my dear daughter"—that Avery wasn't a real colonel. He'd been just a bushwhacker who robbed and probably murdered just to line his own pockets. He'd manufactured a title and a reputation for himself, and he lived a myth of honor and dignity and courage which some who had little to be proud of were happy to embrace. For years Julia had shared her father's contempt for this fraud, but she hoped she'd never shown what she felt. She preferred to ignore Avery rather than provoke him.

It was Esther who told her Avery was a Klansman. She couldn't recall now how Esther knew, but in such matters Esther was reliable.

Was Avery among those who had whipped Azri Peters?

The "Colonel" was gifted with a clarion voice and he was trying to address all the others, but for perhaps a minute Julia couldn't hear what he was saying because many men were talking to each other or to restless horses. At last she heard him say, "We got to do something, men. Charley Williams raped and murdered the wife of this poor man here."

Avery put his hand on the shoulder of the poor man, whom Julia knew. Robert Conkling. She knew him to her shame. She had once advanced cash to Robert Conkling in the expectation that he'd collect sap from about fifteen acres of pines. As Joanna put it, Robert Conkling couldn't even collect his own wits. Julia feared that the whole town had laughed at her. Esther had explained that Robert's wife Mabel, an enormously fat woman, sold herself for two chickens or a suitable amount of other produce to anyone interested — and that was how she and Robert lived. Why should Robert Conkling exert himself to collect sap?

"Button your pants, Robert!" somebody yelled, with the special enthusiasm reserved for village idiots.

Fingering his fly, Robert smiled.

But Avery proclaimed, "My deepest sympathy goes out to you, you poor old boy." There was an aimless shuffling in the movement of horses and a desultory quality in overheard fragments of conversation. She anticipated that Avery would put some insane purpose in words, and that almost everyone there expected just that. Who would question his pilfered distinction, his reputed authority? Also, some men from other towns probably didn't know the Conklings. And those who did might be savoring the irony of Robert Conkling's status as a representative of ravaged white virtue.

Julia rushed forward among the prancing horses to the "poor old boy" who couldn't collect sap, where he sat on an old and grungy mule. And she found her voice, surprising herself with its power — "Robert Conkling, you look me in the eye!"

Her startling call silenced a lot of men.

Robert smiled at her, his watery eyes showing no recognition, but he didn't say anything. Did he remember when she had spoken to him in a somewhat similar tone about his failure to collect sap? Avery's horse was nuzzling his mule, and this engaged his interest.

"Robert, you tell me the truth!" she snapped. "Where is Mabel?"

He was still smiling. Did the very simplicity of her question baffle him? He recited, separating the syllables of his words as a wayward child struggles with learning the alphabet — "Mur-der-ing black dev-ils!"

A stranger shouted, "This Mabel you talking about. She the one got raped?"

Robert went on with his text — "She the best wife I ever had and I'm sure getting a marble headstone from St. Vincent."

"You mean a nigger stuck it in Mabel?"

Avery patted Robert's back, and with this encouragement he went on, "I hope all you boys—"

Julia screamed — "Robert, you talk to me! Tell me — where *is* Mabel?"

"Miz Clayton, can't you see this poor old boy is distressed?" said Avery. "It ain't no time for asking him questions."

"Where is this nigger?" somebody yelled.

"There's matters ain't no business for a lady," Avery continued.

Another man spoke up, and like Avery he was able to get the attention of the crowd. He had a striking pale face and pinkish eyes, and his black hat was obviously new. "Gentlemen, there's reason to think this nigger is hiding in some shanty in Myrtle."

"A lot of you boys got reason to be grateful to Mabel," Robert persisted.

"Mr. Conkling," said the Colonel, sternly, "we're all mighty sorry for you and some other time perhaps we can help you out with the headstone. Just at present we got more urgent business."

There was a hush in the crowd. What they had come for seemed imminent.

In a rage, Julia bawled, "Mr. Avery, did you whip Azri Peters?"

"There's responsibilities for men you'd best not fool around with, Miz Clayton."

Julia's horse whinnied. All the commotion upset her, and she was yanking at the reins which had her tied to the rail. Julia went to her and stroked her nose, quieting her. She was aware of Joshua and Joanna on the porch of the store.

Joshua spoke up — "*You* there. Bascomb Good. If what I hear tell is correct, Mr. Good, you were directed by Tom Clayton in no uncertain terms to leave these parts."

Pale face and pink eyes responded, "I'm still here ain't I, Mr. Dale."

Joshua raised his voice so that everybody could hear him — "I thought over what you told me yesterday — about some man getting out of Wehadke. Haven't heard tell about this from nobody else. And now you're talking about finding him in Myrtle. Ain't likely he'd be there anyway. And all you boys ought to realize going into Myrtle wouldn't be no sewing-circle folderol. Most of the niggers in Myrtle has guns, and they ain't scared to use them. Wouldn't be like whipping some poor old nigger like Azri Peters, alone on his farm."

The man called Bascomb Good sniggered—"Mr. Dale, I can't believe you're standing up for a murdering and raping nigger."

"That story smells like a fish stranded on a sunny bank for more'n a week."

Good nodded at Robert Conkling and spoke with weighty sarcasm—"You ought to be ashamed of yourself, Mr. Dale. This poor old boy is suffering."

Joshua was still speaking in a very loud voice—"*If* a crime has been committed, and *if* anybody thinks he knows who did it, it'd be best for Leroy McIlvey to find him. That's what a marshal's for. Ain't no call for anybody getting shot up over in Myrtle."

"McIlvey ain't home," somebody said.

"I respect Mr. McIlvey for his absence," said Avery.

A few men laughed.

Julia spotted the minister of her church, whom she regarded as a good man but timid, walking slowly from the direction of his house, which was located in the direction of the new loading platform. Would he be able to influence this gang?

But before she could shout at him, Sanford Payne strode around the corner of the Dales' store, followed by a black man who worked for Amos Whitaker and was now leading by the bridle Payne's big stallion. As usual, Sanford was dressed in his neatly-pressed gray suit and gray hat, and he was wearing two guns.

Men backed their horses away from him as he walked toward Avery.

The "Colonel" spoke in a tone that suggested disappointed paternity—"Sanford, I don't enjoy being the man who has to say you and Tom Clayton made a terrible mistake yesterday. You put Mr. Good and these boys from Hamilton County off the trail of Charley Williams, and since that time Charley has raped Mrs. Mabel Conkling."

"He murdered her, too," Bascomb reminded everybody.

In a voice utterly without passion, as though he were merely taking notice of a law of nature, Payne said to Good, "You were told to stay in Hamilton County."

Some men near Bascomb Good adjusted their rifles and shotguns.

"Howdy do, Mr. Payne. I don't mean no disrespect," said Bascomb.

"Sanford," said the Colonel, "I hope that whatever personal considerations stand between you and Mr. Good, a rape and murder gives any white man a responsibility he can't run away from."

"He told me nothing."

"Well, all I know is what Amos Whitaker told me. Tom Clayton just told Bascomb Good and his friends to get out of town and, according to Amos, Clayton has a very commanding way. Bascomb Good went like a whipped dog, and I'm surprised he's back. Looks like he somehow got in touch with Lawrence Avery."

"Then Tom tried to keep all this from happening."

"Yes, he did. He did his best."

Julia felt stunned. How faithless she'd been, feeling estranged, even welcoming Tom's absences! How immense his responsibilities were! For progress. For keeping peace between white folks and black. His responsibilities were inescapable for a man with his rare gifts. The railroad magnate Arthur Wilkins certainly appreciated him. And the President of the United States! How petty she'd been!!

"You'd best go home, Julia," Joshua Dale said. It was kindly of him at this time to call her by her first name. "Hard to tell what's going to happen, and the fact is I'm scared. I'm more scared than I've been at any time since the War."

As she drove the buggy home, having taken Caroline and William from school, remaining silent while they chattered, she thought of Tom striving to control the disorder in the chaotic world of railroads and development, of Tom trying to curb fraud and antagonism between the races, and of herself doing nothing to straighten out the disorder in her own mind. But even while she was terrified of what might be going to happen in Olustee and Myrtle, and while she tried to exult in Tom's capability and basic goodness, she saw again the image of her dream while she huddled in her quilt in the cold dressing room. She realized that the dream-woman in bed with Thorstein Brach was herself.

The dream was especially abominable because her own husband had just possessed her, as was his right. St. Paul said in his Epistle to the Corinthians, "The wife hath not the power of her body, but the husband." Thoughts about what was wrong or right in her own behavior and about Tom swirled in her mind, mixed up with horror, rage and terror brought on by the beating of Azri Peters and by what might be going on in Myrtle. In God's sight her unhappiness in marriage must seem trivial, stupidly rebellious. St. Paul also said, "If a virgin marry, she hath not sinned. Nevertheless she shall have trouble in the flesh." She certainly had trouble in the flesh! But the fact that St. Paul knew about this trouble was comforting. She didn't have to feel ashamed. After all, it was only in a dream that she was in bed with Thorstein. It wasn't real. She couldn't help dreaming. The Bible, St. Paul, was a sufficient guide to faith and practice.

*

Tom Clayton was having breakfast in the kitchen when Sanford Payne walked in and without any word of greeting said, "Bascomb Good's got Avery and his Klan hunting that Charley Williams."

Tom wiped his mouth with his napkin and didn't comment for a few seconds. He showed no surprise. "Well, Sanford, I guess you'll have to take care of Mr. Good."

"I just couldn't start shooting with Avery and his whole Klan."

"Of course you couldn't, Sanford. So—Avery is it?" He'd ridden with Avery and the Klan some years back, they were no doubt jealous of his position and prospects with the Yankee railroad, and so he was in no position to tell them what to do. He couldn't make them stop stirring up the Myrtle blacks, including the best workers on the main line. A race riot in Myrtle could stop construction. He thought of the bonus of twenty-five thousand dollars which Arthur Wilkins had promised him if the line was completed by April First, complying with the contract between the Pamlico and Gulf and the state of Florida. The bonus meant little to Arthur Wilkins. The Pamlico and Gulf Corporation would be penalized twenty-five thousand dollars a day for every day after April First that the line remained unfinished, with freight not moving. This clause in the contract was a sop to populists, but Tom was happy about it. It had pressured Wilkins to offer him the bonus. With twenty-five thousand dollars he could say good-bye to Arthur Wilkins and start his own empire.

Now that the Klan was threatening his bonus, he was particularly struck by the Klan's absurdity. Klansmen saw what-should-be, not what-was, purity of the white race and so on. Even an old agent of the Freedmen's Bureau like Joshua Dale didn't regard the Klan as absurd—he just hated it. Now that the Klan was standing in Tom's way, he came close to hating it, too. But what he had to *do* was cope with it, use it. How?

"They all headed for Myrtle and there's shooting," Sanford went on.

Tom threw his napkin down and strode out, leaving a plate that still had a slab of ham, at least one egg, and some smoking-hot cornbread. And he ignored Lucy, who had given up trying to talk with him and was poking the fire in the stove.

He and Payne didn't talk as they rode toward Olustee. Sanford didn't like to talk, and Tom didn't enjoy conversation with Sanford. The man was a weapon—a whip, a knife, or a gun. No point in talking to a whip, a knife, or a gun.

Tom turned over in his mind what he should do in a number of possible circumstances. The best outcome would be that Avery and his Klansmen, with other hangers-on, would find the black Charley Williams, string him up, and go home satisfied. All over in no time so the Myrtle railroaders would have no reason for not staying on the job. On the other hand, there might be shooting for a day or even for two or three days. Deaths. Black deaths. White deaths, with predictable statewide or perhaps national outrage.

There were some thirty-five railroad bosses who were reasonably capable with a rifle and would follow orders. How could he best use these men in each of the conceivable contingencies?

Below these logical calculations was a bedrock of emotion and habit, especially a belief in his own genius for power that had been ritualized since childhood, when he'd seen that Merion C. Clayton was a whimpering drunk and no war hero, when he'd thereby deduced that the Confederacy itself was a foolish crusade that would have been a glorious and bloody success if he'd lived in the previous generation and had led it. A fantasy of course! But a fantasy that curled his lip like a good brandy, a fantasy endorsed by the reality of growing up as prince of the hard-up Clayton Plantation and learning early-on how to control all others—field hands, house servants, foremen, his father Merion—and now a man like Arthur Wilkins who was ostensibly his boss, a President of the United States childishly eager to accept any parcel of suitable words, and needless to say a wife. He thought of Laura Wilkins, of her sexual look at him and their explosive laughter as he'd said, *"There are people like mules, and people like monkeys, and people like oxen..."* He didn't want to control Laura Wilkins.

He was amazed that this goddess wanted him—in bed, obviously. Her look was plain—as though she'd grabbed his hard penis. It was strange. Nature was turned around. Men desired and women submitted. That was what-was. After years of whores who gave themselves with whimpers or begging that might be provocative or flattering or terrified—did it matter?—and after a wife who surrendered with religious grace, his lungs heaved and his sex throbbed, even while riding along with silent Sanford Payne toward Olustee, just with getting all excited because for the umpteenth time he realized that the direction of sexual desire had been turned topsy-turvy and his own substantial bulk of flesh and bone, a powerhouse that would blow up if it didn't let off steam, was avidly desired by a woman—and what a woman! Goddamnit, according to nature or not, it was one hell of a good thing!

He also had a puzzling sense of danger. How could Arthur Wilkins, no doubt a genius as a businessman, be so stupid and lacking in shame that he could exhibit himself, on the threshold of old age, as the bed partner of a Venus like Laura?

Getting a hard-on about Laura Wilkins while he was on his way to settling this business in Olustee and Myrtle was so futile that he tried to cool off by thinking about Bascomb Good. It didn't help. Thinking about killing Bascomb Good seemed to make his hard-on even worse. A hard-on under circumstances he couldn't do anything about made him mad. And getting mad under the circumstances was futile too, since he couldn't right on the spot do anything about that, either. Talking to Sanford Payne might cool him off—"I been thinking, Sanford—I know how disgusted you was just looking at that Bascomb Good and how it would be just fine with you to put a bullet in his drooping guts, and it seems like he didn't believe me when I told him to get out of town or you'd do just that. So I told him what you'd do, in the hearing of Amos Whitaker and all that trash from Hamilton County too, so word'll get around, that it was you going to settle his hash."

"Yes, it was," Sanford mumbled.

"But it was me he disobeyed," said Tom.

"I told him myself he was to get out of town," said Sanford.

"What did he say?"

"He didn't say nothing consequential. Avery talked."

"I know you got a feeling about this, Sanford. But I hope you won't feel I'm taking anything away from you if I do for this Bascomb Good all by myself. He's been even more insulting to me than to you."

"It's all the same to me, Tom."

"That's what I wanted to hear, Sanford."

He still had the goddamned hard-on. He finally got rid of it by thinking about arrangements so that folks could believe Bascomb Good had tried to bushwhack him. Fixing up a trampled space among some palmettos where a man might have crouched in ambush should be evidence enough. Who cared about Bascomb Good anyway? Most particularly, in Jackson County who cared? In the unlikely eventuality that the matter ever went to law at all, it would be in the Jackson County courthouse presided over by Judge Cooper, who had been a personal friend of Merion C. Clayton.

Bascomb Good was just a nuisance. Ever since at age eighteen when Tom had gone to the Exposition in Philadelphia and talked with politicians there, he'd committed himself, at first without even realizing it, to acquire power in the big world beyond Florida. The New Year's Eve ball in the Alhambra Hotel gave this commitment increased force. It was lucky he was a Florida man. Florida was not just Deep South, like Georgia or Alabama. Florida was Yankee too, with a man like Arthur Wilkins taking over. President Benjamin Harrison, that accident from Indiana, was Florida. Farmers who came from up north and planted oranges and like Julia and her niggers made smudges to keep them from freezing—these were Florida. Poor folks who spoke Spanish and made cigars were Florida. Tourists from Europe were Florida. Florida was a section of the national and international swarm, where Tom Clayton could get the right contacts and right experience for taking the power to which he was entitled by his nature in a world that was bigger but not much different.

He had a sense that what was going on in Myrtle put at risk not just his career but his belief in himself. Not just the twenty-five-thousand-dollar bonus but his power to do what he had to do. Arthur Wilkins believed in him only as he could profitably use him. President Harrison believed in him only as a handy token of that national git-up-and-git that he liked to think he guided. Laura Wilkins was the only human being he'd ever met who knew him right off as he was.

Every house on Olustee's Main Street had drawn shades, except for two that had no shades. They met only two men carrying rifles. One of these, a tall and lanky farmer, knew him. "Howdy, Mr. Clayton," he said, and in a tone of sour irony added, "going over to Myrtle to join the shooting?"

Tom didn't know the man's name, and he chose to overlook the irony. "Howdy, sir. Reckon I'll just look things over."

"Be glad to see it finished and done for," said the man, now serious.

"Your name is Andrews, ain't it?"

"That's my name."

"Your boy works for the railroad."

"That's Bert."

"All us railroaders will be glad to see it finished. Ain't no sense in stirring up a war over one nigger."

"That's what folks here are saying."

As they rode on, he said to Payne, "Got to do something to end this thing quick. Most folks here won't take no part in it, I'm thinking. And the white trash that's come in here to kill niggers won't have the brains to end it."

They left their horses at the new telegraph office in a tent pending construction of the Olustee station. Then they walked completely around Myrtle, most of the way through pine woods. In ambush behind bushes and trees on the side of Myrtle away from Olustee were only a few men with rifles or shotguns. These were the soberest ones, men with hate in their eyes who hoped for human targets. Where most of the attackers were concentrated behind the railroad grade, Clayton and Payne walked back and forth for about an hour, studying the mob and its equipment. Tom had a few words with three men he knew, neither approving nor disapproving what was going on. Sanford never spoke. Most of the men behind the railroad embankment were drunk or had been drinking too much, but they observed the progress of Thomas Clayton and Sanford Payne in reverential silence.

This incident occurred:

"Hey, Kip, whas the state of your coperosity?"

"Biling over."

The questioner slung a whiskey bottle over the embankment toward Myrtle. "There's a right good swaller of firewater in that bottle for the man with the balls to get it."

The bottle struck the sandy ground, bounced a couple of times, and came to rest against a fallen branch. It was not broken.

Kip rose to his feet.

"Keep your head down, young feller," somebody said.

"I na-sceared," muttered Kip. He was a scrawny man with a torn shirt, feverish red blotches on his pale cheeks, and a tangle of blonde hair brushing inflamed eyes. "Nobody can say I'm a-sceared."

He tottered to the rim of the embankment, tripped over a rail, and rolled down the other side.

"Hey, *Kip*! Come back here, you dern fool. There ain't *no* liquor in that bottle."

Kip managed to get up. He took two steps. He did not seem to hear.

From somewhere in Myrtle, a rifle. The lead chunged on the heavy steel of the rail.

"Come *back*, Kip! I got the liquor *here*!"

Another shot.

Kip turned around, clutching his guts. It seemed he now heard the voices from behind the embankment. But maybe he never understood. He stared toward the embankment, his reddened eyes wide, and then went down.

"I *yelled* for him to come back! You all heard me…"

Four men were grouped around Clayton and Payne, probably expecting authoritative comment. One of them said, "Some men don't care much about living."

"I ain't laughing at the fool," said Payne.

"I've seen enough," said Clayton.

"Wonder who's going to do the burying when this is over," said Payne. "Niggers is going to be scarce."

V

Some of the windows in the Dales' store and in the cabin attached to the store had shutters, and some didn't. Some had fastenings and some didn't. The door to the store was latched with a light hook which would come out if anybody gave the knob a hard yank. The kitchen door had no latch at all. There was no lock on the kerosene shed, which was on one end of the chicken house. And the mob might want kerosene.

"We been fools," said Joanna. She elaborated, suggesting that Joshua was the principal fool. He'd got so used to craziness during the War that he couldn't do without it, and he had to settle where there were more crazy people than anywhere else. Because of the reputation he'd made during the War he could have got himself a decent job in Washington. General Sherman would have recommended him. Or he could have started up a store in Connecticut somewhere near her own father and mother. The climate wasn't so bad once you got used to it. And any climate was a damn sight more tolerable than white folks shooting at black folks, and black folks shooting back. All that liquor that folks brewed for themselves drove them out of their minds.

Joshua had nothing to say when she went on like this. Her observations had merit. He was boring holes with a brace-and-bit through the kitchen doorjamb so that he could put in carriage bolts to hold heavy chocks for a two-by-four bar.

"You wouldn't have to be doing this if you hadn't let everyTom, Dick, and Harry know how you was always a red-white-and-blue Union man and proud of it," said Joanna.

He heard shooting over toward Myrtle. First, a pistol and a volley. Then, one shotgun blast. Then, quickly, another. Then, a lot of shooting for about ten seconds. Then, silence.

"Damnation," he said, almost casually. He'd expected something like this. He went on, questioning himself more than his wife, "Just what does that mean?"

She was driving nails through the bottom of the porch shutter into the window sill. She spoke more deliberately than usual, controlling her nerves—"You're the one knows all about shooting and such. Can't you tell me?"

"I was wondering who was shooting which guns, and who got hit the most."

"Can you guess by the sound?"

"In the War, when the shooting started, I generally could. But this situation's different."

She put down her hammer—"Ain't there enough men in this town want to stop it and willing to do something about it?"

She'd had her say about what their lives might have been, and what she said now was as final as a decision to fight a battle. To find men, or even to try to find men, who would be willing to do something about the shooting in Myrtle, could risk the burning of the store, perhaps life. Joanna's question showed she was ready for the risk.

"First, I have to finish making a bar for this door," he said. He found himself trembling, and he couldn't control this. Why had he so often gone out to meet dangers when he could never harden himself to them? When he looked in the mirror, shaving, he saw the wary eyes of a man who'd lived with too much fear.

Joanna raised both arms and poked with a hairpin to tuck a strand of gray hair into her pug—an ordinary gesture and an ancient bit of witchcraft. It struck him like a harsh chime of bells. His eyes watered. He'd been a damn fool when he was young, staying away from Joanna for years on end to go scouting for General Sherman. But the fact that he had done so made the scouting more significant. Leaving her for an hour or so now would be worse than it used to be when he left her for years. She'd been safe in Connecticut then. He couldn't talk. When he tried, his throat tightened. He finished bolting the chocks and trying out the bar. After watching Joanna bang in a couple of nails, he tried again to talk but couldn't. He went inside to the bedroom, to the gun cupboard.

He took out his Army Enfield, also the shotgun. In the kitchen again, he gave out a long breath and found his voice—"I finished putting a bar on the door to the store. Now you got this bar on the kitchen door so you can stay in here if you want to. Anybody trying to bust in either place would have to make an awful racket. I'm leaving the shotgun on the kitchen table where you can reach it easy. It's loaded. If anybody threatens you or even looks cross-eyed at you, blow his head off. I'll be around to speak up for you with this." He slapped the stock of his rifle.

Without waiting for her to say anything, he hurried off to find men who might, as she hoped, want to stop the shooting and be willing to do something about it.

There was nobody in the streets. Men who hadn't gone to the shooting were no doubt inside their homes, doing more or less what he and Joanna had been doing.

He walked toward the railroad and Myrtle. On the deserted road, which led directly from his store to the new loading platform, he was followed by an old dog. It was a fat hound on shaky legs, too old for hunting. Joshua thought: He knows kinfolk when he sees one.

At the loading platform beside the new tracks there were about a dozen people, two women and the rest men. He knew none of them well. Before saying anything, he listened.

"The Colonel he talked first to an old nigger woman making a quilt—"

"He axed her where is Charley Williams."

"Did she tell?"

"Wouldn't say 'sir' 'til she was told."

"The Colonel says to her he says, 'You don want nothing happen to you, do you now? Charley Williams got to die and you better tell where he is at cause iffen you don tell where he is at ever nigger in this town going to die."

"Did she tell?"

"Colonel Lawrence Avery warn't the kind of gentleman—"

The dozen or so people milled about to make way for four horsemen.

"Where you from?"

"Withlacoochee City."

"Out to get that Charley Williams?"

"Going to get *some* damn nigger."

"Did that old nigger woman tell where Charley Williams is at?"

"She say he out in the woods."

"The Colonel he decide she an ignorant old woman didn't know nothing."

Joshua spoke to the stranger who seemed able to report what had happened in Myrtle—"Did you say Colonel Avery *warn't* a certain kind of gentleman?"

"I said he warn't the kind of gentleman to put with an uppity nigger and he warn't."

"Ain't he still the same way he always was?"

"Sir, I reckon you ain't heard. Colonel Avery was killed by a Myrtle nigger."

"No!"

"He was killed when they first went in. Killed when he went to a cabin where niggers name of Richardson lives."

Another man spoke up—"Some nigger fired from between the boards. Then they shot the Conkling feller."

"Is he dead too?"

"Dead? Half his side is missing."

"Surprising thing, ain't it, what comes out a man blasted up like that!"

"That's buckshot for you, buckshot at fifteen feet."

"You wan to take a shot at the Richardson cabin, I advise going over there behind the railroad grading."

"Be mighty careful bout sticking your head up."

"I don reckon there's nobody in that cabin no more."

"If they is, they's deadern a four-year-old ham."

"I live here in Olustee," said Joshua. "I'm more interested in stopping the shooting than contributing to it."

The gibble-gabble ceased for about two seconds. Then—"Mister, this shooting ain't going to stop til the Myrtle niggers is taught a lesson or dead."

"Most of the Myrtle niggers is innocent of wrongdoing," said Joshua.

"If the Myrtle niggers ain't disciplined, the niggers everywhere will start raping and murdering."

What could he say? And at that moment a fight broke out on the other side of the loading platform between a man from Hamilton County and a man from Withlacoochee City. They both had knives. As though this event were happily expected, there came from further along the railroad embankment, from locations behind trees for taking shots, from a nearby backhouse, some twenty or thirty more men, many drunk, many yelling as loud as their whiskey-soaked throats permitted, whether anybody could hear them or not. In the scuffle, the man from Withlacoochee City got cut in the side with his own knife and was laid out on the loading platform. A fellow used *his* knife to slice the man's shirt off for a bandage. Meanwhile, his opponent was distracted by an enthusiastic admirer who forced the neck of a jug down his throat. He spluttered and passed out, probably more damaged by the whiskey than the other man by the knife.

By himself, Joshua couldn't cope with attitudes or fracas. He walked toward the parsonage, still followed by the old dog. For at least a minute he banged on the door of the one man in Olustee whose influence he was sure to need. "Reverend, it's me, Joshua Dale!" he shouted.

Some window curtains twitched, and a moment later the minister's wife cracked open the door. Her voice was thin, frightened and spiteful—"Please don't shout, Mr. Dale. My husband's ailing."

"Ailing or not, I got to talk to him."

"It wouldn't do no good. He's flat on his back."

"If he can't get up, I can talk to him while he's laying down."

With sudden venom she cried, "Very well, Mr. Dale! Come in, Mr. Dale! You want to drive him *more* out of his mind, you can try!"

Joshua found the Reverend not, as his wife said, flat on his back but planted on his knees. He was in the middle of his parlor, on a rug with a bright design of pink peonies, dressed in his black Sunday preaching suit. His eyes were closed and he said nothing, although he must have heard Joshua's shout and conversation with his wife. After an uncomfortable silence Joshua said, "Reverend, I hate to interrupt a man at his prayers, but you and me are the only ones in this town who can do anything practical to stop some killing."

The Reverend opened his eyes but did not look at Joshua. He seemed to see only a picture of the boy Jesus with a very smart expression surrounded by elderly men with very astonished expressions. "God moves in a mysterious way!" he proclaimed, in a loud but toneless voice. Then he clenched his hands, closed his eyes again, and bowed his head. Visible above his preacher's collar, the sinews of his neck stood out like twine.

Joshua spoke very distinctly, hoping for his attention—"Reverend! I want you to ring the church bell and call together your congregation. I want you to talk to them."

The preacher was just unresponsive and shaking nerves.

"Reverend!" Joshua exclaimed, several times.

After it was clear he wasn't going to get a response, the minister's wife tugged Joshua's sleeve and said, "Come out here. I got something to tell you."

In the kitchen, having closed the door to the parlor, she said, "Azri Peters was killed."

"Azri Peters!"

"He was here—"

"Oh—damnation—"

"He was killed here."

"Here?"

"Out where my husband grows corn."

"Who killed him?"

"I don't know. Some men I never saw before."

"May God burn them in Hell!"

"They took him right out of this kitchen. He came for the same reason you did—to ask for help in stopping the killing."

"Where's his grandchildren?"

"Grandchildren?"

"Grandchildren—Bina, Amos and Ruth."

"I never did know their names."

"They need something they generally come to Joanna and me."

"I don't know anything about them. My husband asked those men not to harm Azri Peters. He begged them and they paid no attention. Azri was beaten last night and he was wearing a sheet all greasy with lard. It was Joanna's sheet. I know her stitching."

"Yes, it was."

"They just laughed at him." She began to choke and put half her fist in her mouth.

After she could breathe again, Joshua asked, "Where's his body?"

"Out in last year's cornstalks. They took him out there and shot him, shot him like he was a bear or something."

"What are you going to do about your husband?"

"He had a shock like this once before. After a time he got well again."

"You both can come to stay with Joanna and me, if you want to."

"No, I can manage." She put her fist in her mouth again. "I can manage everything except burying Azri Peters. Do you think you could do that, Mr. Dale? I believe the buzzards are at him."

"Can I find a spade in your shed?"

She didn't seem able to reply.

As he came upon the body, with four buzzards at it, he lashed out with the spade and was able to strike one of the creatures while the rest fluttered off. He didn't want to bring attention by firing his rifle, and a buzzard wasn't worth a bullet anyway. He clamped a foot over its neck and ground its head into the earth with his other foot, at the same time chopping at its thrashing wings with the spade. After about a minute it stopped flopping. He was exhausted, but he had to kill *something*.

The earth was sandy, easy to dig. But it was an hour before he could go back to the Reverend's wife and say, "I buried him deep, by the fence, at the far end of the garden. If you see buzzards, they're just after another buzzard I killed. I hope Azri's in Kingdom Come like he expected."

*

In a bunkhouse for colored men at the construction camp of the Pamlico and Gulf Corporation, lit by a single lantern with the wick turned low, a boy who had run all the way from Myrtle, eighteen miles give-or-take a mile or so, told the railroaders about Ku Kluxes and white trash shooting at folks back home and a few of the folks holding them off by shooting back. "It's a riot," he said.

Riot was a conjuring word. Ku Kluxes and others minded like Ku Kluxes might snatch a colored man and lynch him before enough people could work out some way of preventing it. But a riot was different. In a riot there was time and occasion for drawing the line, and it seemed as though everybody got the idea, all together, that there was now time and occasion. History was coming to Myrtle. In Atlanta over in Georgia there had been a riot. In Springfield in a state called Illinois to which no black person from Myrtle had ever gone, there had been a riot. There had been riots in other states—Louisiana, Arkansas, Mississippi, Kansas. Was there any state in which there had never been a riot? A riot might be anywhere or everywhere. A riot was a foretaste of the apocalypse described in the Bible. Everybody knew what riot meant. In a riot there was an end to choice. What was there to live for?

A guard called Mr. Billy sat with his rifle in the cab of the *Nellie May*, the old balloon-stack engine that hauled the flats and cabooses of the construction train. The fire in the *Nellie May* never went out, and Mr. Billy was sitting next to the firebox to keep warm. This was a regular responsibility for Mr. Billy because he didn't get along with the other white men. Mr. Thomas Ewell Clayton, the biggest boss, along with the Gray Man Sanford Payne, had called together most of the bosses before sundown. It seemed likely the bosses knew about the riot earlier than the railroaders in the bunkhouse. Mr. Billy had not been summoned to the talk with Mr. Clayton. Did Mr. Billy know about the riot?

A young fellow named Mark Richardson rose to the occasion—"I know Mr. Billy. He tell me bout where he live near St. Vincent and get shrimp with a net and plant orange trees that are too young yet to have many oranges. He say I's the only one hereabouts he can talk to."

At this time Mark was only sixteen years old. He'd worked at picking cotton, driving mules and helping a blacksmith before he became a bridge monkey for the Pamlico and Gulf, earning as much as any grown man. Mark always had a good word for everybody, black or white. He was cheerful even with the bosses without seeming to lose his natural self. He was very strong and agile. He could cling with his legs to a pile and catch the swinging end of a heavy beam lowered by a derrick and muscle it for bolting. Older men on the job liked to think they'd once been like Mark whether they had been or not.

Mr. Billy saw Mark by the light of an almost full moon as he crossed a log over the drainage ditch next to the tracks. "You stop right where you're at!"

"It's just me, Mark."

"What you want, Mark?"

"I think this ain't no fit place for you, Mr. Billy. Other white men drinking and talking and sleeping in bunks all night and you alone out here."

"This got nothing to do with you, Mark."

"How come it's always you sitting by yourself—"

"Like I say, Mark—"

"I know this got nothing to do with me if you mean I can't do nothing about it because I's just a black bridge monkey but all the same I got a feeling about you and the way it's always you alone out here in the night and even us black men sleeps in bunks."

"You're a good boy, Mark."

"I always try to be, Mr. Billy. I got a feeling about you when you told about leaving your wife and three chilluns all by theirselves to earn more money working for the railroad than you could get from pine-tree sap and how you couldn't make ends meet. But with the other bosses—well, you ain't no drinking man, Mr. Billy. Being here ain't like being home for you. It just can't be."

"What do you want, Mark?"

"Mr. Billy, there's trouble back in my home in Myrtle. Have you heard?"

"Yes, I heard."

"All us railroaders has to be home, just like you want to be."

"I hope you ain't aiming to make no trouble, Mark."

"No, sir, I ain't aiming at nothing of the kind. It's just we has to be home."

"I don't know—"

"All us railroaders respect you, Mr. Billy, and we want no harm. We want no harm for you. But we gwine home, Mr. Billy, even if you shoot somebody. Can't nothing stop us."

"Come close so I can see you."

"Yes, sir." Mark crossed the rest of the log so that he stood at the step to the cab of the *Nellie May*.

Mr. Billy's hand, holding a lighted lantern, reached out.

Mark held out his own hands, in which there was no weapon.

"Mark, I don't blame you," said Mr. Billy. "And I don't blame t'other niggers want to go home. I heard about white trash shooting in Myrtle. I's going to give you this rifle."

"You don't mean that—"

"I knows what I's meaning. Here—take it!" He lowered the rifle stock first from the window of the cab.

"I can't take it, Mr. Billy."

"You *got* to take it. I's getting out of here. I wants no part of what's going on. Anybody ask, my rifle was took. I won't never say who took it."

"I'll give it back to you, Mr. Billy."

"No you won't! It ain't my rifle anyway. There's burned in the stock P&G for Pamlico and Gulf, and you can give it back to the Pamlico and Gulf if you be so minded, but I don't advise it."

"I don't know—"

"Or you can whittle the letters off."

"That'd be stealing."

"I don't care. Stealing ain't shooting." Billy came down the steps of the cab and thrust the rifle into Mark's hands. "Now you mind what I's saying—"

"Yes, Mr. Billy."

"You let anybody know I's giving you this rifle and I won't never trust a colored man again."

"Nobody going to know, Mr. Billy. There come a time I can do something for you, I will do it."

Billy nodded and ran down the track into the night.

Mark took a couple of steps back on the log and said quietly to the darkness, where he knew the railroaders were waiting, "It's all right."

They jumped or waded the drainage ditch and flooded over the flatcars.

Mingo, a black fireman who had been barred by his color from becoming an engineer, crossed the log and appointed himself to this office. He was helped by a self-chosen fireman. They threw dry hard kindling into the firebox. It exploded in roaring flames, and in twenty seconds the safety valve hissed.

"Bo-ard! Bo-ard!" Mingo exclaimed, quietly. He pulled the throttle. "Man, slam the door of that firebox or the draft'll pull your ears off!"

The door of the bosses' bunkhouse banged open—"Billy! What the fuck you doing?"

The man in the door fired a pistol. He probably wasn't aiming at anybody in particular. Just stating intention.

"Niggers is loose!"

Then there was a lot of shouting and scrambling.

It took a lot of seconds for the old *Nellie May* to gain momentum with all those loaded flatcars.

Some bosses had time to get their guns. There was more shooting.

Boxes on the flatcars held spikes, and the railroaders threw them. A couple of boards were smashed off the bosses' bunkhouse, and in the light that streamed out one boss was kneeling, taking aim.

There was so much shouting nobody could hear words. Some of the older railroaders were slow and had to step lively. They had to get on a flatcar or stay behind. Everybody had to make up his own mind what to do.

Mark rode on the woodpile in the tender. He'd never held a rifle in his hands before, but he knew how to use his mother's shotgun. We all depend on Mingo, he thought. By the light of the moon he could examine the rifle. It was an old Sharps, and it held just one bullet.

Two men on the flatcar behind the tender were hurt by gunfire before the *Nellie May* could leave the construction camp. As they rattled through the moonlight toward Olustee and the loading platform close to Myrtle, Mark could see other men bandaging the injured, trying to ease their pain.

Many rioters were around a big bonfire near the loading platform.

The arrival of the *Nellie May* surprised them.

"It's the *Nellie May*!"

"Niggers got the *Nellie May*!"

One man, a frantic scarecrow against the blaze of the bonfire, rushed toward the cab and pointed a pistol at Mingo. The engineer's job was finished, and he was climbing down from the cab. Mark protected him. He threw the rifle to his shoulder and pulled the trigger. For the first time he felt the solid certainty of a big-bore rifle. He saw the man go down and knew the bullet struck just as was meant.

*

Back at the store after burying Azri Peters, Joshua found Joanna very busy. He couldn't find it in himself to tell her, just then, about Azri's death. She was hurrying this way-and-that. Most of their regular customers were stocking up. They were preparing to stay behind locked doors, guns handy and loaded. Joanna kept running to the barred window on the front of the store, peeking out to see who was banging on the door, and taking down the bar to let some customer in. A lot of them were women, and they didn't take kindly to Joshua's urging them to tell their fathers or husbands or sons what they ought to do. Joanna expressed no opinions and just served them. One woman came from a distance with a mule and her fourteen-year-old son. The boy led the mule while she carried a shotgun. Joseph Rourke came in from Clayton Plantation. He was horrified at what had happened, especially at the killing of Azri Peters, whom he had known. He mentioned that he was worried about his friend Thorstein Brach, who was coming from St. Vincent to spend a few days with him and Esther, and wouldn't realize what he was riding into. Crazy white trash meeting Thorstein and sizing him up as a rank foreigner might regard him as easier game than the armed black people in Myrtle. Thorstein's Norwegian accent was enough to get him stripped, whipped and maybe shot and dumped in a swamp!

When it was dark, Joshua barred the store and kitchen, as before, and then told Joanna about Azri. She was weeping as he went out again, with his rifle. He didn't know just what he was going to do. He was hoping against hope that some new circumstance might give him a chance to do something about stopping the shooting.

He realized that the yarn about Charley Williams, whether there was any truth in it or not, had attracted the scum of the whole region, and that some of them would enjoy the irreproachable murder of a former Union soldier and agent of the Freedmen's Bureau. So he was quiet and sly as a hunting cat. He was crafty in positioning himself so that others were in danger, not he. He found a clump of palmettos near the loading platform from which he could see what was going on and control with his rifle anyone who came close. Fear made him feel more vital, a young soldier again. His nostrils took in more air, his arms and legs seemed more fit for whatever had to be done, and his mind became more agile and assured.

About two dozen men were sitting or lying around a big bonfire, and a few were wandering about, restlessly. There was some drinking but not much talk. One man sang for a few seconds and then shut up because nobody joined in. The rioters seemed tired, sullen.

Joshua was probably the first to hear the *Nellie May*. He could make out that it was slowing down perhaps a quarter of a mile from the loading platform. Beyond the bonfire, a telegraph operator came out of his temporary tent with a lantern. He too must have heard the train. The beam from the headlight streamed along the track.

Joshua stood.

Who would be on the train? What was the purpose? The construction train did not ordinarily move at night. If it went through Olustee on the way to get more rails, spikes or other items, it generally did so around noon. Was the train bringing men to help put an end to the riot? Would the railroad bosses, all acting together, force the white trash and Ku Kluxers to go back where they came from? What he had seen of the mob convinced him that a few good men, steadfast, determined, could send them packing.

Some of them near the bonfire lit pine-knot torches. Joshua wanted no light. It was just common sense to remain inconspicuous. Thank God for damn fools who make it easier for prudent men!

There was a bright moon anyway.

A few of the rioters moved toward the track.

As Joshua expected, the locomotive was the balloon-stack *Nellie May*. Only the construction train traveled the new track beyond Olustee.

Somebody near the bonfire yelled, "Whoa!"

A few were on the track, perhaps drunk. One ran beside the locomotive, making a comic play as if to seize the bridle of a horse.

The engineer leaned from the window of the cab and roared, "Git offen the track, white trash. This man Mingo's at the throttle, and he'll make mincemeat out of you!"

Joshua recognized the voice, that of a friend and customer.

"Niggers got the *Nellie May*!" somebody screamed.

Joshua could imagine just about what had happened.

The train clanked to a stop. Shapes rose from the flatcars and disappeared on the other side of the track, toward Myrtle.

Mingo climbed down from the cab. Damnit, man, go down the other side, thought Joshua.

One of the rioters rushed toward Mingo and pointed a pistol.

Somebody on the woodpile in the tender fired a rifle, and the man with the pistol fell. Mingo ran around the front of the *Nellie May* and vanished. Several shots were fired by rioters. There were iron missiles from the flatcars.

Joshua had learned that in war there can be purposeful unity or, on the other hand, feather-brained chaos. He saw two black men supporting a third who had a bandage around a leg—the man must have been wounded before the train came to Olustee, probably in getting out of the construction camp. These three were the last to drop down the other side of the flatcars and disappear. They would be wallowing across the swamp toward Myrtle.

Where for a wild moment the flatcars were covered with men throwing spikes, now they were bare except for a few boxes and on one of them some rails. The *Nellie May* stood empty, smoke curling from its stack.

But the rioters were not of one mind. They had appeared to be of one mind when Joshua sized them up during the day. Now, a shower of spikes had made a difference. A couple of men lay on their bellies and fired their guns under the flatcars toward Myrtle. It wasn't possible for them to see what they might be shooting at. An Olustee man, armed only with a pistol, walked on the moonlit road toward the town. Events must have persuaded him that it was better to go home and to bed. Three men drinking from a jug hadn't moved—perhaps they took in dimly or not at all what had happened. Others ambled about, not going anywhere in particular.

Joshua strode toward the man who had been shot near the *Nellie May*. He wondered how a railroader from the camp came to have a rifle. He was confident that in the confusion nobody would pay attention to him. He looked and listened.

Some torches spluttered on the sand, and a man bending over the fallen one said, "Can't somebody bring a torch over here?"

"You want a torch you just go ahead and get one."

"I got to see what's happened here."

"Iffen you take a torch you just give the niggers something to shoot at."

"Ain't no niggers no more."

"This man's hurt – "

"How you hurt, Zeke?"

"Zeke! You're all bloody!"

"Damnit, don't bring no lighted torch near me!"

"Put out that damn torch!"

"Jesus! This man's killt!"

"Zeke—"

"Right over his eye—"

Joshua turned away. He could make out a group of men near the tent for the telegraph operator. One of these called out, "Jeb is here, Mr. Clayton. He can work the telegraph for you."

Joshua hurried toward them. Was this the circumstance he had been hoping for? He thought of what Amos Whitaker had told him—how Clayton had told Bascomb Good and the trash from Hamilton County to get out of town.

Someone in the group hailed him—"Who's coming?"

"Joshua Dale." He made out the massive shape of the construction boss. "Hello, Mr. Clayton."

"Mr. Dale!" There was surprise in Clayton's voice. "Come to join the riot?"

"A lot of people here in Olustee want it ended, now. But they don't know what to do about it and they stay home."

"Is that so? What would it take to make them do something about it?"

"Somebody to get them together and tell them what's-what."

"Well—all us railroaders would like to see it ended, too."

Railroaders! Clayton called himself a railroader. The black men on the construction crews called themselves railroaders. Was there sanity in this?

Joshua sounded out Clayton's attitude – "Ain't no sense in having a war over one nigger some says did wrong."

"No sense at all. Could you stay around while I send a telegram, Mr. Dale?"

"Got nothing better to do."

The telegraph operator named Jeb threw back the flaps of his tent. It contained a cot, a chair, a table with the instrument and a box of writing materials and other stuff. Wires reached out and up to a new pole at the other end of the tent. Jeb turned up a lighted lantern.

Clayton went in the tent. There wasn't room for Joshua or any other men. Joshua didn't recognize them.

The operator clicked away for a while, wrote notes while listening to answering clicks, and then said, "I'm all ready, Mr. Clayton. That's St. Vincent on the other end of the line."

"Send this to Arthur Wilkins, President and Chairman of the Board, Pamlico and Gulf Railroad – he'll be at the Alhambra Hotel." Clayton waited for this to be clicked out. "Crews quit. Took over construction train and rode it to Olustee... Niggers now holed up in Myrtle...Big riot here...Best use influence with governor and get militia...Urgent to fulfill contract with state...Clayton."

Clayton turned to men outside the tent – "Mr. McIlvey, you can make use of the telegraph now."

The town marshal came out of the dark – "Hello, Mr. Dale. This is a terrible thing, ain't it? Lawrence Avery killed—my my. I was out hunting when it happened."

"That's too bad, Leroy," said Joshua, with no attempt to keep sarcasm out of his voice.

Clayton, forestalling any possible argument between the marshal and Joshua, said, "Let's do our damndest to straighten things out, regardless."

"This is to be delivered to the governor, who is staying at the Alhambra, too," McIlvey said to the operator. "Don't send this to his home or to the Capitol because he ain't at either place."

While the operator was busy with this, the marshal asserted, "Any public servant has a private life, just like most folks." McIlvey had come from Ohio during the late 1870s, had been energetic and effective in politicking, and regarded a comfortable life as the sole object of his job. He spread a piece of paper next to the lantern and read a long message in toilsome spasms. He described conditions in detail and accurately enough. Finally, he too asked for the militia.

When he finished dictating, no one spoke as the operator clicked away, and as the St. Vincent operator clicked an acknowledgment.

Then Clayton said, "You know, old Wilkins says it's commercial paper builds railroads."

Out of the dark came the unmistakable toneless voice of Gray Man – "He ought to use that there commercial paper for wiping his ass, so it'd be more useful."

McIlvey laughed.

Without paying any attention to Payne's remark, Clayton said to Joshua, "We're going to need the help of Olustee citizens, Mr. Dale—all the men we can get. Will we find you at home tomorrow morning?"

Joshua had mixed feelings about this question and even more about these wired requests for the militia. The governor would never use the militia to control voters as against black men who couldn't vote. The militia would never permit being so used. Anyway, the militia couldn't be mobilized in a hurry. Clayton knew this. McIlvey knew this. Anybody with a brain knew this. Talk of the militia was a way of shedding responsibility for what might happen. It put in question Clayton's sincerity. Was he really trying to stop the riot? Still, Joshua couldn't forget his humiliation of Bascomb Good. And there was no other person with so much influence and power who might do *anything* to stop the riot. "I got no place else to go," he replied.

VI

Thorstein Brach set out early in the morning to ride some thirty miles to visit Joseph and Esther Rourke for two days. He had a good horse, a brown gelding four years old, a saddle bag containing a change of underwear and an extra shirt, toilet articles and a ham sandwich. Also, he had a canteen of water that tasted of sulfur. He was wearing old but intact riding breeches and a woolen jacket which he soon took off and tied in a roll behind him because the cold weather broke and the day rapidly became warm.

He was both tormented and stimulated by recent events.

An affair with the wife of a St. Vincent physician had just ended with the husband beating the wife. She'd showed Thorstein her black eye and shrilled that they must "run away" together. Run? How? Running required more money than either one of them had. Away? Where? Some utopian university that welcomed lovers on the lam? First, Thorstein had pacified her and then had induced gratitude, even a sense of fulfillment, as he'd showed her that she didn't need to have anything more to do with him, that she could even feel good about leaving him. She was grateful because he'd made her "feel more like a woman" (My God as though she wasn't the most magnificent woman!) and also because he persuaded her that she didn't need to lose her security out of quixotic bondage to an economics professor in a fourth-rate college. How many marvelous and enthralling women there were! Not dull like most men but smoldering with discontent and rebellion and passion endemic to their intolerable status as property and readily inflamed by simple affirmations of their unique and phenomenal qualities. Finally, on parting from Thorstein, the physician's wife had exulted—she'd found a man who understood her and their ecstasy had been a victory—"You'll always be my true love, Thorstein!" Having helped her achieve this state of mind, he himself was disconsolate. Did he feel this way because there had been some narcotic pretending, by himself as well as by the woman, both at the beginning, during, and end of their affair? Inevitably, pretending about anything became sickening!

He was riding through open woods of live oak, hickory, and magnolia. Squirrels soared and a fish eagle skimmed the blue sky. No matter how he tried to hoard joyous memories of the physician's wife, the balmy sun was sad. He answered a bobwhite's call with a mournful whistle.

Another event that gave him mixed feelings was a hostile review in *The Nation* of *The Tumefaction of Property*. His book had been out for more than a year, and the publisher had sold the one thousand copies that had been printed. So the review was hostile not only because of what it said but also because it appeared so late it couldn't help sales and warrant a second printing. Edwin Lawrence Godwin, the founder of *The Nation* and panjandrum of American intellectual society, was trying to keep him poor! He could be angry at that! But the content of the review, intended to be devastating, was merely simple-minded. The reviewer, a Yale professor who had once been cool to Thorstein, wrote about the financial and social stability attributable to gold with emotions more appropriate to mothers' milk, and he seethed with commendable indignation that Thorstein sympathized with the advocacy by ignorant farmers of greenbacks, free silver, subtreasuries, income tax, and railroad regulation. The reviewer's irony was coy—was Dr. Brach sincere when he wrote that costly entertainments, such as the potlatch of Indians or the balls of millionaires, attained their best development at the higher stages of barbarian culture? Barbarian? Why, America had art museums and concert halls as well as factories and railroads! Was this barbarian? And behold! Property in these United States and indeed in other non-barbarian cultures was burgeoning like mushrooms. Where was the tumefaction, Dr. Brach? Alas, poor Dr. Brach!

The review evoked one serious question—would it hurt or help his chances of getting a better job? The idea of staying long at Rowland College, doing dormitory duty and trying to keep young aspirants to the ministry from chasing black whores, filled him with gray horror. No university would hire a man whose book provoked the contents of *The Nation*'s review. On the other hand, the fact that he was reviewed at all in *The Nation* was recognition of some importance, and perhaps some university president or department chairman might not bother to read what the review said. Or, naturally, what his book said. Perhaps Godwin was helping him by printing any kind of review, in spite of venomous intentions.

The thought lifted his spirits. He watched the merry flickers of red-wing blackbirds among the tussocks of a swamp, and he recalled again, happily, his evening with the physician's wife in the Alhambra Hotel. The railroad magnate's potlatch was felicitous. No occasion could have served better for kicking over the traces, for purging superstitious reverence for the sacrosanctity of property that underpinned both financial skullduggery and marriage vows. He hummed a folksong of Norwegian immigrants learned in childhood—"Ah vimmins on the velocipede, ah vimmins, ah mens!"

Without dismounting, he ate his ham sandwich.

Riding through primeval pines close to Clayton Plantation, he thought of Esther—how she'd understood with no fuss or feathers that he'd truly needed her room in the Alhambra Hotel. Did she have any idea *why* the Alhambra Hotel, with a potlatch in progress, had stimulated a delirium in both him and the physician's wife? How could he explain? He had to earn a living as a professor—perhaps he should talk like one—"Oh Esther, my dear Esther, what do mortals need? Money—and passionate love. Since only by rare coincidence can both needs be satisfied at once, passionate love requires revolt against the circumstances and culture that provide money. Passionate love and a money culture are implacable foes! You instinctively understand this, Esther. Isn't this why you knew that a man and a woman needing passionate love couldn't respect convention or property rights in a hotel room?" But alas, poor crippled Esther! Bittersweet Esther! How could he ever talk about passionate love, athletic love, to Esther? Impossible—cruel!

He could, he should, he must talk about passionate love with Julia Clayton. How could he manage to be alone with her? After dinner at the Rourkes', could he ask her to show him the garden? Would Esther be offended if he seemed to be flirting with her brother's wife?

What a rare kind of loveliness there was in the woman! The selectivity of his own memory was baffling. Why did she remain so dazzling in his mind's eye, and appear there again and again, just as she appeared inside the doorway of Esther's hotel room, blushing with embarrassment and God-knows-what other emotions? Why did he recall her at that moment even more vividly than the physician's wife? Should he talk like a professor to Julia Clayton? "Was it your electric emotion, Julia, that burned your image in my brain? I toasted you with my red wine, and I toast you again and again with thought after thought of holding you in my arms—good health and all the sunny pleasures, my startled deer, my timid spirit of life! I knew that under that simple purple dress sewed with your own perfect fingers, and under your Sunday cotton dresses at the Rourkes', your flesh is dewy, sensitive, more beloved than you can imagine. Julia Julia, my hands tremble, my mouth moistens – " Hardly the right words, even for a professor! Outlandish! Not so outlandish in the natural order of things as that Yale flunky's claptrap about the gold standard. Indeed, in the natural order of things the plain truth. Still, not right for Julia Clayton. How lucky that we can meet at the Rourkes', out here in the piney woods and cotton fields, and not in St. Vincent. How pretty her teeth, her gestures, her way of talking. How fresh and playful her mind. How innocent and real. Enjoying her double-entry bookkeeping! Laughing at order out of confusion! Not giving a damn that managing her naval-stores business is regarded as inappropriate for a woman like her. A marvel!

Pretending about anything with Julia, even if she became confused and expected it, would be unthinkable. A prostrating thought! He might have to put his whole life on hold until he figured out who he really was!

The pines ended at a swamp, and suddenly, there was the sky again, like an embrace. The warm spell had eased in the spring, never completely at odds with winter. There was a sprinkle of soft green in the gray cypresses, a flash of courting redbirds. If he got a new job and went north, he'd never again possess this splendor, never again bathe in this subtropical fertility. Never again meet a woman like Julia Clayton.

As if waking from a dream, he saw four riders on the narrow sandy road ahead of him. They had rifles or shotguns across their saddles. Hunters? Did four horsemen hunt together? Not the style of Florida hunting. The *Chronicle* had reported violent episodes only a few miles from St. Vincent, and he talked about them with the Rourkes and Julia. He thought of reining about. But his horse was tired from almost a whole day of being ridden. If they really wanted him, they'd catch him.

He continued ahead.

Closer to them, he recognized one of the riders. "Joseph!" he called, his voice high-pitched with relief. He was used to seeing Joseph dressed up for Sunday dinners in white pants with white shirt and red bow tie. Now he was wearing overalls and a shirt so stained and washed-out that it had no special color at all. His rifle was polished.

The three men with him were black—one of them really a boy and not on a horse but on a donkey. He had a shotgun.

Joseph's thin face was dark with unshaven beard, but it brightly expressed his amusement at this strange twist of existence which was bringing the two of them together not for a chatty Sunday dinner but on a narrow road in a swamp, and himself with three armed companions. He guided his horse close and held out his hand – "You're a good lad, Thorstein, but on occasion surpassingly ignorant. Is it you are trying to copy your mode of walking along a street in St. Vincent, or in New Haven Connecticut perhaps? Folks hereabouts are shooting at each other and might be inclined to shoot at you."

"Oh, I'm not worth a bullet!" How could he be so self-deprecating, even as a bad joke? "What's going on, Joseph?"

Before answering the question, Joseph introduced the others, slowly and with relaxed formality. They were workers at Clayton Plantation and all in the same family, three generations—old, middle-aged, and young. "Howdy do," said the grandfather. The father nodded somberly and the boy grinned.

"Anyway, you're here, Thorstein, and in one piece."

"Thanks for striving to keep me this way. I haven't heard anything about what's going on here. I was enjoying the sunshine and thinking about a review of my book in *The Nation*."

"It was only *The Nation* on your mind was it?"

"Mostly – " He couldn't talk to Joseph about Julia Clayton.

"It is only on your bad advice that Esther and I subscribe to that pernicious sheet published by a loutish Englishman from County Wexford in the Old Country. There's English and there's English but none so malevolent as English in Ireland." He glanced along the road, both ways. "We better get out of here. We'll talk when we're in the house."

They rode single-file—Joseph, Thorstein, the grandfather, the boy, the father. The grandfather said, "There be a riot in Myrtle, Mr. Brach." Otherwise, all of them were silent.

At Clayton Plantation there was nobody in the cotton fields, nobody outdoors around the cabins, the gin or the sheds, nobody around the big house. No animals. Even the hogs had been put away somewhere. The grandfather and the boy took the horses to the barn. The father spoke for the first time – "I'll be in the pecan trees, Mr. Rourke. Anybody come I let you know. I shoot in the ground anybody come at all." Then he rode back toward the cotton fields and the forest.

Indoors, a few windows were open to let in warm air and make it more convenient for anybody who had to shoot out. Esther was ensconced in her wheelchair in the parlor. She greeted Thorstein quietly, solemnly, and for a while had little to say.

Piney, the tall black woman who looked after Esther, seemed to be in charge. As usual, she was wearing a yellow cotton house dress and had her long hair tied up in a red bandanna, but she had added a heavy gun belt and holster with a large revolver. Instantly, she was voluble – "There's some your niggers gone traipsing off, Mr. Rourke, and iffen I was you I'd locate them and make them stay put. Ain't doing theirselves no favor staying in the woods. How they eat? How they keep their health cold come again? How they hide iffen trash come with dogs? I's privileged to look in your face, Mr. Rourke, because you is one white man has sympathy for black peoples and gives them guns to protect theirselves. There's lazy niggers you shout at, Mr. Rourke, and they don't understand you protect them all the same. You got to find them lazy niggers, Mr. Rourke, so they don't get theirselves killed. They best off here where some of us has guns."

She went to the kitchen, where she could be heard scolding somebody.

"Did you ever see the like of Piney?" said Joseph. "It's better I'd be feeling myself if I were out in the peaceable woods." He went on to Esther about how the animals were fairly safe from thieves, the three mules were in the barn, most of the hogs were penned and only the big boar that nobody could deal with and one or two others were rooting in last year's corn, and all the hens were shut in their coop. And finally he excused himself to Thorstein with a formality that was grimly comic under the circumstances because he had to go looking for those who had gone traipsing off, just as Piney said he should.

"Sit down here," said Esther, as soon as they were alone together. She waved toward a sofa that faced her wheelchair. Then she changed her mind – "First, open that window, please."

"Certainly."

"I scarcely know how to begin telling you what's been going on here." Uncertainty about anything was not Esther's style. "Oh my my my, how those redbirds sing after a cold snap!"

Thorstein glanced out the window at a stump sprinkled with dry corn and haloed by fluttering wings. "They do indeed sing as though they're beside themselves."

"There's evil men bent on killing," she went on. "They killed the preacher of the church for black people in Myrtle, killed him for no reason at all except they just like killing the way sane folks like food and air and life—first whipped him and then killed him, no finer man you could ever hope to know."

She paused, watching the redbirds without seeing them.

Her words brought to a climax feelings in Thorstein that had been accumulating since he'd met Joseph and his three armed companions in the swamp. The meeting had been so unexpected, so different from anything he could have conceived, that he hadn't at first reacted with apt emotions. He'd simply put himself in Joseph's hands. Now, his scalp prickled and he felt a tightening—rage? fear?—in his gut. If he'd been a victim, along with this preacher Azri Peters, Esther might refer to him as "no finer man you could ever hope to know." So it had been necessary for Joseph to meet him in the swamp. His love for Esther and Joseph could never be adequate. He said, "I can see how killing this preacher wounded you, Esther. What can I say? What could anyone say? Now I'm wounded because you are, and I was never fortunate enough to know the man."

"We were all wounded a long time ago. How could this happen?" It wasn't unusual for Esther to think of many people as being crippled in their minds as she was crippled in her body. But she didn't elaborate now on this concept. Instead, she told what she knew about the local violence in a rather confused and uncharacteristic way. There was a story going around about a black man who had escaped from a prison farm in the next county and had allegedly raped and murdered a white woman, wife of a well-known idiot and herself no better than she should be either in mental capacity or morals. Story might be true and might not be true. Everything so out of hand now it didn't matter. Lot of bully boys from Hamilton County and from all over—kind of men you don't think exist until something like this brings them out from wherever they've been keeping themselves—drinking and shooting and getting into fights. Shooting at Negroes in Myrtle who were shooting back, so that there was a standoff. Ought to stop, but how could anybody make it stop? Joseph found out all about this from Joshua Dale, the storekeeper in Olustee. At some other time, Thorstein might find it interesting to meet Dale. He'd been one of

Sherman's captains in the War—he was a hard man but capable and not given to saying what wasn't so. Dale told Joseph about Azri Peters. It was Dale himself who buried Azri Peters. And Dale told Joseph something surprising—that her brother Tom Clayton had tried to send the trash from Hamilton County back where they came from to keep all this from happening. Esther digressed. She told about Tom taking her to school in the buggy, about his ambition – "He's got a wildcat in his innards that won't stop clawing and all the time he looks steady as a photograph," and about his indifferent treatment of Julia—"No finer woman you could ever hope to know," as Thorstein must be aware! Esther was sure she'd feel a lot better about Tom doing the decent and courageous thing in sending those boys from Hamilton County back where they came if she didn't suspect the reason he was doing it was to keep black railroad workers on the job and not have them get involved in what was going on around Myrtle. Tom had to finish that railroad line on schedule to get a big bonus from the Pamlico and Gulf Railroad. A banker in St. Vincent had told her the bonus would be twenty-five thousand dollars, if he got it. Might be true or might be just gossip. Of course, Tom would never tell her what was going on, and no doubt he hadn't told Julia either. If he had told Julia, Julia would have told her. Anyway, regardless of what Tom had done or tried to do, and regardless of his motives, the shooting was going on, and some of the trash got tired of shooting in Myrtle, mostly without knowing whether they hit anybody or not, and roamed around the woods and fields looking for Negroes easier to shoot, which was how Azri Peters got killed. Joanna Dale—that was Joshua Dale's wife—and sometimes Esther thought Joanna tended the store better than Joshua did—she was so worried about what had happened to Azri Peters's grandchildren! Neither she nor Joshua knew what had happened to them. Esther knew just how Joanna felt because she was worried about Julia the same way. Tom had humiliated some of the riffraff—he'd told them to mind their own business and go back where they came from. Now they'd feel revengeful. They'd feel a lot better if they went to Tom's property and burned down the house, smashed the turpentine still and shot his people. And where was Tom? At home, where he should be? Not he! All he thought about was working for the Pamlico and Gulf. It was a bitter pill to swallow—-admitting that she had a brother who was so unconcerned about his wife, his children, the property that was his because he'd married Julia Richmond. Esther and Joseph were worried about their property and people, but thank God they had Piney. Joseph was a good man when it came to chopping or picking cotton or running the gin and dealing with the Negroes who did the heavy work. But it was Piney who knew which people could be responsible with guns and that you could even depend on a boy who'd do just what his grandpa told him to do. All the people on their place, including herself and Joseph, should be safe if they'd do just what Piney said they *must* do. But Julia had *nobody* to help her. Tom away and her black folks from families who'd been with Richmond Plantation since before the War and never engaged in any fighting.

The style of Esther's mixed-up and savage reportage, comments and digressions moved Thorstein as much as its content. Usually, a calculated irony underscored her passionate longing for rationality and morality in a world that she found mindless in self-deception and sanctimonious in affectations. This expressed a spirit which Thorstein found profoundly congenial—it comported with his own zeal for exposing in his writings the disguised relationships between economics and social custom. But now, Esther's language was rough and direct. He was meeting a new Esther who had crossed a divide between observation and involvement, who was hurt and enraged far beyond use of irony. Thorstein himself was usually stimulated by thinking as precise as the facets of a diamond. But as Esther paused to catch her breath, he jumped up from the sofa, his body tense, and seeming not to think at all, he stuttered from a choked-up throat, "My God—my God—Esther—goddamnit—what can I do, Esther? Julia all by herself you say? Oh Christ! I didn't come prepared for this! Goddamnit to hell!"

She looked up at him from her wheelchair, not speaking for a couple of seconds. With her broad and solemn Clayton face and muscular shoulders above her shrunken lower body, she was like a primitive idol. "Well, Thorstein, I do have in mind something for you to do. I won't try to tell you how happy I am that you're obviously ready to do it." He could see that her eyes were moist. In Esther, this was a miracle. "I want you to borrow a rifle from us, go over to Julia, and give her whatever help you can if she needs it. I hope she won't need it. Even if she doesn't, she'll feel better if you're where my ambitious brother Tom ought to be."

"Of course, of course," he said.

She tinkled a small brass bell – "I'm ashamed of myself because I wondered what you'd be willing to do, Thorstein. With all the talking we've done, with all the pleasure I've had because Joseph and I got to count on you as a real friend, I worried about this and I shouldn't have. I should have known you're a man as well as a scholar and a friend."

He couldn't say anything.

Piney appeared – "What you want, Sugar?"

"Fetch the rifle for Mr. Brach, Piney."

The tall military commander of Clayton Plantation gave him a stern glare – "You ain't going to take our rifle and skedaddle out of here, Mr. Brach? I wants your promise you going over to help Miz Clayton and all the niggers at her place."

"If you give me the rifle, I'll do what I can to protect Julia Clayton, her niggers too."

She went back toward the kitchen.

"Piney and I talked about this," Esther explained.

"Sure, sure."

Piney was back, carrying the gun. "This the best rifle we has, Mr. Brach. You know how to use it?"

He wasn't certain. He handled the unloaded rifle at Piney's direction and had to recount for her his experience with guns—as a grown boy shooting geese with a shotgun on the farm in Illinois, and on one occasion killing a deer with a single-shot rifle. This rifle held six bullets and had a lever for reloading. He soon mastered it.

"This here's the best gun we has," said Piney. "Mr. Rourke got no gun like this here." She faced Esther – "Sugar, it ain't right to let this gun offen Clayton Plantation. I tells you it ain't. I could give Mr. Brach my pistol. I'd feel a heap better with this rifle stead of this old pistol which can't hit nothing furthern you can spit."

Esther became briskly decisive – "Mr. Brach gets the rifle, Piney. We've been over that." She gave directions – how to go to Richmond Plantation, where he had never been.

Piney glowered at him – "I hope you is brave as you is smart."

"You don't need to worry about that," said Esther.

"Thanks," said Thorstein, cradling the rifle. He was aware of the incongruity in showing gratitude for the possibility of a shooting encounter in this wilderness. He spoke with some of the light bantering quality they were used to at their Sunday dinners – "Give my regards to Joseph when he comes back from chasing those who've gone traipsing off. We'll have plenty to talk about the next time we meet."

After he mounted his own horse again, Piney watched where he headed. With macabre amusement he imagined that she'd shoot him in the back as a deserter, and get back the rifle, if he rode toward St. Vincent instead of toward Richmond Plantation. God bless you, Piney!

Thorstein thought of himself as a scholar. For him, this meant piecing together facts and events to show how the business community functioned, and then—going far beyond the perceptions of Adam Smith—describing the coition of financial management and people, both managers and managed. In daily practice, this entailed reading, thinking, and countering the dogmas of his peers. A job for a desk, lots of publications, and a good reading light!

He knew he was a rebel, not respectable, declassed. His early marriage had ended in annulment. His affairs had always ruptured in some kind of disaster. He'd never kept a position long. He was a hounded rabbit scuttling from one hole to another. In contrast with the fierce courage of his book, in his personal life he couldn't stand up to competition and certainly not to any violence.

This self-assessment was a given, but it didn't affect him now. He'd been shocked into disregarding who he was or wasn't. Esther's chronicle had appalled him. Julia alone! Much later he became aware that it was a unique experience for him to curse a husband for being insufficiently attentive to a wife! As he rode he simply damned Tom Clayton to hell as a clod incapable of human feeling. In *The Tumefaction of Property* there was a passage about change in values as men moved from farms or small proprietorships into managerial jobs for monopolies. There was estrangement from previously accepted morality. There was a new code that assured conformity, subservience. Out of loyalty to the Pamlico and Gulf, Tom Clayton, this lap dog of Arthur Wilkins, arrogant in his presumptive leonine and masterful aura, was leaving Julia, precious Julia, at the mercy of vicious men whom he himself had provoked! The passage in his book made a kind of biological specimen out of Tom Clayton's behavior, as though it were bottled in alcohol. It gave no hint as to what the feelings of the author were as he rode through Florida wilderness, his rifle ready.

Julia alone! Esther had made plain the character of the men who might attack Richmond Plantation—they'd accept any yarn about raping and killing as true because it accorded with their own pathological impulses. Their lives were an endless writhing of hatred, and they cherished dreams of raping and killing with impunity. Julia alone—Julia, whose face was light in darkness, whose body was spirit of virgin wilderness, whose mind and heart were unheard song.

Hide, Julia! If anyone wants to burn the goddamned house down, let them do it! That's your husband's business, not yours! For God's sake keep yourself safe, Julia!

He *must* stay calm. It was lucky he had such a good horse. Even after the long ride from St. Vincent, he could move at a fast trot along the narrow sandy road toward Richmond Plantation. Good that he had this excellent rifle! He'd minimized, for Piney and Esther, his capability with a gun. The fact was he'd killed his one deer with a single well-placed shot. He was sure of himself, desperate about Julia.

He heard voices before he saw anyone. Ahead of him on the road, at least two men were talking, almost shouting. Thorstein dismounted. Standing on the ground, no nervous horse under him, he could shoot accurately, if it came to that. Perhaps these men had no connection with the riot and killing. But he had to be prepared for whatever they were. He unbuckled one end of the bridle and snagged it through his own belt so that he could lead his horse and at the same time have his hands free for the rifle. The speakers were moving so slowly that even on foot he could shorten his distance from them. The voices became clearer. He couldn't make out words, but the tone was angry and frenetic.

He came upon a clearing in the forest for the schoolhouse, as Esther had said he would. The men ahead of him were walking their horses, in no hurry. For a minute or so, they halted for conversation, more quiet now. He stayed in the shadow of pines and watched. The short winter day was fading. But he could see that two of them had a rifle or shotgun. He assumed that the third man had some kind of gun he couldn't see. The third man was fat and wore a black hat.

They walked their horses again into the road on the other side of the clearing.

In giving him directions, Esther had said that the road would fork three or four hundred yards beyond the schoolhouse. The left fork led toward Olustee. The right fork, toward Richmond Plantation. The horsemen turned right.

Who were these men? It might be that Tom Clayton, worried to a degree about his wife as well as about his cherished railroad construction, had sent three trusted railroad employees to protect her. If so, he would soon be with them as well as Julia at Richmond Plantation, be introduced, and shake their hands. On the other hand, they might be what Esther feared—men out for revenge because Tom Clayton had insulted them. He might have to shoot them. He was sure he could.

He walked faster. If they turned around and saw him, he'd challenge them. He walked at a distance from them that put him beyond the accurate range of most shotguns but gave him with his rifle a certainty for killing.

The road turned close to the bank of the Olustee River. Beyond a wall of brush rooted in water the sky opened out. On the other side of the road was a swamp. As Esther had described, he must be where the bends in the oxbow nearly met, very close to Richmond Plantation.

From far ahead, out of the silence, a dog howled. As one who had been a farm boy, Thorstein thought he knew dog language. An Indian who lived in a shack close to where Thorstein grew up had kept a dog which howled like that. It was not the hysterical yap of a creature which needed a master's command. It was a summons for other dogs to an attack. At almost the same instant, Thorstein saw in the light from the low sun the shape of a roof. Richmond Plantation, without doubt. From beyond that roof, other dogs howled.

The riders halted and talked for a few seconds. Then they smacked their horses and galloped.

The act resolved doubt. If they were railroad employees sent to guard Julia, or anyone else with peaceful intentions, they'd approach the howling dog slowly and call out. Galloping their horses showed surprise attack.

Thorstein tried to run but was held back by his own tired horse, hitched to him by the bridle snagged in his belt. He tore the end of the bridle loose and let the horse go. Then he ran as fast as he could. All his calculations about strategy went by the board. His ears and heart pounding, all he wanted was point blank.

A heavy shotgun roared.

Ahead of him, the riders checked their horses, which milled about, snorting. One of them reared.

Thorstein ran a few more steps and saw Julia.

She was standing on the other side of a slough, and she was putting another shell into a double-barreled shotgun. In a long light-colored dress, she seemed bright and defenseless as a slender birch in the darkening oaks. He raised his rifle, clear in his mind how he would stand, move, aim and fire, killing as required if any one of these men fingered his gun with the least possibility of using it. He remained in shadow — some hunter's wit served him — the riders would more readily die if they didn't know the source of the fatal bullets.

Julia shouted — her voice was biting, strange, with a sharp and unaccustomed rural accent — "*You*, Bascomb Good! I know you! You git out of here! I wouldn't care no more about shooting *you* than I'd care about shooting a hawk in my chicken yard. Git a move on now! My finger's on the trigger and this gun goes off mighty easy!"

She was aiming at the fat man with the black hat.

Thorstein's trigger finger tensed, too.

Time became a missing heartbeat. Would Julia fire — kill the man with the black hat? If she did, he'd kill the others, whether they went for their guns or not.

The fat man wheeled his horse about. He shrank and slumped down in his saddle as he saw Thorstein. "Don't shoot!" he cried out. "I wasn't intending. Miz Clayton she don't — "

Thorstein kept his rifle raised.

Words failed the man, and he passed.

The others followed. One kept his hands over his head. The other kept his gun pointed away from Thorstein.

Julia had cradled her shotgun.

The horsemen vanished in the forest.

"Julia!" he called.

She came forward on the bridge – "Who is it? Who's there?"

He strode out of the shadow of the pines – "Julia, Julia!"

"Thorstein, I can't believe — oh, I've imagined — " She put the butt of the shotgun on the planks of the bridge and freed a hand to brush a strand of hair back from her forehead.

"Yes, yes, Julia, I'm here." As he strode out of the shadow toward her he repeated, "Yes, I'm here, Julia – "

Her face was drawn and blanched. "Oh yes, I'm *really* seeing you!"

"Are you all right?"

"Oh — Thorstein — " She trembled and had to lean on her shotgun. "I could hardly believe it was you."

Going to her on the bridge, he saw the familiar frank eyes, now strangely hardened. "I've been following those men," he said.

She seemed about to collapse – "It's terrible—I was ready to kill that man."

He put his hand on her shoulder, steadying her, and became frankly grim – "I was ready to kill all of them."

"Even if I had to die myself," she went on. "Oh, it's an awful thing!"

"Thank God you're safe!" he exclaimed. He was conscious of how little these words showed the heat of his feelings, and he had a notion that their readiness to kill had molded both of them, had turned them to clay.

"How is it—" she began.

"Esther sent me—with this rifle."

"Oh yes—Esther—she knew, naturally—"

What Esther knew, and what Julia knew she knew, had to do with the absence of Tom Clayton while murder became the norm. And Thorstein knew, too. He was recovering from his rage and readiness to kill the three men Julia had faced with her shotgun, and now he inwardly raged at Julia's husband, whom he'd never met, because of what must be painful and bitter for her. After taking advantage of several bad marriages, how could he be so selfless regarding Julia's bad marriage? He had become submerged in *her* emotions and life, and his own make-up shocked him. He could feel her shoulder, delicate under the thin cotton dress, shivering under his hand. My God she must have feared dying! What was it, beside the ridiculous fact that he was holding a rifle, that kept him from embracing her? "Yes, Esther knew, and I *had* to be here."

She could barely speak – "Of course."

Her trust staggered him even though he was not surprised. He could only repeat, in a husky voice, "Of course."

Her face softened – "I've thought, oh I've thought many times, about your being here friendly-like, *without* these guns—but who knows? What those men might have done—" She put a hand over his, which still rested on her trembling shoulder, and she inclined her face toward both their hands.

"My dear Julia," he murmured. What he was to her, and what she was to him, seemed beyond the control of either of them. Certainly more than just a friend! Bewildered, distrusting himself, he began an aimless and futile explanation – "When your dog howled and they spurred their horses, I knew—oh Julia, Esther was so afraid for you—*I* was so afraid for you – "

"I'm glad—*glad* you're here!" she interrupted. "You're more *important* to me than anyone, except maybe Caroline and William. The way you talk—

the way you look. When you came running out of the pines just now, the whole world seemed lighted up, and I was able to think thank God I'm still alive." She shuddered and had to stop speaking.

"Christ, you are brave!" he exclaimed. But he took his hand from her shoulder.

A sudden change in her expression, in her steady and questioning eyes, showed him that she was mastering her feelings. Law and gospel! "I must go to my children, Thorstein – "

"Your children, oh yes we must think—"

Painfully practical, she looked behind him – "That's your horse, I suppose."

Sure enough, his horse had followed, dragging the unbuckled bridle, and was chomping a patch of grass.

The last sunshine disappeared. The forest became dusky and still.

Was his stay at Richmond Plantation a part of his actual life and not just a page from a book about someone else, perhaps a parchment from a medieval manuscript with golden letters concerning a knight and fair lady in a dark castle? Some knight he was! Skulking in the brush while fair lady dealt with the dragon! A legend seemed to be playing out, with the impossible and the real all mixed up.

The children and Lucy came from a clump of oleanders, the little boy William gamboling in frisky hops as he rushed to hug his mother – who handed Thorstein her shotgun—the plump girl Caroline who regarded him with blue-eyed wonder as she took and received her hug, and the pretty black young woman Lucy, hugged too and saying, "We was so scared, Miz Clayton."

There was the brightness of the kitchen lit by four kerosene lamps and separated by dark verandah from the rest of the expectant house—an apprehensive but vigilant castle—for the dog named Big Thing would sound the alarm if ogres appeared. William said, "Big Thing knows everything."

There was the strange meal of ham and white potatoes and milk that had been baking in an iron pot most of the day.

There was the grace that Julia pronounced before they took up their heavy forks—she knew he was an atheist but kept the custom of her house—"Grace be unto us, and peace for Caroline, William and Lucy. Hold us in your arms, oh Lord. Protect us. Defend, oh Lord, thy servant Thorstein with thy heavenly grace..."

Why did his lips tremble?

"And deliver from evil all thy children in Myrtle. Amen."

There was another custom – "At supper we always talk about the *good* things that have happened to us during the day..."

The day having been what it was, Caroline and Lucy could think only of being able to hide together, while Mama sent away the men. William had added a new beetle to his collection. Julia's good thing was that Mr. Brach had come.

There was the lamplit procession to bed—Julia with Caroline to her room, Thorstein with William to his room—through dim hallways that whispered with a breath of oranges.

And finally, as a kind of good night and sweet dreams, there was William, a spirit boy in overalls, talking Latin with his mother. How proud he was of this knowledge, this secret charm shared with his mother! Could he translate for Professor Brach? He could, and he promptly piped – "Upon this boy just born, in whose time the race of iron shall first cease, while a race of gold shall arise through the whole world, smile oh chaste goddess of births!"

Julia—Julia—smile, my darling—smile!

VII

After sleeping in fits and starts, Joshua commented to Joanna, "Tom Clayton said he was going to need the help of Olustee citizens. It ought to be the other way around—Olustee citizens ought to be running things and demanding *his* help. It was like that during and after the Great Rebellion—folks who wanted the Union, and wanted freedom for blacks, turned out to be helping a lot of rich men run the country their way. That's why I feel funny talking to Tom Clayton as if I was just languishing to help him out."

"I don't know what to say," Joanna responded.

"Listen! They're shooting over in Myrtle!"

He had to wait for several hours before Clayton sent any message, hours during which horsemen, buggies, and wagons passed the store with more recruits for the riot. The scum of the surrounding counties. When Clayton's message did come, it was delivered by a rioter who had been diverted from the purpose of his presence in Olustee by two bits and the honor of making himself useful to the important construction boss. "Mr. Clayton he says for you to meet him down by the railroad," said the messenger.

"What choice do I have?" Joshua asked Joanna, pointlessly. "Be mighty careful today, and keep the doors barred."

He found Clayton seated on the fresh planks of the loading platform. Next to him was Sanford Payne, who didn't look him or any other man in the eye. And there were a few others. Two were Olustee men who might be there for reasons similar to Joshua's. He'd have to sound them out.

"Good morning, Mr. Dale," said Clayton. "Quickest way of telling you where we stand is to let you read this." He handed Joshua a telegram. It was addressed to Thomas Ewell Clayton and was signed Arthur Wilkins. Joshua read:

"GOVERNOR CANNOT BE REACHED STOP UNFORTUNATE YOU HAVE PERMITTED BAD SITUATION TO DETERIORATE TO THIS EXTENT STOP AM COMING TO OLUSTEE WITH A FEW COMPLETELY RELIABLE MEN STOP WILL ARRIVE AROUND NOON STOP BE AT SITE FOR NEW STATION STOP AM READY TO TAKE ANY STEPS WHATSOEVER TO KEEP CONSTRUCTION GOING AND FULFILL MY PART OF CONTRACT WITH STATE STOP DO WHAT YOU CAN BEFORE I ARRIVE IN OLUSTEE TO PUT CREWS BACK TO WORK STOP WILL SUPPORT YOU IN WHATEVER YOU DO STOP MY FUTURE IN THIS STATE AND YOUR FUTURE IN THIS STATE DEPEND UPON PROMPT AND EFFICIENT ACTION STOP ARTHUR WILKINS END"

Joshua handed the telegram back – "It's after noon now."

Clayton drew his famous watch from his vest pocket, pressed the stem to flick open the cover, looked at what it communicated, and nodded – "So it is." Was he really as calm as he appeared? "It's like this, Mr. Dale – Wilkins don't want the responsibility for doing what has to be done."

"Wilkins seems to hold you responsible for this riot. That ain't fair, Mr. Clayton."

"What's fair ain't important, Mr. Dale. A lot of people will read copies of this telegram, including stockholders."

"Stockholders?"

"Florida people been buying stock in the Pamlico and Gulf and have to see this line completed."

Silence. This information suggested a concept which Joshua found hard to absorb. He made a declaration – "This riot would end if a dozen leaders were arrested."

"Well, we have to wait for Wilkins and his few reliable men."

While they waited, one of the men whom Joshua didn't know well talked about Colonel Lawrence Avery, revenge, honor, and teaching the niggers a lesson. No point in sounding *him* out!

A spry and bearded old man walked by the loading platform. He was admired by four other men because he had around his neck a necklace of thong on which were strung four black ears.

Someone stated the obvious—"Must have broke through somewhere."

At twenty-six minutes past twelve — Clayton consulted his watch again and announced the time — the private train of Arthur Wilkins arrived. The magnate, flanked by men with rifles, stood on the rear observation platform. Joshua didn't like his looks. He was tall, gray-haired and distinguished, but his face was snappish. "Hello, Tom," he hailed Clayton. "I got your second wire. Come in here with us."

"Hello, Arthur," Clayton replied.

"Looks like there may be some people here don't *want* progress, but we'll stuff it down their throats whether they want it or not. What d'you say?" He shook Clayton's hand vigorously.

They went inside the private car, which glistened with enamel touched up with gilt.

Quite a crowd collected.

In about two minutes Clayton came back out on the observation platform and called out, "Gentlemen, there ain't room in Mr. Wilkins's car for everybody. But we want representatives of everybody concerned with ending the riot. So we'd like Mr. Payne to come in, in behalf of the security men of the Pamlico and Gulf - and Mr. Joshua Dale, for the citizens of Olustee. I hope the rest of you gentlemen will wait patiently while we figure out some strategy for bringing about peace and putting the niggers back to work. We're going to need all the help we can get."

Out of the small crowd who were listening, one spat and headed toward Myrtle. Two followed.

Joshua had met men who exercised great power only during the War, when he was young. As he boarded the Wilkins train, he recalled one of these occasions.

He was reporting to General Sherman the disposition of Wheeler's cavalry. He galloped the length of a column. There were mules with pots and skillets, axes and picks and grubbing hoes and spades — an army which lived off the country, which made sense, since the country had to support the army anyway. This way, it was done without middlemen and in a state that hadn't been paying taxes for several years. And there were great crowds of colored folks. The whole length of the column they were singing jubilee songs — "Rooster, don't you crow no more. You are free! You are free!"

The soldiers sang too - "Snap poo, snap Peter, real rebel-eater!"

At first, Sherman didn't hear Joshua's report. "Silence!" he shouted. An aide repeated, "Silence!" And the word rolled all down the line —

"Silence...silence...silence...silence..." And they all *were* silent. The shuffling of feet and the muted clanking of equipment, strangely without voices, kept coming back to Joshua in dreams. The will of the Grand Army of the Republic, of the Union, was a single body. The unity in silence predestined victory. He would always so remember it.

Arthur Wilkins's salon car was paneled in carved walnut with high spots, such as the tips of rose petals or the cheeks of cupids, lightly brushed with gold. It was furnished with enormous overstuffed chairs in green-blue velvet or in dark-brown silk brightly embroidered with scenes suggesting the history of the Pamlico and Gulf Railroad. An enormous oil painting of the Grand Canal in Venice, according to a small brass label, dominated the whole shebang. Joshua thought: as Wilkins rides, he can look at that instead of out the window at drainage ditches. Power? There had been the power of the Grand Army of the Republic on the march to the sea. Now this!

Wilkins rose from behind a spindly and foreign-looking desk, against which leaned several rifles and shotguns ornamented with silver filigree. On a red blotting pad were a few papers, some boxes of cartridges, and a big revolver.

Clayton made introductions.

The railroad magnate's fingers were dry and brittle as pieces of chalk.

Another man remained in his chair but extended a long, thin arm — Dexter Hewitt, general manager of the Pamlico and Gulf, "Some mess, huh?" he said.

A third man of the magnate's party was looking out a window across the swamp toward Myrtle. As he turned, he looked thick and square, like a piece of Mission furniture. The flat top of his head was visible through a short haircut. There were right angles in his nose, his jaw flared sharply before caving in to join his skull, and he thrust toward Joshua a hand with fingers all of a length and ending in thick square stubs.

"Captain Van Bibber," said Clayton.

It was never explained what he was captain of.

Joshua noted that some hidden feeling in Sanford Payne had been touched. As soon as Gray Man entered the salon car, he stopped short, staring about with his wide pale eyes, standing on tip-toe, no more able to tread naturally the tawny golden carpet than he could have trod a pink cloud. The gristle that layered his face softened a bit. Obviously, he felt that he had come "home," as in the songs — he was "saved," as the churchgoers put it—or, as the boys around the courthouse might say, he was "in."

Wilkins was pleased with this reaction. "This is the country for young men," he said. "Go south, young man, I say when I'm up north. But you're already south, young man. Splendid, eh?"

To Joshua, Wilkins said, "Once we settle this trouble and get the railroad established, I expect we'll bring you a lot more prosperous customers than you now have."

Then, with an irascible and petulant rasp, the magnate said, "Now, Tom, give me the whole story."

According to Clayton, the trouble started with Bascomb Good—white trash who didn't want to own up to being white trash. Tried to become county clerk in Hamilton County and couldn't make it. Fixed it with a captain at the Wehadke Farm to let the nigger Charley Williams think he had a chance to escape. Charley was just a patsy, of course. Lawrence Avery might have known that Charley was a patsy, or he might not have known. Didn't matter now that Lawrence Avery was dead and dragged out of Myrtle in the middle of the night by some Ku Kluxers who regarded him highly and buried him in the church cemetery. Of course Bascomb Good was being paid by the Nashville and Mobile Line. If he weren't paid, how could he get horses for his gang and keep them fired up with victuals and drink? And who besides the Nashville and Mobile Line had any reason for paying Bascomb Good?

"This all fits," said Van Bibber. He spoke with an accent Joshua couldn't identify. "Now that you have retained me and my organization, you are entitled to all the significant information we have. We have two agents in Nashville, and we have known about this plan to scare your niggers off the job for about two weeks."

"Why didn't you tell me this?" snapped Wilkins.

"You did not renew the contract with Industrial Services until this morning."

Wilkins snorted.

"It is always cheaper to pay for prevention than for cure," the captain went on. "If my service had been brought in earlier, this cheap little fat man Bascomb Good would never have left his squalid home. The black man would have stayed in prison, or on a chain gang. You'd have no problem about your contract for the right-of-way."

The contract to which the captain referred was a much-debated political issue. Populist voters had enough power to insist on a clause in the contract which required the Pamlico and Gulf to pay a penalty of twenty-five thousand dollars for each day after April First on which the line remained uncompleted. Fair enough, in view of the Pamlico and Gulf's privilege to cut and sell timber from the scandalously broad right-of-way. But the amount, twenty-five thousand dollars, stuck in the craw because Wilkins could handle it so casually.

Was it true that Wilkins would give the same amount to his construction superintendent as a bonus if the line *was* finished on time? Joshua wondered. Twenty-five thousand dollars! Far more than he and almost all other Florida citizens would ever see.

Clayton spoke up – "Let's not assume we won't finish on time. I don't know what arrangement Arthur has made with you, Grotius, but I figured the reason you're here is to help so we *can* finish in the time specified."

Wilkins fixed unblinking eyes on Van Bibber – "If you can deliver the services we need, perhaps we can arrange protection against this kind of thing in the future."

The railroad president and board chairman was wearing a tweed hunting jacket, and from one of the pockets he drew a handful of revolver cartridges, which he arranged in squares within squares on the blotting pad, destroyed, and arranged again.

The other five men watched him in a silence that became uncomfortable. But the magnate just waited. He seemed to be demanding sound thinking.

Clayton said, "Before we decide to depend only on our own men and guns, I'd like to know if we've used up every chance, every last chance there is, of getting a company of militia."

"I told you in my wire," Wilkins said, impatiently, "we'll have to do without the militia."

"We ought to have the militia," said Clayton. "You're a man the state is beholding to."

"It seems that don't make any difference—yet," the magnate responded. "Whatever we do we've got to do ourselves. I wired the governor, but he's on a yachting trip, or so says his wife. That wire your marshal here sent to him never reached him, but it was shown to me. What this state needs is a housecleaning at the capitol. In due time we'll see to that. It could be an opportunity for you, Tom. By God, I admit I'm shocked by what's going on here."

In a somewhat strangled voice Sanford Payne said, "I been hunting that Bascomb Good, Mr. Wilkins, and I aim to hunt him some more. We ain't going to stand for him treating you like this—"

This goddamned hothouse atmosphere makes him feel more than ever like shedding blood, thought Joshua.

Wilkins smiled—"I appreciate your concern, young man."

"Makes me uncomfortable for you, having that Bascomb Good running around free and loose."

Wilkins held up a long and slender hand—"Don't worry about him—not now, anyway." The magnate gave Clayton a questioning glance that meant why-did-you-include-this-fellow-in-our-talk?

But the construction superintendent met this look with a bland stare. He wants Wilkins to understand that he didn't have the men to keep a big riot from happening, Joshua figured.

Captain Van Bibber and Dexter Hewitt regarded Payne with mildly ironical smiles.

"How about new crews, Arthur?" drawled Clayton. "You must have some good section gangs up in the Carolinas."

"Skeleton crews," said Wilkins. "We've been operating shorthanded to get more money for the line to Payhokee. Every road in the Carolinas needs repair."

"How many men do you need?" Dexter Hewitt asked Clayton.

"Two hundred at least, a hundred for each shift, working day and night. Track can be put down at night, though I'm against it when it ain't necessary."

Wilkins destroyed an arrangement of cartridges. "I can't get one-quarter that many, not in the time we have."

"The conditions are such there's only one thing to do," said Clayton. "But before we go into that, I'd like to tell you, Arthur—I realize as well as any businessman from up north it's the nigger problem at the bottom of all the troubles a new enterprise hereabouts has to face."

"Why do you say that now?" asked Wilkins.

"Cause I want to make it clear you ain't to be blamed, and the Pamlico and Gulf ain't to be blamed, for anything we have to do to finish the railroad."

After one of his habitual thoughtful pauses, the magnate said, "When I first came down to Florida, I admit I was worried about the race problem. But I thought the trend of the past twenty years justified some optimism.

The excesses of War and Reconstruction seemed to be over, for the most part. Now I don't know. We're sitting on a powder keg and any cheap crook can light the fuse. I've been trying to interest other men in investment down here. But unless the country is pacified in a hurry, it's going to be hard. We had to fight some selling on the exchange. I'm saying this, Tom, because you seem to think a frank expression of my views is important at this time. Also, I'm telling you this because you're a coming man in this state, and you've got as much to gain or lose in cleaning up this mess as anybody has."

"I realize that, Arthur," said Clayton. "And I ain't thinking only of the generous bonus you offered if the road's done on time."

"I won't go into the losses the Pamlico and Gulf stands to incur," continued the magnate. The fact is he did go into those possible losses. For some ten minutes, he and Dexter Hewitt competed in elaborating on figures. Then Wilkins leaned back in his big swivel chair, his face seamed and white, his bony fingers drumming. He looked exhausted. His gray eyes with their peculiar green speckles focused on the possibility of ruin as though he were seeing a ghost.

Poor feller! Joshua said to himself. Here he is with his railroads, hotels, oil wells, steamship lines, steel mill, and bank—not to mention private possessions such as that marble palace he's building or his house on Fifth Avenue in New York—and he's scared of financial ruin! On the other hand, Joanna and me are worried about a new wagon and another mule so we can get out of this nest of vipers if we have to. Joshua had been waiting for the right moment to suggest a course of action, and he'd been confused by the talk about the financial condition of the Pamlico and Gulf, which wasn't at all what he'd expected. Now, in view of Wilkins's anxiety, the right moment seemed to have come. "I think you worry too much, Mr. Wilkins," said Joshua. "How many men did you bring down here with you – on this train?"

Wilkins was taken aback. But he replied, "Thirty-five. Twenty-one who work for the Pamlico and Gulf, and fourteen of Captain Van Bibber's men."

"I propose we arrest the leaders of this riot and throw them in the calaboose, maybe a dozen or so. If we do that, the rest would go home."

"How many white men are out there in the riot?" asked Van Bibber.

"Eight hundred or so," said Clayton.

"The newspapers haven't said anything about that."

"I haven't read the newspapers. I counted them myself."

Van Bibber turned to Wilkins – "I wasn't told I'd have to deal with a race war."

"You exaggerate, Captain," said Clayton, pleasantly.

Wilkins became harsh – "The only value of your service, Captain Van Bibber, is that it's supposed to deal with all sorts of unpredictable situations."

"It ain't as if there's a real army attacking Myrtle," persisted Joshua. "The men we have to put out of commission is just a mob, and that's different. I learned about mobs during Reconstruction. You arrest a few leaders and the rest crawl back into their holes."

"Some of the leaders of that mob, as you call it, are important men in this part of Florida," said Clayton.

Joshua became angry – "Being important don't excuse shooting at people, white or black."

Wilkins changed the subject. Turning to Clayton, he asked, "Suppose you do get some of your crews back to work, can you finish by April First?"

"I think so," Clayton answered. "We can put down the track without driving every spike. Just fix it so a light engine can go to Payhokee. That would cover your contract."

"Can you get your old crews back?" asked Hewitt.

Wilkins broke in – "If there's going to be shooting, with railroad employees involved, I want it understood I'm in this thing only because I have to be. I don't want any tales going round about the responsibility of the Nashville and Mobile Line, either. I'll deal with them in another way. I can't say I have any love for their president. He's pigheaded and don't have any ability in correct organization. Just the same, the worst thing that could happen would be that people with money to invest, people up north in particular, would get the idea it's commonplace for business enterprise in Florida to use unethical methods."

"The ethical thing would be to arrest them responsible," said Joshua.

"I ain't the law!" exclaimed Wilkins, exasperated. "We got no militia, as I said, and you ought to know, Mr. Dale, how much you can expect from the marshal in this town."

Everyone was silent for a few seconds. It was a way of snapping to attention because the important man was a bit riled.

Joshua had to accept the bitter reality that his proposal to arrest leaders of the mob was futile. Wilkins would have none of it. Wilkins seemed to think he was just as ridiculous as Sanford Payne with his talk about shooting Bascomb Good. The great magnate, with his salon car of carved walnut and gold, and his "few completely reliable men" presumably in the next car, wasn't making this trip to arrest crazed men with guns or deal with trash like Good — or to stop and condemn a race riot. His single-minded devotion to finishing the railroad line and making money put any human concern, good or bad, either to save lives or to end one life, beyond this earthly sphere. Joshua's motive was in cold storage, on the moon. Wilkins's attitude was maddening and frustrating, especially since Joshua was standing in the carpeted and gilded evidence that it had worked.

Clayton said, "I'd like to keep as many railroad workers from getting killed as I can. To do that, we have to end the riot in a hurry and not let it drag on. We have to get the railroad workers out of Little Africa. Ordinary folks here in Olustee, and all over Florida for that matter, want to see this riot finished. They ain't in favor of too much killing either, even if some of them are worked up by this yarn about a rape - "

"Is this yarn true?" asked Wilkins.

"No, it ain't. Sanford Payne found out the nigger Charley Williams is dead and buried on the Wehadke State Farm. Never left it."

"It's easier to make a story stick if there's no way of showing it ain't so," Payne himself commented.

"It don't make no difference," Clayton went on. "We're dealing with men who're persuaded the story is true."

"What do the more responsible citizens think," asked Wilkins — "men who might buy stock in the Pamlico and Gulf?"

"They'll curse the damn Yankees until they can make money doing something more practical. And they'd rather curse the niggers. What they think about Charley Williams just don't count. Getting wrought up over Colonel Lawrence Avery getting killed don't even count very much. When we go into Myrtle, your men and Captain Van Bibber's men, Payne, me and citizens like Mr. Dale if he's willing — everybody in Florida is going to know that when the Pamlico and Gulf hires niggers, them niggers work, and there ain't nobody, white or black, going to keep them from working. Everybody is going to know that Arthur Wilkins don't stand for this kind of foolishness — nor Tom Clayton neither. The responsible citizens won't exactly love you for this, but they'll take their hats off to you. They need the railroad."

Wilkins looked at Joshua as he replied, "They need the railroad all right—if they want to shingle their roofs or wear shoes or put themselves apart from niggers."

Joshua ignored the magnate and said to Clayton, "It ain't clear to me what you have in mind."

"I'm going to burn down Myrtle and drive the niggers out, and we're going to protect any railroad workers we find."

"There's going to be a lot of killing if you do that."

"Not so much as there would be if this riot drags on for another week."

Joshua spoke to the whole group – "I won't have no part in this!"

"I respect your right to make your own decision," said Wilkins.

Clayton studied Joshua for a moment and then turned to Sanford Payne – "Well, let's get the white trash off their asses and charging into Myrtle. There's enough of them. All they need is somebody to start them off, somebody to lead them."

The right-hand man's pale and milky eyes widened and glowed. "Reckon I can start them off, if that's what you and Mr. Wilkins want."

Clayton looked at Wilkins.

"Thank you, young man," said the magnate. "That's bully. I won't forget this, you can rest assured."

"You can make one hell of a big reputation, Sanford," said Clayton.

"You're going to lead that mob?" exclaimed Van Bibber.

"Just control it," said Wilkins.

"You can lend a hand," said Clayton, genially.

But the captain objected to sending his men into battle until he had seen the front lines. Wilkins had to threaten him with dismissal and no future work for the Pamlico and Gulf. The exercise of power made him puff out his chest, and he added, putting this strategy of murder into those moral terms that made him feel comfortable, "If the white trash start a riot and stop work on the railroad, they ought to finish the riot, so the work can start up again."

During this interchange, Joshua Dale was of two minds: should he leave this conclave of buzzards, calculating how to fatten themselves off the production of corpses or should he remain, learn more of their plans, and so be able to do whatever poor thing he might? The other four men were ignoring him. Partly for this reason and partly because he had no other definite thing to do, he stayed and listened.

There was general satisfaction that the best of all possible plans had been approved.

Clayton said to Payne, "Building this railroad is a great experience for us. In a short time it will be done, and whether I earn my bonus or not, you and me are going to take a vacation together, and go hunting."

Hewitt said to Van Bibber, "This should be interesting to you. If you're going to work down here in Florida, you'll want to know first-hand about the race problem." It wasn't clear whether he was being ironical or not.

Wilkins said, "Let's go talk to our troops."

The next car was an ordinary coach. Some men played poker. Some just chatted. There was an air of seriousness although one man, obviously one of Van Bibber's thugs, was giving a forced laugh. The Pamlico and Gulf employees were men with desk jobs—Joshua judged their type—men without political or moral spine, men who had thrown in their souls for a paycheck and were capable of almost any desperate act out of what they would call loyalty. Tailor's dummies. Lice of civilization.

Wilkins was abrupt, commanding – "Men, most of you know Tom Clayton, who's been bossing the construction of the new line to Payhokee-on-the-Gulf. We've been talking over this riot, and I've settled on a plan for ending it and getting the crews back to work. I'm giving Mr. Clayton full charge of carrying out this plan. Assisting Tom Clayton will be Captain Van Bibber, and I guess that all of you who don't know him have heard of him. Good luck, Tom." He shook the construction superintendent's hand formally and sat down.

Clayton spoke for about ten minutes, making it clear to each man what was expected of him. Obviously, he had plans in his mind even before the private train had arrived. He concluded, "There's only one way to end a war, which is what this is. That's to win it. So take all the ammunition your belts will hold and put more in your pockets and meet me outside in fifteen minutes."

Without speaking to any of them, Joshua left.

Near the observation platform of Wilkins's salon car, about a score of rioters clamored for the help of the railroad men in killing niggers.

Any peace-minded citizens of Olustee were shut up in their houses.

Joshua was alone with his rifle.

*

After Mark Richardson fired the old Sharps at the man pointing a pistol at Mingo, he scrambled down the other side of the *Nellie May* and waded into the swamp between the railroad tracks and Myrtle. To his left there was high ground and a road, but somebody in that direction fired a shotgun. Mark called, "Mingo!" But there was no reply.

The water in the swamp was cold, but he had to stand it. He could hear other railroaders wading. They must be standing it, too. The sound of the shotgun told them there was some rioter and maybe more than one rioter on the dry road.

Soon, he was soaked to the waist. He pulled the bottom of his jacket up around his chest and tied the corners to keep it from dragging in the water. He held the rifle high.

The big cypresses in the swamp had been cut, and there was plenty of light from the moon among the small trees that were left. He saw the moving shapes of other railroaders but couldn't make out who they were. He didn't call out to them nor they to him. They didn't want to draw fire. Somebody was shooting into the swamp. The bullets hissed in the water and plunked into stumps.

The mud was stinking, and he was afraid of snakes.

When at last he stood on firm ground, his britches and the tail of his shirt were heavy with slime.

There was a dead horse on the road toward his home, and it smelled. It was swollen and must have been there for at least a day, he figured.

All over, far and near, dogs began to bark. One of them gave a whining yelp and then was silent. Perhaps somebody cuffed it.

For a moment he thought that it was wrong for all the railroaders to go home, splitting up like this. They'd be more powerful if they stayed together, as they had been in leaving the camp and in taking over the *Nellie May*.

And he thought of the man he'd shot. He hoped the man wasn't dead. He'd be changed into a person he'd never been and never wanted to be if he killed a man. Azri Peters once read from Scripture – "Thou shalt not kill!" But the man would have killed Mingo, and perhaps the Lord would balance that against whatever he'd done.

For shooting a white man he'd have to leave Myrtle whether the man was killed or not, and thinking about that was fearsome.

His mother could never leave. There was the cabin. She and the father he'd never known had built the big room before he was born. When he was still a small boy, he'd helped his mother build the second small room for his mother's sleeping. They lived on what they had in the cabin and around the cabin. They had the hogs, the cow, the chickens, the cornfield, the peas, the beans. They had an ax, a saw, a shovel, a hoe. They had the stove and the sewing machine bought with dollars he'd earned as a bridge monkey. They had the two beds with mattresses his mother had made. They even had a shotgun, and in the woods he'd killed hogs nobody could claim. Before he had to run away, he'd have to help drive off the white trash so his mother could keep the cabin.

It was wrong but also partly right that he'd shot the man. So it might be that his punishment wouldn't last. It might be that he wouldn't be long on a lonesome road, begging strangers for some chore to do, so he could eat and sleep somewhere under cover when it was cold or rainy. After his punishment, no longer than the good Lord saw fit to make it, and everybody forgot what he'd done, he'd come back to his mother, he'd just show up without her knowing ahead of time, like now.

There was no light in the cabin, but smoke twisted up from the chimney. His mother knew that somehow he'd come, wet and cold, and she'd kept the stove going. The dog Spook came from under the house, rubbed against his cold legs, and Mark spoke. "Ma!" he called. The riot would make her afraid that someone intending harm might come, maybe a Ku Kluck. "I'm here!"

The door opened. "Mark. Praise the Lord I lived to this time! Bina, put down that shotgun. It's Mark."

She embraced him—she was thin and bony - "You's wet. You's shaking. Take them wet things off."

He heard movement in the dark cabin. "Who's here?"

"The Peters chillun—Bina, Amos and Ruth."

"Amos? Hold this rifle, Amos. Take good care of it."

He felt the boy's hands, and the rifle drifted away.

"Bina?"

"Here I is." Her voice came from a dark corner, near the floor.

"Ruth? Where's Ruth?"

Bina's voice replied - "Sleeping—she sleeping."

He could hear his mother rummaging in a trunk in her sleeping room. He felt for the peg behind the stove and hung his jacket on it. Then he kicked out of his soggy shoes – "I needs these shoes just for winter anyhow, to keep my feet from splitting." He shuddered out of his slimy britches and shirt and ran naked out of the cabin, around in back of it, and dropped them over a sawhorse. Back inside, his mother had dry britches and shirt ready for him.

A narrow moonbeam followed him into the cabin through the opened door, and he could see Bina Peters cross-legged on the floor with his mother's shotgun across her lap.

"Now I's here, the chilluns won't have to tote shotguns," he said.

"I ain't no chile," Bina declared.

"She killt that Ku Kluck Avery," said his mother.

"Bina killt a man?" He expected her to say something, but she didn't.

"Bina and me, we have to—" He was beginning to say that he and Bina would have to run from Myrtle, maybe together. But he didn't want his mother to hear this at this time.

His mother told him what it was needful he should know—how Azri Peters was whipped, how Miz Dale wrapped him in a lardy sheet, how Colonel Avery and his gang came into Myrtle – "The white men were disagreeing amongst theirselves. They talked a long time down the road a piece and then Colonel Avery and another man come on us here. I say, 'White man, don't you come no closer! I has a gun and I will use it!' Other white man shooted at us here. Then all the white men shooted. The bullets come through the boards like bees, and a splinter stuck me. That why my arm all wrapped up. Colonel Avery say, 'Hold your fire. I didn't tell you to do that!' But he take a pistol from under his coat and come on. The splinter make me drop the shotgun, and Bina pick it up. Boom! Right side of me! I look at Bina. She putting in another shell. I look out the door. Colonel Avery flat on his back."

So Bina Peters, not yet a full-grown woman, had done the same as he'd done! What was in her heart about it? "Was Colonel Avery killt?" he asked.

"Killt? Oh yes he killt."

"I'd rather rot in the ground than have a beating," said Bina. "I seed what they did to Grandpa."

Neither he nor his mother had anything to say for a minute. Bina filled him with wonder. "Where is Grandpa Peters?" he asked at last.

His question wasn't answered. His mother was trapped by her memory of what had happened, and by her need to tell her son – "I heard another gun somewhere, and tother man fell over. It were Granny Robinson shooted him. After that was plenty shooting and the rest of the white men galloped out of here fastern they come in. It might be us black folks hit one or two, and one horse was killt. It laying beside the lumber pile, and it have to stay put cause it ain't safe to go and drag it and bury it. Somebody took the Colonel away in the night, and we buried tother one under Granny Robinson's cabbages, where the diggings easy."

"Where is Parson Azri Peters?" he persisted.

"We ain't seen Azri since him and Bina brung the chilluns here. He say he going to the white minister in Olustee. I say it risky, with white trash full of whiskey and shooting. But he say a man of God have to stop the Ku Klucks and all the other sinners. Where you get this rifle, Mark?"

He told her.

"It's all done," she said.

She was harsh, signifying that much besides the man that Mark had shot was done. She talked about the Quinns who lived in a cabin some distance from others in Myrtle, and had been butchered by white trash—Joel Quinn, Nancy Quinn, and maybe all the children. It might be that one or two of the children had hid. She didn't know. Joel and Nancy couldn't always collect all the children to come to church. The Quinn's cabin was burned. All their possessions took. Thinking that one or two of the Quinn children might be alive called to mind a dream she'd had before Mark was born. There had been another child before Mark, a girl who'd lived only nine days. But before Mark was born, an angel came to her in a dream and said, "Not last time but this time!" Sure enough, Mark lived. The Lord might decide she was done, like Nancy Quinn, the cabin too, the hogs, the chickens, the cornfield—done, done. And Azri Peters—she loved Azri Peters as he might have been her man but never was no matter what some folks said—was he done too? What was Azri expecting when he went off to the white minister in Olustee? She couldn't say what she didn't know. But she did know Mark was not done—the angel had told her in the dream before he was born. Mark had a long road ahead of him.

Her words flowed like a river. Did she pause because what she said about Azri might be cruel to Bina and Amos? "Bina? Amos?" she asked. Where were they in the dark cabin?

"I's here, Miz Richardson," said Bina. She didn't regard herself as grown-up enough to call his mother Martha.

"I just don't know," his mother whispered. The Lord hadn't told her about Bina and Amos, whether they were done or not, and she couldn't pretend anything.

Did Mark feel joy because his mother was certain he wasn't done? Did he feel joy because death was a frothing white hound like the mad dog which had been shot after it bit a child who died, a dog that Azri Peters, speaking from the pulpit, had compared to the beast in the Book of Revelations that caused everyone, rich and poor, free and slave, to be branded with the beast's mark so that no person could buy or sell or plant or harvest unless she or he was bitten by the mad white hound. Had *he* been bitten when he got Mr. Billy's rifle? What had Parson Azri meant? Mark knew he couldn't kill the white hound Parson Azri talked about the way the mad dog that bit the child was killed, but the notion of killing it gave him joy.

After it became light enough to see, Mark walked out and found others who felt a kind of joy a little like his, even though they didn't know what he was talking about when he recalled for them Parson Azri Peters's sermon. They worked together chopping down trees which fell across the road from Olustee and blocked it.

Mark found a railroader with twelve paper cartridges for a Sharps, and some used cartridges too. He showed Mark, with empty cartridges, how to fire, eject the fired cartridge from the chamber, and reload – fast. He held three cartridges between his teeth. He was very patient. At last, he gave Mark five of the twelve good cartridges – "Don't waste them, brother. Make every one bite."

Some men talked of driving the white trash out of Olustee.

There was no noise from the direction of the railroad tracks until the sun passed its highest. The attack began when someone threw a kerosene-soaked torch on the roof of a house. Mark was with about a dozen men in front of the church when the burning began, and they all ran toward this first blazing house, carrying their guns. Three were shot down.

The white trash, the Ku Klucks, and a few well-dressed white men began to scream. First there were separate screams as one man or another held high his oily flame and hurled it toward some cabin, or fired his gun with a curse if he missed and yelped with triumph if the bullet struck as intended. In only a few minutes these separate screams mixed into a single screeching roar that hung over the mob like a cloud, following it wherever it went.

There were hundreds of murdering whites. On foot and on horses. Swarming over the railroad grading. Coming with torches and guns through the woods. Nobody through the swamp. They were running from Olustee. Ropes were snagged on the trees across the road, and horsemen dragged them aside.

No feeling of joy could keep Mark from knowing there were too many of them for the black folks of Myrtle. He decided to die.

When they were a hundred yards away they shot a boy who ran from a burning house. Then they shouted at each other in some kind of argument. Mark took careful aim and fired. His target continued waving a torch and yelling, just as before. Mark ran closer to the mob and hid behind a house. He aimed and fired again. Again he missed. A dozen men headed for cover, some on one side of Mark and some on the other. He ran for a tree, and as he ran he saw one of the white men aim at him. They both fired at once and they both missed.

Behind the tree, Mark found himself shaking so he couldn't steady his gun. Suddenly, he was disgusted with dying. He thought of his mother, and of Bina and the children. Dodging to make himself hard to hit, he ran toward home. There was so much shooting by this time that he couldn't tell whether any of it was meant for him or not. A black man near him fell, his chest bloody.

One scene was like a foolish dream:

Sheltered by the church from the gunfire, Richard the Barber was talking to a small crowd, perhaps twenty people, women as well as men. As usual, he was dressed in a jacket that was not a castoff, a fairly new jacket no doubt bought for him by his master, Sanford Payne. Richard's round belly strained at the bottom buttons. His spectacles glittered. With all that fighting going on, his little round body and flabby face seemed more out of place in Myrtle than on ordinary days.

Seeing Mark, Richard shouted, "Run that way!" He threw out a pudgy arm. "Get out of town! The railroad bosses is there in the woods! They's ready to protect anybody works for the railroad, and any other niggers goes to them!"

"Git your gun, man!" Mark answered.

Richard whipped off his spectacles. This gesture was a habit. Whether he did it to see better or simply to take on the attitude and stance of a white professional man, no one could say. "I's telling you how to stay alive!"

Inside the door his mother gave him a hug. She didn't say a word. Bina was standing with the children. Amos and Ruth, on either side of her, were holding her hands. When Ruth saw Mark, she began to cry. "Hush—hush—hush"—with one arm he swept her up and clutched his rifle with his other hand.

"We can't stay here!" Bina declared.

Through the door, Mark could see Richard the Barber trotting clumsily toward the woods, away from the shooting. About a dozen men and women and a few children followed him. At least four of the men were railroaders.

"I wouldn't ever trust that man," Martha Richardson said.

"Bina's right," said Mark. "We got to get out."

His mother gave him an angry look – "I won't leave this house."

"There's too many white men to be fit off. I saw them. They burning all the cabins. They killing all the people. They killing chilluns."

"There no other place I can live."

"I can make a new house. I can't make myself a new ma."

Bina came to the door beside them – "I ain't going to run out of town."

Mark just looked at her.

She pointed – "If the white men reach that shed, I's taking Amos and Ruth, and we going across to the church and hide under the porch."

"There ain't room for a cat under that porch," said his mother.

"Chillins goes under there all the time. They dug out the sand."

"First thing white trash do is shoot under houses."

"Iffen they shoot under the church, won't harm nobody under the porch. Beams of the porch sets right on the ground, and there ain't no place where they can poke a gun."

"Ma, you git under that porch with Bina."

She gave him a kind of look he'd never seen before. In a strange way she was apart from him – "Where *you* going?"

"I got two bullets left. I can git to the woods. I can shoot two of them."

"I got five shells for the shotgun. I's coming with you."

"You can't run, Ma. Your feet ain't good enough."

"I got more bullets than you."

"A shotgun ain't no good. They'd kill you with rifles before you can git close enough."

"I'll hide and wait until they close enough."

"Bina, don't you stay here no longer." He put Ruth down.

She began to cry and he placed a finger on her lips—"Hush."

Bina picked up Ruth – "Amos—you come. When I run, you run."

She's strong for a little woman, thought Mark. Amos scampered after her. As far as Mark could tell, nobody shot at them as they crossed the road. He and his mother watched as they slithered under the porch of the church. It was just a platform standing only about a foot above the ground. The hole the children squirmed through was like an animal's burrow.

"Ma, git over there where Bina went—"

At that instant a bullet smashed into the house. It split a board and struck in a rafter.

"That come from behind," Mark said. "They all around." He clutched his mother's arm and shook her a little.

She drew away from him and took the shotgun from where it was leaning against the wall. "You git you*self* under there with Bina. I's getting the railroad money."

Mark's pay was always put in a small tin lard pail that was hung on a nail between two studs behind a movable cupboard. His mother began to shift the cupboard about to get at it. As he hesitated, she cried, "You go long now!"

Mark ran into the road. He made sure no white man was in sight before he plunged under the porch. His mother hadn't come out yet, but he was afraid to call out. There was shooting on the other side of the cabin, quite close. Somebody was screaming. She'd got to come out now, he thought.

Bina was waving her arm from a pile of dead live oak leaves that almost closed the opening. "You come in *here*!"

Through the burrow, he found himself under the porch in a space between joists. Children had hollowed out a bit in the sand, as Bina had said. He could see Bina's bare feet drawing up in a tunnel under the joist to his right.

Her voice was muffled – "Amos other side of you. I got Ruth here with me."

Some light came through cracks between the floorboards over his head, and through a knothole in the riser of the front step he could see a short stretch of road. "Can you look out?" he asked Bina.

"Just a bit. There's a crack."

"You see ma?"

"No. Where she at?"

"She say she coming soon's she git my railroad money."

He could hear Bina crawling about. "I can't see her," she said.

He felt trapped. His rifle was squeezed to his side, and there wasn't any room to use it, or even any way of looking out, or of poking it out, and then using it. "I's going back for her," he told Bina. There came into his mind some of his mother's words that seemed to show mixed-up notions, maybe including a willingness to die, like his own feeling less than an hour ago. He could imagine her standing in the cabin, looking sadly about, unable to leave in a hurry—perhaps sitting on the edge of the bed where she'd told him he'd been born.

As soon as he had this imagining, he heard the shotgun. The boom came from right across the road.

He bit hard to keep his teeth from chattering. He fought hard to make his body act as it should, his mind filled with a clear picture of what might be going on—or what *must* be going on. He had come under the porch only after he made sure he could do it without being seen. Some white man or men must have seen his mother. Now she would never come.

There was so much shooting he couldn't tell whether any of it had to do with her. Almost all of it sounded from a hundred yards away, or more.

The shotgun blasted again.

She probably wasn't hit yet. She had reloaded.

Mark wormed backward to slide feet first out of the burrow, dragging his rifle.

But Bina pushed her head, shoulder and arms under the joist next to him, and she grabbed the barrel of his gun - "You go out now and you git us *all* murdered."

He gave the rifle a hard yank, but she held on. Their faces were only a few inches apart, and she came for his face with her teeth.

Then his mother's shotgun crashed a third time. He moaned, and Bina drew back. He let the rifle go. The shotgun had sounded from down the road, where there was lots of shooting. His mother had taken to heart his words about a shotgun being no good unless you were close enough.

They didn't hear the shotgun again. The rattle and crash of all kinds of guns were closer. They could make out words in the shouting. From right at hand, out in the road, a pistol barked.

Bina was whispering - "Don't you cry, Ruth. You *must* not cry!"

Mark thought he felt Bina's hand drawn across his face. Was he crying, or was it Ruth?

Shooting. Shouting. Screams. Horses on the road. Crackle from burning. Smell of burning pine. Crash of a collapsing cabin.

"Don't make no noise at all," Bina whispered. "We don't talk no more. We don t move a finger 'til dark. You hear me, Amos?"

"I hears you."

Voices on the road. Feet on the planks over their heads. Feet with shoes on.

"I see that pail soon's you."

"Finders keepers, and I's the one finding it."

"You ain't the only one—"

A man stumbled and fell, or sat hard, jarring the whole porch.

"It's only fair to split this up."

"Just think of a nigger having all this money!"

"You set that pail *here*, right *here*, so I can see what you doing with it."

"You got no call to talk like that!"

"You set it down or you fighting me and no nigger!"

"I's setting it down anyway, and you got no power over me one way or t'other!"

"Well, do it then."

"I's a fair man and I don't cheat nobody, and I don't take kindly to be spoke to like that!"

There was wrangling for a long time. The silver dollars were stacked over and over again. One man was always complaining about another man's stacking. Six hands scrambled the coins over and over again. The three united only when others came by –

"We all found this!"

"Git away from here!"

"We all's splitting up, and we ain't going to have no*body* horning in."

After there were three piles of dollars accepted as equal, there was one dollar left over. The white men agreed there must be some kind of justice for determining what to do with that extra dollar, but it was sure hard to locate. At last they draw sticks.

Then there was some hard feeling over the pail. Two men had no pockets that didn't have holes. Any man unlucky enough to have no pockets without holes ought to be allowed to keep an old lard pail for toting his possessions, and without interference.

But now that each man had dollars, nobody wanted to quarrel any more. The man with the sound pockets showed the wisdom of Solomon, according to the others. He used his knife to slit strips from the skirt of an old dead nigger woman, so the unlucky gentlemen with holey pockets could have something for wrapping their shares, something just as convenient as an old lard pail.

VIII

Thorstein Brach stayed at Richmond Plantation for one evening, a night, one full day, another night, and a morning. It seemed to Julia that this span of time was set apart, becoming life for someone else, a twin who existed in spirit and was always at her elbow.

Only a twin, not she herself, could have faced those three men at the bridge over the slough and threatened to kill them. Thorstein was part of her exultation that she was alive. The power of this rapture was frightening. Only the twin could deal with it.

The shy and gradual spring continued to creep in during the night. There was a smell of jessamine, heavy and moist in the nostrils.

In the morning Julia was all energy, herself. They must see to the animals. All the plantation people except one old woman had hid in the forest. Some wind had reported that black people in outlying cabins were being slaughtered, and the Richmond workers had underestimated the savage determination of their boss-lady. The old woman who remained was cooking victuals and said she couldn't stand laying out in the woods — there was a snake in her liver that told her to stay where she was.

William and Caroline fed the chickens – "Co-ome chick chick chick..." Lucy slopped the hogs.

The three cows were moaning with pain, needing to be milked. Thorstein milked them. When the cows stopped moaning, the folks out in the woods heard that somebody must have relieved the poor creatures, reckoned that peace and security might be restored and cautiously came out of hiding.

A half-crazed young woman from Myrtle came through, crying out about cutting and shooting and burning before wading, splashing and swimming across the Olustee River, headed for nowhere. Her wild and jumbled words suggested things worse than anybody could suppose. Old and young on Richmond Plantation feared an end of their world. What did Julia know—she who knew so much? Or the stranger Mr. Thorstein?

Doing something eased bodies and souls. A man harnessed a mule and plowed the cornfield. It was time to plant. Somebody drove nails for an unknown purpose. From time to time, all day long, there was the sound of a banging hammer.

Julia, with shotgun again, and Thorstein, as usual with Esther's rifle, walked together to the bridge. They must look in the earth for tracks—had anyone prowled during the night? The way to the bridge was dazzling with yellow jessamine that stifled thought with its perfume, and tiny red dots in the greening Spanish moss prickled one's eyes, liberating inner visions, reckless hopes. Why think about the three horsemen, the rage and terror that was over and done with? In the bright new day she could put out of her mind the three horsemen, and her own anger and terror. She clung in her mind to that magical instant when Thorstein rushed out of the pines and seemed about to embrace her. And since not then, why not now? Didn't their shared resistance to the hurricane of murder entitle them to one embrace? The law and the gospel wouldn't drown. The rock of ages wouldn't split.

She talked and talked as though possessed: Colonel Lawrence Avery and her father's opinion of him, Robert Conkling who didn't have all his wits but (laughing at herself) had wits enough to trick her by not collecting sap after taking her money, Mabel Conkling and her loose ways, some black man whose name she'd heard but had forgot and who was said to have escaped from the Wehadke Farm. She talked especially about the Dales—the store, the schoolhouse in Myrtle which Joshua finished building after he was fired from the Freedmen's Bureau—the schoolhouse which became a church on Sundays, where Azri Peters preached, and finally she talked about Joshua and Joanna's son the school principal in Torrington, Connecticut. Joanna was so happy about her son's position in a more civilized part of the United States that Julia had the idea maybe William might someday become well educated and move and have a better life than could be had running a naval-stores business. Times were changing, and it was hard to predict what was going to happen to Richmond Plantation. What did Thorstein think? Aghast, she realized that her tongue had wagged out of control—Thorstein would think she now regarded him just as a professor who knew all about colleges. *Don't listen to me! Hold me, if only for a few seconds!*

"I never knew such a likable and bright little chap," said Thorstein. "But he has to grow up a bit before we face that problem, doesn't he?"

We? What did he mean by we? He'd be a lifelong friend, a source of sincere and reliable advice, especially about education. Why couldn't she speak from the heart? She could weep.

They examined the earth, looking for tracks different and separate from those made the day before. There were none.

Thorstein noticed the sign that Tom had put up years ago—Richmond Plantat...iness or KEEP OUT. Somebody had blasted away some words with birdshot.

Julia had to explain—men out hunting for quail or duck didn't like being kept off the Richmond land. They played with their guns before using them for a purpose. They played with violence.

It was shameful that she lived on the edge of violence. Thorstein was no doubt as repelled as she was but unlike her he might move away from it. Why did she have to talk about what shamed her so much, as though she were responsible? Violence seemed to stand for everything that separated them—her responsibilities for her children and the business—his work as a professor that might take him even from St. Vincent; her marriage—his affairs. She repeated what the Dales had told her about Azri Peters being whipped by the Klan. "I'd die before the Klan could come in here and whip one of my niggers!" she cried.

His gentle manner moved her more than what he said – "You seem to have some good men and women here. They could defend themselves, you too, if they were armed. I just don't want to think any more about you dying, Julia."

She had to tell a story. When she was five years old, one of the Richmond workers came back from the War with a gun and shot another worker in a fight over a woman. The killer had been hanged, not in a lynching but by due process of law. Julia had to ask why the man who made whistles for her out of hollow reeds had gone away, and she was told only some years later what had happened. Her father's moral: the niggers mustn't have guns!

"It's so hard to do what's right!" she exclaimed. Was it right that she wanted him to embrace her?

They walked back from the bridge. The jessamine was as stifling as before, the springtime greening of the moss and the tiny red blossoms were just as inspiriting, but the house—silent, haggard, lowering—faced her like an enemy. *Can't you understand, Thorstein?? I'm lonely here and never knew it before — here, where I was born and have always lived! Help me...*

The dog Big Thing came, snuffled at Thorstein, accepted him, and then followed, panting.

No seconds for an embrace! No secret words of flesh and blood!

He took the shotgun from her. He knew where it was kept and would put it away.

She went to the parlor set aside as the office of the business. She unlocked and rolled up the cover of her desk. Her ledger waited, but she didn't touch it. She was shattered, spent. She'd given up being herself. The mysterious twin had taken over. She herself could never have made those passionate and silent demands of Thorstein Brach!

It seemed that she herself didn't have the strength to rise from her chair. Perhaps the twin helped. Perhaps it was the twin who sat down for supper at the kitchen table and said grace, hurriedly this evening, thanking God for a good man who was protecting them from evil-doers.

With his usual irreverence, in the mood of their regular Sunday dinners at the Rourkes', he said, "It seems that God didn't need to send any man, brave and good or not." He smiled. One of the lamps flickered. Recalling the ominous event of the previous evening silenced the children and Lucy. Caroline comprehended that murder was rampaging outside her home and had tried to break in. William sensed the terror in others. And Lucy? If the horsemen hadn't been stopped, what they might have done with Lucy was unbearable to think about. The girl looked at her with wonder and trust, almost as if she *were* her own child, too. "My God how brave *you* were!" Thorstein exclaimed.

"I don't know how I could have talked to those men like I did," blurted Julia's twin. "I really was ready to kill them, and if one of them killed me before I could load the shotgun again I didn't seem to care."

Tears came. Was it she or her twin who rose from the table, turned away, and wiped her face with her apron?

Thorstein might have a twin, too. She was used to his rough irony and wit, to his curiously buoyant sarcasm, to his habit of singling out truths concealed by pretense. But he was now earnest and warm with exposed emotion — "I was ready to shoot and kill, just like you, Julia. I never could have imagined myself in that kind of situation, any more than you could."

She sat down again and managed to face him.

"Caroline, William, Lucy, what a wonderful mother you have!" he exclaimed.

Although she was not actually Lucy's mother, the thought was in the spirit of the moment. Wonderful? He'd called her that before, when she'd talked about the naval-stores business at the Rourkes'.

"There were three men on horses," he went on, mostly to Lucy, "and I can't tell you what holes they crawled out of — the day had been bright and the sun was going down all red and orange the way it does one good to look at. The birds were singing in the swamps, and I was glad to come calling — but there they were, these three ugly monsters. I had a pretty good idea they were up to no good. Your Aunt Esther had just told me that your daddy tried to make them leave this vicinity and that might be why they came here. They were afraid of your daddy but mad at him, too. No telling what they might have done if they got past your mother at the bridge. But they *didn't* get by your mother, did they! Well, why should I talk about *them*? Why should *anybody* talk about them any more? Let's forget them! Good riddance!" He grinned. He seemed to have turned the three horsemen into a rather scary fairy tale for Caroline and William.

"What I'll never forget is your mother! Oh, your mother is all jessamine and oranges! I think the warm sun looked at her with great pleasure and gave his best rays. I think the sweet water flowed just to give her a good refreshing drink. Don't you agree, William?"

Her little son nodded.

Thorstein seemed wound up. Her mind was a fuzz, but she did realize that he was saying to the children what he'd kept himself from saying to her alone. Was he being honorable because she was married and the mother of two children? Esther would snort at the thought. Where women were involved, Thorstein was a pirate, as she had seen for herself! Why was he so restrained with her? Numbed, she drank his words – "She's not very big, just an inch or two taller than Lucy, but she's strong as that big live oak near the wagon shed. There's no other tree near it — it stands alone, it's shaded Seminoles, and it will last hundreds of years more, like your mother's strength will last in you. And have you noticed your mother's eyes? Have you noticed, Caroline? Your mother's eyes make me think of birds. What do birds see? One thing we can be sure of — they don't tell themselves they see anything they don't see. They don't whine and complain that they *ought* to be seeing what they don't see. Their eyes are honest, completely honest. Just like your mother's eyes. A very dull person can come to life just by looking in your mother's eyes."

William, Caroline and Lucy were looking at her curiously, studying her.

"We must have a toast!" he exclaimed, cheerfully. He then explained that people clinked glasses with other people, then drank, and that this meant they wholeheartedly approved what a person said when he raised his glass. "Come – I'll show you – " He raised his glass of milk.

Julia was in a near-panic. She remembered half-naked Thorstein raising his glass of red wine, sitting up in bed in Esther's room at the Alhambra Hotel, while the head, bare shoulders and breasts of the unknown woman disappeared under the sheet. She felt her face burn, and she knew that Thorstein would notice and would know she was remembering. Worse — he'd know that she was trying to hide her feelings about that moment, and about Thorstein himself.

As he went on speaking, he was no longer just cheerful. His voice became low, more gentle than seemed possible in a man—"To long life and happiness to everyone at Richmond Plantation. Now, William, drink a little milk. You too, Caroline, Lucy—" And last of all, without saying more, he clinked his glass against Julia's and drank every drop.

She hung her head after she drank all the milk in her own glass. She couldn't look at her children, at Lucy, or at Thorstein.

Lucy drank all her milk, too. Perhaps the toast seemed a kind of religious ceremony. "Amen!" she pronounced.

The warm night became for Julia one long tremor of mixed torment and exaltation. She rose from bed and paced her room, then the hallway, dim in reflected light from moon and stars. She paused to listen at the doors of the children's rooms, then at the door of the spare room where Thorstein slept. She heard the distant hoot of an owl. *If only you could stay with me, just stay with me!* The race riot would end, there would be no need or excuse for his protection, he would return to his teaching at Rowland College, and she would see him only at the Rourkes' for Sunday dinners. It was a miracle of chance that he had been able to say before the children what he never would have said before Esther and Joseph. She saw him in remembered sunlight more clearly than she could see anything in the shadowy hallway. She envisioned his hair and mustache, yellow and stiff as fine straw, his wide grin that showed oversized teeth and no consciousness of how he looked, and the way his body functioned, with a playful looseness like the gamboling of a puppy, so that he occasionally bumped into things. An impulse to open the door and go into the spare room—would he be asleep or awake?—was so strong and unnerving that she rushed back through her own chamber to the dressing room, where she lit a lamp.

The quilt in which she'd huddled on the cold night Tom came home was folded on its shelf. And on the shelf above were a few books of sermons and political tracts that she didn't care for enough to keep in her office bookcase with her Latin books from Aurora Academy. The shelf also contained one book that she was ashamed to keep in the office, where people might see it. It was *Sex in Education, the Proper Sphere of Womanhood* by Phineas Oscar Jones, M.D., of Birmingham, Alabama. Her father had given her this book when she started to menstruate. Even though she had no mother to make proper explanations, and even though she might be picking up God-knows-what notions from the black women who worked in the naval-stores operation, daddy had given her through this book a priceless access to expert knowledge. Julia had read the book twice from cover to cover and had referred to parts of it many other times. One passage in particular had worried her—

Women beware. You can readily overstimulate your emotions by overtaxing your minds. The mental discipline of Latin and geometry and science is not for the fair sex. Beware, I say, beware! The woman who aspires to masculine scholarship is lost!

The book opened to this chapter because she had a bookmark in place. But the thought in it made her angry now. Thorstein had smiled, delighted when William recited and then translated his Virgil! She sweated. Her thin cotton nightdress dampened. She propped up the window sash with a stick, tearing a spider's web. Dr. Jones's book plagued her even though she couldn't entirely believe in it. Trembling, she turned to the most forbidding chapter of all, on the duel between the brain and the uterus. She half hoped this chapter would ease emotions that were both irresistible and intolerable. It described the sicknesses of children born of women who indulged in "the vice." She knew what Dr. Jones meant by "the vice"! How many nights, as a young woman at the academy! And what strength of character was required even after marriage—luckily in time, since Caroline and William had always been unusually healthy. Dr. Jones explained that there were uterine, natural women, fulfilling their God-ordained primary function of reproduction—and there were cerebral, sterile, unnatural women, biological castoffs. But both kinds of women were prone to all sorts of diseases. The one capacity common to all women was to be sick. But she was never sick!

She could scarcely see the pages. In the same moment that she thrust the book back on the shelf, she thought of the three horsemen at the bridge — she'd blast to hell any reptiles who came after her children or her niggers! And to hell with Dr. Jones!

Angry, impulsive, she turned down and blew out the lamp, strode back through her own chamber to the hallway, stood listening — some birds were twittering, it was nearly daybreak — and put out her hand toward the doorknob of the spare room. There was something strange in herself, as though she had a different heart. With the passing of her anger, her body softened and seemed weightless. She thought of touching Thorstein's dear sleeping face, of how his eyes would open, expecting, wanting her. *Here I am — I love you.*

Then she just could not open the door. Her knees trembled so that she nearly collapsed, and she choked on a sob. Her thin nightgown was drenched with her sweat and was sticking to her breasts and thighs. The time before Thorstein's door became an age. How was it that her body, which seemed to count for so little and even become repugnant in her marriage, now counted for so much? Her whole life — Caroline and William, the Eden she'd inherited and kept going, the generations of black folks whose care was her God-given destiny — all seemed to dangle from a wispy thread. As the minutes passed, she had to remember who she was — the mother of two children and the boss-lady of a naval-stores business. If she opened Thorstein's door, her body, which she had tried to disregard for years, would commit her to a future that might be more tragic than glorious. The power of this suddenly acknowledged body to make decisions, in spite of common sense and what passed for morality, was frightening. She recognized this power for the first time. It was within her, surprising, irrepressible. What her mind prescribed would follow the empowerment of her body, and this was more awesome than she could bear. If she stood before Thorstein and told him that she loved him, the thread from which her whole life was dangling would snap.

Trembling, terrified by her own thoughts and by far more intricate and inscrutable feelings, she withdrew her hand from the doorknob. *Sleep on, precious guest! Tomorrow — and on other days to come — will you have more kind words for me?*

In the morning the spring persisted, warm and benign. She was able to treat Thorstein with controlled friendliness, and she managed to become busy. What might be going on in Myrtle and Olustee was on everyone's mind, but she wouldn't send anyone on a dangerous mission to find out.

Uncertainty ended in mid-morning. Two wagons from Clayton Plantation rumbled in with much snorting of horses and wolfish baying of Big Thing. Joseph Rourke drove the first wagon with Piney seated beside him and Esther in her strapped-down wheelchair on the planks behind them. A gray-bearded old man drove the second heavy freight wagon now bearing sixteen black men and women, four of them with guns.

Richmond Plantation, prostrate since Julia had turned back the three horsemen, now quickened with the dread need of finding out what must be learned. Everybody gathered around the wagons. Talk was uncannily quiet.

Joseph handed Julia an envelope – "A boy brought me this letter from Joshua Dale."

"Joseph and I, all of us here, are doing what he asks," said Esther. She was wearing her black funeral dress.

Julia drew two sheets of stiff stationery from the envelope. At first she was struck by the quality of the calligraphy and then recalled that Joshua Dale had read for the law. The words scourged—

My dear Joseph,

Myrtle no longer exists. Many people have been slaughtered, women and children as well as men. Some escaped. There are four with Joanna and me. The men who work for the railroad have been shunted away. Every structure has been burned except the schoolhouse and church that I helped to build when I first came here young and hopeful.

The murderers have finished and left. The militia is here later than needed. The Salvation Army is more useful finding people to bury the dead.

I myself buried Azri Peters in our minister's cornfield, and he has donated the whole field as a graveyard for the other victims. This afternoon we hold a funeral service there, and he has promised to officiate since there is no longer a black preacher.

I urge you to attend and bring folks from your farm who have doubtless lost friends and relatives. We are reduced to using a funeral to show that those of us who are still alive stand up for humanity. We mourn, and we demonstrate our determination that white people and black people can go on living here together and in peace.

Show this letter to Mrs. Thomas Clayton if you wish. I do not know if she is in a position to come to this funeral.

Your friend,
Joshua Washington Dale

Julia couldn't speak immediately. She shuffled the two sheets of stationery and read again. Joseph and Esther watched as if they didn't know her. And Piney, grim, her gun belt and revolver in her lap. And all the black people from both plantations. Thorstein too. No doubt all the people with Joseph and Esther knew what the letter said. Her own people knew only that it must be important. "Of course I'll come," she said at last. "All the grown-ups here will want to come. Can you tell me, tell all of us, who has died, who has lived?"

"We know only what Joshua has written," said Joseph.

She handed the letter to Thorstein and said, "Please read it aloud for everyone — but it's not necessary to read the last paragraph — " Interrupting herself, she raised her voice — "Mr. Brach will read a letter which Mr. Joshua Dale, the storekeeper in Olustee, wrote to Mr. Joseph Rourke here. It tells what's happened. We'll be going to a funeral in Olustee. We'd best leave the children home."

While Thorstein read, slowly and distinctly, she turned to Joseph and Esther — "I don't know why Joshua Dale should think I might not be in a position to go."

"I wondered why he wrote that, too," said Esther.

They were speaking softly so that Thorstein could be heard.

"It was fitting that we sent Thorstein to you," said Joseph.

"Yes, you did right," she said. There was no time for talk, and she had no inclination to give an account of her time with Thorstein. She was conscious of her appearance before her work people. Only by staying calm and self-controlled could she prevent an outburst of wild grief and rage — shouts, screams, paroxysms. She didn't know the black people of Myrtle as some of her people undoubtedly did. They had all gone to the church where Azri Peters had preached. She knew the Myrtle people only through chance meetings in the Dales' store. Was the woman who bought the calico with the pink peony design alive or dead? And the boy to whom Joanna had extended two cents in credit because he didn't have quite enough to pay for the three pounds of sugar already weighed out—how about him? Julia's eyes were dry. Did she lack heart? She conceived that she was able to remain so calm because she'd spent all emotion on Thorstein. The thought was a wound. How trifling her desire and ambiguous dreams were! How could she have whined in her mind for an embrace—how could she have crept like an animal, all feverish flesh, to the door of the room in which he slept, while folks in Myrtle were being murdered? She knew her country. She'd had a duty. After meeting Lawrence Avery and all those drunk and armed strangers in Olustee, hadn't she hidden from herself the apprehension that Myrtle would burn, that bodies would strew the sandy earth, that buzzards would flock? Why hadn't she used her time in going from house to house in Olustee, with or without the Dales, exhorting, preaching, arousing men and women to cut off the craze to murder? She was third-generation Richmond, a voice to reckon with, and folks would have responded—perhaps. But she'd been a Cassandra unable to speak.

Thorstein had finished reading Joshua Dale's letter.

There was a lot of movement and talk. Who would go to the funeral? Who would stay on the place to care for the children? There were horses and mules to be harnessed.

Thorstein was speaking to her – "Esther told me that this preacher Azri Peters was murdered. I should have realized that you would know him – I should have told you – "

She felt inside his mind and conscience, and she put her hand on his arm—"What you didn't do isn't important, Thorstein. Believe me, it isn't." Her self-control ebbed and her voice quavered—"This is all strange to you. But it's part of my life to know about killing. My father used to talk about it—the War, the years after the War, the Klan. What I've had to know, what I can't help but know, is like a disease—" She couldn't go on.

From her wheelchair mounted on the wagon, Esther was watching her, listening to her.

She took her hand from Thorstein's arm.

"I used the boy who brought Joshua's letter and sent him back to Olustee with a telegram for Tom," Esther said. "It should reach Tom wherever he is along the railroad—he has an arrangement for that, I understand. I'm *demanding* that he come to this funeral." Esther became harsh, malignant—"I could put it better than you could, Julia. He doesn't stop being my brother because he's your husband."

Even though Esther had never got on with Tom, Julia was surprised that she took this tone now. "I'm glad you sent your telegram," she said. "I don't know whether Tom's presence at this funeral, or the presence of any of us white folks, can be healing the way Joshua Dale seems to expect. Maybe Tom's presence would help more than anybody else's because he hires so many black men to work for the railroad. But I don't know—what is there to say? For myself, I feel I can't do anything right—"

Esther murmured, "All of us feel we can't do anything right."

Julia had no more to say. She went to her room for her funeral dress, which she hadn't worn since her father died. When she came out again, the wagons were ready to roll. Piney was holding the rifle that Thorstein had borrowed. He himself was mounted, his saddle bags packed. She approached him.

"I won't be going to this funeral, Julia," he said. "I don't know the people—they don't know me. And I have my job at the college."

How many times there'd been casual goodbyes after Sunday dinners with Esther and Joseph! She'd never again be able to say goodbye to him in the same way. Mentioning his job combined with what she'd undergone during his stay in her house illuminated as never before the barriers between them. Alone on his horse, as now, or alone in drifting from one university to another, from one lover to another, from one intellectual preoccupation to another, he was wanderer, rogue and prophet. She was alone in other ways. Growing up among mostly black people, she could give her life in an effort to protect them but always remained somewhat apart as predestined by much blood and sweat. She was free of the worst the world offered in Richmond Plantation's secluded ox-bow, and she was also shut off from the best. She expected that Thorstein understood this. Perhaps he knew her passion and was protecting her from it. She held out her hand.

He took it – "I won't say goodbye, Julia."

She couldn't look at him. Were her eyes really honest, as he'd declared before the children? Was she really, to him, jessamine and oranges, a being made out of warm sun and sweet water? With sudden recklessness she pressed the back of his hand against her face—"My dear dear friend!"

As she released his hand, he passed it over her hair.

Joseph flicked his whip, and his wagon moved.

Holding up the long skirt of her funeral dress, Julia climbed up into her buggy and took the reins.

*

When the sun was high and day almost hot, the people from Clayton and Richmond plantations arrived before the Dales' store in Olustee. Joanna went out. She wished Joshua was on hand. Where was he? What was he doing?

Joseph Rourke, driving the lead wagon, spoke to her—"We're here, Joanna Dale, we're here because Joshua wrote to me why we ought to be here, and what he wrote was right and proper."

Piney, the tall black woman who nursed Esther Clayton Rourke, was still seated beside Joseph, wearing a gun belt with a heavy revolver. She said, "Us black folks from the farms and woods don't know who lived and who died, and us has to find out."

Esther herself, from her wheelchair strapped down in the bed of the wagon, added a harsh and uncompromising twist to her husband's words—"None of us could stop the killing, and going to this funeral now is God's joke!"

"I been up most of the night caring for Azri Peters's grandchildren who came to Joshua and me. Oh—they were desperate and scart, I can't tell you! So I know just what you mean, Mrs. Rourke. When God jokes, ain't nothing anybody can do but cry." She'd never called Mrs. Rourke by her first name. Was it because of her infirmity and her not coming to the store much, or was it because of some hard Clayton quality in her character?

"Is my brother Tom on hand?" Mrs. Rourke asked.

"Mr. Clayton?"

"Yes, Thomas Clayton. I sent him a telegram telling him how he ought to be here."

Perhaps this was part of God's joke! Mrs. Rourke didn't know about Tom Clayton's leadership of the murder and burning in Myrtle, as arranged in Arthur Wilkins's prettified salon car—and damn him too! Joanna thought: I'm probably the only soul in Olustee, besides Joshua, who knows what went on in that salon car, because he hasn't had time to tell anybody else. She said to Mrs. Rourke all she could say—"No, I ain't seen him."

Joanna turned away from the Rourkes and strode along the line of wagons. She and some of the black people knew each other well and exchanged nods. But it was no time for talking.

She wanted to speak to Julia Clayton because she didn't like the way Joshua seemed to put on Julia part of the blame for what Tom Clayton did, just because she was unlucky enough to be Tom Clayton's wife. This was wrong of Joshua!

Julia had only one old black man beside her in her light buggy. The sun happened to shine through an opening in the foliage of a live oak and light up her yellow hair, and the effect, with her blue eyes and black dress, as she sat very straight and held the reins, was somehow startling, as though she brought with her another kind of living. Julia was changed. Joanna wondered—why hadn't she ever before paid attention to the fact that Julia Clayton was very beautiful? And why was she so moved? Was it because Julia Clayton's beauty was an assault on the ugly horror of the past few days? Her voice became hoarse as she said, "I'm more glad you're here than I can say, Julia. I don't know if this town can begin over the way Joshua seems to think it might. But if it does begin over, it will be because of you and the Rourkes and a few others."

Julia's voice was soft but decisive—"I can't see the future, Joanna. We just have to love one another and leave the rest to God."

Joshua appeared at the intersection of the road toward the railroad and the lane which led to the church and the parsonage. Two Olustee men were with him and like Joshua were carrying rifles.

Everybody waited.

Joshua was in shirtsleeves. When he'd left the house, he'd been wearing a sweater Joanna had knitted, and he must have left it somewhere. He looked mussy, unkempt. What had he been doing? The two men with him were wearing overalls. He must have persuaded them to leave off what they'd been doing in order to attend the funeral. Or perhaps they'd been helping Joshua in some way. Joanna couldn't remember their names. She'd probably dealt with their wives at the store.

Joshua took a position so that everyone in the wagons or standing around could see him and hear him. He stood very straight, the butt of his rifle on the ground, and he turned his head slowly, taking in with his eyes everyone there. Silence. A horse stomped and harness creaked. He was all certainty—the commander. Not like Esther Rourke or Julia Clayton, thought Joanna, not concerned about God either joking or acting as custodian of the future. She knew this quality in her husband but had never before seen it so starkly.

"Good people," he said, "the cornfield next to the parsonage has been set aside as cemetery for those who died in the riot. We will march to this cemetery through the whole town of Olustee so that all can see there's some who know the difference between wrong and right and will act accordingly. Our Reverend Augustus Blanding is waiting for us to make a proper funeral. Joanna "—he looked at her, captain, not husband—" fetch Mark Richardson, Bina Peters, and the children."

She did so. Mark was stony. Would he remain so—or give way to another convulsion of grief and rage? Bina seemed to scan everyone in sight.

Joshua waved his hand at Joseph Rourke, who cracked his whip, and the procession moved. Joshua led, accompanied by the two Olustee men and Mark. Joanna was just behind them.

One of the Olustee men took in the jacket which Joanna had fitted on Mark and, with some anxiety, the rifle which Joshua had cleaned and repaired. He said, "You might get youself shot for toting that gun, boy. You sure got a right to tote that gun—I ain't saying nay. But I don't want to see you get youself shot."

Joshua said, "If anybody starts shooting, he'll have to deal with me as well as Mark."

They moved past Whitaker's saloon, which was locked up. Amos Whitaker's hound followed them, tongue lolling.

At a crossroads, some men and women of the Salvation Army fell in. Also, two men and four women of Olustee. Two of the women wore mourning. Joshua stopped the procession and made a statement: "I want you all to know—and you can interpret this as you see fit—Colonel Bartlett and his militia refused to take any part in this funeral, or to promise protection for folks going to this funeral."

Then he waved his arm and everybody moved again.

At the cornfield which had become cemetery, Joseph Rourke drove his wagon to unplowed firm ground, and the others followed.

The field was painfully bright under the high sun. Some buzzards circled but didn't come close. The Salvation Army's burial detail, four black men and three black women—Joanna knew all of them—were waiting. Their shovels were standing, thrust into soft cultivated earth. Burial had apparently been completed—a mercy in view of what must have been the condition of some of the bodies. Three members of the Salvation Army, in uniform, stood by. At the far end of the field, near the parsonage, four men of the militia sprawled on the ground. Regardless of what Colonel Bartlett said, did they intend to protect mourners? Or were they merely curious? The minister's wife held a Bible in one hand and seemed to be supporting her husband with the other. Some children of the town came out of nearby pines.

In the field itself was the result of what Joshua must have been doing all morning. There were rows of crosses lined up with precision, as though for soldiers. The crosses were made of two pieces of lath, one long piece stuck in the ground and a short piece nailed across it, and each cross had a half-sheet of Dales' General Merchandise business stationery tacked where the two pieces joined. Joanna knew the origin of the laths as well as the stationery. The parlor in the parsonage was one of the few rooms in any Olustee house that had been lathed and plastered. Nobody had ever got around to lath and plaster the other rooms. So the laths intended for this purpose had been stored in a shed for several years, and now they had a use. Joanna went to the nearest cross. On the half-sheet of stationery was the name of a child she had known.

The black people from the plantations were moving around the field. A few who could read were doing so. There were sobs, curses — usually soft, sometimes shrieked.

Joanna looked for names too — found some. In thinking about people she'd never see again, she couldn't help thinking, at the same time, that these little scraps of stationery would soak, tear, and blow away with two or three storms. So, the names would go. In only a few years the laths would rot. The land here, once cultivated, would invite cultivation again. The corn would grow again, attracting crows. People would forget. But Joshua wouldn't forget! Nor she! The folks buried here would become for them a shared trust. She had a fierce conviction that even though Joshua was an almost godless man in spite of his churchgoing, that the Lord had known him in the womb as He had known Jeremiah, and at that time had marked Joshua as His own.

Joshua was saying something to the minister. Then he shouted across the field — "My friends, let us come together!"

All moved toward him.

He muttered something to the Reverend Blanding, who trembled and shook his head. There was a silence. Who would say what must be said?

At last Joshua spoke—"My friends, come with me for a time." He strode to one of the crosses, and the congregation he had recruited followed. "Brothers and sisters," he went on, "there ain't nobody here ought to be conducting this funeral but the pastor of the Myrtle church. But the Reverend Azri Peters was murdered during the riot, after he was brutally whipped. I buried him myself right here, and that's his name on this cross. It was here his murderers shot him down. Now he's with his congregation here. God will put his soul in Heaven. Azri Peters was a saint."

Joshua continued along the row of crosses until he came to sixth from Azri's. "Brothers and sisters, among all of us here, I'm the only veteran of the Freedom War, except for my comrade in arms Mingo, who lies under this cross. Mingo was brung up by Indians and he was proud he had no other name but Mingo. I first knew him when we were both keeping the Seceshes busy around Tallahassee. That was a company where black and white fought side by side against their enemies, as they should. One of the last things Mingo did was bring the railroaders home so they could try to protect their families. Mingo was my friend for more than twenty-five years."

Joshua then walked back to Reverend Blanding and put a hand on his shoulder. "The minister of the Olustee church will lead us all in a prayer. I will pray that we can all be good people like Azri Peters and Mingo."

But the white minister could not do as Joshua was demanding. Instead, he gave a long sob and collapsed on the ground. His wife knelt beside him—"Augustus, Augustus, you must—" She couldn't say what he must do.

Joshua knelt beside him too, and said quietly, "Have courage, sir. Every black man, woman, and child here has lost somebody close. And they're all standing up."

An old black woman said, "Leave him be. Mourning like that you can't do nothing about."

Joshua rose and said, "Since I'm the steward of the Olustee church and since my minister is struck down, it's up to me to say one thing more. If I'd figured correctly what was coming, what I couldn't do nothing to stop, I'd taken my gun and gone to Myrtle and helped the colored folks. That warn't no black folks' riot. It were a white folks' riot. It were a terrible crime to kill all these innocent children of God, and the ones that did it will burn in Hell, if the justice up There is any better than it is down here. Murder ain't black. Murder ain't white. It's just murder."

IX

Laura and Arthur Wilkins occupied separate three-room suites in the Alhambra Hotel, hers on the second floor and his on the third. Since Arthur had no social life apart from his business, his parlor served as office and conference room. A real office on the first floor served for routine administrative matters and was occupied during the day by Claude Lyman, who sported the title of office manager, and two lady stenographers. Thus, the Wilkins empire of railroads, oil companies, and hotels was operated from a desk and a few files. When the files were filled, paper no longer of current consequence was sifted out and shipped to the permanent office in the New York financial district.

Laura's parlor, a much more richly furnished one than her husband's, with red and gold brocade drapes and a carved cedar ceiling from a Saracen mosque, became the salon to which the magnate and his numerous business acquaintances repaired every evening after brandy and cigars.

The main purpose of Laura's soirees was to sell stock in the Pamlico and Gulf Railroad.

She wore a series of black net gowns of panne velvet embroidered with silver, and at her glistening bosom was generally a bunch of Parma violets in which diamonds sparkled. Laura could see that she disturbed these men not only with her beauty but also because they were unable to pigeonhole her. She was not exactly "good" and she certainly was not "fast." She was respectably married and seemed to have great wealth at her disposal, possibly "in her own right." Great social influence too, in Florida if not in New York. But when they contemplated the marble halves of her breasts above the Parma violets and the diamonds, their voices acquired the resonance of a bass fiddle in a melancholy mood.

This was Laura's cue for saying: "Oh I wish I were a man so I could go into business! My husband tells me you have one of the biggest orange groves in the world" — or: "...so many thousand cattle you can't count them. Why, you're like one of those kings in the Old Testament!" — or: "...an enormous sawmill going buzz-buzz-buzz night and day, with great wide boards coming out. My little heart would burst if I were a man like you! You're a railroad man too, aren't you?...You aren't? I don't understand! If your boards are shipped by rail, you *should* profit from it. It would be only *right*!"

The orange grower or cattleman or lumberman was almost always incapable of perceiving that she was motivated by the ambition she so plainly exhibited. With an ogling gallantry, socially extravagant and sexually perfunctory, the man usually said something like: "I do believe I'll take three hundred shares if your husband can spare them. Any stock issue launched under such *fair* auspices — huh-huh-huh — is bound to yield good dividends."

"Oh, I'm *sure* Arthur can put aside some shares for *you*!"

That her salesmanship and sexuality should move these men, with their hard and brutal faces, to give up between ten and fifty thousand dollars, seemed to be of a piece with the whole fantastic course of her life. She believed that she was gifted as most people were not because she had learned not to expect a logical pattern in human behavior or events.

During the first months of her marriage, she had drawn from the magnate certain confidences regarding the management of his empire, along with stock worth then about twenty-five thousand dollars and currently valued at about sixty-five thousand dollars. At that time he was genial about her enthusiasm for trading, which seemed to make her more languid and pliable in bed. Among his confidences was the remark: "Control is just as good as ownership and sometimes better." Since nobody was sold enough shares to threaten Arthur's control, or her own cut, she felt that any sale amounted to a gift. Also, during that brief period when Arthur was capable of romantic caprice, he had promised her a commission on sales. By scaring him a little she could keep him from going back on this promise. She compared herself to a whore or high-class courtesan but inwardly laughed at the thought. She didn't have to do anything beyond wearing extravagant dresses, showing her bosom a bit, and swaying her body in the amber light of the Saracen Room. She didn't tell Arthur about her accounts in banks with which he never did business.

She realized that her new wealth, along with the sexually-charged homage given her, had changed her manner and perhaps her nature. She was conscious of irresistible charm and graciousness, of power to make men think what she wanted them to think. With the conclusion of each sale of stock, a thousand shifting shades of color, as when one turns mother-of-pearl this way and that, came and went in her glowing skin, so that she blossomed in the Saracen Room like the magical flower of an Indian fakir, which unfurls its petals before one's eyes.

At first, Arthur smiled and called her "my pretty broker."

Recently, he had suggested, twice, that he keep the men with brandy and cigars in the parlor next to the Renaissance Room, and that she entertain just the ladies in the Saracen Room. She could see that she worried him because she was violating one of his favorite general principles — "Never permit any individual in your organization to get too much power." Like an obstreperous vice-president, she was becoming too influential.

One evening, Arthur became heated over some business matter — she could never remember what it was — gesticulated violently, and smashed a stained-glass lampshade.

"Control yourself, Arthur," she said, coldly.

The guests in the Saracen Room were not adept at glossing over embarrassing animosities, and there was an interested silence.

"Don't worry, my pet," said Arthur. "I'll buy you another just like this one."

"I liked this one," said Laura.

Claude Lyman began talking about a new organ which Mrs. Wilkins had presented to the Episcopal Church.

Arthur's skin became white and then a muddy gray. Some cords in his neck vibrated. Which of his public personalities would emerge — the ruthless financier or the Christian gentleman? It turned out to be the latter. "Laura bought that lamp in Paris when we were on our honeymoon," he said.

The wife of one of the stockholders came to the old gentleman's rescue — "How you both must have treasured it! Paris is the nicest place in the world for a honeymoon. Richard and I began our honeymoon in Paris, and it hasn't ended yet, has it, Richard?"

"Our honeymoon lasted one week," said Laura.

The Christian gentleman departed with the guests. His jaw rigid, Arthur barked, "Laura, there's no excuse for the way you behaved tonight!"

Laura tapped her fan against her open palm and drawled, "How you speak! I suppose *I* broke the lamp!"

"You know it was an accident and out of pure cussedness you want to pretend it was something else."

"It wouldn't have happened if you hadn't been jumping around like a jack-in-a-box."

"For a woman who used to empty bedpans you feel pretty sure of yourself, don't you!"

"You tricked me into marrying you just so you could fling that in my face!"

"So *I* tricked *you*! *That's* it, is it? I suppose *I* was tricking *you* when you were taking care of Katherine and walked into her bedroom and my bedroom at all hours of the night in that shameless nightgown you wore then, using your body to take advantage of me!"

"You little — *thing*!" She raised her round white arms.

Arthur shrank, but his eyes glittered — "Laura, bygod I won't stand for this – "

"You were under my feet like a hungry cat!"

"You're going to make me — "

"I couldn't give your former wife her pills, change her sheets, or do anything at all without you following me around with those sad eyes of yours, like a calf's with the rheumatism."

"You'll regret this!"

"I don't think you'd ever seen a woman before!"

"I'll have to teach you your place."

"My place? *You*? Teach *me*? D'you think I'll kiss your big toe every time you speak, as if you were the Pope in Rome or something? You're jealous, Arthur — just jealous because I persuade so many of your friends to buy stock — "

"They'd buy anyway. They make you think they'd buy only from you just to flatter your vanity."

"Oh, *do* they? Why don't you make them flatter *your* vanity?"

"I'm not a pretty woman."

"If I were a man who owns what you own, I'd make them bow and scrape."

"The object of commercial enterprise is not to make men bow and scrape."

"All your life you've used people who have abilities you don't have. That's your one talent, Arthur. You're using people now, me for one, and others. Tom Clayton's an example. People think of you as the great Arthur Wilkins, people who don't know you. With me you'd better sing a different tune!"

"You're the one who's going to sing a different tune, and damn soon!"

In all their quarrels a moment always came, sooner or later, at which some dazzling inspiration gave Laura the power to destroy the brittle righteousness of Arthur's outlook. It came now. With a complete change of mood she howled with mirth—"How vulgar we are, how utterly vulgar! Oh my god! Ha-ha-ha…"

Arthur became somber and polite—"Good night, Laura." But as he left, he slammed the door.

"Vulgar vulgar vulgar!" she cried after him.

Every evening Arthur sent her flowers for the Saracen Room. There they were, inevitable, mostly pink roses this time, in a vase on a taboret. She smashed it in the fireplace. As a nurse, she had learned the curses that pain can wring from an underground of rage or sexual calamity, and she spat them now at the empty room. When she closed her eyes, she saw waves of red.

After a few minutes she became afraid. She imagined herself beaten by servants.

Feeling driven to the wall, she even began to think about love. She sat for perhaps an hour on the largest sofa and mused about her grand ambitions when Arthur proposed, some of which had been attained. She told herself she was after all the loyal and loving wife of this multi-millionaire, and that she should appear to show him a certain consideration. Without even throwing a shawl over her bare shoulders, she went upstairs to his suite and banged with the brass knocker.

No response.

Since only the parlor-office of this suite opened to the corridor, she realized that Arthur had probably gone to bed in his chamber and couldn't hear. She banged and banged.

On the other side of the corridor a door opened and a young man appeared, garbed in a long nightshirt. On seeing Laura, he ducked modestly out of sight and then poked his head around the doorjamb, a pink head plastered with black hair and adorned with popping eyes. It was Arthur's valet. "Oh, Mrs. Wilkins, it's you. Hope I didn't startle you. Beg pardon. Didn't know what to think, you know. Knocking at Mr. Wilkins' door this time of night."

"That's all right, Luther. Don't be disturbed."

"Have to be careful, you know. Always sleep with one eye open, taking care of a man in Mr. Wilkins' position."

"Go back to bed!" snapped Laura, and banged again.

This time Arthur opened the door.

She saw immediately that he had overheard her conversation with Luther, and that he understood she had come to sing a different tune. He puffed out his cheeks, he pursed his lips—his enjoyment of his triumph was sensual.

Laura shut the door behind her. "Oh Arthur, I'm so sorry for what I said I couldn't sleep." Tears came into her eyes. With a soft finger he wiped a tear from her cheek and murmured, "Like dew on a full-bloomed white orchid." Then he joked—"The servants will have a great story tomorrow—you coming up here in the middle of the night and banging on my door."

On the next morning, as planned, the private train again set out from St. Vincent across the state—this time all the way, bearing in the salon the magnate himself, Mrs. Laura Wilkins, the Governor, the Governor's wife, the president of the First National Bank in St. Vincent, the banker's wife, the English viscountess who as Laura's guest was being put up in the Alhambra Hotel, a French gentleman of no occupation attached to the viscountess, the second vice-president of the Pamlico and Gulf Railroad, the second vice-president's wife, the second vice-president's daughter, the editor of *The St. Vincent Chronicle*, the editor's wife, and the office manager Claude Lyman. The Atlantic to the Gulf! The line was finished. Following the private train was a freight engine upon which Laura was scheduled to smash a bottle of native scuppernong wine and christen it, as Superintendent Thomas Clayton had quaintly suggested. A gala occasion.

The brass bell, into which Arthur had dumped thirty silver dollars when it was cast, cling-clanged merrily. Roses perfumed the whole train. How beautiful, how primitive, how exotic, how rich the land! Interminable forests. Flatcars on sidings stacked with fresh lumber. New loading platforms with crates of oranges. Roaring past the loading platform in a town called Olustee prompted discussion of a race riot that had made Arthur Wilkins "absolutely mad with anxiety" for almost a week, according to his wife. Everybody had read, or knew somebody who had read, an editorial written by the editor of the *Chronicle*. Since the editor himself was present, its language was now recalled and savored: "The thunderstorm has cleared the atmosphere…" There would be "a long era of amity between the two races," and "a favorable climate for a golden age of opportunity." While "deploring the violence of the rioters," along with "the loss of business that resulted from the interruption of normal trade," the people of Olustee "were breathing more freely." "Negro bumptiousness" was said to have disappeared, and "many appeals for assistance from Negro refugees" were said to have "created new sympathy for this child-man among us. In this light, indeed," the editorial concluded, "the trouble at Olustee may well be a blessing in disguise, for the Negroes have been taught a needed lesson, even by the indiscriminate violence of the mob."

Laura went to the rear observation platform for air. In every village, which they passed in seconds, were humble souls, white and black, busy or idle one couldn't say, but there were mules or oxen ploughing, dragging carts…No suggestion of the kind of thing the *Chronicle* had editorialized about. She waved at humble souls, and on two occasions one of them waved back. Most of them stood like posts to watch their lightning passage. "We must seem very strange to them," she said to the viscountess and the gentleman of no occupation. The bell gave its silver cling-clang, and oh, the sunlight, the perfect splendid sunlight that radiated from an azure sky so soft and brilliant she felt like weeping.

The ceremony at Payhokee-on-the-Gulf was a bore. She smashed the bottle of scuppernong wine and pronounced, "I christen this locomotive *Nellie May*." The *Chronicle* was going to say this was symbolic. The new locomotive would take the place of an out-of-date balloon-stacker destroyed after the riot by some ignorant white men who somehow acquired a box of ammunition that didn't fit their own guns and so disposed of it in the firebox to find out what would happen. The symbolism had to do with progress in spite of setbacks.

The Governor talked for about twenty painful minutes.

Arthur took over after a pattering of applause. He referred to the one hundred and fifty thousand dollars in compensation due to the state of Florida because the line wasn't completed on schedule. "Fortunes of war," he commented, smiling. "That race riot delayed us." But he wasn't worried. Financially, the Pamlico and Gulf was solid as granite.

As the group gathered for the symbolic christening broke up, Arthur turned to the man most affected by not finishing the line on schedule – "I'm sincerely sorry you can't have that bonus, Tom. That money has to help pay the state. But don't worry about it. They can't keep a good man down." He gave his construction superintendent a jolly punch in the biceps.

Laura was furious. "They"! Who were "they" that presumably couldn't keep Tom Clayton down? "They" was just Arthur himself who was behaving like the petty skinflint he was!

The construction boss was standing in a group of men whose hard-bitten faces, creased by years under a hot sun, and whose poorly-fitting suits, no doubt their Sunday-best for the occasion, identified them as natives. With the ceremony over, he was shaking their hands. Now each one would be looking for another job. Tom Clayton too.

He was wearing an elegant blue serge suit with the jacket unbuttoned so that a pale yellow and satiny vest, with a heavy gold watch chain, bulged over his burly chest. His auburn hair, almost the same color as her own — a sign of something! — puffed out under a glistening white Stetson and together with his red beard framed his tanned face. A lion among jackals and hyenas! His expression was affable as he distributed farewells among men who had apparently been his lieutenants. She was suddenly elated with the inspired notion that Tom Clayton, the men around him, and the two thousand-or-so others working under these men, both black and white, were the true males. Arthur and the men in the party on his private train were paper and dust. Her perception was imperial!

Arthur, the Governor, the Governor's wife, the editor of the *Chronicle* and his wife had already walked away from the rest. They were headed for the private train which was on the pier so that they could look out over the Gulf while dining. Besides humiliating her with his foolish admiration, Arthur was still putting her down because of their quarrel, and he hadn't even offered her the courtesy of his arm. That Tom Clayton was not included in the intimate group on the private train insulted her, too. Arthur could never forget how she toasted Tom on New Year's Eve in the Alhambra Hotel, before the President of the United States — *to the great builder of the main line to the Gulf — to Tom Clayton: good health and happy days!* Since the magnate no longer needed a man who could *really* build a railroad, Tom would dine in the Wentworth Hotel, which was really just an old-fashioned boarding house, with the hoi polloi. What would the great Arthur Wilkins choose to do with him, if anything?

Those who had come to Payhokee-on-the-Gulf on the private train but were not included for intimate dining were heading for the Wentworth Hotel. They had to be careful so they wouldn't trip over rails and ties. The viscountess hiked up her long skirt and leaned on the arm of her gentleman of no occupation. She wasn't included for intimate dining because she was in the party as Laura's friend! Anyway, she could take a lover as she chose!

"Come along, Laura," Arthur called, pleasantly.

"One moment, if you please," she replied. Tom Clayton had noted Arthur's call and was watching her—even at a little distance she sensed a smoldering fusion of anger and desire. She hurried toward him and held out a hand as though she were bidding him good-bye and perhaps saying something nice about what he had done, or perhaps about it being his idea that she smash a bottle of scuppernong against the new *Nellie May*.

How big and hard his hand was, the skin surprisingly silky. She used both hands and kept her hold. She knew that her eyes and a quality of breath in her body added sexual force to her words—"I don't like sham and I don't like shilly-shallying, Tom. I know what I think you know, too—we'll be together in the future, in every way you can imagine. I can't say more now. Come to me in St. Vincent. We must talk, make plans. I have my own money. I believe in you, want you. Goodbye for now, Tom."

Immediately, she felt unburdened and happy. She was amused that he was taken aback. He was as aware of their feeling for each other as she was, she was certain. But her blunt invitation did surprise him. He didn't even reply.

"Coming, Arthur, coming," she called, gaily. Holding up her skirt, she trotted over the rails and ties to where Arthur, trying to conceal his irritation, was waiting with their guests.

X

Summer came, scorching, familiar. To Julia this was incongruous, a divine joke, because she was so unlike what she'd been in other summers. Also, everyone else seemed different. Was this only because *she* had changed? She wasn't sure, and she worried. There was anxiety in the hum of bees, foreboding in the mourning of turtle doves.

It was obvious that her world had changed. There were aftershocks from the destruction of Myrtle and the final crash of the railroad through the wilderness to Payhokee.

Naval stores went to St. Vincent by railroad freight instead of wagon.

Someone tried to burn down the Dales' store. The young bridge monkey Mark Richardson prevented it. Ever since the Dales took him in during the riot, along with the Peters children, he'd been sleeping on the counter in the store. One night, when he heard someone piling sticks on the porch facing the street, he knew immediately what was going on. He'd run out with a hoe, chased the man away, and scattered burning kindling. His shouts had brought Joanna and Joshua, who threw pails of water.

Lucy spread her story of how Miz Clayton drove three men away from Richmond Plantation with her shotgun. Soon the whole town realized that one of those three men was the fellow Tom Clayton had sent packing out of Amos Whitaker's saloon. Miz Julia had protected her property, and her husband's, from some bum out for revenge. Fine woman Miz Julia Clayton! The Dales knew what the whole town knew and they admired her, but Joshua's attitude toward Tom was puzzling. One day, at the store, he remarked, "I have to say Miz Julia – Arthur Wilkins and all his railroad men, including your husband, could have stopped that riot." He was studying her, obviously curious about how she would react.

"You can't be sure of that!" Joanna snapped.

Joshua shrugged.

Startled, Julia said, "I'm sure Tom would have stopped it if he could."

Joanna continued to her husband, "You found out for yourself it ain't easy to stop something like that once it gets going."

Joshua persisted — "All I'm saying is the railroad mustered a lot of men, and if they'd meant business they could have done just about anything they wanted to do."

Julia became heated — "Are you saying Tom didn't really want to stop the riot?"

"It ain't like that."

Joanna broke in — "You got no call going into this with Julia."

Joshua answered his wife — "I guess you're right. Julia's Julia and Thomas Ewell Clayton is Thomas Ewell Clayton."

"Look, Mr. Dale, Tom's my husband!" Why was she irritated? She couldn't stand her husband. At the same time, what had happened in Myrtle gave her a confused sense of guilt because she hadn't foreseen it and tried to stop it, an even stronger feeling of responsibility toward her own work people, and resignation to what she regarded as her destiny in a violent land. Her indissoluble marriage to Tom was part of this destiny. In criticizing Tom, Joshua Dale seemed to suggest that she was answerable in some measure for whatever Tom did or failed to do — just because she was Tom's wife. She didn't need to be reminded of this bitter fact. Mr. Dale was pointlessly cruel. But what she said to him, without thinking, might suggest she did indeed regard herself as answerable, and that wasn't what she intended at all!

"I don't want to get you all riled up, Julia," said Joshua Dale. "If this whole sniveling town had just a pinch of your courage, there'd never been a riot."

Subsequently, Joshua was gruff but more friendly than ever. There was a little bewildering apology in Joanna's manner. What the Dales were thinking was presumably too complicated for explanation, and Julia was afraid to question them.

Every Sunday she went to the Rourkes'. Thorstein was always there. There was enough new understanding between them so that Julia could marvel at how little she understood herself, and could wonder whether Thorstein understood himself. There was no doubt about her desire, which she tried hard to ignore. For a few hours each week she imagined herself and Thorstein as married. The Sunday conversations flourished.

One Sunday they talked about Sir Walter Scott. When she was an adolescent, her father had tried to instill in her an aspiration to perfect womanhood as suggested in the novels of Scott, his favorite author. She should hope for a gentleman all courtesy and respect and devotion, ready to lay down life to protect honor, his own and especially his lady's. And what should a perfect lady do? She should wait, just wait! What tricky shuffling in mind and spirit could explain such a pusillanimous notion in an energetic and practical man of business like her father? She had no clear answer, and her confusion was compounded by the thought that her father had been moved by love, by hope, by determination that she have a life more transcendent than possible. At age thirty, with an eleven-year-old daughter almost as tall as she was and just as heavy, what did she know and feel that her father hadn't known and felt? He wouldn't have seen a gentleman in the half-naked man in the bedroom of the Alhambra Hotel, in the author of *The Tumefaction of Property*. He wouldn't have seen a perfect lady in the piteous creature, paralyzed in her sweat-drenched nightie, unable to turn a doorknob.

Julia couldn't be forthright about all this in conversation with Thorstein, Esther, and Joseph. But they did discuss *Ivanhoe*, in which the hero opted for the nonenity Rowena instead of the vibrant Rebecca. Poor Ivanhoe! Poor Scott!

Around the dinner table and in the relatively cool shade of the live oak they talked a lot about concepts in Thorstein's book. He cited the New Year's Eve celebration at the Alhambra Hotel as an example of "conspicuous consumption," the disease, the tumefaction, which infected the whole world from Paris to New York, from St. Petersburg to St. Vincent. Immoderate property met no bodily human needs but merely enhanced prestige and power. Thorstein studied Arthur Wilkins and his circle as though they were insect specimens under a magnifying glass. They were like certain barbarians who demonstrated superior status by burning valued possessions. Did the great magnate in effect burn a million dollars by crowning his wife with that diamond tiara and by adorning her nearly-naked and ample bosom with that necklace and pendant of pearls and emeralds? What use were those fatuous jewels? Thorstein made a grisly joke: wives like Laura Wilkins lived on burning pyres as widows in India died on them—the body of the magnate's wife remained intact while her soul was cremated.

Julia thought: Tom was aspiring to this world of cremated souls.

How did Thorstein come to think this way? She asked and he answered. Esther and Joseph were fascinated, too.

He was the son of Norwegian immigrant farmers, female as well as male since his mother along with his father plowed, harrowed, spread manure, cultivated, weeded and harvested. English had been such a burdensome second language that he'd had to think about what he was saying much more painstakingly than those who'd taken in mother tongue with mother's milk, unreflectively, and so unruffled by the bromides which any language can vomit. Were Norwegian immigrants in Illinois a little like the colored folks in Florida, presumptively inferior to manufacturers, bankers, and merchants of the old white American stock?

Thorstein demurred—"We were fortunate. We weren't massacred, like the colored folks in Myrtle, or the Indians. But on occasion we were starved, frozen and worked to death."

We! Thorstein always spoke of Norwegians, poor folks, and black folks as *we*. Julia felt that the irony in *fortunate* and the covenant in *we* both expressed and concealed his special passion that had grown with years of commitment to his study and writing. He felt about the whole world as she felt about the people at Richmond Plantation she knew so thoroughly. It was wonderful but the loneliness in his mind must be terrible!

Summer heat fostered a smoldering torpor. The charmed foursome, dressed in thin white cotton, remained in the shade of the live oak, sipped lemonade, and nibbled fish cooked in cream sauce. Could Julia show Thorstein that she understood, that he was not alone? What could she do?

She danced a Latin verse. Her hands fluttered like hummingbirds in the hibiscus and her thin dress stuck with sweat to her breasts, unconcealed by any corset. She knew she was seducing Thorstein, that her impulse was terrifying because in some unforeseeable way it might lead to the destruction of both of them, and she couldn't help herself. She was shameless and also aware of being strange, eccentric—

Felix qui potuit rerum cognoscere causas,
atque metus omnis et inexorabile fatum
subiecit pedibus strepitumque Acherontis avari—

"I'm just an ignoramus from the Old Sod—" Joseph began.

"It is like music, isn't it?" said Esther. "But good heavens, Julia, you'll have to translate."

"Thorstein—he is very very happy. He's been able to learn the causes of things. He's stomped under his foot all fear and inexorable fate, and the big racket of greedy Hell."

"I wish I could," said Thorstein.

He knew her need for one lasting mate, and he feared what he knew! She sometimes wished she could go merrily to bed with him, have a glass of wine with him, and then go her way while he went his. But she couldn't escape from what she was, and she knew that he knew she couldn't.

During the whole spring, after the new railroad line was finished, and then during the summer, Tom was at home only on four separate days, calm and pleasant enough on the rare occasions when he spoke to her or to the children. He'd been in St. Vincent, Atlanta, Washington, and possibly other places he didn't bother to mention, looking for "the right opportunity." He didn't explain what this might be, and his kingly manner discouraged inquiry. Also, Julia didn't much care. Caroline pestered him a bit, but when he stopped talking to her she remained content with just being near him, knitting something for him. He sat in a rocking chair on the porch, fanned himself, and drank a moderate amount of whiskey.

Julia lied that she was ill and evaded him. She was able to sleep in the spare room until he came on one very hot night in August, just after the Sunday when she danced for Thorstein. "Goddamnit, Julia, there's nothing wrong with you some good old rutting won't fix up." He was a little high but not drunk, and he became gallant—"You look sweet as honey and maybe this heat will make you melt." He caught her wrist and dragged her to the bedroom. He was browbeating her to laugh, but she didn't. Yet, terrified and ashamed, she didn't resist much. She *was* his wife! Naked, slippery with sweat, she went into the sagging bed and gave herself to him as he seemed to prefer—that is, she threw her legs over his heaving back without being ordered to do so and remained still. There might have been some recognition of who she was if he'd shown some dissatisfaction with her supineness, but he didn't. If he'd known who she was, he wouldn't have dragged her to bed in the first place! Anyway, he wouldn't have cared what she wanted or didn't want. After he went to sleep, she went to the room for the necessaries, sponge bathed, washed her chafed genitals, and retched with tears and disgust. Then she went to the spare room.

Tom departed in the morning and hadn't come back. She was pleased to note that William didn't care.

The following Sunday morning, before going to the Rourkes', she listened to a sermon by the Reverend Augustus Blanding, who had recovered from his collapse during the funeral for the Myrtle victims and was now able to preach with his former vigor. He had chosen a text from Leviticus because of unlawful lusts in his congregation—"Thou shalt not lie carnally with thy neighbor's wife, to defile thyself with her." Everybody in Olustee knew that a professor from Rowland College had spent two nights at Richmond Plantation during the riot, and that Julia saw him every Sunday afternoon at Clayton Plantation. Was the sermon aimed at Mrs. Clayton, perhaps among others? Julia didn't care very much. It occurred to her that neither Leviticus nor Mr. Blanding mentioned women defiling *them*selves, as she had done just the previous Monday night! For Leviticus and Mr. Blanding, were women defiled no matter what they did or didn't do? Did Leviticus and Mr. Blanding regard all women as ipso facto unclean?

If Tom ever tried to drag her to bed again, she'd fight!

What a fool, what a moral cretin she'd been! That she'd even had to think about Sir Walter Scott and Leviticus meant that she was stuck in their dogmatic mud! Perhaps her kind of thinking about almost everything was her curse! If something ugly in her mind hadn't turned her to a jelly, would she have let Tom drag her to bed? And wait wait—what was she waiting for?

The September dry spell came. The sky glared, cloudless. Julia's horse and buggy, proceeding on a Sunday to the Rourkes', roiled up a fine dust. The birds did not sing.

After dinner, served by Piney under the brittle leaves of the live oak, Julia said, "I would like to have Thorstein take a walk with me."

She knew that he was not surprised. He rose from his chair and put out his hand, which she took.

Esther and Joseph were probably not surprised, either. Esther said, "We have just put out new seed beds in the vegetable garden." Joseph said, looking at Thorstein, "If you walk that way, please be careful. Walk between the beds, not on them."

A stand of Clayton Plantation's great primeval pines loomed just beyond the vegetable garden, and there was no better place to walk. Both Esther and Joseph understood the inevitability of what she and Thorstein were doing, and for a moment Julia felt grateful. Also, she sensed their concern—they knew her nature, her bent toward commitment, and they knew Thorstein's piratical past. But they shouldn't worry! She and Thorstein, together, would flout the past, both his and hers. Her legs trembled so that she could walk only quite slowly, but his rough hand was gentle and strengthening.

They unclasped hands so that Julia could lead along the narrow paths among the seed beds, and then clasped hands again as they came to a broad area of earth where sweet potatoes had been dug. She saw that his face shone as she'd never seen it—emotion deepened lines that made him look both severe and inspired—older. They'd be lovers forever! She'd rejoice in his nature forever—his adventurous and myth-challenging mind, his rather cheeky habits of eating as if there were no tomorrow, of dressing as if all clothes were idiotic, of harnessing and controlling his horse with brusque efficiency as if even the beast had to know where he had to be and when, so that he could most deftly feed or whet his mind. She refused to think about any practical obstacles to their becoming lovers forever. She threw her arms around him. He held her tight, secure, and she sagged with all her weight against him. How slender he was—vulnerable, she thought, with momentary alarm. The sinews in his back seemed unbearably vital and precious.

He kissed her lips, and she responded so desperately that he kept kissing her until she could become utterly and serenely sensual.

They were still standing in the open vegetable garden, which merged on one side with Clayton Plantation's many acres of cotton field. They looked at each other, they looked about—some children were walking across the cotton field—they smiled, and they continued toward the pines.

The great trunks soared before the tufted branches curtained the glare of the September sun. They walked upon the spongy needles in twilight. It was an awesome place for lovers, but were they aware of this?

Their bodies were bright, defying the twilight.

She wept—why hadn't she known Thorstein when she was a dreaming virgin at the academy? Is this really love? Oh the years in which she hadn't known this glory, this life!

Then she could smile, savoring half-guessed-at expectations, as they caressed and kissed away the pine needles that stuck to their moist bodies—to backs, in hair, to parts usually hidden by idiotic clothes. Again and again, tenacious, acquisitive, tireless, they could coat their moist bodies with pine needles! Then caress and kiss them away.

How strong she was! Never again would she go sweating and anxious to the little room for the necessaries, huddle with or without the guilt, read Dr. Jones's book. Never again would she whine about who she was or should be. She'd be proud as an animal, self-assured, mated.

*

The enchanted Sundays seemed to end with that most enchanted Sunday of all. Esther had a heart attack. It was a shock. Her health had seemed no worse than usual. A boy on a mule brought the message that there would be no Sunday dinner. The new Olustee telegraph had been used to inform Thorstein.

Then Tom came home. Julia slept in the spare room. Was it her austere manner or his own involvements that kept him from bothering her?

On a hot and dry Wednesday, five days after the heart attack, Esther invited Tom and Julia, commanded them in effect, to visit her about a matter which the boy on the mule didn't and no doubt couldn't explain.

She was propped up on many pillows on a sofa. The huge desk which was the center of her working life, somewhat similar to Julia's, was across the room. Her wheelchair was at her elbow, with the crutches in the rack which Joseph had made. There were distinct red patches on her cheeks, like the tinting done by an undertaker on a corpse.

Julia felt her own heart tighten. She was prepared to say something encouraging, reassuring. But Esther's appearance stopped her. Esther hated pretense.

"Good afternoon, Julia—Tom." Esther didn't smile and her voice was curiously high-pitched. To Piney she said, "Fetch Joseph. Tell him my brother and sister are here."

Esther had never seemed so withdrawn and despairing. Was this the effect of the heart attack or of what she intended to talk about?

While they waited for Joseph, she asked Tom about his many trips.

He replied pleasantly and with apparent candor, "I can't say I found what I'm looking for, but I don't want to be a hired man no more. If I'm going to build another railroad or anything else, I want some equity in it when it's done."

This was more than he'd told Julia all spring and summer. He must be determined to be agreeable, for the moment at least! No doubt he wanted to consider Esther's "matter," whatever it was, without giving offense and to his own advantage.

Esther said, "It's a shame the big riot in Myrtle held you up so you didn't get that big bonus Arthur Wilkins was ready to give you."

"What big bonus?"

"If you choose not to tell me, it's all right. Joseph and I hear things when we do our banking in St. Vincent."

Tom moved to the window and looked out. He wasn't going to talk about the bonus. His effort to be agreeable didn't extend that far.

Piney came in again—"Mr. Joseph coming. He washing up now." She put her big hand to Esther's forehead and said, "You a bit warm, Sugar. I's going to get you a glass of water, and I put just a little peppermint in it."

Once this was done and Piney left, Esther said, "What have I ever done for Piney except give her a cabin for herself and her son? Why shouldn't I live in the cabin and move Piney in here? Why shouldn't I tuck Piney in white sheets and bring her a little water with peppermint in it?"

Tom was examining a collection of medicines on a bookcase.

"I don't know the answers to such questions," said Julia. "I wish I did."

Esther flashed her sunny smile. For a moment she was her old self. "Come right down to it, I don't know why you should. You don't know what it is to have but not deserve a husband like Joseph, day and night looking after me, *me* what am and have always been a sick wreck."

After all their years together any undercurrent in whatever Esther said was clear to Julia. Now Esther was saying in effect that in contrast to the good fortune that she, the sick wreck, had enjoyed, Julia, her lusty nymph of the piney woods, was tied to Tom, the stony-hearted brother she scorned. "I find it hard to bear your talking like this," said Julia.

They continued to wait for Joseph in silence.

In about a minute he came in, wearing clean work clothes. He looked grim.

After brisk greetings Esther said, "Let's not waste time. We must talk about Clayton Plantation, what's to be done about it."

"Your place and Joseph Rourke's," said Tom.

Esther blazed—"When you say things like that, I can't tell what you feel. All our lives I've never known what you really feel. Father would have willed the place to you if you'd been interested, if you hadn't gone scooting around the country like some moaning lost bull, and if I weren't a cripple he thought needed a nest."

"Well, you've made a go of it."

"We have our troubles, which we have to talk about, but Joseph and I have done as well as we could."

"It's your brains keeps us going at all," said Joseph.

Esther waved her hand in a gesture that said enough of these amenities or irrelevancies. "I've got a simple request to make, Tom," she said. "I'm very very sick. Foolish, isn't it, to dwindle here on this sofa and say I'm sick, as though you couldn't see? But it's not just being crippled like I've been for so many years—" her voice became strident, forestalling any denial of reality—"my heart is giving out. I'm like a lump of dough with the yeast forgot, so it won't ever rise. It's got so I can't move from here to my trusty wheelchair without the help of Piney or Joseph. Thank God for doctors who are so dull they never learned how to lie. They tell me what I know. I don't have much longer. Next week? Next month? Tonight? I've talked this over with Joseph and he agrees with me..."

Joseph said, "No matter what you say the doctors *don't* know—"

She silenced him with a look and went on, to Tom, "If you side with us and do what's right for Clayton Plantation, you can have a partnership when I go—"

Tom was seated in Esther's swivel chair by the big desk. He turned a little away from Joseph and spoke as if his brother-in-law were not there—"Partnership with Joseph Rourke?"

"Wait till I've finished, Tom. You must know that our cotton doesn't cover our costs. Maybe you know and maybe you don't know we've borrowed money to put up a steam sawmill and get other necessities for lumbering. We've been cutting the pines, way across the creek, far from here. If you become partner, you'd have little to do besides fighting for us before the Railroad Commission or go into politicking for a new commission."

"If Esther wants your help—" Julia began.

Tom interrupted, ignoring her—"What do you want from the Commission?"

Esther hesitated before replying—"I feel ashamed of myself, and of you, that you ask. And this has nothing to do with the Railroad Commission—I'm sure you know what *they're* up to. I feel ashamed for what twisted us both when we were children, so we vied with each other and took opposite roads."

"You were always the good one," said Tom, lightly. It was only with Esther that he exhibited a certain playful etiquette, larded with compliments, that actually suggested arrogance and hatred.

Julia became angry—"That's no way to talk!"

But Esther ignored her, too. "Here are the facts," she said to Tom. "We owe the bank more than twelve thousand dollars we borrowed so we could buy the sawmill and some other—"

"Oh, do you really *have* to cut the pines?" Julia cried.

Moved, Esther almost whispered, "It will probably be some time before we have to cut the stand near the vegetable garden."

It seemed that Piney had been waiting within earshot—she came in and gave Esther another glass of water, presumably with a little peppermint in it.

Joseph stood by the open window, waiting, looking out.

Tom clasped his hands in his lap and twiddled his thumbs.

"Our mill can turn out about four thousand feet a day," Esther went on. "But we're being choked because we can't move it profitably to market. And we can't meet payments to the First National Bank in St. Vincent."

"That's Wilkins's bank."

"Joseph and I didn't know that when we arranged for the loan."

"Perhaps it don't make no difference. Wilkins is supposed to be a reasonable man." Tom's flat tone was emphatically ironic.

Esther was calm, keeping her temper without apparent effort—"We don't count on any quality or purpose of Mr. Wilkins beyond an unappeasable appetite for gobbling up the whole state. We have to pay forty-two dollars a carload to move lumber to the dock in St. Vincent. I know of two other lumbermen who pay only twelve dollars a carload, and they're farther from St. Vincent than we are."

"Have you notified the Commission?"

Esther smiled at Piney and sipped her peppermint water—"I've filed a complaint."

"What's happened?"

"Nothing. You probably know why better than I do."

Tom shrugged—"You ought to've known Arthur Wilkins owns the Commission."

"Well, I didn't. I've talked this over with Joseph and he agrees with me—"

Joseph muttered, sullenly, "I ought to've known, like you say, Tom—" He was trying to be conciliatory but was angered by Tom's disdain.

Esther went on—"What success you could have in making the Commission act with justice I don't know. But Joseph and I would like to make it to your interest to try. As things stand, and with the price of cotton so low, we're being crushed between the Wilkins bank and the Wilkins railroad. You know Arthur Wilkins, you know your way around with men like him or connected with him, you know men at the Capitol. All Joseph and I know is cotton and lumber. Say yes and the partnership's yours."

Tom looked at the ceiling, and for a few seconds nobody spoke.

Enraged, Julia demanded, "What are you thinking? What *is* there to think *about*?"

Esther continued—"Of course Joseph will have to be boss here. He knows how things are run. The colored folks respect him. But the whole place can go in time to William. I can put that in my will, and Joseph can put it in his."

Tom made a dry comment—"A will signed by a wife of a surviving husband ain't worth the paper it's writ on."

Joseph made no further attempt to conceal his anger—"I don't give a good goddamn about the legalistics of wills and such. I ain't conversant with the law. What Esther wants is law enough for me." Then, abruptly, in what was almost a howl—"I won't *tolerate* more talking of dying and wills."

"Very sensible, Joseph," said Tom.

"I'm proposing a way for Clayton Plantation to stay in the family after all," Esther said, without apparent emotion. "One day William will take over. I'm putting all the cards on the table, Tom. This is the way I would like it."

"Suppose Joseph marries again—" Tom began.

Julia raged—"How can you talk as though Esther's gone? Good heavens, Tom, she's just asking for your help!"

But he paid no attention to her and went on, "He's a young man still. And he's going to have the best farm land in Jackson County as well as the lumber."

"There is no cause at all for saying that," Joseph growled. "Such notions do you no credit, Tom Clayton. It's not that I'm resigned to Esther failing anyhow. The doctors don't know everything—"

Esther's mouth, rather thin like Tom's, writhed with a hurt that might have been either mental or physical, or both. "We have to face it, Joseph.

Look here, Tom, we're making you an offer because we'd like to save Clayton Plantation. I'd like to keep it in the family, and I don't want it to be took by the First National Bank of St. Vincent, no matter who owns it. If you want to help, you can profit and make sure of an inheritance for William. I don't see why you can't at long last come out and admit that you do have some kind of loyalty to your origin. I'm not trying to reproach you because we've never got along. I'm a dying woman, and if I can lie here and tell you this and ask for your help and be willing to give you something in return, the least you can do is give me a straight answer."

"All this talk is hot air," said Tom. "Like Joseph says, we don't know you're going to die. You'll probably take care of the old farm a good many years."

Joseph turned his trembling back on all of them and looked out the window.

Julia knew his agony and what he must be thinking—she herself was probably thinking about the same thing. That Tom should use Joseph's passionate denial of Esther's condition as justification for not replying to his sister's dying request was an unbearable incongruity. Their feelings were opposite. The obvious artifice in Tom's cheery optimism about Esther's health had ghastly force, actually suggesting satisfaction with her approaching end. Julia suddenly understood that Esther, knowing her brother well, would not have risked this painful impasse with him unless she felt driven, with death near. And for the first time Julia, having for so many years known and loved Esther's bent toward unsparing realism, now had to accept, with Esther, the certainty of her imminent death. She had been denying too, like Joseph, and she no longer could. She wept.

No one spoke.

Julia couldn't avoid the thought that time was on Tom's side. Since Esther was dying, she might feel forced to offer Tom better terms. Was the alternative losing Clayton Plantation to the bank? What was Tom bargaining for? For sole title to Clayton Plantation with Joseph as foreman again, as just a hired hand? But she couldn't say outright what she was thinking. She cried, "By heavens, Tom, why can't you do what Esther wants you to do? You could at least help out with the Railroad Commission without expecting *anything* in return. Can't you just be kind to your own sister when she's sick? Do you have to keep on being so distant from her?"

Tom ignored her, and the faces of both Esther and Joseph were frozen, as though she hadn't said anything at all.

After another silence Esther said, quietly, "You will never control this plantation, Tom. There are thirty-six souls here. There's Piney, and Piney's son. After what you did to the folks in Myrtle, Joseph and I will not put you in charge of folks here."

Julia was staggered. "Did to the folks in Myrtle?" she repeated. "What are you saying?"

Esther was both tender and wooden—"Talk to Joshua Dale."

"I have. He respects me—"

"Of course he does. Anyway, I blame Arthur Wilkins for what happened in Myrtle even more than your husband." Unwilling to veer from her purpose, she turned abruptly to Tom again – "If you don't agree to what I've proposed, the plantation will probably be split up. The bank can repossess the sawmill, which Joseph and I shouldn't have got anyhow. Joseph will try to sell off some land and make do with whatever he can keep."

With sardonic hostility, Tom bowed to Joseph. His meaning was clear: congratulations, Hobo, you've done well!

Joseph took a nervous step. For a moment it seemed as though he might strike Tom.

Esther continued as though nothing had happened—"On the other hand you could make an honest effort at the Capitol and Joseph and I will sign over a forty- percent share of Clayton Plantation while I'm still alive. Get a fair rate on freight charges and you'll deserve your share. You'll get right here that equity you've been chasing in Atlanta and Washington and God-knows-where."

"Jackson County won't amount to a hill of beans in my lifetime," said Tom.

Esther was so exhausted she could barely speak—"If you don't like our proposal—well, the Yankee railroads are taking over the state anyway."

"You're very reasonable, my dear sister. I'll have to give thought to all you've said."

Esther closed her eyes—"If I don't have your answer in a week, I'll assume you're saying no."

*

On the following Sunday there was a hurricane on the coast. In Jackson County there was strong wind that felled trees and stripped loose boards and shingles from every human shelter. The rain whipped and slashed.

Neither Thorstein nor Julia could visit Esther—or see each other.

The storm lasted three days, and on Wednesday Julia drove in her buggy to see Esther and tell her that yes, Tom was still at home and that she and Tom had never been so "distant" from each other, which was "just as well." *Distant*! He was distant from his sister, too. Was there anyone from whom Tom was not distant? No, he had not mentioned what he'd do about the Railroad Commission, if anything. She and Tom were so distant that she hadn't asked.

Esther felt stronger – she'd moved to her wheelchair without help, and she'd even used her crutches. She referred by indirection to Thorstein and Julia as lovers by commenting on her own condition. Everybody was such a prude, and she herself was the biggest prude! She'd never talked about some matters, but now she could. No one should imagine she was without sexual feeling because she was a cripple! She believed that for years she had tried to make up for her infirmity by telling herself that she was even more sexual than healthy people. Was what she told herself true? Who could say? All she *could* say was what she'd learned from her few years with Joseph, that sex was the seasoning of life and every warm-blooded creature should savor it. "I told Joseph that after I'm gone he must find somebody new, a woman with good legs. And how my poor lover cried – I should have bit my tongue. Oh there is never time enough for lovers, but true love turns hours into eternity!"

She seized Julia's hand. Was she hinting that Julia too would never have enough time? For a different reason, of course! Probably because of Thorstein's nature – he'd never stayed long with one woman. Was Esther advising desperate love no matter how brief, regardless of any sad consequences?

Joseph came in, back from a lumber negotiation in St. Vincent, and he had harrowing news that added force to what Esther had said. Joseph had talked for a few minutes with Thorstein, who was catching a train north. He'd obtained a brief leave from Rowland College in order to arrange publication of his new book on business combinations. Also, he was applying for a better job at the University of Chicago. He'd be back in two weeks.

Events were driving spikes into Julia's mind. What would she become without Esther – and without Thorstein, who would inevitably leave Rowland College sooner or later, with herself anchored in Richmond Plantation, finding as much solace as she could in caring for Caroline and William, in perpetual bitterness evading her loathsome husband.

And fate was not done with her.

OVERHEAD THE SUN

She was more energetic than ever in running the naval-stores business. The inventory was cleared out, and there was demand for more turpentine. At the same time, fall crops had to be put in—turnips, beans, carrots, cabbage. Cane had to be cut. A mule tramped in its circle from dawn to dusk, turning the sugar mill. Work was as endless for humans as for the mule. Even the children, including Caroline and William, did a little. The storm had kept everybody under roofs for three days. The delay had been intolerable—both the business and the season were making emphatic claims. For which she was grateful.

Three days after she saw Esther the sky was blue, the birds sang as though demented, and the children were off to school. Since she was too busy to take them in the buggy, they would walk. But she could race them as far as the bridge. Their feet rattled its planks at the same time. In the windless morning they could hear the school bell.

She went to the stable on the way back to the house and her big desk. She was concerned about the health of an old horse. While there she heard galloping on the road from Olustee. A moment later, from the stable door, she saw Sanford Payne's big stallion hitched to a post before the house.

The personality of Tom's right-hand man chilled her. She didn't like the way his face hardly ever changed expression. She didn't like his gray suits which suggested a masquerade, as though he was hiding his character and had to play at being a gentleman far more exquisite than he really was. When he spoke, she generally didn't like what he said. She'd heard him described as a killer, and while she didn't know what she should believe about him, she did sense a benumbed inhumanity.

She was relieved to confirm that the old horse probably had another year or so before he would have to take his last walk into a swamp.

It was weakness in her that she remained patting the horse to put off meeting Sanford. Slowly, she walked back to the house. Gray Man and Tom stood on the verandah. They stopped talking as she approached them.

When she was quite close, Tom said, "Julia, there's some very sad news. Joseph Rourke's been shot."

"Shot? It can't be! Is he hurt bad?"

"He's been killed."

XI

During a hypnotic exchange of stares with the eyes in the mirror, Laura Wilkins began her toilet in preparation for going to breakfast and her day. With light fingertips, on which the skin was now thin and pearly—it had once been rough from hard work and harsh soaps—she stroked her whole body with a delicate white ointment purchased in Paris, a cool liquor that smelled like overripe grapes. She found peace in the reflection of her own subtly shaded flesh with its magical brilliance that both absorbed and gave forth the golden light from a linen lampshade. The vitality in the opalescent image was tremulous and challenging. You are peerless, unique, said the goddess in the glass.

She and Arthur were in New York, staying at the Waldorf. In a petulant fit Arthur had sold the limestone palace on Fifth Avenue. Since they were rejected by the Four Hundred, Arthur flaunted democratic manners, especially when they stayed at the Waldorf. They even ate in the public dining room. "Sassiety," Arthur said more than once, using a provincialism to underscore his scorn, "ain't worth a moldy pickle."

She must make Arthur return to Florida.

She took deep breaths, her large breasts swelling upwards, her small nipples budding out pink and hard—"Ah—ah—ah..." The Viscountess Mary Burleigh had said she was an absolute Rubens and had gone on and on about seductive curves in arms, breasts, hips, necks, lips—about infinite petal shades in skin. The viscountess had scandalized St. Vincent by wearing a continental one-piece bathing suit. After she and Laura laughed about this, she'd declared that ingrained American Puritanism was leading her absolute Rubens by the nose—-"You could make men surpass themselves, my dear!" She'd neighed her rough laugh. "When will you admit you have a lover?"

Laura had become angry—"I don't!"

"Then you are absolutely mad!"

The eyes of the Venus in the mirror became large and fierce. Her words to Tom Clayton had been carefully chosen — *"We'll be together in the future, in every way you can imagine."* He was hers after that moment, if not before. But she'd managed their meetings in public as she might have used a whip. No consummation. The body in the glass was right for an empire builder, nothing less. Tom Clayton had been scouring the whole east coast for months without result. No "right opportunity" — his words! She had money to invest and he didn't — yet. When he clutched her in the courtyard of the Alhambra Hotel — they might have been discovered — she'd pushed him away but at the same time had grabbed his right hand and crushed it against her breasts. Oh he was hers all right! Arthur had seen his unique quality and had used it. The President had seen it. She herself saw it as those men couldn't — she was the only one who knew the meaning of the great hard body and the hand like steel wrapped in silk. Ouija promised him to her.

Her whole life proved that bodies and sex fit money and power like feet in shoes. The sick and dying she'd attended as a nurse had shown again and again a unity of frustrated lusts and unrealized ambitions. Whimperings of *little* people! Not for the body in the mirror, which had made the great Arthur Wilkins babble about making her his queen. But as the viscountess guessed, her glorious body harbored unexpended force. Arthur's pathetic fumblings could never release it. No more than his petulant fury because she'd been so successful selling stock. There was violence in Tom Clayton's blue eyes with the glinting yellow cast. The face in the mirror bared its teeth.

She put on a suit of green woolen with brown velvet pleats and went down to breakfast.

She was glad she had breakfast with Arthur in public. It crimped his boorishness. He was already at their reserved table, a plate of sausages and eggs before him, a folded *Tribune* beside it.

"Good morning, my dear," he said, louder than necessary, "you're looking very chipper."

She was aware that eyes turned to follow her bewitching progress to his table. By all means let Arthur enjoy showing her off! "Good morning, my darling," she replied. "I trust you slept well?"

"Tolerably well. I have here a letter from Claude Lyman may interest you." He drew it from a jacket pocket and handed it across the table.

She put it beside her plate and picked up a menu. After she ordered sliced Florida oranges, an egg, a croissant, and coffee, she turned to the letter. She knew that the office manager in St. Vincent had instructions to write anything he regarded as significant to Arthur at the Waldorf, bypassing the communications sequence in the Wall Street office.

The letter conveyed the information that a man named Joseph Rourke had been murdered. Lyman reminded Arthur of his interest, some months ago, in acquiring some pine timber owned by Rourke, and that Rourke was having trouble making timely payments on what he owed to the St. Vincent bank (data enclosed). He informed Arthur that Rourke's widow was so sick she wasn't expected to live and suggested that the bank might get the timber at a bargain price. He suggested that the timber might be sold by the bank to the railroad for money acquired from new shareholders, and then that the timber might be marketed along with what was being cut along the right-of-way, with opportunities for profit with which Arthur was familiar.

"You don't need to bother reading the whole letter," Arthur said. "Just look at the next to-the-last paragraph."

"Oh very well—"

> Now for an astonishing development – the widow Esther Rourke, who is Tom Clayton's sister, has been saying it was Tom who murdered Joseph Rourke. This seems insane since it is certain Tom was at home with his wife when it happened. But Mrs. Rourke has taken advantage of some local jealousy of Tom Clayton (because of all you did for him) and got a grand jury to indict him. So there will be a trial.

Laura put the letter down and ate a slice of orange. She was aware that Arthur was studying her.

Did Tom really have anything to do with the death of Joseph Rourke? Whether his sister died or not, could he somehow lay his hands on money from the sale of that timber? In spite of Arthur's flunkies in St. Vincent! "What a terrible thing," she said, with just the proper amount of shock. "I remember the Rourkes—that crippled woman."

"I remember *him* very well," said Arthur. "He was the fellow at our table on New Year's Eve whose mother took in washings."

"He said some very stupid things. But that doesn't mean it's any less terrible he's been murdered. If everybody stupid were murdered, where'd we be?"

"Mighty lonely, no doubt."

"Are you really interested in buying this timber?"

"I'll buy anything in Florida if there's a profit to be made."

"I can't imagine Tom Clayton killing his brother-in-law, even though he was a stupid man."

Arthur grunted.

"Do you expect to work with Tom Clayton again?"

Arthur slapped his *Tribune* down—"Work *with* him? I *hired* the man!"

"Of course—"

"The question is: will I *permit* him to work *for* me again?"

"Will you?"

"I haven't made up my mind. A lot of the value of a man like Clayton is that people in Florida feel he's one of them. I'm not. I've had in mind grooming him for governor. The machine they've got at the Capitol is old-fashioned and inefficient. It's corrupt in obvious ways. A man like Clayton could give it some push. But a trial like this, insane or not, makes people talk and now I don't know."

Arthur did not usually expose his thinking about any individual in or close to his empire. That he did so now reflected his awareness of her special feeling for Tom. Well, she certainly hadn't concealed it! But Arthur still didn't know how special it was! The time would come when he'd have to accept that their marriage was a public affair of state, and that like any queen she could select a lover as she chose. But not yet! Regarding Tom merely as Arthur's hired man was outrageous. And in derogating Tom, Arthur was also belittling and vulgarizing her own aims, even though she wasn't clear exactly what they were! He was smirching her mind and heart! She hoped she was concealing her anger—"It doesn't matter what the hoi-polloi think of Tom Clayton."

"He ain't worth a plug nickel to *me* unless he keeps a good reputation."

"He probably doesn't care one way or another whether he keeps a reputation that might be useful to *you*."

"If that's true the man's a fool. He's a nobody without money unless he works for me, even if they do talk a lot in Florida about old families and all that twaddle. To do him credit, I never heard Clayton talk about old families. He's got too much sense."

"Ah well, he has loftier qualities than the kind of sense you're talking about."

Her husband studied her—"How much money have you invested in that sugar company he's trying to start up?"

Her surprise was genuine—"Sugar company?"

Arthur smiled—"I see you don't know about it."

"No, should I?" There was chaos in her brain—serenity and common sense, she hoped, in her voice.

"No—no reason why you should."

"Who told you about this sugar company? What do you know about it?"

"It ain't a sugar company yet. It's just Tom Clayton's idea."

"Do you think it's a good idea?"

He shrugged—"Can't say. Haven't looked into it enough."

"*How* do you know about it?"

"I have a little bird that flies around and peeps to me."

This playfulness was his way of putting her in her place. He wasn't going to tell her how or what he knew about Tom's plans. But apparently he was keeping track of what Tom was doing. It was hard to bear the humiliation that he knew more about Tom than she did. For a few minutes they ate their breakfasts in silence. Arthur flipped his *Tribune* over but didn't seem to read it intently.

Suddenly, he chuckled—"Let's just suppose that Esther Rourke ain't quite so crazy as Claude intimates in his letter. Suppose Tom Clayton really is behind this killing, even if he didn't do it himself! What then? What will we have to say about Tom Clayton *then*?"

"I don't know what we'll have to say. All powerful men have a streak of cruelty."

"That may be so—"

"Julius Caesar cut the ears off the Gauls."

Arthur laughed and stood up, throwing his napkin back on the table—"Be careful Tom Clayton don't cut *your* ears off!"

*

Sanford Payne surprised her by becoming gallant—"Ain't no colored man handy and so I'll hitch up for you, Miz Clayton."

Actually, both Sanford and Tom hitched her horse to the buggy.

"Don't tell Caroline and William about this," she said to Tom. "Unless they hear about it in school, I'll be the first to tell them. I *must* be the one who tells them."

He nodded and gave her his hand to help her up into the buggy.

She glanced at Gray Man—"Thank you, Sanford."

He bowed a little.

"I'd go with you," said Tom, "but you know how Esther feels about me. It's best you go alone. Tell Esther I'm truly sorry we don't get along better and I'm ready to do all I can. I'll deal with the Railroad Commission, and she don't need to bother about me getting anything out of it. Will you tell her that?"

"I don't know what I can say to her right now. Oh my God how terrible, and her own time so short—" She couldn't bear to have Tom see her grief, and she shook the reins.

Her horse knew the way to Clayton Plantation—skirting the marsh by the river, past the schoolhouse. She couldn't predict how she might try to help Esther to deal with her loss. But, alone in the buggy, she saw her own bond with Joseph as never before—their shared physical care of Esther, their kindred feeling for hard work, their voracious appetites for intellectual challenge after spotty or skewed educations. Joseph read *The Tumefaction of Property* even before she did. Child of Ireland and wanderer, how had be become so much like her, nourished in her ox-bow of the Olustee River? How hideous it was that she'd never shown, without restraint, how friendly she felt. She'd never talked with Joseph as spontaneously, as freely, as with Esther. There was a strange barrier between women and men, even the husband of a best friend, that was accepted with smiles but was actually cold and ugly. *Live again, Joseph, so that we can speak together*!

The charmed Sunday circle, a concentration of life, would become a diffused memory. She had to tell herself that there was no sense in thinking that the death of Joseph somehow meant that Thorstein would go away and that they'd never see each other again. It was pure superstition to suppose there was a ruthless Jehovah who made them pay for their Sundays, and made her pay for her love, with death and loss.

Most of the colored people of Clayton Plantation were sitting or standing about in front of the big house. The tragedy was compounded by their presence. With Joseph gone and Esther's days numbered, what of their future? Without employment, without property, what would they do?

As Julia stepped down from her buggy, a man she didn't know caught the reins and held her horse, mournfully stroking its nose.

Piney was seated on the front steps. She stood as Julia approached and looked down at her—"Miz Esther she in the bedroom where we laid out Mr. Joseph. She don't want to see nobody, Miz Julia, but I think she will see you. Yes, I am certain she will see you. You come with me."

The best parlor on the ground floor in the big house had become Esther's bedroom so that she wouldn't have to cope with stairs. Piney cracked open the door and said, "Sugar, Miz Clayton here."

Esther's voice was quiet, almost normal—"Tell Julia to come in. Nobody else, Piney."

"Yes, Sugar."

Piney stood aside and Julia entered.

Joseph lay on one side of the bed. It might almost have been someone else. Most of his head was wrapped in thick bandage. Only a gray nose and part of a gray cheek were visible. He was dressed in the white suit he'd worn on many a Sunday, an affirmation of pure intellect in contrast with his weekday overalls. Julia turned away, conscious of Esther in her wheelchair and fierce in determination not to show horror or despair.

She heard Esther's voice again, steady, soft—"I want to talk to you, Julia."

It seemed a grace that Esther was so self-possessed. She was her usual dignified presence in her wheelchair, dressed in a white shirtwaist with a long blue skirt over her legs. Her blue eyes were dry. Julia's words came in a rush—"What can I say to you, Esther, now, with what's happened, except I love you? I've loved you ever since we were girls together in the academy. All these years we've both struggled with our plantations I've loved you. All these past months, the wonderful hours with Joseph and Thorstein—ah-h, Esther, the older I become the more I love you. I'll always love you as long as I live."

Esther put out her arm—"Take my hand, Julia."

The fragile fingers were cold.

Then Esther asked, "Who killed Joseph?"

Shocked, Julia repeated, "Who killed Joseph? Why—I don't know. Does anybody know? Who did? Do you know?"

"Leroy McIlvey was here," Esther said. She kept her hold of Julia's hand.

With her other hand Julia dragged a chair closer to Esther and sat. The Olustee marshal was a nodding acquaintance. "Does he know who did it?"

"He says he does."

"What does he say?"

"He says Mark Richardson did it."

"The young colored man who's staying with the Dales?"

"Yes"

"That's impossible—"

"It certainly is."

"I've talked with Mark. He couldn't—"

"McIlvey already has a posse out hunting Mark."

"That's crazy! With Joseph—" She couldn't say more. As she sat, still holding Esther's hand, the body of Joseph, behind her on the bed, became a presence that scorned irrationality and absurdity, as in life.

Esther persisted—"McIlvey says somebody saw Mark shoot a white man when the *Nellie May* brought all the colored railroaders to Myrtle. At least, this somebody says he's pretty sure he saw Mark do this. That's what McIlvey says. McIlvey says he'll take his oath on a stack of Bibles any colored man who shoots one white man always pines to shoot another."

"McIlvey is plain foolish! Isn't it terrible enough that somebody did shoot Joseph?"

"It's terrible enough," said Esther.

Julia felt Esther's calm as a reproach. How could she have let her tongue run away, putting Esther in a position so that she had to say that Joseph's death was "terrible enough"? "Mark Richardson's mother was shot during the riot," she said. "Joanna Dale told me."

"Joanna told me, too."

"I can't hold it against that young man for whatever he did during the riot, with bloodthirsty drunks running loose and killing his own mother. But that has nothing, *nothing*, to do with—" Julia checked her voice. She couldn't mention the shooting of Joseph again.

Esther could mention it—"I'm just as certain as you are, Julia. Whatever Mark did during the riot has *nothing* to do with shooting Joseph. McIlvey isn't right in the head."

"When such a terrible thing happens, a man should take particular care to be sensible."

"You ought to talk to McIlvey. Perhaps *you* could make him be sensible."

"Yes—yes, I'll do that." She tried to withdraw her hand, but Esther held her.

"You asked me if I knew who killed Joseph," said Esther.

"Why, yes—"

"I do know who killed Joseph."

"*You* know? You?"

"Yes, I know."

"Who—"

"You will have to be very strong, Julia." The cold hand tightened its grip.

"What do you mean?"

Esther leaned toward her. Her voice was gentle—"I mean this—Tom killed Joseph, murdered him."

"Tom? My husband?"

Esther's eyes were clear, unwavering – "Yes – Tom."

Julia pulled at her hand, but Esther used both of her hands and wouldn't let go. "Yes—Tom," she repeated, "Tom, your husband, my brother."

Was this Esther? Esther, whose mind had actually seemed sharpened by the pain of infantile paralysis? Esther, who had been more energetic and lucid in her wheelchair than other people with two sound legs? Had she been overstrainingly stoical for years about her crippled body, lately about her own approaching death, and now about her only lover lying on the bed with his blasted head almost obliterated in bandage—had her mind been in limbo, as in an airless respite before a hurricane, so that cumulative tragedy had at last ravaged her proud and vivifying resistance and blown away her reason? Julia added her other hand to the one already clasped, making a nest of hands in Esther's lap. She almost whispered—it was unbearably sad even to mention this accusation—"Oh Esther, Esther, you can't think this—you can't believe this."

"I don't just *believe* this, Julia. I *know* it."

"Esther, Tom has been at home—when did this happen?"

"The day before yesterday."

"Two days ago? And you didn't let me know? I—Sanford Payne just came—"

"It didn't seem necessary to send a message to Richmond Plantation."

"Oh, Esther!"

"I had to see a number of people, and I don't have much time myself."

Esther had become awesome, and Julia was not inclined to question her about whom she'd seen, or why. "Tom has been at home for four days, and just like me he didn't know Joseph was shot until Sanford Payne told us, just a couple of hours ago. You believe *me*, don't you?"

"Yes, I believe you."

"Tom has scarcely set foot out of the house. He sits in the dining room we hardly ever use, all wrapped up in some kind of plan, with papers and maps. He doesn't tell me anything, and, well, you know how it is with us, and I don't ask. But he *couldn't* have killed Joseph. He's hardly been out of my sight for the four days he's been home."

"Tom has always been artful in using other people for his purposes."

Julia didn't know what to say.

"You mentioned Sanford Payne," Esther went on.

"I know you don't care for him, and neither do I. He and Tom hitched up the buggy so I could come here."

"That was real courteous."

"Don't you see, Esther? Tom didn't come because you and he haven't got along, and he didn't know how you'd take his coming. He wanted me to ask you, for him, if there's anything he can do?"

"Oh my God, my God!"

"He meant it, I'm sure. He said he'd deal with the Railroad Commission as you asked, and he doesn't want anything in return. I think he's sorry for the way he acted when you asked for help about Clayton Plantation. And I must say he should be!"

"He'll never have it!"

"Does it matter now?"

"Where was Sanford Payne the day before yesterday?"

"I don't know. He said he didn't like to be the one to tell me and Tom about Joseph being shot."

"I wouldn't have thought Mr. Payne was so sensitive."

"We've had such glorious years together, Esther. It was you who made them glorious. Your mind has been like the sun. You've always lighted up everything while other people grope around not knowing what's what. Please, Esther, for my sake, for Thorstein, for Piney too and all the folks around you, be yourself in spite of all. You have no *reason* for supposing that Tom somehow managed to get Joseph killed, and you've always had to know reasons for everything!"

"I have my reasons."

"What reasons? Oh Esther—"

"I've known Tom through and through since we were children."

"Still, you're just imagining—"

"Imagining isn't so bad. At times it's necessary—"

"I should be angry with you, Esther. But I'm not. With Joseph lying here—how dear he was to me and I never said or showed it enough, to him, or to you either—please, Esther—" She couldn't say more. It would be monstrous if she gave in to her emotions, wept, carried on, while Esther remained calm as a portrait.

"There's an iron logic that connects what people are and what they do," said Esther. "This gives me my reasons for knowing that Tom killed Joseph."

"Let me say what I think. I've never talked about Tom with you. I've told you just about everything in my whole life except that. But I'll tell you now. Tom and I have no marriage any more. I don't go to his bed. He seems to know how I feel and he doesn't force me. He has a woman or women somewhere I suppose, and I'm sure you can understand what my marriage has come to when I tell you, honestly, and I know you'll believe me, that I just don't *care* about Tom and other women. Let him go to the devil with other women! Maybe you've known this even though I've never told you in so many words."

"I've seen what your life is. I've never felt worse about anything than being the one who introduced Tom to you, so many years ago now."

"I'm telling you straight out how it is with me and Tom so you can see I wouldn't excuse him for anything. You hate Tom, I know. I have more reason for hating him than you have, but mostly he makes me want to just forget him. I've found Thorstein and I wish I could see some kind of loving future to make up for a past that made me feel my existence was mostly just duty and my body was foul and now, at my age and with two children half grown I find thank God it isn't. Oh, I don't know, Esther—what I want you to see is I'd never defend Tom for any crime he's actually *done*, but I have to say it's not *just* to accuse Tom or any man of murder just because you think you've known him through and through."

Esther's face showed that she was not moved by Julia's words. "I expected you'd come to me today," she said.

"Yes, of course—"

"I told Piney the only person in this whole world I wanted to see was you."

Julia was not to be put off—"You *must* see—it's wrong to accuse Tom—"

Esther's hands crushed Julia's fingers and silenced her. There was first a spasm of pain in Esther's self-controlled face and then a jolting contortion as she declared, "Enough, Julia! *Leave* Tom! That's what I have to say to you!"

"Leave? Leave Tom? I wish I could, but—"

"Take Caroline and William and go!"

"Go? Go where?"

"You said you loved me, Julia. Love me enough to listen. I don't have much time. Take to heart what I'm saying—"

"But what are you saying, really? This is mad, Esther—"

"I know this beautiful state of Florida doesn't allow divorce, but no matter. Marriage isn't made on paper. Take the children and go to Thorstein."

"You don't know what you're saying!"

"Don't pretend to me, with Joseph lying behind you, that you haven't thought about going away with Thorstein."

Julia shuddered. At that moment it seemed almost frightening that she and Esther shared a feeling that in some unfathomable way the body of Joseph made truth inviolate. "I don't want to pretend anything. If I lived with Thorstein, he couldn't keep a position—"

"I can see you really have considered going away with him."

"Yes, I have, but I always put the thought out of my mind."

"*Don't* put it out of your mind!"

"But to go with him, with Caroline and William, to desert all the folks who work in my naval-stores business! And if Thorstein left me, how would I earn a living?"

"I don't think Thorstein would leave you, but if he did you could teach Latin or get a job as a bookkeeper."

"Well, maybe. I'm not hiding anything from you. I often feel desperate. Thorstein got to know the children better in a couple of days than Tom knows them after being in and out during their whole lives."

"Look behind you, Julia."

Julia turned. Esther's command seemed almost to resurrect the body in the white suit, to give life to the swathed head.

"You can see the hollow in that bed where I lay beside Joseph every night—" Esther was so calm she might have been talking about food or weather. It was her way of insisting on solemn truth. "How we talked! Often we talked about you and Thorstein. Joseph could read hearts the way other folks read *The St. Vincent Chronicle*. He talked about Thorstein looking into your soft blue eyes like he was searching for a shelter in the long road ahead while he talks and writes sense for unfeeling gentry bent on preserving wooden hypocrisies, a shelter from infectious ignorance and from desperate bodies joining for sport but not for loving. He talked about the dampered appeal in your eyes, you being a woman with a naturally loving heart. He talked about the gentle motion of hands that say more than fearful tongues, and about the gallant yarns concerning all that was seen and heard since last you and Thorstein could be close to one another. He talked about the generous moon that gave you extra hours with Thorstein, and gave him extra hours with you, so you both could stay here late before going back to plodding weekdays, the road being clear and shining in the sweet-smelling night. Oh, you couldn't fool Joseph!"

Julia covered her face with her hands. She couldn't bear to see Joseph's body, or the bed. She couldn't doubt that he'd said what Esther reported, reclaiming the very style of Joseph's speech. "I just can't think of *myself* now," she cried. "Please don't ask me to do anything about myself. What can I do for you, Esther?"

Esther reached out for Julia's hand again, which Julia gave. But she didn't look at Julia. She looked past her at the presence on the bed, gave a very low moan, and then said, carefully, distinctly, "We'll be at the Clayton burial ground tomorrow at nine o'clock. You can best judge whether you should bring Caroline and William. But don't let Tom come. I don't wish to see him there, and anyway, Joshua Dale will be there, and there's no telling what might happen if Joshua Dale and your husband meet."

"Does Mr. Dale think—" Julia began, then choked off what she had been about to say. Did Joshua Dale, like Esther, think that Tom had murdered Joseph? But it would be too painful to bring up this delusion again. "Very well," she said, trying to be matter-of-fact, "I'll see to it Tom doesn't come."

Esther reached for the crutches in the rack which Joseph had attached to her wheelchair.

Adeptly, from long practice, Julia helped her up. It was custom for Esther to accompany Julia to her buggy, after their Sundays or on any other occasion.

Piney was waiting in the hall. In her eagerness to see Esther when she arrived, Julia hadn't noticed uncompromising judgment in Piney's look. Piney probably thought as Esther did, that Tom murdered Joseph. So what could Sugar possibly have to say to the presumptive murderer's wife? What could the wife have to say? Piney's stern eyes asked these questions. No doubt Esther would enlighten her.

But it was Julia, not Piney, on whom Esther leaned with one arm while managing the crutch with the other, so that they passed together through the hall, across the verandah, and down the steps to the waiting buggy. From her seat, taking the reins, Julia looked down at Esther, standing for a moment alone, waiting for Piney's help. The lack of animation in her face hurt.

Then Esther said something so conventional and banal, so alien to the character that Julia knew and loved, that she felt again they were both trapped in madness as well as in death. "Oh I can't stand this endless blue sky!" Esther exclaimed. "I can't wait for rain!"

"Yes, I wish it would rain, too," said Julia, like an automaton. "It would help the plantings."

Tortured in both shared and separate ways, they were withdrawing inside their own minds and depersonalizing all that had made them closest friends for years and years. Help the plantings? As though either she or Esther cared!

*

During the afternoon of the same day, Julia was trying to find peace by working with her ledger in her office when Tom entered, followed by the sheriff of Jackson County, an elderly man named Cyrus Kirby whom her father had known well.

Tom dropped a sheet of yellow lined paper over her ledger and said, "You might as well read this, Julia."

Julia was somewhat irritated by the abrupt intrusion. She rose from her chair and held out her hand to the sheriff — "I didn't hear you come, Mr. Kirby." Then she mentioned how her father often spoke of Mr. Kirby and for a minute or so, putting off what Tom had told her to do, told how and what her father had said about Mr. Kirby.

Then she picked up the yellow lined paper and read the penciled elaborate script on it:

State of Florida
County of Jackson
In the name of the Sovereign State of Florida
To the Sheriff or any constable of said county:

Whereas Donald Ashley has this day made oath before me that Thomas Ewell Clayton on the Eleventh day of October a.d. 1890 in the County of Jackson in and upon one Joseph Rourke in the peace of God then and there being, feloniously, willfully and of his malice aforethought did shoot the said Joseph Rourke, and in the manner aforesaid the said Thomas Ewell Clayton then and there did kill and murder. These are therefore to command you forthright to arrest the said Thomas Ewell Clayton and bring him before me to be dealt with according to the law.

Given under my hand and seal this Fourteenth day of October a.d. 1890.

H. L. Cooper

Judge Cooper had drawn a circle and had written *Seal* in the center of it. Julia silently reread the warrant.

"I can believe you are as amazed by this document as I am," said Mr. Kirby.

"My dear sister has raised a ruckus with a grand jury," said Tom.

Julia recalled Esther saying something to the effect that she had to see a number of people — *after* Joseph was murdered. A strange circumstance, but in the agony of that time in the bedroom with the body of Joseph, she hadn't considered asking Esther whom she had seen or why.

Julia said to Mr. Kirby, "Tom was here, busy with some kind of plan, during the whole day when Joseph Rourke was murdered."

"Well, don't you worry yourself too much, Miz Clayton. The reason Judge Cooper acted so quick-like is he don't want something so foolish to drag out. It's just a shame Miz Rourke is so sick and makes such trouble for your husband."

While under arrest, Tom was in effect a guest in Mr. Kirby's house in Withlacooch.

XII

The day of the trial was clear, the temperature balmy, with a breeze that smelled slightly of the salt and fishy Gulf, although the county seat was twenty-five miles from the coast, as the eagle may be said to fly but doesn't.

Before the courthouse was a wide expanse of road, dusty from dry weather, which was called Courthouse Square although the demarkation of a square was haphazard. Here a crowd had begun to gather at eight o'clock in the morning, Julia heard. The trial of such a well-known gentleman as Thomas Ewell Clayton, on the sensational charge of having murdered his own brother-in-law, was bound to make legal history, or so said *The St. Vincent Chronicle*, and so repeated many folks in Courthouse Square, sitting in carriages, wagons and carts, buying lemonade at stands of boards set up on sawhorses under the live oaks, or devouring some of the delicious crab cakes which an enterprising Negro woman had brought from Payhokee-on-the-Gulf. It was calculated she must have netted at least eighteen dollars for a half-day's work, an amount of money for a colored person that led many to doubt that God was in His Heaven. She was as much spoken of as Thomas Ewell Clayton.

Another enterprising individual, a backwoodsman from the Lord knows where, had arrived the evening before, dug a pit in the sandy soil, accumulated a lot of oak coals which from time to time he shoveled into the pit, and over the heat which flooded upward had spitted the carcass of an enormous hog, which he turned occasionally, and at about ten o'clock, when portions of this animal were browned and drizzled copiously with a peppery but sweet sauce, sliced off tidbits with a Bowie knife and held them out on the point, so that customers got pieces of meat real clean—the backwoodsman didn't even touch what he was barbecuing, so deft was he with sauce ladle and Bowie knife and a couple of stout sticks with which he prodded his great beast, rolling it over and over so that drippings of fat exploded in the coals, and one could smell the delicious odor of barbecuing pork over a half-mile downwind, even above the odor of horses and so many human beings, at least three hundred in Courthouse Square at the same time, most of them in holiday clothes from which strong homemade soap could never be perfectly rinsed, and many of them moist with the smell of nervous excitement.

Hard to tell what so many people all together might do, or so reasoned certain philosophers, were it not for the God-given talent for song and story which some folks possess—for, mingling with the crowd were men and women, both colored and white, with guitars or banjos, who sang songs, some of them proudly, just for the fun of it, and others with a kind of shame, before passing a hat. The tannery and both sawmills in Withlacooch had shut down. If the railroad branch line had reached the county seat, no telling how many people would have come, and the philosophers figured it was just as well the railroad hadn't come to the county seat at that time, because there would have been three thousand people in Courthouse Square instead of three hundred, and if there were that many people in one place at one time, and all of them thinking about something as unhealthy as murdering a brother-in-law, it was a certainty that there would have been the worst trouble, and the militia would've had to be on hand.

Julia had these impressions even before her horse was unhitched and tethered. Then, following instructions, she gave a boy two pennies to go and inform Tom's lawyer and Mr. Kirby of her arrival. It was deemed important for Tom to escort her into the courthouse, as though this were an ordinary social occasion. While waiting, she had more impressions. It apparently got around who she was and some individuals made loud remarks, hoping to provoke an interesting response from the defendant's wife. Since this intent was obvious, Julia took care not to look at anyone. Perhaps because she saw no individuals, the crowd as a whole seemed to be animated by a single soul. The arguments that flourished seemed like disorders in a common psyche. What would Thorstein have to say about it? There had been nothing in his conversation or in *The Tumefaction of Property* that explained this phenomenon.

Thorstein was back in St. Vincent. The publisher wouldn't print his book, and the University of Chicago didn't want him. He was able to borrow the cottage of a fellow faculty member at Rowland College, and they met there every Thursday. Seated in her unhitched buggy, waiting, she dreamed of their lovemaking, repeated their conversations in her mind, and listened to what was being said near her in anticipation of telling Thorstein next Thursday.

A strange belief about the murder of Joseph Rourke obsessed the common psyche: that Thomas Ewell Clayton had killed Joseph Rourke because Thomas Ewell Clayton was still working, secretly now, for the Pamlico and Gulf Railroad. Somehow people in general had come to believe what it had taken Esther Clayton Rourke several bitter months to find out—that the Pamlico and Gulf Railroad was using the First National Bank of St. Vincent as its agent in order to get possession of Clayton Plantation. That dragon—the railroad. That creature of darkness—the bank. Who controlled them? The Yankees? The Jews? A rich nigger in Atlanta? Wilkins? J. P. Morgan?

Anyway, Tom Clayton was an agent of some sinister power, a young native son gone wrong, having succumbed to evil foreign influences. These influences were building hotels and railroads, and were buying fruits and vegetables through commission merchants who were never their own masters but were always working for somebody else, and even when drunk they were never sure who—and finally, these influences were poisoning the old simple life of Florida with a crazy greed. Wealth was rank as swamp grass and none of the original settlers' families had any. A man's life and actions had to be affected.

Some raised the question: *should* the deceased have departed? After all, Joseph Rourke was just an Irish hobo. Yet, he was also in debt—he was a farmer. Those who found Joseph Rourke's decease desirable believed in Tom Clayton's innocence—and vice versa. Those who hated Tom Clayton as one who would go to any lengths to serve Wilkins or the Yankee Jew Morgan, at the same time feared him as the devil. Some who feared Tom Clayton the most were certain that Joseph Rourke had been killed by Mark Richardson, the nigger that old carpetbagger Joshua Dale took in after the riot in Myrtle. It figured—Mark Richardson had a rifle when he came out of the riot and must've kept aching to use it. He'd shot the first white man he could find alone by himself in the woods, and that man happened to be Joseph Rourke.

Tom came with his lawyer and Mr. Kirby. He helped Julia down from the high seat of the buggy and she clung to his arm as they entered the courthouse, behaving as a wife should. The lawyer muttered in her ear that she had nothing to worry about. The whole thing had been settled in a pretrial conference.

*

The door of the judge's chamber opened, Judge Cooper entered, and the clerk shouted, "All rise!"

Tom looked at his watch as he stood up. He clicked open the elaborate case, apparently noted the time, snapped it shut, and put back in his waistcoat pocket this famous instrument, which almost everybody knew was loot from the War Between the States. The action suggested he was impatient but nevertheless resigned to these proceedings. He didn't like wasting time. Julia was irritated. Tom's time hadn't seemed particularly valuable since work on the railroad's main line had ended.

Judge Cooper sat, a suitably grim expression on his red face, rapped his gavel, and thereby seated everyone else. Tom sat somewhat slower than the others so that his tall body stood out for a moment. He was wearing his blue serge suit which Julia had pressed and delivered to Mr. Kirby's house, along with his polished best shoes and fresh shirt and clean underthings. His size, red hair and beard, and clothes of the best quality made him easily the most distinguished looking person present. He was using his appearance as a statement that he had nothing to be ashamed of.

Julia observed that the people in the courtroom were different from those outside. Most of the men were in suits, and the women wore fashionable dresses. But clustered around Joshua Dale were a few men not so well-dressed, tobacco chewers in work clothes, sullen and silent, expectorating into brass spittoons where the floor was stained by many years of those who had tried, rather casually, and missed. This faction didn't talk much and avoided looking at Gray Man Sanford Payne, who leaned against a wall, looked the crowd over, and then sauntered out, with an expression which suggested the proceedings were beneath contempt. During his brief inspection he violated two rules of the court: he was smoking a long black cigar, although every other man was respecting a sign which said no smoking; and he had entered the courtroom wearing two guns, although guns were supposed to be worn only by law officers.

The clerk stuttered as he read the indictment, but no one needed to hear him anyway since Tom rose again and said in loud and heavy bass voice, "I am innocent."

After some gibberish between judge and clerk, the prosecutor, a Mr. Edward Smallstock, rose, hunched his shoulders, and reckoned he had some questions to ask the accused.

"Just a minute," said Judge Cooper. "Ain't you the son of Major Ephraim Smallstock?"

"I am, your honor." The prosecutor was a beefy man, probably in his late thirties, and he had a nervous habit of thrusting his left shoulder before his chin, as though he were protecting himself from a punch.

"Wasn't Major Ephraim Smallstock a personal friend of Captain Merion C. Clayton?"

"He was, your honor. Major Smallstock, my-father-that-is, and Captain Clayton were comrades in arms through the whole War Between the States, from Manassas to Appomattox, or almost—Major Smallstock, my-father-that-is, was seriously wounded by shell fragments in the Wilderness."

"Isn't it true that in their hot-blooded youth both of these gentlemen frequently called on Patricia Giddings, who later became Mrs. Smallstock, who became your mother?"

"Indeed it is true. There was once an exchange of pistol fire in a duel, to their mutual satisfaction."

"And did the late Captain Clayton once write a poem, under the pseudonym—" Judge Cooper bethought himself of the jury, turned to them, and said, "Boys, pseudonym is something you call yourself when you don't want to say straight out who you are. Now, Mr. Smallstock, did the late Captain Clayton once write a poem under the pseudonym Perseus?"

"He did, your honor. I would respectfully suggest that since Thomas Ewell Clayton, the son of Merion C. Clayton, is in the courtroom, he might answer questions about the poem better than I can."

What *was* Tom's role in all this?

Tom stood up and said, "Your honor, that poem, *To Andromache*, was written by my father, just like Mr. Smallstock says he did. I want to add that he retained feelings of respect for both Major and Mrs. Smallstock until his death. Of course, after Miz Patricia Giddings became Mrs. Smallstock, his feelings were refined by delicacy and honor, for God never made a purer angel than Mrs. Smallstock."

Julia was reminded of Tom's language during his courtship, which along with virginal derangements had overwhelmed her at the time. Now, she had to throttle a howl at the base of her throat.

"Gentlemen," Judge Cooper was saying to the jury, "these are facts you got to be acquainted with so you can understand what's going on here."

"Thank you, your honor," said Mr. Smallstock.

For what?

Cooper continued, to Smallstock—"In view of these family associations, can you declare that you will prosecute this case fairly and squarely, without fear or favor?"

"I can, your honor. My first duty is to the law."

The judge addressed Tom's lawyer—"Mr. Dingell, are you satisfied that Mr. Smallstock will prosecute the case according to the best traditions of the law?"

Clyde Dingell was a slender man, clean shaven, with thin features of the kind that were generally called aristocratic. Julia happened to know he was born in a one-room shack. He had a thick bush of black hair combed straight back and Byronic tendrils around his ears. He constantly exhibited perfervid mannerisms involving peculiar and strained angles of head, wrists and fingers. Some of these were on display now as he rose and said, "Your honor, I am satisfied that the distinguished Mr. Smallstock always serves the best traditions of the law as he sees them."

Prosecutor Smallstock bowed.

One of the sour-faced companions of Joshua Dale let fly a wad of tobacco juice that made one of the spittoons ring like a bell. It provided a kind of sardonic comment, and there were a few laughs, even from some of the jurymen.

Judge Cooper banged his gavel. But he kept order not so much by his invested authority as by representing a social consensus. "My, that barbecuing pork does smell good!" he suddenly exclaimed. "Mmmmmmmm-hmm! Boy! Go out to the pump and fetch me a glass of cold water. Work that handle and make sure it's cold. Bring two pitchers for the jury while you're about it, and some glasses too."

While everyone waited, Smallstock and Tom had a low conversation, Dingell leafed through a sheaf of papers, and Judge Cooper talked about the weather with the jury.

After his drink of cold water, Cooper again turned to Smallstock—"Now, I understand you want to put some questions to the accused."

"Yes indeed, your honor."

"The grand jury's indictment mentions a Donald Ashley. Ain't you going to question him?"

"Nobody knows where Donald Ashley is."

"Nobody knows?"

"Nobody I know."

"Where was he when the grand jury heard what he had to say?"

"The grand jury never rightly heard what Donald Ashley had to say."

"Never heard? But his name is set down here in the indictment. Who in tarnation *is* Donald Ashley?"

"He's just a colored man tries to make himself useful around the livery stable."

"Did he do the shooting?"

"Nobody has said so, far as I know."

"How did the grand jury come by his name?"

"He was mentioned by Mrs. Rourke, the widow of the deceased."

"What did she say about him?"

"She said he was an honest nigger."

"I must say, Mr. Smallstock, I don't see where this is getting us."

"If you please, your honor, if I can just start questioning the accused, we can clear everything up."

"Well then, proceed, Mr. Smallstock."

After Tom took the oath and identified himself, formally, since everybody already knew who he was, Prosecutor Smallstock asked, "Where were you on the morning of the shooting?"

"Home," replied Tom.

At this point Julia had her only active part in the trial. Smallstock looked at her, held his gaze until everyone in the courtroom looked at her, so that she had to nod, confirming Tom's single word—*home*. It was the truth. He'd been home. After nodding, she hung her head.

Smallstock turned again to Tom—"Do you know whether your brother-in-law had any enemies?"

"He had no enemies, far as I know."

"Do you have an opinion as to who shot Joseph Rourke?"

"Very likely it were some Myrtle nigger. Only shooting we've had hereabouts in recent months had some connection with the big riot in Myrtle. No reason to believe the shooting of Joseph Rourke was any exception."

Judge Cooper interrupted the questioning—"I take it that is your considered opinion, Mr. Clayton."

"It is."

Judge Cooper turned to the jury—"I keep a position of impartiality in this courtroom. Just the same I can't help having great interest in the opinion of Mr. Clayton because that is, in case—the present defendant is found innocent."

"Thank you, your honor," said Mr. Smallstock.

Julia marveled that Mr. Smallstock, the prosecutor, should be so grateful when Judge Cooper said what would obviously move the jury to acquit Tom. Smallstock was merely an actor in a ceremony. She thought of a passage in *The Tumefaction of Property* concerning ceremonies, which according to Thorstein became more complex, flamboyant and meretricious as the urgency for disregarding reality increased. He'd cited laws underlying economic monopoly, debates in the Senate, Presidential inaugurations, and royal weddings to support his thesis. Julia's need for him became an ache. With Joseph gone and Esther strangely alienated and perhaps unstable, she was alone in her mind except for Thorstein.

"Keep going, Mr. Smallstock," said Judge Cooper.

"Your honor, Mr. Clayton is now Mr. Dingell's witness, if he wants him—"

Uproar.

"Silence!" roared Judge Cooper. "Only folks as is recognized by the court has a right to speak!"

"Well, recognize me goddamnit! I'm Joshua Dale and you've known a good many years who I am, Henry Cooper!"

Companions of Dale shouted, "Let him speak!" and other words to that effect. Judge Cooper banged and banged his gavel.

One of Dale's companions drew a knife from a boot, and a well-dressed gentleman flourished a derringer. The shouting was at its loudest when the door from Courthouse Square was flung open and a yapping of dogs and stronger odor of barbecuing pork flooded into the courtroom. In the doorway, supported by her crutch under her right shoulder and by a steely Piney holding her left arm, stood Esther Clayton Rourke. She was so pale and drawn that her large eyes seemed to become her whole presence.

Appalled hush.

After a breathless second Judge Cooper said in a kindly tone, "Mrs. Rourke, the court took your testimony at the pre-trial hearing."

"That ain't proper law and you know it, Judge Cooper!" snapped Esther.

Working her crutch and helped by Piney, Esther cradled herself toward the bench. She gave a ferocious glance at Dingell, who tossed his mane of black hair like a startled horse. Then she singled out Edward Smallstock. It was strange that such a strong and healthy-looking man should have those eccentric mannerisms—he actually shook, pulling his head down between his thick shoulders and thrusting it out again like a bated turtle. "You'd better ask me some questions," Esther said.

"Mrs. Rourke, the attorneys must make up their minds as to what's relevant in this case," said Cooper.

"Call *me*! I'm a witness!" Esther commanded Smallstock.

"Mrs. Rourke, I will have to scold you a little bit," said the judge. "With the state of your health you ought not to be here at all."

"Will you stop that drivel!" Esther cried. Then, to Smallstock again—"Are you going to call me or aren't you? Do I have to stand here all day?"

Before speaking, Smallstock looked at Tom, who returned an inscrutable smile. Then he spoke to Esther in the tone of a doctor at a bedside—"Mrs. Rourke, as Judge Cooper says, we heard you at the pre-trial session, and the grand jury heard you. In my judgment you have no evidence at all that can stand up in open court—"

Esther almost screamed—"No evidence! The motive! Are you going to call Joshua Dale? Sanford Payne? Richard the Barber? Will the court find Donald Ashley?"

"Mrs. Rourke, Mr. Edward Smallstock is an honorable attorney highly respected in his profession, and he'll call whom he sees fit so that justice can be done."

Esther continued to address the prosecutor—"Are you going to call Joshua Dale?"

"Mr. Dale made a brave attempt to catch the murderer," said Smallstock, "but he has admitted that he never got a good look at him—"

Julia gasped at Smallstock's insinuation that he and no doubt the other men who were managing this ceremony might have some evidence who the real murderer was. It was because of Esther's illness, because everyone realized she had not long to live, because of pity, because she was a Clayton and so required respect, that Tom, and she too, had to endure this charade. And oh God how ugly and sad it all was!

"You Pharisees!" cried Esther. "If I could live long enough, I'd make you more afraid of me than you are of Tom! I'd make you *eat* your fear of Tom! With your fear of *me* you'd split like rotten squashes!"

"Because of her condition I do not wish to order an officer of the court to remove her," said Judge Cooper. "So I ask the jury to disregard what she is saying."

Esther pointed while a sphinx-like Piney held her shoulder—"You—you, Judge Cooper. You wouldn't dare to hang Tom Clayton. Look in your own heart, Judge Cooper. Ask what the cowardly years have done to you—respect for the Ten Commandments, manly courage. Oh, you will soon enough put some helpless black man on a chain gang—"

"Mrs. Rourke—" Cooper began.

"You—you—" Esther pointed at Smallstock, who stood paralyzed like a toad held by the eye of a rattlesnake—"do you suppose I don't know what you're up to?"

Perhaps she spoke quietly to Piney. If so, Julia couldn't hear her. Anyway, Esther turned and with Piney's help slowly swung herself out.

Silence.

As Esther was in the doorway, Joshua Dale strode toward Smallstock.

Sheriff Kirby rose from his seat in a corner, his hand on his gun.

Dale spat at Smallstock's feet—"Judas!"

Sanford Payne was now in the doorway, and one of his pistols was half drawn.

"Not here, Sanford, and he ain't armed!" Tom shouted.

Joshua pushed past Sanford.

Julia was on her feet with everyone else. She could see through the open doorway that someone was holding Joshua Dale's horse—he must have foreseen that he might want to get away fast. He slithered on its back like an Indian without bothering about the stirrups, and he was gone.

Judge Cooper announced a recess, and he recommended the barbecued pork.

*

After the recess Judge Cooper said, "I hope that we have no more interruptions of the orderly processes of justice."

Indeed, everything now seemed to proceed according to those arrangements the judge and attorneys had made before the trial began.

Sheriff Kirby was questioned briefly. Since Julia, as the wife of the accused, could not testify, Sheriff Kirby declared that she had vouched for Tom's presence at home on the morning of the shooting.

Sanford Payne was called and questioned—"for the record," as Judge Cooper said, inferring that he was *not* questioned because Esther Clayton Rourke had demanded it. Mr. Payne, who had been in Amos Whitaker's saloon on the morning of the shooting, said that his servant Richard the Barber had disappeared, and he opined that Richard the Barber had stumbled on some knowledge of the shooting, and realized that knowing what he knew might make staying around kind of risky for *him*.

Was it possible that Richard the Barber might be the guilty party?

"Richard the Barber," said Mr. Payne, with a contempt that might have included the questioner as well as the subject, "is a fat pig. He could no more handle a rifle and hide behind a tree than he could do a waltz."

"Did you ever see Richard the Barber try to waltz?" asked Smallstock.

Judge Cooper joined the laughter.

"Any ideas about a nigger can handle a rifle?" Smallstock asked.

"Nigger named Mark Richardson took up by Joshua Dale. Everybody in Olustee saw him with a rifle."

"Where is this Mark Richardson?"

"Probably hunting Richard the Barber because that pig saw him do it."

Having made his contribution, Mr. Payne retrieved his temporarily surrendered guns from Sheriff Kirby and went outside again.

Finally, the most entertaining part of trial came—the questioning of Tom and the speechifying by the dashing Clyde Dingell. Clearly, Mr. Dingell regarded himself as the leading man in this drama. He paced back and forth for more than two hours, sometimes speaking in a kind of hushed stage whisper, sometimes eloquently declamatory, sometimes roaring with righteous rage. One might forget that Tom was on trial, that the proceeding *was* a trial. It was entertainment of a high order for a county seat that did not often enjoy the like. The open door and windows were crowded with relatively poor folks not quite up to being admitted inside. But whether outside or inside, faces glowed with rejuvenation by the great Dingell's oratory.

Tom had provided the theme with his opinion that some Myrtle nigger had shot Joseph Rourke. Not only had the savage slaughtered a white man in cold blood but had also ravaged the mind of the man's poor invalided wife! As everybody in the court had seen! He spoke of the honorable association of the Smallstocks and the Claytons, of the service to the Confederacy of Colonel Lawrence Avery, of a time when knighthood was in flower, of how hearts were touched by what happened to the Conklings even though they were humble folks, of Jesus Christ driving out the money changers, which almost but not quite suggested Joseph Rourke, who got property just by marrying into an old Florida family. And by way of climax he evoked grisly images of rapine and plunder if, *if,* the *Nellie May* had crossed the whole state and the savages had fallen upon an unprepared and unforewarned St. Vincent.

The great Dingell plucked nerves as a guitarist plucks strings. Outside and inside the courtroom there were sighs, moans, snarls...

Julia felt as though drowning in a sea of quackery, corruption and horror. The grief and despair and mystery of Joseph's murder was compounded by this ugly nonsense. How could Tom tolerate it, even though it diverted the jury from even thinking about the question of his guilt or innocence? Did he really believe that Joseph had been murdered by some colored man who had been driven out of Myrtle? Did he really suspect, like Sanford Payne, that Mark Richardson did it? Impossible! As she'd agreed with Esther! Was Donald Ashley, mentioned by Esther, the small and thin colored man who worked at the livery stable and was so good with horses? She'd ask the Dales about him, about Mark Richardson too, about other matters. But would they talk to her now?

With revulsion, she thought of her arrangement to drive Tom home in the buggy, after the trial. He'd been confident of being found innocent, of being set free by the court—which just meant he could go home from Sheriff Kirby's house. How could she have refused? Yet, the thought of him sitting beside her in the buggy sickened her.

Her suffering did not end with Dingell's speech. Judge Cooper had the duty of explaining to the jury that the killing of a human being without the authority of the law, by poison, stabbing, shooting, or by any other means or in any other manner is either murder, manslaughter, or excusable and justifiable homicide according to the facts and circumstances in each case. He outlined in a fashion that fascinated the jury and the public how such facts and circumstances operated to determine the correct designation— murder in the first degree, murder in the second degree, manslaughter in the first degree, manslaughter in the second degree, manslaughter in the third degree, manslaughter in the fourth degree, and justifiable homicide. Each of these was described in minute and scholarly detail until Julia wanted to scream but knew she wouldn't.

Judge Cooper concluded, "The jury may very well find that the defendant didn't kill anybody at all, unless it was some no-count nigger in Myrtle, in which case he should of course be found not guilty, and the gentlemen of the jury can be spared the trouble of determining any guilty designations or degrees whatsoever."

The jury filed out. If Julia looked about, smiling faces assured her that the verdict would please her. So she looked down at her hands. After a few minutes, while the court buzzed with cheerful conversation, the jury filed in. "We find the defendant not guilty," said the foreman.

There was a patter of applause. Judge Cooper banged his gavel—"I want to remind the gentlemen present that we have not yet found the truth as to who killed Joseph Rourke. And what is truth? As Plato said, truth is a series of shadows in the great dark cavern of life. That's philosophy, by gum! Court's adjourned."

XIII

Six months after the so-called trial, during a humid June, Laura met Tom Clayton in the small town of Fort Harrison in southern Florida. They both kept the meeting secret from everyone connected with them. They rented a cabin on a small passenger and freight boat, the *Pocohontas*, which navigated a stretch of Gulf coast and Lost Man's River. They would look over, together, the illimitable acreage they were buying "for a song" from a man whose title dated from military conquest of the Seminoles.

They both knew that they could now become lovers because Tom had got some money and was ready to go into business for himself, with her partnership. Love would seal the deal.

In Laura's disastrous affair with the Boston physician before her marriage to Arthur, she'd learned that she must never be dominated by any man. She'd been used for brief, rough, frigid, and uncommunicative sex — then dumped. Hardened, using her wits, she'd snared Arthur. She'd got status of a sort, power in a measure that troubled her because she always had to reckon how much, and even considerable money "in her own right," as people said. But all the time she was aware of her own frustrated sexuality, which sometimes kept her from thinking straight, sometimes made her terrified of going insane. As a nurse she'd seen what thwarted or deflected sex could do to people, and in her friend the Viscountess Mary Burleigh she found a model of a strong and free woman taking a lover as she chose. She herself had really chosen Tom Clayton during the New Year's Eve ball for the dedication of the Alhambra Hotel — but had only half realized it at the time. She wanted the powerful body — she felt compelled to possess this man so capable of ruling thousands of other fierce but lesser men, as both Arthur and the President of the United States had attested. At last she'd have the pleasure to which her own body, more beautiful and sensual than any other woman's, was by nature entitled;

she'd chosen as lover one whose instinct for power matched her own; and she herself would call the tune.

He carried her valise to their cabin, and they had the same impulse at the same moment—they grappled in a fierce hug, he squeezing her breath out with one arm while clutching at her breasts and genitals with the other hand, she clawing his neck and buttocks. Then, in a few seconds, she supported and balanced her back against the upper berth, drew up her legs, put her feet against his chest and, exerting all her strength, thrust him out in the passage. By God she was going to enjoy and control this crowning sexual experience! She laughed like the pealing of many bells.

"Laura! Goddamnit!" he shouted, banging at the locked door.

"Oh you naughty man!" she mocked, laughing. Then she gasped, "I'll be on deck in a few minutes."

Lost Man's River rarely had banks. It wandered through channels in sawgrass prairie or among cypresses that reared from ridgy knees out of water that sparkled like jet in the wash from the *Pocohontas*. Occasionally they rammed a floating mass of vegetation and pushed it into a backwater, then reversed into the channel again, the paddles under the box stern slapping heavily. Vines and roots often tangled in this paddle, which creaked and groaned until a Negro deckhand balanced on its frame and chopped the obstructions loose with an ax.

At a dock next to three ramshackle cabins, a naked little black boy had a fat catfish.

"That's a right fine fish you got there, boy," said Tom, tossing him a penny. "Take it to the man through that door." He pointed to the galley.

"Is that good to eat?" asked Laura.

"A lot of people like it. I have doubts about the food on this craft. Might not be healthy for you."

"Why, Tom, you *care* about me!"

They both laughed.

"Arthur Wilkins seems to think you had something to do with the murder of Joseph Rourke," she said, abruptly.

"Is that so? What makes him think that?"

"He had Van Bibber make an investigation."

"That Dutch feller—"

"Yes."

"Everybody gets suspicious when a man comes by money, and Wilkins ain't no exception."

"Did you come by a *lot* of money?"

"I came by enough so I can pay for whatever up this river we want to buy."

"How much is that?" She was annoyed because he'd never stated a precise amount, but she asked pleasantly.

"Don't know. Still have fees to settle up. I didn't get anything when Joseph Rourke was killed, nor anything right off when my sister died. She made a will giving Clayton Plantation to her servants and field hands, and I had to get it overturned."

"Van Bibber looked into that, too."

"Did he now?"

"Arthur doesn't lose interest in you."

"Mighty flattering."

"Was your sister really insane?"

"I ain't a doctor. Did you see the poem Clyde Dingell wrote about her?"

"I didn't know Clyde Dingell wrote poetry."

"He's almost as well known for his poetry as for his law practice." Tom opened his light linen jacket, showing a shoulder holster with a revolver close to his left armpit and an inside pocket with a huge wallet close to his right armpit. He drew a clipping from the wallet—"It's from *The St. Vincent Chronicle*."

Laura read:
> Ode to a Wounded Nymph
> If with the music of some ancient bard
> There echoes in my heart a solemn ring,
> 'Twas but an earnest of the calling card
> Which Death of late did in our doorways fling.
> There was a wounded nymph—be still, my Soul...
> This nymph, associated with an historic plantation and virgin pines, had been shattered like a crystal vase too rudely met with craggy rocks of life. Ultimately, God healed the wounds and turned the nymph into a healthy angel.

"This is horrible," said Laura.

"You mean it ain't good poetry?"

"It's dreadful."

"When Clyde read it at the hearing, it was decided the will was no good and I was the one who had to get Clayton Plantation."

"Then this bad poetry seems to have been good law."
"Seems so."
They both laughed.
"Who was it bought the plantation from you?"
"Don't Arthur Wilkins tell you *nothing*?"
"He just tells me what he thinks will make me mad."
"Maybe you guess anyway. I sold to a corporation headed by the trustee who was appointed by the court when I challenged the will."
"Who was the trustee?"
"You must know him—president of the First National Bank of St. Vincent."
"Arthur's bank."
He nodded.
"How much did you get?"
"Twenty-three thousand dollars."
It was the first time he'd given her a precise figure. She squeezed his arm—"For all that pine and land for cotton?"
"He's an old man and won't last."
"But that's oatmeal and skimmed milk!"
He laughed away the possibility that he might not have made a good deal—"I wanted the cash. You know why. I feel good about giving up Clayton Plantation—too much foolish dreaming connected with it, too much about what ought to be and not enough about what is—my father, Esther, Joseph Rourke." He shrugged—"It just ain't what we need."
Laura thought that she needed him and that they needed each other, not Clayton Plantation! As they talked, standing in the prow of the *Pocohontas*, his huge hands, at least twice as large as hers, rested on the rail. She trembled in thinking of those hands on her during that moment in the cabin before she forced him out, teasing him and making him burn. What else might those hands do? Smiling, she said, "Arthur had even more to gain from Joseph Rourke being out of the way than you did."
"That's true."
"I wish Arthur were capable of killing, but he's not."
"He wouldn't have to do it himself."
"I suppose not."
"Arthur's no fool. He wanted that pine."
"I can't imagine Arthur planning a shooting."
"He didn't have to plan it."

"Are you saying that Arthur really was behind this shooting?"

"I don't know as how I can say that for certain. All I'm saying is he wouldn't have to plan it if he wanted it done. There's always a man who can plan a shooting—my right-hand man Sanford Payne for example. Or me myself—I had to plan some shooting to end the riot in Myrtle. Arthur couldn't plan it himself or even suggest it. But it had to be done and he benefitted from it." Tom smiled.

"Oh, I know he's a timid man—underneath his rude little spasms of anger."

"Now, take Sanford Payne," he went on. "He just might know something about the killing of Rourke. Even though he's responsible to me, and he's felt this way for years, he's on the Pamlico and Gulf payroll." He was teasing her with this speculation, and it seemed almost sexual, as she had teased him.

"How do you know that?"

"I just know Sanford. He boarded and roomed at a saloon in Olustee for a spell. It warn't fancy enough for him and he moved to someplace in St. Vincent. I haven't seen Sanford since he showed up at my trial in Withlacooch."

"A strange man," she commented. But if Tom knew Sanford so well, surely he must know whether Sanford had anything to do with the murder of Rourke. He knew more about the murder of Rourke than he was telling her, and he knew that being mysterious about it excited her. What must she do to make him tell her what he knew? She didn't know whether she was annoyed or aroused. But she didn't like a feeling that she was losing control, and she changed the subject, casually—"Let's explore our ship."

The *Pocohontas* was a small imitation of the dream palaces that puffed up and down the Hudson and Mississippi. A lower deck was occupied almost entirely by cargo, and below that was a shallow hold and engine room. The miniature salon in the center of the upper deck had once been glorious in red and green paint and gilt, and still had perceptibly red brocade on the sofas and chairs with which it was over-furnished. A wheezy old dog thumped off one of the sofas to greet them, wagging its tail. Laura rumpled its coarse hair—"Hello, boy." Why should this seedy old boat and friendly dog, out of a world so different from what she had fought for and won, suddenly move her so much? Against her will her eyes moistened.

A black man in a frayed white jacket came in and set tables for supper. They sat, and since they were in public she could titillate and bewitch without losing control of either Tom or herself. Beside themselves there were only the wife of an upcountry settler and a drummer in the salon. The drummer didn't dare glance at Laura, fearing the formidable Tom. The wife didn't dare either, perhaps fearing that Jehovah might know her thoughts. Laura waved her round arms about, primped her auburn and disorderly hair, and unbuttoned her blouse to show the rounds of her breasts, damp in the tropical warmth. She caught his greedy gaze with her own burning eyes and absorbed every inch of him.

"Do you think men ought to dominate women, Tom?"

"Well, that's nature, ain't it?"

"Is it now?"

He laughed and pawed her thigh under the table.

She thrust her arm under the table, too. But instead of pushing his hand away, she reached his groin and squeezed.

He yelped.

She roared—"I do enjoy going into business with you, Tom." She made him talk about their sugar company, but she scarcely listened. Her whole body prickled with salty sweat.

The supper was excellent, better than what she could get at the Alhambra Hotel. The catfish was fried and then doused with a sauce of parsley, lemon and butter. Boiled yams with a little orange juice could have nothing wrong with them. Spinach had come aboard that afternoon. The pecan pie was luscious. She dragged out her eating, sucking interminably on catfish bones and dabbling over the pecan pie, inflicting something like pain on herself and scarcely caring any more what she was doing to Tom.

And after supper she insisted that they sit on a bench before the wheelhouse. The sun had set, and on the wheelhouse roof in an iron brazier a fire of pine knots blazed. This threw a yellow glow some hundred yards ahead. Moving toward them as on a wave of dim light the jungle advanced. The little ship seemed to glide uphill, with a surge of trees and vines rolling to engulf it.

"I want to be swallowed!" Laura exclaimed. Her own voice seemed disembodied—"I've been here before, in some other life!" She had bizarre notions for which she had no words—that in some occult manner she was swallowing her own past, that this phantasmagorical slide into jungle and night, with her chosen lion-like lover by her side, was a voyage to becoming in deed as well as dream a new person, or more likely the one she'd secretly been all along, regardless of regimentation either by harsh poverty or by a marriage of convenience to imperial wealth.

"You're happy," he observed.

She fingered his red hair, so much like her own.

"Been here before, have you?" He chuckled, enjoying her fantasy, perhaps sharing it. "Well, it's right for us. And there's a lot of land can be had for nothing, just for the taking."

She still didn't choose to talk, and he went on, puzzling over what she'd said—"Life? Life is what-is. Life is us."

"Money!" she exclaimed. Her thoughts jumped unpredictably. "There has to be money—"

"Money?" he repeated, surprised. "Well, yes, there has to be money—guns too, bosses, niggers, cleared land, sugar. Money? Our money will multiply like mosquitoes."

She seized his big hand, so hard and silky, into her own, led him to their cabin, and with a laugh preceded him inside. This cubby was about eight feet square with room for only upper and lower bunks and a couple of shelves. She turned up the lamp—she wanted lots of light. How hairy he was! She kept delaying the removal of clothes with convulsive embraces and then delayed even more by pushing him away to manipulate her garments. After she'd taken off everything except a silk chemise, he knotted this flimsy wisp in his big fist and tore it off.

She ripped down his drawers, surprising him and pushing him down on the narrow area of floor.

He gave a belch of laughter—"Lord, you're strong!"

She grabbed him in fierce clutches by one muscle after another, wrenching them as though she would tear them out.

Their union was as rough as one of his construction jobs.

At their climax she cried, "Plow! Plow me—plow—plow!" and she screamed.

On succeeding days and nights, she expressed her feelings in ways she might have invented at age fifteen, fitting silly phrases to her turbulent emotions. "My footsie itches itty-bit!" she wailed and then commanded harshly, "Kiss here—here—dammit dammit dammit *here*—" and as he seized the tingling foot and gave it a smack, rubbing his coarse beard over the heaving and trembling flesh of her legs, she gave inarticulate shrieks.

The first of their daytime bouts attracted the attention of the boat's captain, who knocked timidly — "Is everything all right?"

"Get the hell away from that door!" roared Laura.

She had always thought of her beauty as something poised and statuesque, as a quality inspiring not only a vulgar heat but also a veneration that was almost religious, since it could not only arouse men but also subdue them into a hopeless passivity, as in a customary churchgoing mood, for loveliness such as hers was not for ordinary mortals! But now — and to hell with what she had been! — she became a delirious witch, a fury. She bucked like a tree in a tempest. She cursed. She choked on a froth in her throat. She jumped from bunk to floor and back again, banging him and herself in the confining space, getting bruises. Sometimes she invented comic games, wild melodramas of feminine terror. She clutched thrown-off clothes to her breasts and genitals, exploding — "Where can I fly?" Then she sprang on him and punched hands and feet into his massive body.

He wasn't hurt. He bellowed with laughter.

She knew that being wild was something new and ecstatic for him.

He was always capable of fresh responses, astounding caresses, kisses that became little prickling bites, joinings with savage thrusts and withdrawals and more thrusts. He was strong and she was violent.

After she was exhausted, she rubbed her hard breasts against him and became foolish — -"My Hercules...my darling Barbarossa..."

Then, during their sixth coupling, she discovered, to her astonishment, that her sensations were even more intense if she were a little less violent.

And how wonderful! How amusing! Tom Clayton was capable of sentiment! "Fair Laura," he murmured — he was tired, too. "Laura so fair, so fair." His silky hand was gentle.

She could sleep, spent and certain he was hers. But was her own satisfaction a snare, unsuitable for an empress? *Don't think about it*!

*

Thorstein Brach was not satisfied with how he lived, but he never had been satisfied with how he lived, and he expected no future without continuous struggle against causes for dissatisfaction. He liked this struggle and was generally cheerful about it. People who hoped to live without struggle were cattle!

Unable to struggle against death, he couldn't deal with it. At Esther's funeral he'd broken down, sobbed and sobbed, a wreck of himself. Thomas Ewell Clayton, the brother of the deceased, was solemn and composed. Julia Clayton, weeping and careless of appearances in this extremity of agony and grief, had steadied Professor Thorstein Brach, clung to him—didn't even speak to her own husband.

Almost a year after the murder of Joseph, and not more than four months after the passing of Esther, Thorstein was able to confront new causes for dissatisfaction, to struggle again—but sometimes with an unaccustomed and rather unhappy ferocity.

Every day, from hour to hour, he had to cope with some new dissatisfactions related to his work. He couldn't obtain a new position that would enable him to leave Rowland College. Presidents, administrators and department chairmen in prestigious universities, with money, knew about *The Tumefaction of Property*, evaluated the views of the heretical Dr. Brach, and took pleasure in rejecting him with a smile. Opinion regarding his iconoclastic book hadn't seeped through to some lesser universities, but these had no money for hiring an extra economist. At Rowland College he shirked his dormitory duty one night in order to be with Julia, and some students, who ordinarily visited whores in shacks on the outskirts of St. Vincent, brought two of them into their rooms. There was an orgy all night. Where was Dr. Brach? He invented complicated lies to keep from being fired. If he were fired from Rowland College, the lowest of the low in academia, he'd never be able to go anywhere else and earn a living by teaching.

But his most poignant dissatisfaction with his work had to do not with what he did to get money, but with what he did that usually required spending what little money he had. He had to buy paper in order to make an extra copy of his new book on business combinations, get postage, correspond, even travel. Two publishers had seemed about to print it. But in each case an editor, responsible for checking punctuation and spelling and therefore forced to read the book carefully, discovered that *Business Combinations* did not, as the title had suggested, help enterprising businessmen make more money. Instead, the book showed that business combinations inevitably became giant and depersonalized institutions goaded by greedy, vulgar shareholders and by self-serving, rapacious managements into bringing about industrial serfdom, with consequent resistance, repression, violence and perhaps anarchy. And Dr. Brach seemed such a gentle and rather humorous fellow!

How was it possible that he should feel any dissatisfaction at all related to his affair with Julia? Certainly not with Julia herself! He couldn't help comparing Julia with other women he'd slept with. He'd loved the other women, would never forget endearing habits and qualities. But he'd come to know Julia in a different way. There were the months when they were not lovers, at the Rourkes', with a play of minds that brought about a more profound affection. There was the unbearable threat of death and readiness to kill at the bridge to Richmond Plantation during the Myrtle riot. Could it be that two such gentle and peace-loving people as he and Julia had become indissolubly linked by shared savagery? Then the mystic two nights and a day at Richmond Plantation, the grave parting as she left in the procession for the Myrtle victims. And their grief as well as their joy in Joseph and Esther had been about the same. No other woman would have been like Julia in all these circumstances! And finally, beyond whatever he might think about Julia and the pure chance in what they'd experienced together, he was shocked by a change in himself. Why did he, so readily intimate with attractive women, find himself gnawed with dissatisfaction because circumstances in both his life and hers might tear them apart? He wasn't used to worrying much about the future. Why did he do so now?

He and Julia had arranged a way of living which they could generally *pretend* was purely satisfying. On a Friday every fourth week he went by train to Olustee, where Julia met him at the station with her buggy. She disclaimed any worry about scandal. It was known that her husband had deserted her and was starting up a sugar company in south Florida. If she chose to have a gentleman friend visit her about once a month, this was her business and if folks didn't like it let them lump it! William, Caroline and Lucy as well as Julia made these Fridays idyllic, and in the middle of the night, while the big old plantation house slept, Julia crept to his bed in the spare room. She didn't want her daughter to observe that her mother slept with a man to whom she was not married.

On Thursdays, a fortnight between the Fridays, Julia came from Olustee to St. Vincent on the train, took a room at the Alhambra Hotel, and dealt with a commission merchant, suppliers, or the bank on Friday morning before going back home. Thorstein spent these Thursday nights with her.

Another year went by.

On a Thursday evening in January, Thorstein mingled with tourists in the Alhambra Hotel and then proceeded to Julia's room. She opened the door immediately after he gave the usual two sharp knocks.

He had an instant's vision, as on all of these Thursdays, of her smile, her glowing eyes, her cornsilk hair in a proper bun for her St. Vincent business, her prim white shirtwaist puffing out her arms and slender body—

the ineffable presence of her—and then they were in each other's arms for uncountable minutes. She moved a little as they both pressed themselves together, fitting their bodies like pieces of a puzzle, anticipating gratification of continual desire and need during the two weeks while they were not together. She smelled of pine with a mysterious suggestion of something else, perhaps the oak that burned in order to operate the turpentine still, perhaps oranges. It was the winter smell, and for the briefest of moments, even while he held her and caressed her hair, he thought that another season had passed, time was a swamp in which he was trapped, and his inability to share his perception of the American destiny together with his failure to create a way of life for constant and daily love, not just these snatched hours every two weeks, meant that he was becoming a cipher. And what was he doing to Julia?

The thought passed as they stood apart and smiled at each other, and he became again, as he usually was, the most fortunate among men.

They had turned their Thursday nights in the Alhambra Hotel into something like a ritual, for what is a ritual anyway but a condensation of time, an extraction of life in essence?

Julia opened her carpet bag and drew out a tin box covered with a design of holly leaves and berries. Apparently, it had once held some delicacy that could serve as a Christmas present. The room, one of the most inexpensive available in the Alhambra, contained a large walnut dresser consisting of two large drawers, two small drawers in separate box-like structures on either side of a large mirror, with surfaces covered by blue-veined marble. She had already covered one of the surfaces with a napkin she'd brought from home, and she set out on this the treasures from her tin box: two small plates, two knives and forks, delicate slices of smoked ham, a piece of cornbread and a soda biscuit for each plate, butter and guava jelly in two tiny jugs, and two oranges.

Thorstein had his own treasure, as usual. His daily recreation from his teaching and dormitory supervision was exercising his horse. He'd recently discovered, about four miles from the center of St. Vincent, an elderly Negro woman who made a superb wine from white scuppernong grapes—not too sweet, like most scuppernong wines, but just right, slick and light on the tongue. Julia delighted in a little wine, *only* a little, since she wasn't used to it and she wanted to be in full possession of all her senses during every minute with *him*. She took two small glasses from the tin box—the big tumblers provided by the hotel, and set out on the marble-topped washstand with crockery pitcher and basin, were always dusty, enough to turn one away from any nectar.

So they arranged their supper, slowly, from time to time touching each other, kissing...

On this particular Thursday evening Julia had the most to say. Lucy was pregnant, and nobody at Richmond Plantation knew where the father was. He was an itinerant preacher who came through Olustee months ago because there was no church for the colored people since Azri Peters was murdered. It was "wonderful, kind of glorious," Julia felt, how Lucy looked forward to having her child, and how her parents the Johnsons looked forward too, even though they were angry with the father for having gone to parts unknown. Julia spoke with special elation—"I'm a lot more in tune with how Lucy feels than I would have been a few years ago. I know how her spirits must have flown like a whole flock of birds when the young preacher came and everyone sang and danced and Lucy was so proud of her young body, and the preacher proud too, of his youth, his fiery words. When they cried out about giving themselves to Jesus, they were really giving themselves to each other, I'm certain as can be. I know just how Lucy feels because *I* feel young again and sure of myself, sure we can somehow manage—if I become pregnant with our child, I'll be purely happy, just *happy*!"

He could only hold her in his arms again, could only say, "Julia, Julia—" No other words could contain both his love and his unspoken anxieties.

But Julia, apparently confident that love could solve all problems, could talk and talk. Since Tom was distant from Caroline and William as well as from her, she'd come to feel that they were only her own children, not Tom's in any way whatsoever. Caroline was troubled, yearning for a father in Tom, a father who'd never been. Julia was troubled because Caroline was troubled. She was aware that Caroline regarded Thorstein with a certain bewilderment—would Caroline always be utterly confused about her own feelings? On the other hand, William had from babyhood a miraculous grasp of what every human being, including his own father, really was. William didn't give a thought to Tom, and he obviously looked forward to Thorstein's visits. Caroline and William were bound to become attached to Thorstein in their own ways, and she would never want them to feel left out if she and Thorstein had their own child.

He said what he honestly felt, which was at the same time what she expected to hear—or most of it probably was. He hoped he'd never let either Caroline or William feel left out, no matter the circumstances, no matter whether Julia and he ever had their own child or not. If he kept searching, he *had* to find *some* university which could give him a better job than he had at Rowland College. Perhaps he'd be in a state that had a civilized, or more nearly civilized, law providing for divorce. Whether she could get a divorce or not, whether they could ever marry or not, they'd live so as to be closer to one another. He imagined a variety of housing arrangements, which might not offend primitive sensibilities regarding wedlock and which might be affordable out of what a big university could provide for the author of two significant books, passing over in the stress of the moment that the books might do more to deflate than to recommend. Dreams!

Julia surprised him by revealing a new anxiety of her own, a new reason for prompt and effective action. Two gentlemen had shown up at Richmond Plantation to look it over—they might buy it. It seems that Julia's husband intended to sell. She had no legal right to do anything about it. She'd talked this over with a lawyer named Smallstock and had learned that whatever property a wife brought with her in marriage became her husband's, to be disposed of as he saw fit. Presumably, Thomas Ewell Clayton wanted more cash for expanding his sugar company.

Then it seemed as though Julia was not so much worried about herself and Thorstein, invulnerable in love, as about the nineteen black people at Richmond Plantation who lived so well by prevailing backwoods standards. "I think about what might happen to Lucy's father because of his stiff joints and him not doing much work any more, and Lucy's mother with her bad feet. Anybody but me might not treat them right." And there were all the others whom Thorstein himself had seen during his visits every four weeks, without comprehending how indispensable each person was in her remote and precarious small world.

The relationships of the twenty-two souls at Richmond Plantation, including Caroline, William and Julia herself, were intricate and delicate and weighty, requiring sensitive but positive and unhesitating adjustment after inevitable and quite frequent disturbances. What would happen if the fire under the turpentine still went out, if shakes were not split for replacing those blown off during the big wind, if the pork was not properly smoked, if the corn wasn't hoed, if the cane wasn't cut, if the hens weren't fed, if the hay for the horses, mules and cows was not dried as it should be and pitched in the loft of the big barn? The tasks were special and endless, and in the center of it all stood Julia, obtaining what cash was needed through selling naval stores in St. Vincent and at the same time assuring the constancy of necessary work continually under siege by unpredictable nature and human frailties. Julia could conceive of no other life for herself, she'd inherited it from father and grandfather who had predestined it, with freed Negroes, even before the War Between the States; she had lived this way of life despite the fraud of her marriage; and—Thorstein understood clearly, for the first time—her love for him did not change her in this respect.

He saw in greater depth why at the time of the Myrtle riot she had stood at the bridge with her shotgun—*You! Bascomb Good!...I wouldn't care no more about shooting you than I'd care about shooting a hawk in my chicken yard!*

He now sensed the feeling behind the controlled solemnity with which she mentioned the possibility of the sale, and in reflections obviously in her mind but not explained while she did mention, cheerfully, that it was Lucy who made the soda biscuits and a man named Jeb, whom he couldn't quite place, who had smoked the ham.

He'd been a self-indulgent clod! How could he have been so absorbed by publishing his book and getting a better job? What was love without understanding, and he'd understood Julia so little! Had his philandering dulled him to what a woman could be? He kept looking in her face, now smiling and now serious but always trusting, confident in their love, and he felt unable to say anything meaningful or healing about how she might deal with the loss of Richmond Plantation, about Caroline and William not being "left out," about living arrangements, about having a baby. He felt inadequate and lumpish. It was probably for the best if he didn't say anything about what she might be able, mercifully, to put out of her mind—while they were together.

He was in a strange mood, out of himself, but he was more stirred than ever, moved by exultant impulses a little like creative inspiration, as they went to bed. She faced him as she undressed, her slender body in eloquent lights from the turned-up lamps, and she smiled at his adoration. She spoke, quietly, gaily, of how she always went to sleep in her lonely bed at Richmond Plantation while thinking of him—him needing, needed, warm.

He couldn't drift into sound sleep as he usually did after their lovemaking. Time brandished a whip. For him, St. Vincent, Florida, was a prison. He must try harder to break out. Befuddled, perhaps half asleep after all, he murmured, "Everything's going to be all right, my darling. You'll see." Perhaps she didn't hear him.

XIV

Tides and river and westerly winds shaped the island like a banana with the inner curve facing the Gulf of Mexico. A ridge of sand with the pulverized remains of sea creatures rounded the center of this banana, which from eons before the time of white men had been seized as suitable for human life. Why it was suitable could never be explained by talking about man and nature but only about man and man. All nature gave man was lots of fish, along with mosquitoes that could kill anyone lost for a single night in the adjacent and endless swamps, and a summer sun that burned up everything green except sawgrass, palmettos, and cacti, and on the sheltered side of the island some mangroves and other strange little trees with leaves that felt like leather.

A storm sometimes opened an ancient mound to disclose that in the day of the stone ax there were those who preferred this scorched and forbidding strand to battling for the more gentle savannahs further north. For comparable reasons, refugees from both justice and injustice came to settle here in the day of commercial paper.

One schooner-load of driven but hopeful people included Joanna and Joshua Dale; Bina, Amos and Ruth Peters; and Mark Richardson.

After four years, following the riot in Myrtle and the shooting of Joseph Rourke, the Dales' store was no longer a going proposition in Olustee. Not enough customers, especially ones with means. Bolstered by the railroad, the town grew. Another store opened up, where men could sit on the porch and chat or doze with the approval of a respectful and like-minded proprietor. The few black people left in the vicinity continued to trade at the Dales' store, Julia Clayton bought supplies for Richmond Plantation there, and a few white people who didn't care about appearances spent a few pennies. The men who ran the lumber company that took the place of the old Clayton Plantation went to the new store, but their days in Olustee were numbered anyway. The trees were about gone, with the irreplaceable yellow pine ending up in cities and towns most Olustee citizens had never heard of. The pristine wealth of the land became dollars that went elsewhere, leaving the inhabitants, old families and newcomers alike, engaged in producing ludicrous articles or buttering with vain services an aspiration to ridiculous status. An enterprising woman made gewgaws out of egret feathers. A quack combined acrid ointments, libidinous rubbing and religious fervor to cure heebie-jeebies. Attitudes as desolate as the squeak of rocking chairs on the porch of the new store became law. Whatever goals existed became hazy, absurd—therefore vitiating. The Reverend Augustus Blanding noted spiritual decay but despaired of doing anything about it. Why should grown men torture cats?

Joshua Dale became a disagreeable crank. He stopped selling chewing tobacco, which he said was dissolving men's brains. Some women's, too.

Joanna wrote twice a month to their son, principal of the high school in Torrington, Connecticut, and her letters frequently said, "Yore father thinks that..." This was in the main how the Torrington principal knew the Olustee storekeeper. So—well-intentioned, himself stirred by people out of work in Torrington, son sent father for Christmas in 1893 Edward Bellamy's *Looking Backward*. All fired up, Joshua subscribed to *The Nationalist*, the organ of groups fostered by the book. At last he found a comprehensive explanation for what had gone wrong with the country since the Freedom War conferred little or no freedom. He had to talk—and how he talked! The country was going to Hell in a passenger coach and everybody in Olustee had a seat! Prices and wages had hit rock bottom, there were four million unemployed, the Pullman workers had struck for a living wage and didn't get it. Was it any surprise that the old Richmond Plantation was in trouble? Who could afford paint or varnish? Grover Judas Cleveland sold bonds to Wall Street and the likes of Arthur Wilkins, now building a marble palace on the East Coast, and then sold *out* working men and farmers, who needed silver or some other kind of money in return for their labor—not just gold, which come right down to it was useful only for fixing teeth. The Attorney General of the United States quashed prosecution of the Sugar Trust in which Thomas Ewell Clayton, formerly of Olustee, had a voice by virtue of a land grab in south Florida made possible first by riding the coattails of Arthur Wilkins and then by a murder which was never properly investigated—and right now—*The Nationalist* provided details—was getting rich fast from the labor of colored men, women and children in his cane fields under conditions worse than slavery. In general, the country had a new law more powerful than the Constitution—wealth for cruel crooks and goddamn the innocents! There was no hope unless folks could learn how to live in a Brotherhood of Humanity, black and white, distinguishing human nature from brute nature.

Joshua's fuming and railing were most heated through the bad year 1894. Some of what he said about the rich touched a responsive populist nerve, but the way he wrapped up what he said in a doctrinal package required the kind of thinking that was worse than a toothache. On the porch of the new store, men commented that Joshua Dale had not only joined with niggers after the Myrtle riot but had remade his henhouse into a cabin for niggers who lived there a lot better off than a lot of white folks. Joshua was eased out of his honorific stewardship at the church. Clearly, most of the new Olustee spawned by the riot and the railroad did not want the Dales. Lest they fail to comprehend, somebody fired a gun through their kitchen window one evening, just missing Joanna.

It was prudent to move. But where?

Mark Richardson influenced their decision. He kept going away and coming back again—because of Bina. In 1894 he no longer looked much like what he'd been, silent, well-dressed in Joshua's jacket, during the funeral for the Myrtle victims. The hair which his mother used to cut had grown into a large bush, and he had a mustache clipped in the Spanish style. There was a lithe and ominous elegance about him in spite of the fact that he wore only stained cotton britches, shirt and sound shoes. He'd kept only one article connecting him with life in Myrtle, and death in Myrtle—the clean and polished Sharps rifle. But he never carried it around Olustee. An unfathomable eye at odds with his smiling mouth made the rockers on the porch of the new store pause, consider, and let him be. Besides, he was staying with Joshua Dale, and while somebody might shoot through the Dales' window at night and then run, nobody wanted to monkey with Joshua in the open.

In the Dales' kitchen Mark talked about his travels. He'd worked on three boats. First, on a steamship that went as far as New Orleans in one direction and Key Alva in the other, with stops between. He'd loaded and unloaded cargo and helped the cook. Next, on a river boat, *Pocohontas*, he'd used an ax to chop away vines and driftwood that got stuck in the paddle. Finally, on a sharpie fishing boat out of Payhokee.

He'd seen new towns and villages along the Gulf. Joshua considered. Might new stores be needed? Supplies for building? Tools for clearing and cultivating land? Commodities for home cooking? He left Olustee for three weeks to explore.

Mark hadn't mentioned that the country was lawless. No doubt it was because white men and black men stood equally firm or mushy depending on natures and conditions, and Mark was certain how he stood. Joshua witnessed a stabbing nobody did anything about. The nearest sheriff was in Key Alva, miles away across open water. There were no roads. Joshua feared violence but reflected that it had always accompanied his best hopes — bushwhackings and hangings along with Father Abraham's call for volunteers, guerrilla fighting and no prisoners along with jubilee songs, and in Olustee the Klan along with healthy attention to naval stores, cotton, oranges and lumber.

At the end of his three weeks' exploration he returned to Olustee feeling he'd made the right choice. He was conscious of advancing years and was the more determined to recapture the spirit of youth and daring. But he knew that he and Joanna would never make another move.

Joanna shared Joshua's hopes and kept worries to herself. She felt responsible for Ruth, Amos and even Bina, who was no longer a child. A small woman, she had prominent breasts and walked with a self-consciously dignified and stately grace. Joanna once said to her husband, "I never seed a young woman so proud of menstruating. She has to show her rags to Amos and Ruth and brag like a hen what's laid an egg." Joanna didn't see how she could move with the Peterses next to the home of her son the high school principal in Torrington, Connecticut. People in Torrington lived different from people in Olustee and weren't used to colored folks. She herself liked to go barefoot and wear nothing but a cotton dress in hot weather. It would be hard to be dressed up all the time. Not seeing her son was an ache but bearable because she had no choice — it was life: little ones flew away and made their own nests. What was her granddaughter like? Her son reported in a letter that she had her grandfather's sharp eyes. In Joanna's mind there were misty pictures. But the Peterses were real, on hand every day, hour by hour. Amos never stopped chattering. Ruth followed her wherever she went, silent, smiling. Bina spent whole days with Mark inside the cabin that had once been a henhouse. Joanna said, "Won't be long before Bina's pregnant, and her and Mark ought to have a better place than an old henhouse even if we did fix it up pretty nice." She herself had been pregnant before she and Joshua were wed. She sighed, breathed hard, closed her eyes, relished memories. Then she snapped, "If we going to move we ought to do it and git it over."

There was sweaty labor for two months. Joshua and Mark took apart the store board by board, rafter by rafter, stud by stud. They used part of the lumber for crating the stock. Most of it was sorted and stacked for moving to their new location. They even saved and bundled the best shakes. Joshua got a tent by mail order, and they moved into it while taking apart the kitchen and bedroom. Finally, the remade henhouse. Joshua listed inventory for both commerce and living in a notebook. He was fussy, military.

Even the remaining trees in Olustee seemed to sigh with relief. With the departure of the Dales free thinking would expire. The Reverend Augustus Blanding wouldn't have to mediate quarrels after church on Sundays. "May the Lord bless you and guide you to the Canaan you be hunting for," he said to Joshua.

Julia Clayton didn't like to see the Dales go but was resigned. She told Joanna she expected to leave Olustee too but didn't know where she would go. Everybody knew her husband had deserted her and was making money hand over fist with a sugar plantation, mill and refinery. Everybody knew Tom Clayton was trying to sell Richmond Plantation and figured he hadn't found anybody who'd pay what he asked. Everybody knew the professor from Rowland College came to see Julia Clayton, and a lot of folks wondered what might come of it. Would it be right for Tom Clayton to shoot the professor since he himself had left his wife? What would be proper law in a situation like that?

In January 1895 everything the Dales owned that was worth keeping was stacked on a flatcar for transportation to Payhokee-on-the-Gulf—the lumber, the furniture, the stove, crates with eight remaining hens and a rooster, the tools, the clothes, the tent tied over the shuck-and-grass mattresses. In Payhokee, all was shifted to the schooner-rigged sharpie on which Mark had once worked. The sharpie was beached on the desolate island of Chokoloske at the mouth of Lost Man's River. Chokoloske was central, settlements got their necessities by boat and it seemed a good place for a store.

Within three months *Joshua Washington Dale—General Merchandise* reopened. Joshua said, "Here we be, Joanna and me, taking a stand on the edge of the Republic. There ain't no further to go."

Bina and Mark had their first child, a boy named Azri after his grandfather. A black preacher who had known Azri Peters made the trip all the way from Payhokee to marry Bina and Mark in a ceremony on the porch of the store. "We ain't no slaves going to be satisfied with jumping over a broom," said Mark.

"I hope to see a hundred years," said Bina. "My chilluns will all have chilluns, and us going to have a whole town here, all related."

Even during the first year they did tolerably well. They built a pier, and Joshua persuaded a steamship company to make stops.

It was great time for alligator skins. Mark and Amos made a skiff and often headed back into the swamps at daybreak. When they found a burrow, Amos thumped with a club until a gator showed itself. If the tail showed first, Mark grabbed it and yanked the beast out. Some of them twisted their long snouts and snapped—they were savage but clumsy. Amos, jumping around to avoid the jaws, planted an ax as carefully as he could in the forehead just above the eyes, trying to kill the creature without spoiling the skin. Even if a buyer wanted a whole skin, stuffed, the gash could be mended with a few stitches.

As soon as one was killed, they skinned it on the spot. So they spent their days like workers in a tannery. They dried the hides on frames that covered a sandbar a hundred yards from their new cabin and to what was generally downwind so that the stench was faint.

Joshua handled the marketing and shipping for a ten-percent commission. Alligator shoes, belts and novelties, including little gators stuffed and mounted on shellacked boards, were in demand. That first year Mark put away five hundred dollars.

During Mark's traveling he'd had his best time on the fishing sharpie, and he decided to build his own. Now he was able to buy lumber, hardware and paint. He got dimensions of a boat he liked and a freehand plan from a builder in Key Alva. It didn't take long to knock together the simple hull.

On a crisp January day in 1896, a little over a year after the move from Olustee, almost the whole town of Chokoloske—whites, blacks, three Cubans, a Greek who'd fished in the Mediterranean Sea—all men and women who for a freakish variety of reasons shared an urgency for space without government—helped with the launching.

Joshua was with some thirty others. He put his stiff and wrinkled hands under the chine—"Heave!"

"Hee-*vah*!"

Joanna watched. Bina too—she had Azri in a sling across her chest.

"You got youself an up-and-coming man, Bina."

"Iffen we knowed the work of making a sharpie, don't knows we'd done it. What am I saying? Don't pay me no mind! I's crazy today! Course we would've done it!"

On log rollers the hull began to move.

"Hee-*vah*! Hee-*vah*!"

The launchers were splashing in shallow water.

"Yeah, he an up-and-coming man, Joanna. You put it right. He ain't a man can be kept down."

The flat-bottomed unballasted hull was floating.

"Look at it bobble!"

"Hit's a mighty pretty boat."

With a yank and thrust of his arms, Mark landed on the deck—"Bina! Wade out! Come, git on! Amos! Come on up, Josh. Don't you feared, Ruth. Stretch out your hand, girl. Bina, lift Azri to me. You just got to come on deck. We all got to come on deck…"

On that same day the *Pocohontas* made one of its last trips because worms had eaten the undersides and it was about to be scrapped for salvage of the topsides. At the dock in Chokoloske it disgorged a boy small enough to hide in a locker and so escape from the Clayton Sugar Company. He confirmed what was supposed—that the cane fields were about ten miles long, that more and more prairie and jungle were surrendering to drainage ditches and plows, that a narrow-gauge railroad was being built for moving cane to mill, that bossmen carried rifles. He summed up—"Folks work 'til they drop. Then they paid with a bullet."

*

After Laura knocked, Captain Grotius Van Bibber admitted her to Arthur's suite in the Alhambra Hotel. The magnate was seated behind his desk and did not rise. "Make yourself comfortable, Laura," he said.

"Good morning, Arthur," she said, pleasantly. His polite and rather formal manner made her wish she'd found some excuse and hadn't come.

He continued—"The captain has been putting Industrial Services to good use, and he has some information about one of your investments that you ought to know about."

Laura both feared and hoped that this discussion with Arthur would have to do with herself and Tom. She'd been discreet—her periodic absences from the social whirl had no doubt aroused speculation, but the Viscountess Mary Burleigh was the only person who knew—Laura couldn't bear being put down by the viscountess for not having a lover! But she never expected to keep her secret from Arthur forever. It would relieve anxieties if he knew and if he accepted how she chose to live her life. "Very well," she said. She selected the most sumptuous sofa and stretched out her feet.

"Permit me to find some papers," said Van Bibber.

Laura shrugged—"Why not?"

The Industrial Services chief opened a file drawer and thumbed through some folders.

The magnate looked out the window at the bright ocean and said, "Had a very peculiar and frightening dream last night."

She felt hopeful. Arthur hadn't ventured this kind of personal confidence for at least a year. Perhaps he was prepared to be agreeable. She hoped she wasn't showing her reaction. "You still dream frequently?" she asked.

"Not so much as I used to—but occasionally."

"What was your dream?"

"I was right at this desk, where I am now, but there wasn't any noise. Listen just for a moment, and I'll tell you what I mean."

The magnate froze. To oblige him, so did Laura. Van Bibber made a little flip-flip-flip in the file. Then, becoming aware of what they were doing, he too became motionless.

There was a distant whush of quiet surf, a creaking cart in the street, somewhere a door closing, somewhere a voice.

"Right now I can hear you breathe," said Arthur. "Lots of other little sounds that you hear, too. In my dream there were no sounds at all. I went to the window and looked out. Then I found I wasn't here. I was looking out of my window in my old boyhood home—there was the catalpa tree and there was the clothes line. It was silent still. I had the damnedest feeling, like all the machinery in the whole world had stopped. Then I saw that the backyard was full of gray worms, and they were eating up my boyhood home. I thought: *sans culottes*—worms don't have pants. Absurd and frightening. I woke up shaking all over."

Van Bibber gave his twisted cynical smile and repeated, "*Sans culottes*? But no guillotine? A dream like that makes one think!"

"It certainly does," said Arthur. "I thought of that crazy anarchist who shot a pistol at Frick. *There* was a thoroughgoing *sans culottes* revolutionary!"

Laura had to smile—"It's so peaceful here in St. Vincent."

The magnate grunted—"Men keep their pants on. But not worms!"

Laura laughed.

The way he looked at her showed that she hadn't responded to his confidence about the dream in the right way. "Ah well," he said, "let's tell Laura what you found, Captain. Do you have the file?"

"Yes. I scarcely need the file. It concerns the operation of the Clayton Sugar Company, in which I understand Mrs. Wilkins has invested."

"I'm all ears," said Laura.

"Three months ago I sent one of our agents to the Clayton Sugar Company, an experienced man named Desvernine. He disappeared. A month ago, I sent another man named Appelbaum, who came back just yesterday. Nobody there would talk about Desvernine. This fellow Clayton is remarkable. He makes his own Devil's Island in south Florida. Mosquitoes, muck and death. Horrible. Appelbaum is sick. I reprimanded him for not getting information about Desvernine. It did no good but for discipline. Among us here, Appelbaum is a good man. If he says Desvernine disappeared off the face of the earth, Desvernine *did* disappear off the face of the earth."

"You assume that Desvernine is dead?" Arthur asked.

"Yes."

"This is all very interesting," said Laura. "What's it have to do with my investment?"

Arthur frowned.

Van Bibber replied, "I could answer that question in great detail. But in brief—Clayton finds it profitable to give jobs to criminals. If law officers ever made the arrests they might, they'd destroy his company."

Arthur put in, "A journalist disappeared there about a year ago, a man writing about peonage."

"Well, this is all news to me," said Laura.

"He was not an important journalist," observed Arthur. "He worked for that populist rag *The Nationalist*."

"I still don't see what all this has to do with my investment," Laura protested. "You told me once yourself, Arthur, that criminals ought to have a second chance."

"Tom Clayton seems to be giving them unlimited chances."

Laura remained casual—"My little investment in his company has paid off very well."

The two men studied her. Their faces were noncommittal.

Do they know I am lying? she wondered. Actually, her dividends had been spasmodic and paltry. Profits had been ploughed back into more equipment. "What's Appelbaum's view of how the company is doing?" she asked.

"It's expanding rapidly—" Van Bibber began. Laura asked questions as though she were merely an objective investor, and Van Bibber provided some information she didn't already have. There were about two thousand acres under cultivation, a big new house, dormitories for the peons, numerous cabins, a sugar mill, a dock on Lost Man's River, a warehouse, even a narrow-gauge railway. Most of the land was simply taken, but some had been acquired for twenty-five cents an acre from a gentleman whose sovereignty dated from the time the Seminoles were driven further into the swamps. The whole establishment was run by gunmen with Winchesters. Up Lost Man's River, it was too expensive and dangerous to enforce the law.

"Then Tom Clayton can be his own law," declared Laura, not troubling to conceal her pride.

"I don't believe a man, or woman, can disregard ethics for an indefinite period and get away with it," said Arthur.

"Has Tom Clayton done anything you haven't done?"

"It's a matter of proportion. A man can't get where I am and remain pure as the driven snow—I acknowledge that. But I've done a lot more decent than questionable things."

"Are you the one who decides what's decent?"

Arthur stood up. Usually, his anger was choleric, nervous. But her quibble about his authority in ethics seemed to have tipped a cauldron. His cheekbones were white with red spots and his nostrils were dilated. He was frightening, terrible, even though he was a skinny old man and his voice was shaky because he was choked up—"The more wealthy and influential I become, the more I find myself forced to make decisions involving all sorts of complicated moral pros and cons."

His rage is not appropriate to what he is saying, Laura thought. He knows about my affair with Tom, sure enough. She had decided that when Arthur found out, as was inevitable, she would win some slight advantage by telling him before he could tell her. "There was a time when you would have been embarrassed talking like this," she commented, with scorn. Then she immediately realized that she had been caught up with what her husband was saying, and that she had lost the opportunity to speak first about her affair.

"Laura, I am *ordering* you to have nothing further to do with Tom Clayton," he blurted. "By this, I mean you are to sell your interest in the Clayton Sugar Company for whatever you can get, whether it's little or nothing. You are to end your personal association with him. I won't become sordid about this unless you make me. I hope it's enough for you that I know about your trip to Havana on the liner *Okefenoke*."

If she had been alone with Arthur, she would have struck him. But Van Bibber was standing by the magnate's desk, the file in his stubby hands, taking in everything they said, impassive, waiting like a stopped clock that needed only to be wound up.

So she controlled her impulse.

Arthur pursued a kind of advantage—"Grotius, could you give Mrs. Wilkins some details about that pearl necklace called The Wealth of the Ocean?"

"Certainly. Last August, as Mrs. Wilkins is of course aware, she sold this necklace to the jeweler Niveau on Fifth Avenue. Last month—December Seventeen to be exact, to be *al*ways exact—The Wealth of the Ocean was worn by a certain duchess at a grand ball in Venice. The duchess purchased this necklace for eighteen thousand dollars, which compares most favorably, for her, with the twenty-two thousand dollars paid for it by Mrs. Wilkins."

"There's twenty-two thousand dollars that's wound up in the muck," said Arthur. "We're going to have a thorough audit to find out what you've done with all your money, and possessions too."

Laura was able to remain cool—"It's time we talked about a number of matters. We must clear up where we stand regarding each other. You see, I have my own kind of Industrial Services. I don't have the talents of a man like Captain Grotius Van Bibber. Nevertheless, I have ways of finding out what I want to know. For example, I know about a bungalow with a wide verandah, not far from here on a lonely beach. There are young women, girls I should say, white and colored, who present — how should I describe their activities? — amateur theatricals, let's say —"

Her husband snatched a heavy glass paperweight from his desk and threw it at her. It grazed her shoulder, caromed off the sofa, and crashed against the wall. He had hurled it at her head with all his strength, bent on murder.

She went for him, clawing.

Van Bibber was slow in putting down the file, and she gashed Arthur's face before she was hauled off. As the director of Industrial Services clamped her arms behind her, the magnate slapped her.

She aimed a kick at his groin — "That stung you, didn't it!" She managed a sardonic laugh. "You stinking pig — "

Van Bibber threw her to the floor and wrenched her arms until she feared they would break. But she refused to cry out.

Arthur gave a hoarse whisper — "In the old days a man would have killed you!"

Van Bibber was kneeling beside her and keeping constant pressure on her arms. Her face was crushed into the carpet. For a few seconds no one spoke. She realized that Arthur, with just a look, must be commanding Van Bibber to go on twisting her arms. There was a burning in her shoulders, elbows, wrists, back. She would not cry out, would not give Arthur *that* satisfaction. Her hatred of him had never reached such a pitch — the acid stink of his body, his contempt for flesh and blood, his rapacious concentration on slippery manipulation of his stocks, his contracts, his bonds, his money — and the ridiculous poses he struck because he loved himself so much! If he made Van Bibber kill her, she still wouldn't cry out!

At last she heard his voice — "Are you ready to behave like a human being?"

She was able to turn her head so that her mouth was clear of the carpet, and she forced herself to speak in a calm and clear voice — "I have always been the one who insisted on civilized conversation."

Van Bibber gave her arms a harder wrench. It surprised her and she gave a soft, sharp "Oh!"

"Let her up," said Arthur.

By willful effort she could stand straight, easily and gracefully. She refrained from looking at Van Bibber. It was a way of dismissing him. The pain filled her eyes with tears, which nourished her rage because Arthur might have the pleasure of seeing them.

He was holding a handkerchief to his face.

"I have only one thing to blame myself for," she said. Her voice was rough and unnatural but distinct. "I am ashamed of nothing, but I should have told you earlier about my relationship with Tom Clayton. When you are willing to sit down and discuss the whole thing, calmly, I'm ready."

Arthur did not reply or give any sign to Van Bibber as she went to the door and found it locked. There was only a latch, no key. Van Bibber must have known that her talk with her husband required privacy. Perhaps he anticipated approximately what had happened. Arthur's instructions to his Industrial Services chief must have been so crawling, so contemptible, so complacent in the frailty of his approaching old age. She turned the latch, opened the door, and spoke again—"I suggest we meet publicly, at dinner. I know you would be ashamed to have your flunky try to break my arms, in public."

XV

Now that Thorstein finally got himself a better job at the University of Wisconsin and moved there, Julia found it hard not to become disheartened. Perhaps she and Thorstein should not have sacrificed meeting every two weeks in the hope of living together at some time in the future, either married or pretending to be married so that Thorstein could keep his conventional academic job in Madison. Perhaps it would have been better not to scheme or plan, not even to think about uncertain prospects. She hadn't foreseen that separation would be so painful.

They wrote long letters to each other every week.

Thorstein was optimistic — or was he just pretending, trying to keep up her spirits? Already he'd become head of the Department of Animal Husbandry, he liked his students — his "young cheese-makers," and he was inspiring them with such "pearls" as "All America sucks at the teat of the dairy cow."

Wisconsin wasn't Florida, and under Wisconsin law Julia would be able to get a divorce. If he sold his horse and buggy, he could afford to pay her rent for a separate home until they could marry.

Julia wrote back that she hoped to save money and be able to pay her own rent. The whole idea of paying rent was strange. She was also trying to save so that she could send Caroline to Aurora Academy for Young Ladies in September. But business was not good. She did her bookkeeping and sent a consolidated financial statement to Thorstein, asking for his comment. He wrote back that for the life of him he couldn't suggest anything she hadn't already done. She just couldn't compete with other companies that cut costs by using peon labor—

> I know you would find it morally intolerable to starve and perhaps beat the colored folks who collect sap and do your other chores. Here at the University of Wisconsin my colleagues feel quite righteous about such situations, and their standard prescription is that everyone should be moral, so that there is no peonage in semi-frontier locations like Florida. And if people aren't moral — well, that's not the fault of economists in such idyllic pastures as the University of Wisconsin. But I hurt inside. No sympathy for me is

required—on occasion all economists ought to hurt inside, so that they are goaded to deal with reality rather than remain content with goofy self-indulgence.

She wrote back summarizing all her thoughts about what would happen if Richmond Plantation went bankrupt, or if her legal husband sold it. She hoped Caroline would find Aurora Academy the same kind of wonderful experience she herself had there, with Esther, so many years ago. She described the one-armed Confederate veteran who taught Latin—in a way, she'd loved the man! She wrote of what the colored folks in her employ might do, if a new owner was not acceptable. One man, hard-faced and energetic, had come with a lawyer from St. Vincent, all primed to buy. Somebody had trapped a cottonmouth moccasin and dumped it where he was sure to walk. The lawyer stepped on it but luckily was not bitten. She'd shot the viper. The hard-faced man was discouraged, and at present there was no buyer for Richmond Plantation.

Thorstein wrote that it happened to be an unseasonably warm day in Madison, the snow was melting and the icicles outside his window were dripping. He was reminded of the Florida mix of winter and spring, with jessamine in the air...They must wait no longer! At least, they could see each other for a week, during his Easter vacation. He proposed that they meet in Washington.

A variety of chores kept Julia occupied on the day she received and read this letter. Finally, in the evening, she lit a lamp in her office and sat down to write a reply. Yes—she would meet him in Washington...

> I can imagine how much you need me because of who you are, like no other man, and I won't try to write how much I need you. I feel that just waiting to be together, even for a little while, is too cruel—no matter what hopes we have, no matter how heartfelt we speak to each other across the whole country but just on paper.

As she was writing, she heard the squeak and rattle of a wagon outside and a male voice shouting whoa. She stuck her pen in the inkwell, rose from her desk, and went to the window that faced the road. With a shock that had the quality of a nightmare she recognized Tom—the bulky shadow in the dappled moonlight under the oaks was unmistakable. He was stepping down from the well-known wagon in which Amos Whitaker transported his wares, and then he reached in back for a satchel. His deliberate and authoritative voice resounded in the still night—"I'm mighty grateful to you, Amos. I would have enjoyed staying with you and Mrs. Whitaker, and I sure will miss those breakfasts your good woman serves—like I always said there ain't no better breakfast in the whole state, and I hope you tell her I said so. But I have to see what can be done about this old plantation back here, this old lost cause."

"I'm happy I can help out, Mr. Clayton." Julia knew this voice well—the Olustee saloon keeper had never lost his northern accent.

"We're here, Obadiah," said Tom. "Can you get yourself up?"

A head and shoulders rose from the bed of the wagon.

Tom set his satchel down, reached into the wagon, and with one heave stood the owner of the head and shoulders on the ground. "Steady now, Obadiah."

Amos Whitaker stepped down from his driver's seat and took from the bed of the wagon another satchel. "He ain't up to toting this, Mr. Clayton."

"That he ain't."

"Can he walk by himself?"

"With a good hiding he might. Obadiah goddamnit!"

"I'll bring the bags, Mr. Clayton," said Amos.

"Much obliged."

Supporting the man called Obadiah, who seemed to be drunk, Tom headed for the house, Amos Whitaker after him with the luggage.

Julia hurried back to the desk, pulled down the rolltop, and locked it with a small brass key which she slipped into her shoe. All of Thorstein's letters, her recent accounts, a copy of the consolidated financial statement she'd sent Thorstein with a previous letter, and her own unfinished letter to him were under the rolltop. She could feel almost sick with the thought of sharing anything with Tom now. She realized that he must have come by train from St. Vincent or from Payhokee-on-the-Gulf and that he had given Amos Whitaker the privilege of transporting him and this other man from the station to Richmond Plantation.

Carrying the lighted lamp, she met them as they came in.

He didn't greet her but said, "Obadiah, can you get your wits about you and say good evening like a true Yankee gentleman to my good woman? This is Mrs. Clayton—" and without looking at her he went on—"and Mrs. Clayton this is Obadiah Giles who is bookkeeper for my sugar company and knows his figures even if he can't hold his liquor."

"How do you do, Mr. Giles," she said, coldly.

"Good evening," muttered Mr. Giles and then, to Amos – "what's her name did he say?"

"Mrs. Clayton," Amos Whitaker replied, louder than necessary, and then spoke in his natural voice to Julia, "I'm very sorry to be coming in this way."

"Don't pay no mind," said Julia. Then she said, briskly, impersonally, "Hello, Tom."

He nodded.

It had been more than a year since she'd seen Tom, and his appearance had changed. His face was more tanned and more stony, more unconnected than ever with what he was saying, whether being polite to Amos Whitaker, scolding Obadiah Giles, or referring to his "good woman." In the light as she moved her lamp, his blue eyes with their yellow glints shone like jewels in his dark face. He was wearing a dark green topcoat and broad-brimmed green hat which he could not have obtained in Florida. His clothes enhanced his aura of unique authority. His features seemed less fleshy, harder. He was frightening, a hostile stranger in a dream.

Obadiah Giles was a small thin man perhaps sixty years old. Suddenly he stood without Tom's help, erect and dignified, and he spoke with unexpected clarity—"How do you do, Mrs. Clayton."

"Why, I'm well," she said, impersonally.

"We'll put Obadiah to bed in the spare room," said Tom.

"I ain't ready for bed yet," said Obadiah, in an alcoholic blaze. Perhaps he was wobbling between a drunk withdrawal from reality and desperation to maintain a sense of his own importance and freedom.

There were four bedrooms upstairs. William and Caroline occupied two of them. Tom would take her room, her bed. With Mr. Giles in the spare room, where would she sleep?

"I'm fit as a fiddle, Mr. Clayton," said Mr. Giles. "Ready to do what you want me to do, ready to do what you got me here for. What time is it?"

Tom ignored him. For the first time he looked directly at his legal wife—"It's been a long time, Julia, and I darn near forgot what a beautiful woman you are." His expression didn't change. His tone was imperious, weighty.

With horror Julia realized that he was suggesting his rights as a husband before these toadies, that naturally he and his wife would share the one remaining bed. Both Whitaker and Giles knew that she and Tom had been separated for years. But regardless of this separation, Tom was demonstrating that he could come and go as he wished, that he could take his "beautiful woman" as he was so inclined. Making his intention clear before these witnesses showed his commitment. His authority must never be diminished in the eyes of other men. It was a matter of honor.

In a second Julia's horror turned to rage—"I shall sleep where I please!"

He clucked his tongue with disapproval and stepped toward her, expecting to embrace, to kiss, to give the other men something to drool over.

She backed away, rigid with defiance, holding the lamp between them.

And in the same instant, from the dark stairs, came a querulous sound, almost a whine—"Daddy!"

Julia redirected the glow from the lamp. Standing on the stairs, a gray blanket held about her nightie for warmth and modesty, was Caroline. She had heard the wagon and voices. She didn't move, uncertain what to do, uncertain who she was in relation to what was going on in the downstairs hallway. Her blonde unbraided hair swirled before part of her face, and she peeked through it with large inquiring eyes.

Julia moaned—"Caroline—darling—"

"Come down here, girl," said Tom.

Caroline descended slowly, fidgeting with her blanket.

"Ain't she a beauty?" Tom went on. "Brush the hair out of your eyes, girl, so we can look at you. My but you are grown up now. How old are you?"

"Sixteen," Caroline murmured. "My birthday was last week."

"Sixteen—well well well—you look like you might be eighteen or nineteen. Don't she, Amos? Calls to mind that picture you got hanging over your bar. There'll be men buzzing around *her* like flies after honey."

In pushing her hair back Caroline lost control of the blanket, so that it opened to show a maturing body under the thin nightdress.

Tom laughed, with no change of expression—"Take a look, Obadiah. You're seeing something ain't no lost cause, like the rest of what's here."

Julia gave Caroline a serious look so that she stopped smiling and rearranged the blanket.

Tom's reduction of his daughter's young body to something like the picture behind Amos Whitaker's bar demonstrated a sexual nature that chilled Julia. The father of her children! The man who'd shared her bed from time to time for years—what had she been that she'd permitted it? Well—now that she had Caroline and William, he'd served a purpose in spite of what he was. Let him get out of her life!

Amos Whitaker was still standing by the door, his red face wooden. "There ain't nothing more I can help out with, Mr. Clayton?"

"I'll let you know if you can," said Tom. He made this sound like gratitude for the ride from the railroad station.

"Always glad to see you when you come through," said Whitaker. He kept his face turned away from Julia, and she sensed that he knew her distress at Tom's attitude regarding Caroline, and he was embarrassed. "Good night, Mrs. Clayton," he said. "Me and Mrs. Whitaker are always very happy when we happen to meet at the post office—well, good night." He was known as a particularly polite man.

"Go back to bed, Caroline," said Julia. "You'll see your father in the morning."

"Good night, Daddy," said Caroline.

Tom did not reply to her. He was speaking to his bookkeeper—"You got your brain ticking again Obadiah?"

"Yes, sir, Mr. Clayton."

Outside, Big Thing had become aware of the unusual night-time activity and was rushing toward the house with thunderous roars.

Julia thrust the lamp upon Mr. Giles and hurried out.

Whitaker was scrambling up to his seat on the wagon.

Julia whistled and called—"Here! Big Thing!"

The monstrous dog snuffled around Whitaker's wagon and then went to Julia.

"That's a mighty ferocious-looking beast you got there, Mrs. Clayton," said Whitaker. "Thank you for calling him off."

"Yes—yes—" Her mind was already on what was going on inside her house—"good night, Mr. Whitaker."

"Good night again, Mrs. Clayton." He flicked his horse with a light whip.

Tom and Mr. Giles, still carrying the lamp, had gone into the office. Tom was jerking at the locked rolltop of her desk. "You got your accounts in here?" he demanded.

She hoped she was concealing her anger at his arrogance, at his being there at all, at what he was. Years ago, she had acquired a habit of deviousness in dealing with Tom—and was ashamed of it. But she said, automatically, "Can't this wait until morning?"

He studied her. "You hiding something in this desk?"

His assumption that whatever was in the desk was his, and his obliviousness to what the desk meant to her, made meaningful talk impossible. For years, this desk was where she'd done a large part of the work needed to keep Richmond Plantation going. Also, it was where she wrote her letters to Thorstein, and through gossip Tom must know about him. Tom had never had anything to do with this desk. It was a desecration for him to paw through the results of her labors and even more if he happened to see her unfinished letter to Thorstein. She hesitated, not knowing what to say.

Mr. Giles spoke. He had not only recovered but seemed suddenly high-powered, fueled with alcoholic energy. He was holding the lamp high so that he could look at her. In the same diffused glow she could look at him. His eyes were large and shining behind his spectacles. His voice was crisp and coherent, acid with a Yankee twang—"Mr. Clayton can't wait 'til morning. It's not practical. We have to catch the train for St. Vincent which picks up passengers in Olustee at ten minutes past seven. I have to see your accounts now so I can explain them to Mr. Clayton."

"You haven't looked at my accounts for years," Julia said to Tom, "and you never did understand them."

"Obadiah has to see them," he said.

"What do you want to know?" she asked.

Mr. Giles answered for his employer—"Mr. Clayton has somebody almost certain to buy this property, but he won't buy until we show him what the property can take in. Facts and figures is what we need."

Julia had been poised for so long between the catastrophe of losing Richmond Plantation, abdicating from how she had grown up and what she had become, and on the other hand the need to make a break so that she could arrange a life with Thorstein, that she could react now only with a feeling of exhaustion. Decision was probably being taken out of her hands. How could she be sad and exultant at the same time? All she said was, "Well—so—do you feel sure that this sale will really go through, Mr. Giles?" She didn't want to talk to Tom.

"I would say it's just about certain," said the bookkeeper.

Tom still had his hand on the handle of the rolltop, and she thought that it would be best if she opened the desk herself. She'd put away the unfinished letter to Thorstein and produce her ledger for Mr. Giles. And she might show him the copy of the consolidated financial statement she'd sent for Thorstein's comment about two months ago. The bookkeeper could make his own copy if he wished. Also, she thought that she must make her own sleeping arrangement. Could she hope that Tom had forgotten his chatter suggesting that he was going to sleep with her? "I hide the key to this desk in my room upstairs," she lied. "I'll go get it."

There was a row of shallow drawers above the rolltop of the massive desk, and on the surface above them was a second lamp which she indicated with a nod—"You'll do well to light that lamp too, Mr. Giles. There are matches next to it." She hurried from the room.

In the small room for the necessaries she took a quilt and an extra blanket from the broad shelf. Downstairs again, she rushed past the door to her office. Mr. Giles began to speak to her—"Mrs. Clayton—" She ignored him and ran to the kitchen, where she dropped the bedding on a chair. She'd drag out the cot later. The stove was banked for the night. So she opened the draft, put in a couple of dry sticks, and set a kettle to boil for coffee. She'd appear gracious, accommodating to Mr. Giles. By behaving nicely, she'd retain a measure of independence. She retrieved the key from her shoe and rushed across the cold verandah, through the dark hall, and back to the office, now bright from two lighted lamps.

"I've put up water for coffee—"she began, with false cheer, and advanced toward the desk with the key.

She was interrupted by what she saw. Tom had yanked up the rolltop, breaking the lock, and was reading her letter to Thorstein. His hard and empty face, after this evident wild impatience, struck her as brain-sick.

She sprang at him, snatching for the letter.

He tore it and dropped the pieces on the floor.

She scooped them up—"You have no right—"

He raised his hand as though he would strike her.

She stood still, not backing away.

He lowered his hand and said, with stern rectitude, "You got no call to meet this Thorstein feller, in Washington or anywheres else. You and me are married, Julia—seems like you've forgot." He seized her wrist and twisted her toward him.

Frantic, she swung her arm and broke loose—"You've gone your way and I've gone mine. You can't come in here and take me like I'm one of your whores."

He stood aloof, lordly, sure that he didn't need to assert his rights at this moment, and he actually smiled—"You're out of your head, Julia. Seems to me I'm saving you from being a whore, with you planning to go with this professor feller. I remember him, stringbean sort used to talk nonsense with Joseph Rourke and my sister." With ironical deprecation of whatever she might feel he asked, "Hain't you got nothing better to do than write to a feller like that? And making promises!"

"It's not for you—" she began.

"I have a new house on Lost Man's River," he said. "I'm going to move you into it."

"Move?" She almost shrieked. "Move me? Move me and the children?"

"It don't look right me being without my wife in my new home," he said.

This was so obviously not a plausible reason for taking her in his new home that Julia's head swam. What did he have in mind? "You know it's impossible—" she began.

He went on, with a false propriety that was at the same time droll and threatening, "Now your wedded husband has a new house for you a million times better than this old barn, and you're talking and acting in this foolish and scorning way. In front of Obadiah, too!"

"It's none of Mr. Giles's business!" she snapped and then almost screamed, "Stop smiling, Tom!"

"The time will come when you'll smile too, Julia. You're all riled up now, but I don't care. It sets you up proper. The fact is we have a lot in common—Caroline—goddamn she's growing up pretty—"

"Leave Caroline out of this!"

"William too. He must be taller."

She spoke fast, trying to establish with her words the reality of their relationship—"I'm not going to your new home, Tom. Whatever you do, I'm not going. I'm not complaining that you're selling Richmond Plantation, even though God knows I have a right to complain since it just came to you through marrying me. My ledger is there on the desk and in the center pigeonhole is my statement that shows the condition of the business as of the end of the month before last. Mr. Giles will understand this if he's as good a bookkeeper as you say he is."

"It's going to take me a little time—" Mr. Giles began.

"I need somebody I can trust in my sugar company," Tom interrupted. He did stop smiling and for the first time seemed to speak seriously, with sincerity—"The only person in this whole stinking universe, man or woman, that I can trust, and who has the brains to add two and two and make four is you, Julia, and you're my wife and by the Almighty it's up to you to do your duty and come with me to my company up Lost Man's River and oversee Obadiah's books and see to it I'm not being cheated right and left the way I been for more than two years now."

"Mr. Clayton—"Obadiah began again.

"Shut up!" growled Tom.

Julia suppressed a half-hysterical laugh. Tom needed an auditor, not a wife. Bookkeeping had always baffled him, not because he wasn't smart enough but because he regarded it as demeaning to involve himself with so clerkly a chore. Through this incongruous need for her, his omnipotence was cracked. She had a fleeting thought of Thorstein and his ironies concerning the strange perversions of spirit wrought by property. Tom had married her for property, and now he wanted her to protect his profits from his new property! She suddenly felt that there was nothing pitiable or tragic in the wreckage of her marriage—it was merely ludicrous, absurd. "We've talked enough!" she exclaimed. "I'll leave you and Mr. Giles with my ledger and statement, which will keep you busy for a while. You ought to get a good price for Richmond Plantation in spite of two bad years." And she hurried out.

But as soon as she was alone she was chilled and terrified. It shouldn't take Mr. Giles very long to look over her bookkeeping and tell Tom what the figures showed. Then her documented husband would come and drag her to bed, using whatever force was required. If she resisted it would be just a joke, a titillation. She sensed that his dependence on her auditing made it all the more indispensable for him to do as he wished with her body. Tom lived by a governing principle—he must always, every hour and minute and second, *appear* to be in charge, even before a flunky like Obadiah Giles. From Tom's appearance issued his reality. Most people, wide-eyed and easygoing, were taken in. This was a part of that tumefaction which moved Thorstein to both ridicule and despair. Not to be taken in by Tom's artfully touted authority was intolerable rebellion, identifying his enemies. Julia thought of Esther and Joseph Rourke. She wondered about the magnate Arthur Wilkins, who seemed to have severed any connection with Tom. Now, she too was his enemy. Her letter to Thorstein and her refusal to go to Lost Man's River made this clear. Obviously, once he and Mr. Giles had finished with her bookkeeping, he'd deal with his uppity wife.

She was still holding the torn scraps of her letter to Thorstein in her left hand, and she hid them on a shelf behind a bag of flour. Then she banked the fire again and pushed the kettle to the back of the stove. Coffee was now out of the question. Dragging out the cot and sleeping in the kitchen was out of the question, too. Tom would promptly find her. She took the sweater which she kept on a peg by the kitchen door, put it on, wrapped a warm knitted shawl around her shoulders, picked up the blanket and quilt she'd left on a chair, and slipped out.

At first she didn't know where she'd go. She thought of the Johnsons' cabin. She could make up a pallet on their floor. Then she realized Lucy would object, would never permit this. She'd insist on giving Miz Julia her own bed and take to the floor herself, with her baby. Also, Julia reflected bitterly that she was a little like Tom in that she valued her appearance of authority. Her leadership as boss lady of Richmond Plantation would be debased by word going around that she'd had to hide from her husband. She feared that she'd pay in a hundred subtle ways for exposure of this ignominy. For a moment she felt she was paying for being white, for a destiny that cursed her into a kind of isolation from the black folks of Richmond Plantation.

The winter night was cold. She didn't need a lantern because the moonlight was unsparing. Big Thing came to mind. Her dog could protect her from Tom. But she knew Big Thing's habits and realized that by this time her great beast must be at least a mile down the road toward Olustee. Big Thing always followed any outsider leaving Richmond Plantation, and at that moment he was no doubt trotting beside Amos Whitaker's wagon, tongue lolling, with a baleful eye and occasional low growl warning the man on the wagon seat he'd better keep going, and no tricks! Even her dog had an instinct for property. Big Thing was an Irish wolfhound given to her as a puppy by her commission merchant in St. Vincent, who'd got him from God-knows-where. Standing on his hind legs with heavy front paws on Julia's shoulders, he towered over her so that he had to lower his shaggy head in order to lap her face with a tongue rough as a file and big as a saucer. She thought of Big Thing tearing and gashing at Tom—she might be unable to call him off if he got started! She tried and was able to put these bloody visions out of her head. Anyway, Big Thing probably wouldn't be back until morning, perhaps after killing a coon or a deer.

There seemed to be only one place where she could rest, perhaps even sleep, until Tom and Mr. Giles left early in the morning. It was the wagon shed. The broad bed of the freight wagon was well above crawly things on the ground, and the roof kept off most of the dew. She spread her quilt, folded the shawl to make a pillow, cocooned herself in the blanket, and lay down. By turning her head, she could see the lighted window of her office in the big house. Early in the morning she'd rouse up Lucy to get Tom and Mr. Giles their breakfasts and then take them in the buggy to the railroad station. She'd never see Tom again—never.

She was exhausted but on edge. Tears came in spite of telling herself that self-pity was contemptible. Tom's coarse suggestion of his rights as a husband, before Giles and Whitaker, had evolved naturally from his empty sentimentality when he courted her. Why had she been taken in? Was she one of the horde, awed by his trumped-up appearance of authority? Was she led by the nose because she had a warm body and saw no other men? What a fool she'd been—Daddy's flower in the secret garden of Richmond Plantation, the pre-eminent Latin scholar of Aurora Academy! Sickened, she thought that she'd actually shared Tom's brutishness in refusing to acknowledge, to herself, that from the very beginning of their marriage he'd used whores and was no doubt happy about his long absences from home so that he could find it more convenient to do so. Even the way she quarreled with Tom brought out how poisoned she was by her years of degradation.

An owl hooted, again and again. She tried to shut out all thought and sensation beyond listening to this incomprehensible statement. Was the owl derisive because she was lying in a hard wagon instead of in her soft bed? She found peace in the thought that her very life was inconsequential—the pines would sough, day and night would continue to swap places—and she almost slept.

Then, after what might have been hours or only minutes, her body turned to ice and she was aware of Tom. There seemed at first no sound, no shadow. But she knew he was in the shed before she heard the crunch of his step on the sandy earth, before she differentiated his breath from the slight breeze in the foliage and Spanish moss outside, before she recognized his special smell, somewhat like that of a cat.

His shape appeared, spectral in reflected glow from the moonlight outside. The wagon shook a little from his weight. He was leaning on it with both hands and looking at her. "You are one crazy woman, Julia," he said. His tone was impersonal, fitting for a statement of fact.

"Leave me be, Tom," she moaned.

He groped about her legs wrapped in the blanket until he found her foot, which he clamped in a hard grip. "You're coming to bed. You ain't going to spend the night in this old shed."

"It's no good you saying that. If your bookkeeper didn't take the spare room, I'd be there like I've been before when you come around." There was fear and anger in her sarcasm as she went on, "I hope Mr. Giles is comfortable."

He began to drag her by the foot.

With a violent convulsion she wrenched loose and slid back in the wagon until she was cornered against the back of the seat.

With one bound, like a cat after a mouse, he landed beside her on the wagon and gripped her shoulders. For a moment his face was clear in a ray of moonlight, and its very lack of expression was far more frightening than any grimace of anger or lust.

She whimpered—"No, Tom, no—it ain't like we're proper man and wife anymore."

He released her shoulders and tore away the blanket. His hands were heavy, methodical.

She had the momentary hope that she'd spring out of the wagon and run into the woods, but he was heaving her about as he pulled at her dress. So she went for him with her nails, hardly seeing him. But she could feel that her left hand made a scrape.

There was a blow on her face and her ears rang. Frantic, she tried to kick, scratch, gouge.

She was lifted free of the tangling quilt and flung against the wagon bed. Her head struck hard. Half-conscious, weak, she thought, "You'll do what you have to do. You'll do as you are. I'll live through it." She managed to gasp aloud, "I'll live, damn you!"

She could feel her bare legs forced apart, was aware of his strangely insignificant but painful male organ, heard the hoots of the owl again, and wept.

Her mind came to life again when she heard the familiar half-whine half-growl of Big Thing's conversation. Her loyal beast, her useless protector, had returned earlier than she expected but not soon enough, and having smelled her out was now panting happily, his paws on the wagon bed, ears cocked expectantly up from his enormous shaggy head. She rumpled his fur, and he lapped her hand. "Where were you, you bad dog?"

Moving made her realize that she was uncovered and shivering from cold. There were aching bruises on her thighs and shoulders. Her head throbbed. Putting her hand to her face, she could feel swelling. Semen on her thighs and abdomen made her feel soiled. There was despair over the whole course of her life in the thought that she'd once welcomed Tom's semen because she'd hoped for children. The change from what she had been to what she had become seemed to be triumph in spirit and disaster in fact. She rearranged her underwear and dress, eased herself down from the wagon, draped the blanket and quilt over her arm, and headed back to the big house.

Big Thing did not try to follow her into the kitchen.

She lit a lamp, opened the stove draft, and put a kettle of water on to heat. If she did what she had to do very quietly, nobody—not Tom, Mr. Giles or the children—was likely to intrude. The tub for baths was hanging on a nail. She took it down and placed it by the stove. Then she removed all her clothes and folded them over the back of a chair. She couldn't get clean clothes from her room because Tom was there.

When she had lukewarm water, she put some in a teapot with a small amount of soapsuds, lay in the tub with her legs raised, and eased the nozzle into her vagina so that she could pour. She must not become pregnant by Tom!

Then she bathed herself all over, dried herself slowly by the hot stove, and dressed.

After emptying the tub and hanging it up, she went silently to her office for stationery, pen and ink. Back in the kitchen, she took the torn scraps of her letter to Thorstein from behind the bag of flour, sat down at the kitchen table, fitted the scraps together like pieces of a puzzle, and copied what she had written on a new piece of paper. The act of copying channeled her mind on its usual forthright course again, even while her body seemed damaged beyond recovery.

She wouldn't tell Thorstein how Tom had read and torn her letter. She'd *never* tell Thorstein what happened after that. She'd always told Thorstein everything important—it had never occurred to her that she might hold anything back. Now, the need to spare Thorstein and never tell him that Tom had attacked her made it seem as though the injury would never heal, would last forever.

She concealed her anguish by continuing her letter in a practical vein. She reported that Tom had come with his bookkeeper, that they almost certainly had a buyer for Richmond Plantation, that she would soon be moving to Madison, and that they could make plans for how she could best get herself settled when they met in Washington. She'd have William with her, but she hoped Caroline could be entered in Aurora Academy for the rest of the school year. She was concerned that they live so that they could steal time for love and at the same time not jeopardize his position with the university. She was counting the days before the Monday after Palm Sunday, when they would meet at the Willard Hotel in Washington.

Thinking about how she and Thorstein would cope with workaday problems brought a sense of being alive again. She sealed and addressed the envelope, which she hid behind the bag of flour. She'd go to Olustee after Tom left and mail it. In her office, replacing stationery, pen and ink, she squinted at her clock. Twenty-two minutes past four. Allowing an hour and a half for driving in the buggy to catch the seven-ten train, and half to three-quarters of an hour to dress and have breakfast, Tom and Mr. Giles would have to rise in a few minutes. She must ease their going.

She put on her heavy sweater again, lit a lantern, and went to the Johnsons' cabin. There were two rooms and a loft. Lucy slept in the chamber next to her parents, her baby next to her. The two boys, one of them a runner with William, slept in the loft. The stove was warm in the room where they all cooked, ate, bathed, talked…What would happen to the Johnsons after Tom sold Richmond Plantation? Would they stay together?

Their gentle assent in being rousted out of bed at about four-thirty, while it was still dark and cold, brought tears to her eyes. What had she ever done to deserve such helping hands? She felt like sobbing, showing her pain, reaping the sympathy they would certainly give. But she held her lantern so that they couldn't see her swollen face, and in an unnatural voice she said, "Lucy you get Mr. Clayton and the man he brought with him some breakfast. Make plenty of coffee. I'll help your father harness up the buggy. I do not wish to see Mr. Clayton this morning."

"Yes, Miz Julia." There was silence as the Johnsons pondered the meaning of her wish not to see her husband, and no doubt they were recalling the past visits of Thorstein.

Sooner or later they would see her bruised face.

After the horse was harnessed to the buggy, she stood by the wagon shed and watched the big house, which she wouldn't enter until Tom left. Lamps had been lit in the upstairs bedrooms as well as in the kitchen, where Lucy and her mother bustled about. After a time the lights upstairs disappeared. Tom and Mr. Giles must have gone down to the kitchen. Were Caroline and William up too? They would wonder why she wasn't sitting down to breakfast with the father they rarely saw, and with the guest.

She waited, impatient even with the minutes that deferred an end to this dead part of her life. Caroline came out the front door with a lantern. Then Lucy, who climbed into the buggy and took the reins. Lucy's father, who had been holding the horse, walked back toward his cabin. William, with his own lantern, came out the kitchen door, saw her, and walked slowly toward her, every hesitant step expressing his wonder and uncertainty. He was wearing only a thin shirt and jeans, indifferent to the chill of the morning, and he was barefoot. He was slim and tanned, like a colored boy except for the mop of blonde hair, and his tentative steps had a delicacy that almost choked her. At the same time Tom and Mr. Giles, holding their satchels, came out the front door. They stood for a moment, talking—had they forgotten something?

William, close to her, suddenly wailed, "Ma! What's happened to your face?"

She couldn't think up a proper reply. "I don't think I shall ever be able to tell you," she said.

He handed her the lantern, stared at her with widening eyes, froze for a moment, like a startled deer, and rushed to the shed. Hanging from a nail, just inside, was a bucket of spikes, useful for repairs. William seized a handful and dashed toward the house.

At about ten steps from his father, William hurled one. It hit the skirt of Tom's long dark green topcoat.

Tom tossed his satchel in the back of the buggy and took a menacing step toward his son. Julia exclaimed—it was terrifying.

But not to William, it seemed. Light, quick as an otter, he threw a second spike. It struck Tom in the belly but because of the coat and jacket probably didn't hurt him much.

Tom did what was necessary. He'd never catch William. So he climbed in the buggy and sat next to Lucy. William couldn't throw more spikes without fear of hitting Lucy.

Mr. Giles climbed into the back of the buggy.

Lucy flicked the reins.

William ran beside the buggy for a few steps and looked Tom in the face. Defiance! Hatred! Let there be no mistake!

For Julia, this seemed a final agony of Tom in her life. What William felt should be and should not be. He was only fourteen years old.

XVI

Amos Peters was standing in front of the Dales' store in Chokoloske and listening to his brother-in-law Mark talk. Amos dug his bare toes in the earth out of restlessness—he enjoyed what Mark had to say but wished he could speak himself and have folks so attentive. Three others were listening to Mark—Joanna Dale, in her rocking chair and fanning herself; Joe the Greek and Litt Young, side by side on the bench, friends who agreed they'd done no wrong but had to get away from the law anyhow.

It was an unusually warm day for February and Mark was waiting for the late afternoon breeze so that he could go out in the sharpie with Joe and Litt, spend the cool of the evening catching fish, and sell them on a Fort Harrison dock early the next morning. Mark would keep half the money while Joe and Litt would divide the other half. Mark needed more to keep the sharpie going. Already Mark had a piece of calico wrapped around his head to shield himself a little from the sun, and stuck in it were six fish hooks he'd got from the ashes of his mother's cabin in Myrtle. He never used those particular hooks for fear of losing them.

Amos knew he could go with Mark if he wanted to, and Mark would figure some share of the money for him, but for no reason Amos could put into words he had to do something by himself. He shared the money from alligator hides, but Bina took some of it for feeding him and giving him a place to bed down. Almost grown, he was like a child in the cabin of Mark and Bina, which they kept building onto to have room for Azri and more babies Bina hoped to have, for Ruth, who would always have to be looked after, and for one extra and unnecessary man—himself! He should be like Mark, important in Chokoloske—by some, feared. Mark owned a sharpie. Mark and Bina got along—Amos heard their noises in the night and thought he'd go crazy. There was a sweet girl in Fort Harrison…Mark had shaved off his beard but left a mustache clipped in the Spanish style, his eyes never wavered when he looked at any kind of white man, and every time he moved it was for a purpose. He'd said that if Bina had a manchild the name would be John Caesar, after a Seminole chief, and Bina had been pleased. When Mark went hunting, he never used more than one bullet.

Mark's words flowed while Miz Joanna, Joe and Litt listened, very respectful. He went on and on, quiet and calm as the Gulf on a still morning, with underneath a shark after something—"That Nick who were living here in Chokoloske since before I come here myself, it's *that* Nick I's talking about. Nick had a fiddle but a big wind blowed down his cabin and smashed it. That were for Nick like losing arm or leg. So when the Clayton Sugar Company were looking for men Nick got notionate. He allow he going to work for the Clayton Sugar Company. He allow he get money and go to New Orleans and get hisself another fiddle. It warn't no use warning Nick against the Clayton Sugar Company, how they haul in men, women and chilluns too, like throwing out a net and pulling in shrimps—getting them drunk and banging them on they heads in Fort Harrison, in Key Alva, in Payhokee, maybe far as Texas and Cuba. I seed it myself when the Clayton Company's schooner *Bonefish* and my own boat were waiting for wind, close together as here to that stump—I seed four colored men and two colored women with tongues swole like they innards coming out, with blood on they heads, lying out on the deck in the sun like fire and the boss men don't give them no drink of water. Them boss men wanted no nourishments or power in they arms and hands till they ready to cut cane. They had to be kept *weak* while they on the *Bonefish*. I seed this. I seed these four men and two womens. I seed two boss men with pistols. There was no wind. The sun were hot—ooo*ee*, hot! Folks moaning, trying to put tongues on lips all shriveled up and not able to do it and saying, 'Oh captain won't you give me just a little water—I's going to die 'less you give me just a little water.' I tell all this to Nick like I's telling you. Just the same he say, 'I's going to get me another fiddle. I had a fiddle once could make folks jump' he say, 'but it got busted and now I got to get me another.' I warn't able to convince Nick he better stay put. Nick he don't listen. So he went to the Clayton Sugar Company—warn't even hauled there. He still there I reckon. Whether he cutting cane and digging muck or whether he under the muck I can't torectly say—"

Was it Satan himself who made Amos remark, "I figure Nick got money and went to New Orleans for his fiddle."

For once, Mark couldn't speak.

Joe the Greek and Litt Young both sat up very straight to get a better look at Amos.

Joanna Dale stopped fanning herself. "Tain't likely, Amos," she said at last. "If Nick left there and got his fiddle we would've knowed. Only one I knowed or ever heard of got out was the boy hid hisself on the *Pocohontas* and come here the day the sharpie was put in the water."

They could all see the *Pocohontas* as she spoke. It was tied up at the Chokoloske dock, water gushing from a hose, spilling bilge so the old hulk could stay afloat. Somebody was working a pump. Litt Young remarked that the *Pocohontas* might last two or three more months, maybe even a year, and after that anybody wanting to go up Lost Man's River, if anybody that big a fool to want to go up Lost Man's River could be found, would have to go in the Clayton Sugar Company's schooner *Bonefish* or in the Clayton Sugar Company's fancy steam launch *Laura*.

The change of subject made Amos squirm. They were shaming him for his remark that Nick probably got out of the Clayton Sugar Company and went to New Orleans for his fiddle. One boy had come *down* the river on the *Pocohontas*. Why not go *up* the river *with* the *Pocohontas*, making use of it while it still made the run?

He left those on the porch of the store without another word, walked to the dock, and pitched in with a man who was loading firewood. When the *Pocohontas* cast loose and headed upriver, Amos was permitted by way of compensation to hitch a line and get towed in the skiff that he and Mark used when they hunted alligators. All he had to do was steer with a paddle so he wouldn't swerve and hit stumps. In no more than an hour he was farther from home than he'd ever been except for when they all moved from Olustee. He found he could steer the skiff by standing and shifting his weight so that he slid like a hooked fish in the wake of the *Pocohontas*. *Pocohontas* could be eased in on the other side and tied up. Amos had never seen such a place. Among oaks and palms back from the river was an immense house painted green, with wide screened verandahs and many windows, those which were not shuttered blinking in the shadowy light. Flower beds dotted a sweep of green grass from this house to the river, and a colored man was pushing a contraption for mowing it. There were no bushes at all, no place to hide the skiff. Upstream, beyond the dock, was a long warehouse like what he'd once seen in Payhokee during the time for moving. Beyond that a tall chimney belched black smoke.

Amos unsnagged the line from the *Pocohontas* and paddled desperately toward the far bank, which was cleared only for one small cabin.

Then, from the dock, a harsh voice—"Hey, you! Boy! Where you going?"

Amos kept paddling.

A shot, and a bullet skipped in the water.

He stopped paddling and turned around.

On the dock was a tall man cradling a rifle and standing out in a bright red shirt.

"I's fishing," said Amos.

"Bring yourself in here."

"I's just fishing," persisted Amos.

The rifle jumped, and some splinters spun away from the skiff.

Amos paddled to the dock.

Another man, shorter, with a blue handkerchief tied around his neck, walked out on the dock.

"Where's your fishing pole?" demanded the tall man.

"I's after crawfish," said Amos.

"You won't need no crawfish. You got yourself a job."

Amos thought he might ask the tall man how much he'd be paid for whatever needed doing. He might ask if he wanted to, but he guessed he didn't want to.

"Hold out your hand, nigger," said the short man with the blue handkerchief.

Amos did as he was told.

"If he can pick up crawfish he can swing a cane knife."

"My sister spects me—" Amos began but was then silent, angry that he'd started to say something that showed weakness. Mark would never have done that.

"You are going to learn to keep your mouth shut, nigger," said the tall man. "You are going to do just what you are told to do, you're going to do it right off, and you ain't going to say nothing. Pull that skiff of yourn up here."

The two boss men talked about using the skiff for a target or chop it up for kindling but finally just let it sit.

The tall man turned to Amos again—"You walk along behind me, nigger. This here man's your boss now. Mister Sanderson. You got that name? Say it."

"Yessir. Mister Sanderson," said Amos.

"You are going to cut cane. You're going to get yourself more money'n you ever see before."

Mister Sanderson grunted.

"This is your lucky day, nigger."

*

During the week following the invasion of Tom and Mr. Giles, and being raped, Julia constantly fought depression and anxiety by working harder than ever, trying to heal herself since what she did for the naval-stores business was now pointless. Worry about money made things even worse. She ran the business and took care of almost negligible personal needs with a checking account in a St. Vincent bank. She wanted to provide her people on Richmond Plantation with a big bonus at the time of the sale so that they would be a little more free in deciding what to do with their lives. She wanted to send Caroline to Aurora Academy. She wanted to arrive in Madison with enough money so that Thorstein wouldn't have to support two establishments until they could marry — or *if* they could marry. Her bank balance showed that what she wanted to do was out of the question.

Thorstein wrote an ecstatic letter in which he informed her he'd arrive in Washington three hours before she would. He cited timetables. She thought of how much going to Washington would cost — the railroad tickets, the hotel. . . But she had to go.

She was astonished at receiving a letter from Joanna Dale. Julia had written to Joanna a short time after she and Joshua moved from Olustee, but there had been no reply. A quick look at this letter showed why. Joanna was almost completely illiterate. It had obviously been a painful struggle for her to write. Her message was garbled. Her spelling was purely imaginative. Her penmanship was almost illegible. But Julia studied the letter until she was sure she understood it. Joanna knew there was "nuthen" between Julia and her husband and didn't hold it against her that a professor had been seeing her. She wouldn't say what was going on between Julia's husband and the wife of a rich railroad man because she wasn't certain what was true. She didn't want to hurt Julia's feelings in bringing all this up — "I alles likd yu as yu air a good wuman." But she hoped Julia still had influence with her husband. Amos Peters, like a grandson to her, was being forced to work at the Clayton Sugar Company, where folks were "brooted horribul" and Joanna was "skeerd to deth" what would happen to Amos. Could Julia prevail on her husband, no matter how distant they might have become, to send Amos home?

What a time for this appeal! She'd have to hurt Joanna by explaining that there was no possibility of her having any influence with her husband—she couldn't do anything about Amos. She didn't want to write this, but since she had to, she did it immediately.

The next day she went to see her commission merchant in St. Vincent and had another surprise. Tom had seen the commission merchant and had told him that he was taking personal charge of Richmond Plantation business. So the money from the last sale of turpentine had to be paid to him—as it was. Julia had been counting on this money, and she felt desperate. Could Thorstein support a woman with two children besides taking care of his own needs? Even if he could, would the stress affect their love? She thought of a passage in *The Tumefaction of Property* which showed the connection between happiness in marriage and security of money and property. She was aware that lack of money, the impending loss of Richmond Plantation, and being raped frayed her mind so that she was uncertain about herself, about Thorstein, even about love—and inwardly she howled with the need for seeing him.

She continued to work harder than ever. Beside having her ledger in perfect order, she checked tools and equipment, supervised minor repairs. She wanted to cherish a memory of an ideal Richmond Plantation.

A week after she got bad news from the commission merchant, late in the afternoon, Big Thing roared, sending her in a rush from the office.

A man was arriving in Amos Whitaker's wagon, and her first impression was style, a citified look. She calmed Big Thing and held the horse while he stepped down.

"Mrs. Clayton?" he said, very bright and cheerful.

"Yes, I am she."

He whipped the reins around a verandah post so that Julia wouldn't have to keep holding the horse. Then, with a little bow, he drew a card from a fawn-colored waistcoat pocket and handed it to her.

She read:

Lawrence H. Eddy President
PELICAN BANK
36 Sunset Avenue
Fort Harrison, Florida

John Ashworth

Your Money Is Safe With Us

How young he was! Scarcely more than a boy! He was slim, clean-shaven, handsome, elegant, utterly out of keeping with Amos Whitaker's wagon and rough-hewn Richmond Plantation. His expression was intelligent, friendly and vivacious. His light brown suit was perfectly pressed, fawn colored gloves that matched his waistcoat fitted his slender hands, and a brown derby floated on thick curly hair the color of golden sand. Julia was conscious of her flowery housedress, like what the colored women wore, and of her knitted shawl which through many washings had lost its blue dye.

"It's a pleasure to meet you, Mrs. Clayton." He made it seem as though it actually was!

"Why, I'm glad of that, Mr. Eddy. You're surprising me, coming here so sudden-like—"

"Of course I am. Not unpleasantly, I hope. I do have some business with you, Mrs. Clayton, a proposal which I expect you'll find quite satisfactory, quite to your taste."

From considerable experience with business gambits, Julia was cautious—"Well, we shall see, Mr. Eddy. Let's go into my office."

But as they went up the verandah steps Caroline screamed, "Who is it, Ma?" She and William were just coming from school.

"A visitor, Caroline," Julia called. "Business—nothing for you."

Yet it did seem lucky that Caroline was dressed properly for receiving their urbane and dapper visitor, even though her mother wasn't. The belle of the schoolhouse was wearing a rusty pink woolen dress which Julia had made, there were matching pink bows on her two flaxen pigtails, and she was carrying a bouquet of blue wild iris. She must have persuaded William to wade in a swamp for them. He was barefoot, his britches were rolled above his knees, his legs were muddy, and his shoes dangled by the laces from his neck.

He did as Julia had taught him—he held out his hand and said, "Howdydo, Mr. Eddy."

Mr. Eddy peeled off a glove and shook hands—"How do you do, William."

Casual, unimpressed, William asked his mother, "Is the still working? I didn't see no smoke. It ain't broke again, is it?"

"I don't think so, William. Why don't you go see?"

William tossed his shoes on the verandah and left.

"The still for the turpentine has been acting up," Julia explained to Mr. Eddy. Then she turned to her daughter.

Caroline's face was as pink as her dress, she seemed to have stopped breathing, and there was a perceptible stain of sweat between her breasts. The impact of this visitor was electrifying, to say the least! Julia saw her own wilderness girlhood in her daughter, her own ignorance and helplessness when she was courted by Tom. She understood, pitied, hoped, feared, despaired. How many dreams of handsome lads with a variety of faces, arms, legs, bodies, voices—rapturous companions of sleepless nights—could become flesh, clear identity, beau ideal in Mr. Eddy! What disasters might follow from such carnal expectations?

"And this is my daughter Caroline, Mr. Eddy," Julia said, crisply.

Caroline hung her head and murmured something.

"Caroline, *Miz* Caroline," said Mr. Eddy, "*my* but that is a lovely bouquet you're carrying. Let's see, the blue is just the color of your eyes. Please look at me without blinking, Miz Caroline. There! I knew it! Isn't it so, Mrs. Clayton? *Aren't* Miz Caroline's eyes and those blue flowers a perfect match?"

Was Caroline going to faint, fall down?

Julia put her arm around her daughter and replied in a cool and matter-of-fact tone, "Yes, I suppose they do match." She passed her hand over Caroline's damp brow, brushing back a few straggling hairs, and then had to smile—"It pleasures me that my only daughter is so lovely, but she mustn't become vain—" Brusquely, she changed the subject—"It's late afternoon, Mr. Eddy, and we have your business to talk over, and after that, with you coming all the way out here, I hope you'll stay for supper."

He grinned—"Why, thank you. You're being very hospitable, Mrs. Clayton." He showed boyish enthusiasm.

Julia realized that she was somewhat captivated. "Can't let you go hungry," she said. "Caroline, Caroline dear, are you listening to me?"

Caroline looked at her but probably didn't see her—"Yes, Ma."

"Can you get Lucy and rummage something up for supper? Set the table in the dining room. But you better help Lucy serve."

"Yes, Ma."

Julia explained—"Our housekeeper Lucy is a very young woman and she has a little baby to look after. So it's best Caroline helps out."

Mr. Eddy spoke so that Caroline, now at the door to the house, could hear him—"I can *see* that Miz Caroline's as good as she is pretty."

How could Mr. Eddy say something so mushy without sounding stupid?

What business could he have with her? Pelican Bank of Fort Harrison? She'd never heard of it. She led him into the office, had him sit on the one extra chair, seated herself at her desk, and said, pleasantly but firmly, "*Well*, Mr. Eddy."

"I have so many interesting things to say that I've thought and thought how to begin," he said. His tone was the same as it had been when he compared Caroline's eyes to the wild iris. Whatever his business was, he was enjoying it. "And now I've met you, Mrs. Clayton, I'm positive about the right way to begin. I can see you're a person takes hold of the whatever and does the needfuls. I'm quoting my uncle who started me in the banking business when I was fourteen."

"Since you and your uncle intended to describe a good quality, I hope I have it," said Julia.

"Oh you do, Mrs. Clayton, I'm absolutely sure. I expected to meet a person who takes hold of the whatevers and does the needfuls even before I came here, and now we've met—" He completed this thought with a sunny smile. "You see, I heard about you in Fort Harrison, from Edward Smallstock."

"Edward Smallstock?" She was startled. What remained in her memory of the man was his unfortunate habit of hunching his shoulder as though he had to ward off a blow. "Why, that's the lawyer who prosecuted my—" She was about to say husband but corrected herself and said Mr. Clayton.

"He prosecuted because he was the state's attorney at the time. Of course, he knew Mr. Clayton was going to be let off—"

"He acted as though he knew—"

"Oh, I wish I'd been there." Mr. Eddy squirmed with pleasure at what he imagined. "But I was nothing more than a half-grown sweet potato at the time, and I wouldn't have knowed from beans what was going on."

"I'm not sure I knew what was going on. What's Edward Smallstock doing in Fort Harrison?"

"He's opened his law office there, and he handles stuff for Mr. Clayton."

"After that trial I should have thought Mr. Clayton would have nothing to do with Mr. Smallstock."

"Oh no. Mr. Clayton knew that Mr. Smallstock was *really* on his side. Anyway, the Claytons and the Smallstocks have always been like kinfolk."

"So I've heard."

"I just mentioned Edward Smallstock because he fixed up the paper I've brought you."

"Paper?"

Mr. Eddy thrust a slim hand into an inner pocket of his stylish jacket and drew out a folded document, which he handed to her. "This," he said. "Please read it, Mrs. Clayton."

On the outside was a fancily printed title—POWER OF ATTORNEY. Julia unfolded it and read. She was informed that she had power of attorney to represent her husband, Thomas Ewell Clayton, in all matters pertaining to the management and operation of the Clayton Sugar Company, and that she could with her own signature deposit in and withdraw from the account of the Clayton Sugar Company in the Pelican Bank in Fort Harrison, Florida, dealing with both profits and expenses of the Clayton Sugar Company according to her own best judgment. Tom had signed with his full name. She recognized the handwriting.

She put the document on her desk and was silent. There must be some appalling trap in this POWER OF ATTORNEY! What was it? Mr. Eddy was as bright and seemingly as immune to personal involvement in the delivery and consequences of this suspicious piece of paper as a bird eyeing a bug. What was there to say?

After a moment he said, "Mr. Clayton's all steamed up about this. He declares you are the only one in this whole stinking universe he can trust. That's his way of putting it, not mine."

Again there was silence. Mr. Eddy waited.

At last she asked, "But why does Mr. Clayton want *me* to manage his sugar company? What's *he* doing?"

"Now I have to tell you something confidential, Mrs. Clayton. I want your word you won't tell a soul what I'm about to tell you."

"Oh all right," Julia said, impatiently. "You have my word."

"Well, it's like this, Mrs. Clayton—Mr. Clayton's being held on a prison farm, up in Georgia."

Yet again, Julia had nothing to say. Tom in prison! It was both just and unbelievable. She studied the young banker, who grinned as though this astounding information suggested experiences, sensations, and perhaps entire ways of living that were adventuresome and enchanting.

"I know this takes some explaining," he went on. "You see, Mr. Arthur Wilkins has it in for Mr. Clayton."

"You'd better tell me everything," said Julia.

Mr. Eddy proceeded to do just that. He spoke for about a half-hour, occasionally pausing in his narrative to answer Julia's questions. There were mixed-up relationships. First, Mrs. Arthur Wilkins—*Laura* Wilkins—was a silent partner in the Clayton Sugar Company. Mr. Wilkins didn't like it. Mr. Eddy hinted that Mr. Wilkins didn't like another kind of relationship between Thomas Clayton and Laura Wilkins but couldn't do anything about it because Thomas Clayton and Laura Wilkins were the kind of people who'd do as they wanted no matter what anybody, even a man like Arthur Wilkins, might have to say about it. Mr. Eddy blushed because he had to say this—he had to make sense for Mrs. Clayton! Now—Mr. Clayton had a right-hand man named Sanford Payne (So Mrs. Clayton knew Sanford Payne—good!) and Mr. Eddy had something more he had to say even though he didn't like doing it. Just this: Mr. Clayton was worried about Mr. Payne because he just went around with a fat little nigger called Richard the Barber and never had to do with ladies. Mr. Eddy blushed again and hoped he wouldn't have to give "dee-tails." (Since Mrs. Clayton insisted, he would and did give "dee-tails," even though they weren't very nice!) Anyway, Mr. Clayton wanted to straighten out Sanford and took him to a place in Key Alva where sailors went, but Sanford got upset and slashed a woman's face. So the sheriff in Key Alva, a man named Burlitt, arrested Mr. Clayton. (For what Mr. Payne did?) Now—here's where Mr. Wilkins comes in again because he wanted to put his railroad on trestles and across keys to Key Alva, and so he'd prepared by getting property in Key Alva and making it his own town. You might say Mr. Burlitt works for Mr. Wilkins, and Mr. Wilkins wanted Mr. *Clayton* arrested and didn't give a damn (Excuse me, Mrs. Clayton) about Mr. *Payne*. Now—Mr. Burlitt has a brother who is warden of a prison farm in Georgia. So by way of helping out Mr. Wilkins, who just wanted Mr. Clayton put away with no fuss in newspapers or anywhere else, Mr. Burlitt the sheriff loaded Mr. Clayton on a boat and shipped him to the care of Mr. Burlitt the warden in Georgia, where he'd have to stay for a while, probably until both he and Laura Wilkins cooled down. (But why wasn't Mr. Clayton jailed in Key Alva, since Mr. Wilkins was running the place?) Well—Key Alva is handy for anybody with a boat, and the Clayton Sugar Company has a schooner named *Bonefish,* and Burlitt was worried it might arrive in Key Alva one fine day, loaded with gunmen who worked for Mr. Clayton and would shoot up the place to get Mr. Clayton out of jail and back up Lost Man's River. (But what about the law?) Fresh-faced Mr. Eddy had to smile. Now — Mr. Clayton would have to be ransomed off the prison farm in Georgia so that both Burlitts would be compensated for the trouble they'd taken. In the negotiations Mr. Smallstock was representing Mr. Clayton and a Mr. Van Bibber was representing Mr. Wilkins. But it was clear that Mr. Wilkins was not prepared to settle soon, and in the meantime Mr. Clayton was worried about what might happen to his sugar company during his absence.

That was why Mr. Clayton had Mr. Smallstock prepare this POWER OF ATTORNEY for Mrs. Clayton.

Julia made Mr. Eddy tell his story again, from the beginning. He did so, without inconsistencies that might show he was making something up.

She was thinking that she might use this POWER OF ATTORNEY to get some money. After the trip to Washington she'd have only about six hundred dollars for entering Caroline in Aurora Academy and going with William to Madison, Wisconsin, to find work and settle. Caroline and William were Tom's children after all, and whatever she might take for their support from the account of the sugar company in the Pelican Bank would be only her just due. The POWER OF ATTORNEY at this time was a godsend! Yet, a long commitment to managing the company was out of the question. What would a further delay in going to Madison do to Thorstein? This long separation, with only a meeting of minds through letters, was a kind of death. Could Thorstein stand being a widower even longer? She couldn't put out of her mind that she might lose him. "How long do you expect Mr. Clayton will be in this prison farm?" she asked Mr. Eddy.

"Hard to tell..." He described the frustrating ransom negotiations at greater length.

"I have to think over all you're telling me," Julia said at last. "I'll let you know after supper what I'm going to do."

Caroline was transformed. She'd wrapped her pigtails in a coil on top of her head in mama's style. Scarcely able to speak when she and Mr. Eddy were introduced, at the supper table she gushed observations, memories, fantasies, questions. What questions! How unlucky she hadn't always known Mr. Eddy! Nothing would do but he must reveal every tittle of his days at the bank, every smidgen of by-play at the boarding house where he took his meals, every secret and treasured hope for himself and — as he surprisingly divulged — for Florida. He had to overcome a certain shame in order to express his idealism. It was more fitting for a young man to think only of himself and not have grandiose dreams about Florida or anything else. But Miz Caroline's onslaught melted him. He'd never been regarded as so special, so precious, so desirable. And by the daughter of a man who was making a fortune in sugar, even though he was temporarily in jail!

Julia was both amazed and fearful. Her sixteen-year-old daughter — usually placid, more compliant than most girls, regarded by everyone as a lovable child — was suddenly a buxom witch. Flushed, bosom heaving, she wove promises with arms, fingers, neck, body — she prickled and goaded with words like sparks.

Did Mr. Eddy feel amorous or ambitious, or both?

Julia knew what she would tell Mr. Eddy after supper. She must be able to send Caroline to Aurora Academy, so that she could grow into an age of reason and not throw herself at a man she'd just met. But she guessed that the Clayton Sugar Company up Lost Man's River was a violent place. Would it be safe for William? Would she be *able* to manage it? And she would have to tell Thorstein, while she was with him in Washington, what she had decided. Was it right to hurt him as well as herself? If he took her decision as rejection and gave her up, could she stand a life without love? How bitter it would be if she had to go on for years with the best of life existing only in memory!

XVII

Music—it seemed that only music made it possible for Laura to live during the intervals between her social triumphs as wife of the magnate Arthur Wilkins, her amorous triumphs in Tom's arms, and her spiritual triumphs of being self-sufficient while he was in prison. Her life in music was more vivid than society's admiration or envy, and possibly more than what her aroused body tried to tell her but never quite did, no matter how desperate and violent it became. Her natural self lived in music—a creature of perfumes, bright colors and song, naked and embracing her lover on some deserted sea strand.

On a warm spring afternoon, almost a month after her lover was beaten and sent to prison, she arrived before the Episcopal Church in St. Vincent—"Wilkins's church." Her protégé Johann Mowrer, whom she'd attached to herself during a New York period, was to give an organ recital. Her carriage was shiny and black, the cushions from which she rose were of orchid-colored velvet, and she herself was clothed in the lightest and most delicate possible white velvet, with trimmings of handmade lace like vapors following a wind-torn cloud, and the old Negro driver, who was dressed in a cutaway coat and striped gray trousers and a tall silk hat, lowered the steps with a bow, so that she could float down in her delicate velvet and frothy lace, with her white parasol above her great white hat, which was trimmed with the same velvet and an egret plume, fold her parasol with a piquant click, and mount the steps of the church, which was a hybrid of Florida gingerbread and Viollet-le-Duc Gothic.

Oh, the flowers before the altar! And the hats of the ladies brilliant as the cannas! The pews held rows of undulating plumage as though the birds of the whole world had lighted and then, as the organ twittered, had found a common song.

Johann Mowrer was behind a red drape which screened him from the congregation, for he insisted that organ music should not be accompanied by awareness of the personal frailties of the performer. Poor Johann, with his haunted eyes and guilty slouch. He did have plenty of frailties. He struggled with drink, lived alone, was married to his art, admired Laura and joked with her.

A musician who was a Pan and a Moses and some coarse Negro bellowing on the waterfront! He came to tea and played waltzes on the piano with the tenderest of feeling, only to replay them in a manner that made fun of them and snort, "Filth!" A small man with a bald head, with something of the hawk and something of the snake in those incredible deep fierce eyes, with bags under them and hoods over them, he could glower one moment and simper the next, and then become — Laura had to hunt in her mind for what he did become…One among the endless stream of people who passed through the Saracen Room, including some wise people and a normal percentage of idiots, considering her wealth, was an ardent philosophy professor from Columbia University. He'd used the word Promethean in describing the colored folks. Johann Mowrer was Promethean, too. Was it possible for her to envy Johann on that account? Johann was master of a world she merely glimpsed. But by making Arthur present the church with this new organ she was the source of what he could do. That wonderful organ — with its vast range, with whatever the ear might absorb in quality of sound, in height and depth, in timbre and hollowness, in wood and brass, in strings and voices, in shouting and praying and cursing! She pulled and pushed stops too, but stops for a queen, not for a musician.

The twittering stopped. Johann had warmed up himself and the organ with a frivolous improvisation. The ladies examined the program with a pink rosebud on the cover — *Prelude…*

The first notes lay soft upon the air like feathers drawn across one's cheek, like the breath of sleep, yet a sleep that brings restless dreams — notes wandering with monotonous repetition in some wooden stop, in casual tryout of shepherd pipes in a lonely pasture — notes emerging from nothingness, from infinite mystery, into being, awakening what had never before been heard. Why was a plaintive high treble, single and clear in a flowing line, so evocative? Why was she discovering an ocean floor in her own nature which she had never apprehended before her affair with Tom, an ocean floor on which she reclined, drowned but not dead, while Tom was in prison? How was she so enlightened by Johann's music? Her conventional role as the magnate's wife was as foolish as the sentimental church music she'd known in girlhood. Johann satirized such music with hate and bawdiness. It was necessary to enter into this hate and bawdiness, to reject all weakness and sentimentality, before she could travel with Johann along that clear treble line, before she could rise, reborn, from her ocean floor.

After *Prelude* there was a pause. The birds roosting in the pews stirred, and there was another pause while all the birds realized that Johann Mowrer would not proceed until there was perfect quiet—for should a clarinet statement become a duet with rustling programs, clicking fans, nervous whispers, or the whush of itching bodies in uncomfortable clothes?

Then *Fugue*.

Who composed the fugue of her life? Not she, certainly. Destiny, no doubt. But she must understand. *Fugue* found concord in contradictory themes, showed that understanding was possible. If there was a chasm between the knowable and what she actually knew, she'd soar across it like Venus on a winged horse.

Arthur didn't know himself as she knew him. But something in Arthur remained hidden. Couldn't he see that by condoning her affair with Tom he'd obtained great satisfaction? Hadn't she become an ideal wife, a dazzling social success? Arthur could have other satisfactions if he lived in harmony with his own nature. Why couldn't he realize that a flowering of his own nature was all that she asked of him? She went to him not with demands but with gifts. He could act out with her the fantasies of his puritanical boyhood—and forget the bungalow on the lonely beach. They hadn't quarreled seriously since she scratched his face, and his apparent adjustment to their new relationship made her feel quite tender toward him. She'd be happy to take him to her bed and let him play with her breasts and enjoy any little thing he chose to do. She'd dance for him, if that's what he wanted. But he'd be terribly embarrassed and might even fly into one of his old rages if she made even the smallest gesture toward such charming sport.

It was sad when a man with Arthur's talent could not act in accordance with his most agreeable impulses. Was it obsession with money that made him so rigid? Since she was his wife, was every thought of her polluted with practical considerations?

With Tom, the theme of practical considerations combined in glory with the theme of their passion. There was a savage intercourse of spirit in the burgeoning empire of Lost Man's River and in their Cuban venture—there was still a perceptible bruise on her thigh from their last encounter before he went to prison...Ah! a tune in the flute, and another in a bass stop of string-like timbre, and soon so many of them she couldn't keep count, weaving like the tracery of branches outside the window, all logically growing from the same unseen root. It sounds as natural and inevitable as though even before Johann began to play it has been beating in the heart of music all the time, unheard and unknown...

...like what beats in her own heart now, more real than her pulse during the turbulent and queenly and numb exertions of her body. What does she remember and what does she make up?

Their steamer for Havana runs into a gale. The sailors stretch lifelines and order all passengers below. But she and Tom disregard regulations and promenade on the hurricane deck. During one wild pitch the steamer *Okefenoke* thrusts its blunt bow into a trough so that a comber thunders on the first deck and a spiraling offshoot of this smashed wave, several tons of green seawater, slops with a crash on the hurricane deck and races aft where she and Tom cling to the lifeline together and take the impact of this water, which for a few seconds is four or five feet deep. The torrent sweeps them off their feet and she loses her hold. Both are buried in brine and foam, and only Tom's arm around her waist and Tom's big tight fist on the lifeline hold her. If she were carried away and drowned, Tom would inherit all her investment in the sugar company, not because she has named him in any will but because there are no documents at all to show that she has given him the use of her money, which has been deposited in the Pelican Bank in Fort Harrison. She is jolted by the thought that he might let her go, or that they both might be swept away. Either way, the prospect seems strangely sweet rather than terrifying.

The *Okefenoke* shudders, the propeller grinds in the air for long seconds, the tons of water cascade off, and they run to the deck below. She laughs. He has a smiling glint in his blue eyes, with their carnal yellow glint.

"You might have become the sole owner of the Clayton Sugar Company," she remarks.

"That ain't what it's all about," he replies. There is no reproof in his tone. Dripping with salt water, surrounded by sailors who don't dare to reproach him, he is lordly—casual and just a bit mocking. Then the music of his flesh—his coarse skin with freckles on the shoulders, the stiff red-brown hairs, almost like horse hairs, on his chest and in the crotches of his heavy muscled reddish body, and the glorious lion mane she rubs between her breasts and over her belly. "Centaur! Beast! Shall I ride you? Or you me?"

The afternoon wears on toward six o'clock. Many of the birds droop and look pleadingly at the patroness of this recital. Will she start a movement to go home?

Not Laura!

More compositions, not even mentioned in the program with the pink rosebud. One can understand why. This pipe organ, not more than a mile from a salt lagoon, responds to changes in the humidity, so that Johann sometimes curses it and sometimes worships it. Today there is a climate for worship. But at last he seizes upon the whole afternoon's collection of themes and twines them again and again with his own variations and magic, so that a sunrise of hope and glory erupt, and Laura floats on the back of her winged horse toward an opening in the blue sky where her lover, smiling, his red hair and beard like copper in the sun, opens his arms.

Silence. And the special sadness that always accompanies the end of music.

Johann pokes his bald head over the top of the red curtain, his hawk's eyes glittering, and says gruffly, impersonally as though he is drugged, "This is all I'm going to play until after supper."

After supper indeed! says a flurry of hats. After four hours of organ music, who would come back for more?

Johann. Johann alone at his organ.

And Laura. Laura alone in her pew.

*

In Chokoloske, Joshua Washington Dale schooled himself to be less outspoken than he'd been when he and Joanna tended store in Olustee. At their time of life they couldn't stand being run out of town again. Also, business was good. The dock near the store made deliveries convenient, and they sold wholesale as well as retail. The area was booming. The great cause for which Joshua had endured constant fear of death during his young manhood became an unshared secret.

He felt old and helpless when Joanna talked about Amos Peters. What could he do about Amos Peters? He was no longer a captain. He had no soldiers for moving into the Clayton Sugar Company and fighting it out with the armed thugs who were employed there.

His prosperity and his weakness made him courteous even to customers he didn't like. One of these was Wheeler, who had his own business making rum out of unrefined sugar from Clayton's company, which was directly across Lost Man's River from his own cabin and distillery. He sold his product to bosses in the sugar company and perhaps because of this service was able to hold on to his little property. Some other settlers in the locality had moved or disappeared. Joshua himself took some of Wheeler's rum on consignment and sold it.

It was Wheeler who brought the news that reignited Joshua's dormant democratic principles, intolerance of human bondage, and consequent feelings of personal responsibility.

Wheeler was very large and fat, his feet always ached, and he sat in the one chair for customers as soon as he came into the store. Joshua bustled from shelf to bin to barrel to icehouse putting together his order.

"Some very tasty sugar-cured hams just come in," said Joshua, agreeably.

"Give you a bottle of rum for one," said Wheeler.

"No, no, I couldn't do that..." They haggled, pleasantly enough.

Mark Richardson came in the store. He needed rope for his sharpie, and Joshua served him. Serving a black man in the middle of a conversation between two white men made Wheeler frown, and he asked, in an extra-loud voice, "What was that you was saying?"

Joshua knew Wheeler had heard and was just demanding undivided attention. But he wasn't in business to point out people's mental incapacities. So he repeated, "I said I'd give you a ham for two bottles of your rum, or two hams for three bottles if you prefer. I can't get more than sixty-five cents a bottle for your rum, a dollar-twenty for a jug, and I have to make it worthwhile to bring in these hams. I have to pay for ice, too. I know you ain't going back up the river for a while and I'm glad I can make you comfortable for thinking it over while I get Mark his rope. Mark here is a busy man and has a growing family to look after, and his fishing boat he needs this rope for is his main means of support."

"I ain't got all day, neither," Wheeler growled.

"The rope is all I needs, Mr. Wheeler," said Mark. "I do preciate your patience while Joshua gets it for me."

They were all silent while Joshua measured the length Mark wanted, cut it from a large roll, handed it over, and took payment.

"You heard about Tom Clayton?" Wheeler asked.

Mark Richardson was walking toward the door, his rope draped over his shoulder, and he stopped.

Joshua Dale became curt—"Heard *what* about Tom Clayton?"

The storekeeper and his black friend stood like stumps, waiting for Wheeler's reply. He took his time, gloating over their undivided attention. They'd made him wait—let this persnickety storekeeper and this uppity nigger do the waiting now! He mopped his brow with a bandanna, put it in his pocket, and drawled, "Well—it happened two—no, almost three weeks back."

"What happened?"

"I'm mighty surprised you ain't heard."

"The pleasure of surprising me and Mark is all yours," said Joshua.

"You all going to have a hard time believing what I'm going to be telling you," said Wheeler.

Joshua and Mark waited.

Wheeler squirmed uncomfortably in the customer's chair.

"Seems like you're having a hard time spitting it out," said Joshua.

"I am—I am having a hard time," said Wheeler. "The fact is—Tom Clayton was arrested in Key Alva, and he's been shipped off to a prison farm in Georgia."

Both Joshua and Mark absorbed this news in silence, studying Wheeler. Joshua figured he hadn't really wanted to tell them, but he had trapped himself into doing it simply to get undivided attention—he was that foolish because of Mark getting his rope before Joshua settled with him what to do about hams and rum. Now he was worried that Tom Clayton might somehow hear about him spreading this news and wouldn't like it. Joshua became crusty—"How'd *you* hear about it?"

It was difficult to pin Wheeler down. Even though Tom Clayton was in jail, Wheeler had to appease his menacing spirit by boosting the Clayton Sugar Company. It was a terrible thing that a man like Tom Clayton, who was making fields of sugar cane out of wilderness and swamp, should become the victim of crazy circumstances, which Wheeler claimed he couldn't rightly describe because the truth of what happened wasn't clear.

He tried to change the subject by mentioning a man named McLevy, whom he delineated with a wealth of detail suggesting a much greater degree of sympathy than he would admit—McLevy, a sailor who'd come home from the sea to go up Lost Man's River and become a lost man himself—"Nobody's seen hide nor hair of him for more'n two years. There's nigger field hands in what's left of his cabin with the roof caved in on one end and the trees and brush dug up or yanked out and burned to clear for cane." What visions were stored behind Wheeler's wide and unblinking eyes? Was he speaking of McLevy or worrying about his own fate as he muttered, "God rest his soul!"

"Dammit, Wheeler!" cried Joshua, "I'm asking you a simple question: how'd you know about Tom Clayton being arrested and sent up to Georgia?"

It came out in bits and pieces: Long Algy, a boss at the Clayton Sugar Company, heard about what happened from Lawrence Eddy, the young fellow who ran Clayton's bank in Fort Harrison. Then he heard more, but not exactly the same story, from a "fat little nigger everybody calls Richard the Barber," a servant of the famous gunman Sanford Payne, who was living in the big new house up the river and sort of taking charge for the time being.

Then Wheeler spewed one additional piece of information with no anxiety at all, since it couldn't possibly be interpreted as a detraction of Tom Clayton: "Mr. Payne's little nigger told me Tom Clayton's got a wife somewhere in the northern part of the state, and she's coming down here to help out—"

"Julia Clayton's going to that hellhole?" Joshua exclaimed.

"I'm told she knows bookkeeping," said Wheeler, alarmed at Joshua's vehemence.

Joshua went to the back door and shouted, "Joanna! Can you stop what you're doing and come in the store?"

She replied and in about half a minute did come in, wiping her hands on her apron.

Mark Richardson hadn't been saying anything. He just sat still on the barrel, studying Wheeler, not showing in any way what he felt. But he said, "Good morning, Miz Joanna" in a tone that made Joanna Dale give him a sharp look and then become very serious.

Joshua took just one bottle of rum for a ham. Now that Wheeler had told what he would—perhaps not quite as much as he knew, perhaps more than he knew—Joshua was in a hurry to have him leave. After getting what Wheeler wanted, Joshua walked him out the door.

"We just learned what makes me hope we can find Amos," Mark said to Joanna.

As Joshua turned to his wife and to Mark, he could feel the hairs on the back of his neck prickle. He astonished himself. At his age, after so many years, the recent ones all taken up with peaceful business, was he sweating with fear, expecting a battle? smelling nervous horses on this gritty island where there were no horses? hearing a bugle and jubilee songs where there was no march for freedom? He became very quiet, sober—"Yes, Joanna, I hope we can find Amos. We have a lot to talk over. Bina ought to be here. What do you think, Mark? Was Wheeler telling us the truth?..."

XVIII

When Thorstein moved from St. Vincent to Madison, he expected that Julia would follow him within a month. Then, partly because Julia had little money and didn't want to be totally dependent on him, and partly because it was hard for her to give up her life and responsibilities at Richmond Plantation, the month became month after month and ultimately ten months. Their letters became more and more rich in detail as to what they were doing, feeling, and thinking. They were offhand, reflective and even philosophical. It seemed that nothing was withheld. The letters added a dimension in how they knew each other. There was a certain desperation in the intimacy of the letters, reflecting loneliness and the unexpressed dread of both of them that they might lose each other.

For the first time in his life, Thorstein knew constant depression, which he took pains in his letters to conceal. He had to reject the superstition that a malign fate was depriving him of his only monogamous kind of love as a punishment for his philandering.

But he was painfully enthralled by the spirit and beauty of women who were not Julia, and he had a disastrous affair with the wife of a dean at the university. She responded to him because she hated the dean and because he talked to her without condescension—she had brains, grace, and a subtle sensibility. They'd met on weekday afternoons at a lakeside cabin that was occupied only on Sundays during the winter. For years he'd carried wherever he went a small satchel that contained notes on research, drafts of writing, and books. In Madison, the satchel also contained letters from Julia. At the lakeside cabin he messed up some papers, and the dean's wife discovered Julia's letters. She raged—"Damn you! Damn you! Damn you!" Her sarcasm blazed—did he find love by correspondence better than love in bed? "What kind of a man are you?" she demanded. Then she sobbed in undisguised agony—"I can't ever see you again! I can't even look at you again!"

He'd just stood like a post as she stormed, naked in the frigid cabin, unaware for some time that he was shivering. He'd never known such remorse and shame. She'd regarded him as her property in reaction to how she herself was regarded in her dismal marriage, but he couldn't help recognizing that this explanation of her feelings was a thick-skinned violation of her spirit, a way of shedding responsibility for the pain he'd inflicted.

He'd never felt so guilty after an affair. Had sex turned him into some kind of monster? How had he begun an affair that had to end in such cruelty? He loathed himself for his insensitivity, for his complacent lack of feeling, for his inability to share the suffering of the woman.

But during the journey from Madison, Wisconsin, to Washington, D.C., with four changes of trains, shunning the conversation of strangers, alone with the kalacking of wheels, Thorstein got rid of his guilt and shame. He was about to be with Julia again! Now that Richmond Plantation was being sold, they'd have to figure out some way of living so that they could see each other every day. Memories of Julia persisted and obsessed him, and he marveled at how quickly memories of other women faded. He'd never again become the careless lover he'd once been. His dependence on one woman was somewhat terrifying!

On the Monday after Palm Sunday he arrived in Washington a little after six in the morning after a night on a sleeper. Julia's train was scheduled to come in at a quarter to eight.

They'd booked separate rooms in the Willard Hotel. He'd been to Washington once, and it was his choice. He liked the bustle of politicians and lobbyists. But the city was expensive. The rooms cost thirty dollars a night. There was news of hotel detectives harassing indiscreet lovers. So they were making a concession to presumptive morality and taking two rooms instead of one. He registered, went to his room, and was discomforted by its false sumptuousness. A plain bedroom on the Florida frontier, with the walls unplastered and the birds singing outside, would be more suitable.

Then he walked back to the station to meet Julia. He felt buoyant. Trees were leaved out in fresh green, and occasional tulips bloomed in little squares of earth before row houses. The streets were noisy with cheerful farm wagons.

The railroad station was an immense neo-Gothic structure of granite and brick built to last for centuries. But already there was talk of demolishing it because it was located in the wrong place. The tracks crossed main avenues and there were accidents. Also, the style of the building clashed with the dream of classical empire embodied in the Capitol and the White House. So it wouldn't do. Great corporations and governments indulged in capricious and conspicuous consumption just as individuals did. The Washington railroad station might be a cautionary paradigm. It seemed auspicious that he had a useful thought for his writing as he was about to meet Julia.

But he was almost in a panic when the train that should be bringing her rumbled in. What if for some reason—some botch of connections, some Florida catastrophe, or even a failure of nerve—she hadn't come? What would happen to her? Would his own life crumble? Could he go on with his great task? Could he teach any more? Could he live like a sexless monk?

Then, just as the train finally stopped, with a clanking of brakes and locking of wheels, she appeared, holding her long skirt and handbag with one hand and with the other swinging herself down from the high step. Far down the platform her grace was unmistakable.

He ran toward her. She was wearing the same straw hat she'd worn when they'd met for the last time before parting almost a year ago in St. Vincent. She saw him a second later than he'd seen her, and she picked up her skirt with both hands to run toward him a few steps before he could embrace her. He had an instant's sight of her face he'd never forget—her eyes wide and smiling, her mouth a little open for his kiss. She smelled of soot, not jessamine!

"We could go to breakfast," he said, uncertain.

"Oh no, I want to come to you in your room."

He gave her the number.

She smiled, was serious, and said, "It's been sinful how I've kept myself from you all these months."

He found a hack so that they could move her trunk to the hotel. During the short ride she said, "Something's happened and I can get more money. It will make it easier for me to move and make it better for you. I'll be able to send Caroline to Aurora Academy. I've been worried–"

He interrupted, "I hope there's no more delay—"

"Oh no—or not much anyway—"

She was diverted because the hack was being guided among wagons and other hacks to the curb before the Willard Hotel. "I'll tell you all about it," she said, smiling.

In his posh and depersonalized hotel room, waiting for her, he was aware of loneliness and then was amused at himself because he could bear to recognize this feeling, now that he would see her in a few minutes.

But a soft knocking on his door was like rain after a drought. As he opened she stood still for quite a long moment, her eyes smiling and hungering as she took in his face. Her hair was darkened and damp—she'd bathed, dried herself hurriedly, and changed into a summery dress with a pattern of small blue and pink flowers. She rushed to him.

It was she who had to turn, close the door, and turn the key. She'd brought her handbag, and with an odd kind of qualm she put it on the ornate bureau. Then she was strangely passive, her arms around him in a trust that was scarcely sexual, in a child's kind of embrace.

He was surprised. During the many months of lovemaking at either Richmond Plantation or the Alhambra Hotel, she'd become exuberant, open about her desire. He sensed something like fright and thought that the months apart had been even worse for her than for him. As during the first time they'd made love, under the pines, she seemed merely to be giving herself, as though this was the most she could hope for as a woman. He knew well this state of mind, which at times for sober reflection he attributed to the bleak, savage, ancient tradition of regarding women as things, as property—a tradition that bamboozled women themselves as political demagoguery duped voters. That she could regress to this abasement of herself was intolerably sad and touching. His own desire became tuned to what he sensed, to what he felt in the backward tilt of her head as he kissed the fluttering pulse in her throat.

As her hands went limp on his shoulders, he undid the buttons on the back of her dress, turned her, put his right hand under her dress and chemise—she wore no corset—and caressed first one breast and then the other. Her nipples stood out hard in his fingers and she breathed so heavily she was actually sighing, and she gave a soft cry. How could this simple love-play be so intense? Had she been subjected to a pain he couldn't comprehend, from some wound more severe than what he attributed to the galling loneliness for both of them in being apart for so long? The sheer wonder of her controlled his caresses. But a thought bobbled on the surface of his passion—his own sexual life had been childish—he'd been a poor thing as a man to have become thirty-eight years old before he could feel as he did at that moment. He'd heard that robins mated for life and shied away from all others. Miraculous, if true.

They stood for some time, his hand upon her breasts. Her breathing set a rhythm for them — they had half a lifetime ahead of them. This was a kind of second wedding. She pressed her hands against his through the fabric of her loosened dress. She had to keep his hand, to prolong this healing of what had wounded her.

The morning sun passed the edge of their one window frame and streamed on them. Reflected in the mirror over the bureau, her face was confident, trusting, dazzling. Her eyes met his in the mirror and widened. When he kissed the coil on top of her head, she took out hairpins, her eyes never straying from his, and slowly and deliberately undid her hair. The concentration of their emotions was almost frightening, as though they were aware for the first time that some internal rupture had been bleeding. She took his hand from her breasts, turned to press herself against him, moved the hand along her side and hip to invite other caresses, and whispered, "My dear." She threw her arms around him in her first strong hug and then her breath, warm and tremulous, was on his face as she took off his necktie and unbuttoned his shirt. She pressed her face against his bare chest in a long embrace and then spoke so softly he could barely hear her, as though a regular speaking voice would be dangerous. Her face was radiant, but she was not exactly smiling — "My dear, my dear, do you suppose we could lie side by side on this bed, without these dismal clothes?"

Her words, her apparent need to utter them, and a humble quality in the soft tone of her voice suggested that she felt unworthy of their lovemaking — she had to ask! He was shocked, felt more than ever driven to revive her from whatever had injured her during their months apart, and caught her up in a long and passionate kiss. She responded but then stood motionless, her eyes closed and her arms raised, as he removed her dress. He kissed the carnal hair under her arm which had the same golden color as the hair on her head. Time and desire seemed to have set her free at last — she gave a soft laugh and began to caress him with the openhearted delight of their past lovemaking. And no more worrisome thoughts for him!

The sun moved from east to west, and the beam through their window moved from west to east.

It was late afternoon before she could say, "I started to tell you how I can get more money so I can settle in Madison, and do it without worrying you—"

"Nothing will worry me when you're in Madison."

"Well, I want to be practical and do what's best for you, for both of us, really. I have to think about Caroline and William, and I don't want us to become a burden—"

He told her that she was a burden for him as long as she remained in Florida. Worrying about her, wanting her near him every day, loving her from an ugly distance, he couldn't even think straight—he couldn't get on with his work. He could explicate the culture of the gilded age as no one else could. He must finish a new expansion of *Business Combinations*, in which he was exposing in new ways the shams in generally accepted assumptions that justice and morality were inherent in existing property relationships. For his sake, so that he could get on with his great work, she must take from his shoulders the terrible burden of their separation—she must come immediately from Olustee to Madison, and of course bring along Caroline and William. He inquired about Caroline and especially William, who might soon be entered as a student in the university. William gave her a good excuse for coming to Madison, if she ever needed one! They would see each other every day! Against his better nature—and hers too, since God knows it was revolting that they should have to pretend anything—he was prepared to be reasonably discreet until she got her divorce and they could marry. *Marry*? Could he stand it? Could *she* stand it? "Will you respect me after we become institutionalized? After all I've written to show up marriage as the economic cage it is, especially for women! Oh Julia, I'm becoming the most disgusting and lily-livered kind of academic—I blink at my own insights!"

She kissed him, laughing.

Then he talked about a four-bedroom house he might rent for her, and about a lawyer who could arrange a quiet divorce.

They were dressing so that they could go out for supper, and they were both yeasty. She mentioned their need for money but as though they had only to pick it off trees, like oranges. How much *was* the rent of the four-bedroom house? And how about the lawyer's fee, his own board and room, his salary? She *must* send Caroline to Aurora Academy, where she and Esther had such good years. Could they afford it?

It was clear they'd have to scrimp.

"I haven't told you how I can get the money we need," she said, smiling. "Married or not, I've had some good luck so I won't be stuck in any economic cage! Or let you be stuck in one either!"

He was moved by her spirit but didn't expect that her presumed good luck would make much difference. They would be poor, he'd grown up poor, if he hadn't been poor he wouldn't have acquired the wisdom to see through the elaborate ideological screen that rationalized a system in behalf of the wealthy. Being poor was life at its best in a way. Being poor was bitter and real. So the hardship of poverty, and any futile attempt by Julia to deal with it, was best faced with a joke—"Well, my darling, I hope that you will support me in a style to which I've never been accustomed!"

She smiled but went on, brightly and at the same time seriously, "A strange thing has happened—Tom's in jail." She told what Lawrence Eddy had told her.

She smiled at his astonishment and patiently answered his questions. She had to go over some details two or three times, especially those concerning the likely responsibility of the magnate Arthur Wilkins for what had happened. At last it became obvious that the power of attorney might give Julia a chance to get some money, and also that taking advantage of this power would delay again her coming to Madison. This made him skeptical about the whole proposition and no longer able to joke—"There must be some limit on how you use this power of attorney to get money just for yourself."

"Yes, there is, but not much," she said. "I've demanded a salary as manager, Lawrence Eddy has passed on my demand to Tom in his Georgia prison, and he's agreed. If he didn't agree, I wouldn't take the position, and he knows it!"

"Why does he need you so much?"

She told how and why he'd wanted her to audit, even before he went to jail. "He knows his sugar company will be mismanaged and probably robbed blind if somebody reliable doesn't look after it. He thinks I'm reliable." She gave a harsh and angry laugh he'd never heard before. It startled him.

He knew that she'd made up her mind to become the manager of this sugar company and that he could never dissuade her. He sensed a rage behind her determination, and he felt ashamed that he lived in the presumably dignified austerity that was the accepted standard for college professors, so that extra money became so important for her, in fact for both of them. "This cannot be for long, Julia—" he was both pleading and commanding. "It's no life for us apart, and in no time at all you'll have to choose between money and life."

"There's no need for me to be greedy," she said. "I don't expect to be a sugar company manager for more than two months. Don't worry, my dear—I'll choose life."

He was skeptical, feared that in some unpredictable way she'd be trapped, but didn't want to disparage her intention. "How do you know you won't be cheated?" he asked. "How can you depend on him to keep paying you what you demand?" He couldn't refer to her husband by name.

She was sitting on the edge of the bed, busy with the long laces of her shoes. "I've insisted on an advance, and I've got it," she said. "My handbag's on that bureau, dear. Open it—please, you will see—take out the money—"

He could only do as she asked. He took out a thick roll of bills.

"There's over six hundred dollars there," she said, "more than I've ever had just for myself in a whole year of work at Richmond Plantation. It came to me out of the Clayton Sugar Company's account in the Pelican Bank in Fort Harrison. Lawrence Eddy sent it to me in a little box, by parcel post, because I wrote to him I had to have it. Believe me, I won't be victimized by Tom Clayton!"

There was a savagery in her tone that reflected something more than the anticipated endurance of another two months apart. Taking the sugar company's money seemed to express rage at her legal and long-departed husband. It was a torment that Julia should still have any kind of emotional involvement with Tom Clayton, even rage, and not just wipe him out of her life.

He seized the handbag in order to replace the roll of bills and was surprised by its weight. With automatic concern as well as curiosity, he reached inside and drew out a large revolver—"My God, Julia, what are you doing with *this*?"

She stopped lacing her shoe and covered her face with her hands.

He put the revolver on the bureau, sat beside her on the bed, and put his arm around her—"My darling, really—"

She spoke softly through her hands, still over her face—"I was afraid of Tom until he went to prison, and in a way I'm still afraid—"

"You had this gun—for *him*?" The accumulation of her responses to him, and to something hidden in her own mind, all through the morning and afternoon, suddenly acquired a new and spine-chilling meaning. He experienced again, and as a whole, her first insecurity in their lovemaking—the suggestions that she was injured not only by their separation but also by something else—her apparent feeling, contrary to what he had known in her, that her body was unworthy, that lovemaking must be healing as well as expression, along with need—an anger at Tom Clayton she'd never talked about or expressed in any way—and her raging satisfaction in taking the Clayton Sugar Company's money not only to make their own lives together easier but also because taking it was a way of striking back at her legal husband. Then, there was the nature of Tom Clayton, whom he'd never known. But in view of Clayton's inability to appreciate and love Julia, he must be perverted even beyond the norm! From all that Thorstein suspected about the man, it would be like him to assert the ultimate property right of a husband over the body of his legal wife. "Julia, Julia, look at me, please," he said. "Has Tom Clayton attacked you?"

But she wouldn't look at him—or reply. She wept, she had never wept before in his presence, and he felt a rush of tears in his own eyes. He put his arms around her, and after a time she returned his embrace, burying her face on his chest. Then, after more time, she was able to look at him. She'd stopped crying, and with a delicate finger she wiped tears from his face.

He sprang up, went to the bureau, seized the gun, and put it in his handy little satchel. He felt as though he were being throttled, and it was hard to speak—"This is for *me*, not you! Where is this prison in Georgia?"

She followed him and grasped his face with both hands so that their eyes locked—"No no no! It's impossible, and I couldn't bear if anything should happen to you!"

He banged his fists on the wall.

She turned to the bureau, reached in his satchel, took out the heavy revolver, and put it back in her handbag. Her face was blanched, her words inexorable and fierce—"This gun is for me, not you. I don't expect ever to see Tom Clayton again. But if it happens that I do see him, I'm going to be prepared."

After such flagellation by what had happened along with such anxieties and hopes about what might happen, how could four more days in Washington become a love idyll? Yet, it had to be. Circumstances they hadn't been strong enough to control had kept them apart before—what unforeseen disaster might keep them apart again? Would there be some inescapable predicament so that they'd never see each other after these four days? Besides making love in their impersonally elaborate rooms, eating together in lush dining rooms—for Julia had plenty of money from the Clayton Sugar Company—they strolled, almost unseeing, talking and talking and talking, through insensate streets, parks, government buildings. What did these architectural recollections of the Roman empire, these row houses suggesting exclusion and a worried respectability, these deifications in marble and bronze of politicians and warriors, have to do with them?

XIX

Richmond Plantation was sold. Julia moved out in May two weeks before the new owner would take possession. She distributed the remaining cash from her own earnings to matriarchs of families who had been with the Richmonds for three generations. There was a lot of weeping. Some families, including the Johnsons, would stay put, tempting fate with the new owner. Others took a look at his face — "Like he a lizard," somebody said — and traveled.

Julia stored a few valued possessions in a corner of the Reverend Blanding's shed previously taken up by the laths that had been used as markers for the graves of the Myrtle victims.

Caroline went to Aurora Academy for the remainder of the school year. She knew that the loss of Richmond Plantation meant that her future would be very different from what she had expected, but she felt incapable of doing anything about it and so became apathetic, with occasional bursts of misdirected anger. She was sullen about going to Aurora Academy. Julia was distressed. After Caroline made new friends among young women her own age, and discovered how exciting study could be, would she wake up? Would she become enthralled by finding unexpected powers in her own mind?

Julia wrote to Mr. Sanford Payne, General Manager, that the company's steam launch *Laura* must be at the pier in Payhokee on May 14 to transport her son William and herself to the new mansion on Lost Man's River, which must be readied for her arrival. She trusted that Sanford didn't know much about her actual relationship with her legal husband, that in spite of the apparent separation he would assume that whatever she wanted would probably be agreeable to Tom. She was not wrong — he sent the launch.

Her days with Thorstein in Washington made her feel specially courageous and clearheaded. She felt sure she understood Tom. In raping her body Tom thought that he'd raped her will too, that she'd do just what he wanted her to do, that she'd take meticulous care of his company during his absence, in effect even manage it since Sanford Payne was obviously not the kind of man who could, regardless of his title as general manager. For Tom, raping her body fulfilled a law of nature. He couldn't imagine that she might flout it.

*

Mr. Benjamin Burlitt, the warden of the prison farm in Georgia and brother of Mr. Edward Burlitt, the sheriff in Key Alva, always treated Mr. Thomas Ewell Clayton with punctilious courtesy. He hoped for money to obtain Mr. Clayton's release, of which he might keep a reasonable percentage as compensation for his time and trouble.

Mr. Clayton was sensible about his situation. He accepted the standard gray prison garb and did a little work in the fields, under no obligation but just enough to ease his restlessness. He lived in a cabin by himself and prepared his own victuals, which were purchased and brought to him by a guard, using money provided by Mr. Clayton's banker in Fort Harrison. Mr. Benjamin Burlitt took it for granted that a white man of Mr. Clayton's standing couldn't be expected to mix with niggers, and doing right by him as much as was proper under the circumstances was a natural way of smoothing a business transaction, which was being handled by his brother Edward in Key Alva and a Captain Van Bibber who worked for the Pamlico and Gulf Railroad, with a lawyer named Smallstock and the young banker Lawrence Eddy representing Mr. Clayton.

The warden was eager to have any hint of progress in these negotiations. So he summoned his prisoner to the living room of his neat frame house and gave him a lemonade—the warden was a teetotaler. Then, trying to show polite disinterest, he handed over two letters, one postmarked Fort Harrison and the other St. Vincent. The envelope from Fort Harrison was thick and no doubt contained cash for Mr. Clayton's victuals. But what party in St. Vincent was interested in Mr. Clayton? Mr. Burlitt made pleasant conversation—"It be hot as the devil's frying pan, and I hope your well ain't going dry."

"No, it ain't, and I do appreciate your concern, Mr. Burlitt."

There was an unsmiling formality in these courtesies. Regardless of the special treatment for this prisoner, there were guards with rifles and an understanding that they'd shoot, probably in the legs, if Mr. Clayton attempted escape. He was an investment that had to be protected.

"You don't have to go out in the fields at all unless you be so minded," Burlitt went on. "August ain't no time for a white man under the blazing sun."

Mr. Clayton rumbled, in quite a friendly way, "I'll just douse myself with well water and read these letters."

He knew the handwriting on the envelope of the letter from St. Vincent. It was Laura's. He sprawled in a hammock slung in shade between two live oaks next to his cabin, and read. She wrote that she had sold a painting to raise more money for his ransom, and she had ordered Eddy and Van Bibber to bribe the sheriff, the warden and also a judge in Key Alva so that he could be freed. Also, she reported that Arthur was fixing the legislature so that Florida would have a law making divorce possible, a law drafted just so he could get rid of her, not that she wouldn't be the happiest woman in the world to get rid of him!

Tom put the letter in the hammock and went into the cabin for whiskey, which he mixed with well water in a large tumbler, doused himself with a bucket, and went back to the hammock. His first thought about a divorce for Laura was that she probably wouldn't have funds for making their sugar business expand. Then he realized that he didn't care very much. His greatest satisfaction in life couldn't be measured with money. Years ago he'd put it right, and in a way that brought him and Laura together, in the Ponce de Leon Room of the Alhambra Hotel: *There are people like mules and people like monkeys and like oxen*...Naked, sprawled in his hammock again, sweating, drinking whiskey and water without effect, he couldn't help thinking that Arthur Wilkins had put a ring in his nose and was yanking him as he chose.

Reading on, Tom learned that Laura had talked with Clyde Dingell, who was doing more and more legal work for Arthur, that she had got him to feel gay and confidential, and that he admitted Arthur hadn't changed the will in which he left almost everything to her.

All alone, in his cabin shaded by two oaks in the middle of broad cotton fields, Tom roared with laughter. It was too much! First he thought of Laura *without* money and then, only seconds later of Laura *with* money, and he was crazy for her both ways. But better with money, since that was what might be! Laura didn't need to suggest what should happen to Arthur before he got around to changing his will! She wrote:

"That man cannot tear me so easy out of his measly little mind and heart."

That Laura had not given him up during the past year, that she kept scheming to get him out, that she seemed to think of him as a part of herself, seemed so strange, such a new kind of experience in his life, that he said aloud to himself — who else was there to talk to? — "She's crazy!" She was thinking in terms of what should be and not in terms of what was. He wrote a brief reply to her letter, concluding:

> When I am out of here I will do for you and you will do for me and then we will both do in a different way for that rascal Arthur.
>
> Yours forever
Tom

*

In September, the sugar company's bank account showed a new deposit of $15,000, and Julia had seen no check for that amount. Where had the money come from? She went to Fort Harrison and talked with Lawrence Eddy at the Pelican Bank.

"Miz Wilkins sent this money," he said.

"Miz Wilkins?"

"She wants us to have enough cash on hand so we can ransom Mr. Clayton right off."

"Perhaps we won't have to borrow after all," Julia responded. She spoke in a business-like fashion, but she could feel her face flush. She and Thorstein had been separated longer than she had predicted, and she was desperate about ending this toil for the sugar company. But she had taken on humane as well as financial responsibilities that she couldn't just drop.

Lawrence, astute, was aware of her emotional reaction but seemed to regard it as due to her feelings about Laura Wilkins. He went on, "Miz Wilkins wrote in the letter with her check that what's been done with Mr. Clayton is worse than the devastation in Cuba. She wrote like she'd real mad. She put it that Mr. Clayton is a king of men the way a lion is king of beasts and it's a shame he ain't doing what he wants to do."

"If she'd sent the money straight to me, I'd've kept things straight on the company books," said Julia.

"Oh, she couldn't've sent the money to you," said Lawrence. "She don't know you."

"That's so," said Julia. The queenly Mrs. Wilkins could never have unburdened herself to her lover's dispensable wife as she had to this sympathetic young banker.

Lawrence continued, "I don't know but maybe you know how much Miz Wilkins has invested in the sugar company. It may be Mr. Clayton and Miz Wilkins know but they ain't telling me or nobody far's I know. Do *your* books show who put in what?"

"No."

Lawrence grinned. This irregularity contributed to the adventurous climate in which the Clayton Sugar Company operated.

By no coincidence, Julia felt sure, Lawrence bought a large new house in Fort Harrison. Since he was the only person who handled and seemed likely to know how much Laura Wilkins thought she was depositing in the company's account, he'd obviously skimmed off what he needed to make the purchase.

After church on the first Sunday in January, he showed Julia and William through the freshly painted empty rooms and asked advice about furnishings. Perhaps he'd skimmed off enough for furnishings, too. Regardless of how busy he seemed to be with trying to negotiate the ransom, no doubt he was actually happy to keep Tom where he was for a while so that he might continue to dip his greedy fingers in the ransom money, as opportunities arose.

"You're an extremely provident young man, Mr. Lawrence," Julia observed, careful to keep any ironical inflection out of her voice.

As Julia had more years than Lawrence, Lawrence had more years than William. He gave William a playful punch in the biceps—"A man wants to make something of hisself can't go on living in a boarding house. Ain't that so?"

"I guess so," William mumbled.

"You must have been saving your money for years to buy this house," said Julia.

Lawrence laughed and even slapped his thigh. Then he declared that both the banking business and the sugar business were good and that her salary as auditor should be raised to $400 a month. He was buying her collusion.

She agreed, surprised at her own corruption. To hell with Tom's business!

*

At six o'clock in the morning, in the office of the Clayton Sugar Company up Lost Man's River, Julia worked with Obadiah Giles at calculating the previous month's retained earnings. The office was about a hundred yards from the mansion in a three-room bungalow—an anteroom; the office for the president, now occupied by Julia and by Sanford Payne when he was so minded; and a living/bedroom for Obadiah Giles, so that he could serve as watchman as well as bookkeeper. At ten o'clock Obadiah had a headache, retired to his room, and drank rum.

Julia heard the bottle clatter as he kicked it under his bed, and then his rattling snores. She went to Obadiah's room, looked at him for a moment, and gave up. There was a nauseating smell, probably from insects and possibly scorpions which had crawled into the empty bottles under Mr. Giles's bed and died there.

As usual, Julia had her main meal of the day at noon. She sat at one end of the long table in the mansion's huge dining room, with Sanford Payne on her right hand and William on her left. Sarah the cook served, silent and morose as always.

"Mr. Giles is drunk again and I can't catch up with what ought to be done," Julia complained. "I keep getting bills for what was bought before I came here. There are still some receipts and unpaid bills all mixed up in boxes and drawers. Mr. Giles just doesn't have the get-up-and-get to file them right and mice have got at some."

"You need a good cat," said the general manager.

"Wouldn't it be nice, Mr. Payne," she went on, "if you could meet up with Tom when he gets out of prison and tell him just how the company is doing? Wouldn't you be most gratified, as general manager, if you could show him figures and tell him his company has done even better than before he was sent up?"

Her words touched Sanford Payne in a way she hadn't expected. "Aw Miz Clayton," he exclaimed, "I miss Tom. He's the best old friend a man could ever have. And I feel particular bad because it was something I done

I oughtn't to've done that gave that Sheriff Burlitt and some of his boys in Key Alva an excuse to get their hands on Tom and lock him up and then send him to Georgia. Don't ask me to tell you what I done Miz Clayton but I never been more sorry about anything. If you could please do me a favor Miz Clayton and tell Tom when you write to him how sorry I am."

"You and Tom know each other well enough so he must understand how you feel," she said. Sanford had seen her in the office writing a letter to Thorstein and must have assumed she was writing to Tom.

"I ain't much for writing or I'd tell him myself. If you'd please write for me I'd feel real peaceable. Seems like I can't do nothing nights but lie up in bed hearing the singing of the mosquitoes and it ain't nothing ought to worry me 'cause I make Richard go round the room every day and if there was a mosquito in the room I'd give him what-for. And I get to thinking about all the things could happen to Tom. They're holding Tom in a little old wooden cabin. Suppose somebody nailed the door shut and set it afire with Tom inside. I can't tell you, Miz Clayton, how many times I worked hard to keep from thinking about Tom on fire. And Tom's a proud man, Miz Clayton. Suppose he answered back to some guard. There's guards as soon shoot a man as spit. And there's diseases—"

Julia interrupted—"We're doing everything we can. We don't want to bankrupt the company in paying for Tom's release. He wouldn't want that."

Gray Man couldn't see through this humbug. His lifeless eyes were focused on how Tom might die.

"You're such a good friend to Tom," she went on, sentimentally. This notorious gunman was seeing in her a kind of mother, and she was encouraging this delusion. It was a hoax that had already been useful. When she doled out silver dollars to the bosses on paydays, he wore two revolvers as he stood behind her. "You're a very sensitive man, Sanford—oh yes you are! I'm surprised now we've come to know each other better how very sensitive you are!"

"I don't know, Miz Clayton—I'm all burned up inside."

Her association with Sanford Payne had begun as cold-blooded and self-serving sham, but with time she'd become uneasy and concerned about his strange impulses that made him alternately brutal and icily playful with his obsequious and revolting servant Richard the Barber, alternately deathlike with self-disgust and then agog with renewal of himself as the immaculate and fearsome Gray Man. His suffering was palpable, and she pitied him even while he horrified her. She sensed a secret shame far more agonizing than his worry about Tom, a shame that had nothing to do with guilt for killing people. He was proud of that, as the notches on his gun showed! What was it that burned him up inside, as he'd said? What gave him the hate that fired up his achievement as a gunman?

She put her hand on his arm, and although he shrank away from her she believed he was moved. "You must always tell me how you feel, Sanford. I do respect you and I do appreciate your concern for Tom and how you protect me. I can see this has been your main responsibility here, and with the kind of dangerous men who've been taken on here—oh I can see the kind of men they are—I know how much Tom needed a loyal and brave friend like you..."

She worked on him intuitively, without plan. He responded by agreeing to fire Obadiah Giles—not realizing, of course, that Julia, with sole oversight of the company books, might fix them to suit her own purpose. She also prevailed on Sanford to fire one of the most brutal bosses—not because he was brutal but because he had passed out with drink while a black man thrashed around with a hammer in the mill and broke a casting. Sanford had to draw his gun in order to get rid of this boss.

Oh God, the mixed-up meanings and motives in her relationship with Sanford Payne! Where did hypocrisy end and openheartedness begin?

*

On a balmy day in October, after Julia completed business at the bank in Fort Harrison, she had the launch *Laura* tie up at the Chokoloske dock so that she could visit Joanna and Joshua Dale.

The store, *Joshua Washington Dale—General Merchandise*, looked almost the same as it once did in Olustee. Julia recalled how Joshua and Mark Richardson had dismantled it and sorted the lumber for shipment, and she had the thought that in a manner of speaking she too had been dismantled, shipped, and made over.

Joanna was sitting in a rocking chair on the porch. Her hair was whiter. After a moment of bewilderment she stood up—"Why—Julia Clayton!"

"Yes, it's me, Joanna."

They embraced.

Joanna was emotional—"For a long time—it's almost three years ain't it?—I never hoped to see you again. Then I heard you're right up the river and I worried it was easier for you to go there than come out."

"I went for what seems to me a good reason, and I can come out whenever I want to."

"I hope you can. My! You're all dressed up!"

Julia was wearing her starched white shirtwaist. Joanna was wearing a housedress and apron, and she was barefoot.

"I'm here only because Tom's in prison," Julia said. "He and I don't get along, as you know, but he figures I'm the only human being can run his company without stealing while he's put away. That's the long and short of it."

"Rest yourself," said Joanna, nodding toward another chair.

"Where's your good man?" asked Julia.

"Out back somewheres. Josh-u-ah!" shouted Joanna.

They listened and heard only some children's voices from among the shanties and cabins of Chokoloske.

"He'll be around," said Joanna.

"I haven't been to see you before because I'm ashamed I can't find Amos Peters," said Julia. She described her position in the big company up Lost Man's River—her oversight of money but only a peek at what was going on in the fields of cane and in the swamps or on the hammocks that were being ditched, cleared and ploughed for more fields. "I thought I might find Amos Peters when I agreed to work for the company, but it's not at all like what I expected—"

She didn't continue because Joshua came out on the porch. He didn't look quite as she remembered him. He was still thin and wiry, and his fierce eyes hadn't changed. But he staggered and his hand shook as he clutched the post of the porch for support. Had he had a stroke? She stood up—"How do you do, Mr. Dale. Won't you sit with us? I've been taking your chair."

He made a gesture that commanded her to sit again and said, "I never thought I'd see you here, Miz Clayton."

Joanna was angry—"That ain't no way to say hello to Julia after all these years. You're a hard man, Joshua. She don't have no connection with Tom Clayton except doing what she can up the river while he's in prison, and she's trying to find Amos."

"Are you going to find him?" he demanded, harshly.

Julia sat. Must she be subjected to this? She responded coldly—"I hope so but I can't promise." She went on with what she had started to tell Joanna. There were sixteen bosses, the worst kind of men hiding out from the law for reasons she never dared to discuss, men who on paydays got silver dollars they were supposed to share with their work crews but no doubt rarely did. She'd withheld pay from one boss who she believed had paid a man with a bullet even though other bosses, grinning at her, swore he hadn't. Sanford Payne had stood by her with his guns while she denounced the man, and although Sanford apparently had instructions from Tom Clayton to protect her so that she could do her honest bookkeeping, she had some question in her mind about how long the protection would last. In accusing a man of murder she was going beyond bookkeeping! Nobody could answer questions about Amos. The bosses didn't know the names of most of the black people and they thought it was a big joke that she should ask about some boy called Amos. They couldn't even tell her how many were doing the work. She guessed it was about two hundred. She had no horse and buggy for going miles and miles, the crews were constantly moved about to different jobs in different areas, she didn't remember what Amos looked like and wouldn't recognize him if she saw him, and Sanford Payne had warned her against going out in the fields at all because some boss who didn't like what she was doing might hide in the cane and shoot at her, and nobody would ever know who had done it. Sanford also kept William from going in the fields because her offenses against the old way of operating the Clayton Sugar Company might be charged against her son. So William hunted, fished, and collected botanical specimens in the primeval swamps.

Why was she explaining to the Dales? She wasn't beholden. Was it because she hadn't seen Thorstein for months?

Joanna's responses were cryptic—"Is that so?...I declare!"

Joshua was silent, probably suspicious, perhaps hostile.

Julia exploded, appealing and defiant at the same time—"I'm telling you what it's like up the river, Joshua Dale, because you and Joanna are the only people I still know who were with me in Olustee when we went to our minister's cornfield to honor and hold a service for all the innocent folks who died in Myrtle. We were together then and that makes us kin. I feel you're kin too, Joshua Dale, the same as Joanna, even though you don't seem to trust me because of what Tom Clayton's done. I know Tom Clayton even better than you do, and I can believe anything about him! I know you think he somehow started the worst killing in Myrtle, and from what I know now about Tom Clayton he probably did. I know you think he had something to do with killing Joseph Rourke, and although he was home with me at the time and Sanford Payne was at Whitaker's place, I've come to agree with you, just from a feeling in my bones and still not knowing just how it was arranged. I know things about Tom Clayton I won't talk about, but the worst is what's going on up Lost Man's River and you know something about that. I do what I can but I can't entirely stop it. Believe me I'm in no bed of roses, but for me it's nothing like so terrible as what goes on out in the fields and swamps."

Neither Joshua nor Joanna had an immediate response. Joanna rocked in her chair. Joshua looked out across the estuary of Lost Man's River—was he turning away from Julia to conceal how he felt?

Finally Joanna spoke—"Ain't you going to say anything, Joshua? Seems to me you ought to!"

He had to clear his throat before he could speak. Then he was quiet, calm—"The law ought to be going up the river, Julia—not you. I ought to be going up there myself, and I keep thinking of what I could do if I had just one squad of troopers like I had in the war for freedom. But I'm a foolish old man now, and there ain't nothing I can do."

Joanna walked with Julia back to the launch *Laura*. Near the dock a sharpie was beached and tilted on its side so that the bottom could be repaired and painted. Joanna nodded toward the man who was working on it and said, "There's Mark Richardson."

Julia would not have recognized him as the young man who had walked beside Joshua in the funeral for the Myrtle victims. He was stripped to the waist for hot and sweaty work with a tool for scraping off sea growth. He was slender and vigorous, with corded muscles. He'd grown a mustache in the Spanish style and had a red bandanna around his head. He looked up. As she would not have recognized him, he did not now recognize her. His quick glance took her in—her white shirtwaist, her laced-up shoes. No doubt he'd looked over the launch *Laura*, its polished mahogany and shining brass highfalutin compared to his rough fishing boat. Perhaps he'd tried to speak to the Greek immigrant who ran the launch and had almost no English.

Julia understood why Joanna couldn't recall for this young man who she was, even though he might remember hearing that she was the white lady who'd stood off white trash with her shotgun. Making long and complicated explanations would be too difficult and probably embarrassing. What was the use? Her name was Clayton.

XX

The year came to an end. Another year trudged, dogged. Julia and Thorstein met in Washington during his academic vacations—at Christmas, for the second time during Easter week, in August, and then for a second Christmas together. They registered at the Willard Hotel as Mr. and Mrs. Brach so that they could stay in the same room. They tried to make up for weeks and months apart, for intolerable longing in solitary beds, for brains become strangely bloodless, no matter how efficient and practical.

Julia's expectation that she was going to manage the Clayton Sugar Company for about two months mocked them. Had she chosen money instead of life? They talked about this choice. They had to admit that what she was doing up Lost Man's River was far more than a matter of "money," and that "life" was even more far-reaching and propulsive than being with one's mate in the same house. Admitting this became an additional intensification of their intimacy, they hoped.

There was a special new impetus in Thorstein's "life," too. During their second Christmas together, he spent two afternoons correcting galleys of *Business Combinations*. He attributed the acceptance of his book by an obscure publisher in Omaha, Nebraska, to William Jennings Bryan, who had seen the manuscript and liked it, even while he deplored the absence of religious spirit. The great orator might have been moved by the fact that Thorstein began his book with reflections on the nature of money, and in this context quoted Bryan respectfully from his speech before the Democratic convention in 1896: "You shall not press down upon the brow of labor this crown of thorns, you shall not crucify mankind upon a cross of gold."

Already, Thorstein had a concept for a third book. He'd call it *Leviathans*, acknowledging a debt to the seventeenth-century English philosopher

Thomas Hobbes, author of *Leviathan, or the Matter, Form, and Power of a Commonwealth, Ecclesiastical and Civil*. Thorstein's subtitle would be *the Matter, Form, and Power of Monopolies, Economic and Political*. He saw monopolies attaining a preponderance of power over prices, costs, technology, consumer tastes, military expenditure and government policy. Meanwhile, almost all people saw only the economic relations of familiar small institutions — the local grocery store, the farm, an artisan's shop, a cottage industry...But there was a conflict of interest that Thorstein intended to show. It wouldn't be easy: "Men who can believe that Joshua Dale with his general store and Arthur Wilkins with his railroads, his oil companies, his hotels and god-knows-what besides are brothers under the skin can believe anything!"

Julia saw that his face had new lines — his face was older and at the same time more moving. He searched for evolving truths about people and their worldly goods with the happy absorption of a child observing the shifting colors in a kaleidoscope. Her love became overwhelming, beyond possibility of expression.

But her "life" at the Clayton Sugar Company lacked the purity of direction that Thorstein found in his work. Her motives were mixed. She hated Tom and wanted to ruin his company. She did want money and was getting it. At the same time, she strove in a hundred ways to undermine the peonage in the Clayton Sugar Company, occasionally with risks to herself that terrified her. Were her ambiguous emotions and contrary impulses making her ugly? She sometimes wished she'd become pregnant and have again the simple happiness of being a mother, as when Caroline and William were little. She'd have a reason for leaving the brutal and profitable enterprise up Lost Man's River. She described her "life" there, expecting more understanding from Thorstein than she had for herself.

It was remarkable, she declared, that the Clayton Sugar Company continued to produce and sell sugar as though the imprisonment of Thomas Clayton himself did not matter. The company survived the utter incompetence of Sanford Payne and her own lack of a profit motive. The bosses continued to patrol with their pistols and rifles. She had cut back in operations to clear and drain new fields. But as formerly the crews of men, women and children kept ditches open, plowed, layered the cuttings, and cut the cane. The narrow-gauge dinky made its daily runs. The tall chimney of the refinery smoked. Barrels of molasses and sacks of sugar were loaded on the *Bonefish*, which sailed as usual to railheads in New Orleans,

Mobile or Payhokee. Market prices were good on account of the destruction of so much Cuban cane in the insurrection there. The company's own fields in Cuba had been burned.

Finally, after a year, she'd taken on enough authority so that she could insist on seeing the fields. She'd had a chair nailed down on one of the flatcars of the dinky and so had toured the route for bringing cane to the mill. She didn't tell Thorstein that Sanford Payne and William, with rifles, kept watch to discourage any disgruntled boss from shooting at her. She did describe the stinking barracks, the brush piles and snakes, the sickness, the universal macabre indifference to the suffering of her peons, probably peppered with outbursts of whipping and shooting that nobody told her about. She was happy that some peons had found a way through the swamps to Chokoloske, where most of them settled in a new shantytown, surviving mainly on fish. But many had stayed behind, perhaps out of fear of being shot for trying to leave, just as object lessons. It was incomprehensible that a tall and strong woman asked for lumber so that she could build a cabin for herself and three small children. Did she fear some hell outside the Clayton Sugar Company even more than what she endured inside? Julia had given the lumber, and she tried to explain to Thorstein her misgivings that by so doing she was helping to perpetuate the use of whips and guns.

She talked about her past and present with black people. She missed Lucy, they couldn't correspond because Lucy couldn't read or write, and so she stopped in Olustee on her way north to see Lucy. There were big changes at Richmond Plantation. Lucy had her second child by the Lizard and had moved into the big house, her first child by the itinerant preacher staying with grandparents in their cabin. Lucy had become harsh and bossy with other black people. She was obsequious toward Julia, trying without success to conceal her hostility. She'd needed Julia as Julia had not needed her. Her cold eyes belied her smiling lips. She blamed Julia for leaving her and so for condemning her to a hard and unhappy life. Up Lost Man's River, Julia had little to do with black people, even though there were hundreds all around her. To the peons in the field, she was the faceless authority behind their suffering. She had her own unknowable purposes for doling out lumber or special victuals. Even Sarah the cook, who served her and William and Sanford Payne two meals almost every day for over a year, looked at her with eyes of stone. Sarah was such a talented cook that she knew she would never be fired. So Sarah could openly show that she didn't like the white woman in the starched shirtwaist who talked in such an easy and friendly way with Gray Man. Julia didn't like Sarah very much, either.

What could Thorstein make of all this? She herself had no explanation for the tormenting unrest of regarding herself as responsible for freeing the anonymous black people up Lost Man's River.

Thorstein couldn't explain either. Some matters were beyond the scope of *Leviathans*. But just talking about it with him brought a feeling of peace — or was she just basking in the warmth of their rare time together?

No black people at all in Madison? Strange, very strange!

*

Before the church in Fort Harrison there was a flourishing banyan tree, and after the service on a Sunday in February Julia walked among the multiple trunks with Lawrence Eddy, Edward Smallstock and William. Lawrence had just come back from Georgia, where he'd delivered spending money to Tom and sounded out the warden Benjamin Burlitt concerning his attitude toward the new and higher offer for his prisoner's ransom.

Lawrence moved with great care, not bending his upper body, and he explained that there was a plaster over his side — "Mr. Clayton's like a lion in a cage he's that impatient. He pushed me against the side of his cabin and cracked one of my ribs. Then he laughed and gave me a big glass of whiskey so I wouldn't feel nothing — "

"That's terrible!" Julia cried.

"I'll heal up," said Lawrence. He showed no hostility toward the man who had cracked his rib and had also given him his chance to make something of himself.

Smallstock became lawyerly — "Why didn't you just mail him the money? Under the circumstances even a man like Benjamin Burlitt wouldn't take it for himself."

"Sometimes I do mail it. Other times I see for myself how he's getting on and I hope he appreciates it even though he don't say he does. And coming back from Georgia I call on Miz Caroline at Aurora Academy."

Smallstock hunched his shoulders. "And how is Miz Caroline?"

"Kind of homesick. But maybe that ain't the right word. She feels she don't have a home right now. She can't seem to think of that big old place way out on Lost Man's River as home."

William was grinning. Lawrence Eddy calling on Caroline prompted fascinating speculations. Earlier, in church, he'd whispered to his mother as Lawrence came in, "Caroline's sweet on that fellow!"

Julia disregarded William's smirk. She worried about Caroline, who was unhappy at Aurora Academy. The Latin teacher whom Julia had loved was an old grouch. Almost all the other girls came from cities—Charleston, Savannah, St. Vincent—and they had clothes different from what her mother had sewed. "Let's not speak of Caroline now," she said. "We have to talk about getting Mr. Clayton out of prison."

"Indeed we do," said Smallstock. "I'm glad the three of us—" he corrected himself, nodding at William—"the four of us are all together under this banyan. This-here's a good place for talking private-like."

Lawrence laughed, then winced. His cracked rib must have hurt. But he hadn't lost his capacity for delight in intrigue, in adventure. "How much do you think we ought to offer, Mr. Smallstock?"

Instead of answering his question the lawyer said, "Mrs. Arthur Wilkins, Laura Wilkins, paid me a visit yesterday."

"She did? She was here, in Fort Harrison?"

"Oh yes indeed she was here. Mrs. Wilkins and I talked the better part of three hours. I never been alone with such beauty before. Her eyes were brighter than the rings on her fingers." He glanced from behind a hunched shoulder at Julia.

You poor stupid man, she thought. Do you expect me to be jealous of Laura Wilkins? Then Julia had a more consequential thought. Laura Wilkins had probably told Smallstock the amount of the check she'd sent to Lawrence, for use in ransoming Tom.

Lawrence exclaimed, "Miz Wilkins didn't see me while she was in Fort Harrison!"

Of course not! No doubt she suspected Lawrence's theft!

And now Smallstock too had a pretty good idea how Lawrence got the money to buy his house. But Smallstock never saw the company's books or the bank account. So he didn't have proof of the difference between the amount of Mrs. Wilkins's check and the amount deposited in the company's account. He addressed Lawrence as though he were an obviously guilty defendant—"Mrs. Wilkins didn't want to see you. She's mad at you."

"Mad at me?"

"She thinks you aren't doing your best to get Mr. Clayton out of prison."

"How can she think such a thing?"
"She sent you a check—"
"That's why we can spend more to get Mr. Clayton out."
"—a check for twenty-two thousand dollars."

Julia did simple subtraction. So Lawrence had skimmed off seven thousand dollars from Laura Wilkins's investment in Tom's ransom. Enough for fancy furniture as well as the house. Julia couldn't help thinking of Lawrence's theft as an almost laughable peccadillo. Instead of picking on Eddy, why didn't Smallstock attack her for presumably doing her best for the Clayton Sugar Company? Its existence was a gross felony. She spoke brightly, disregarding Smallstock's litigious manner—"We can now spend enough to free Mr. Clayton, but we mustn't let Mr. Van Bibber and the Burlitt brothers know we can. Their demands would become even more exorbitant."

Lawrence became voluble—"Mrs. Wilkins has got no call for saying I ain't done my best. All I can do is talk with Benjamin Burlitt. And it's me takes or sends money to Mr. Clayton so he can be treated right. Mrs. Wilkins ought to be grateful for that!" Lawrence went on at some length about his conversations with the warden. Benjamin Burlitt had three times treated him to delicious dinners of roast pork and sweet potatoes—the prisoners on the farm raised as good victuals as could be found anywhere; the warden had sent his wife packing so they could talk man-to-man; and he hadn't said straight out but had almost admitted what he needed to cover his personal expenses in providing Mr. Clayton with his special accommodation and with the best victuals on hand, the same as what he himself and Mr. Clayton's banker enjoyed. Four thousand dollars, Lawrence Eddy believed, should be enough for the warden. Then, instead of defending or even mentioning his handling of Laura Wilkins's check, the young banker called attention to the lawyer's slow performance. After all, Smallstock was doing the most important negotiating. Smallstock was the one who conferred in Key Alva about what the sheriff and the judge required for their time and services. It was Smallstock who talked with the proprietor of the house that couldn't profit so much from the woman with the slashed face. And most important, Smallstock met with Captain Grotius Van Bibber, who represented Mr. Arthur Wilkins. Lawrence pronounced the name of the magnate with respect, even reverence. "Mr. Wilkins is set on having law and order in Key Alva, as is only right," he concluded.

Probably out of regard for what he assumed were Julia's feelings, he did not mention the real reason for Mr. Wilkins's hard feelings toward Mr. Clayton. Both Smallstock and Eddy regarded her in a simple-minded way as an aggrieved wife, and they assumed that she used her power of attorney conscientiously in Tom's interest, with perhaps some piddling shady dealing for some no-account feminine purpose. She said, "We are depending on you, Mr. Smallstock, to advise on how much we should offer now."

William disrupted their discussion. Did he sense the cockeyed and belittling notion that his mother was a pathetic deserted wife yearning to retrieve an errant husband? Neither Eddy nor Smallstock had even implied this in so many words, but somehow the thought was in the air. It had been in the air ever since Julia had taken over at the company. Why else would she work so hard? Anyway, William, fifteen years old, taller than either Eddy or Smallstock, acting like a man in his good man's clothes since he'd just come from church, felt that his mother was being run down and that he had to stand up for her. He blurted, "Ma and me ain't going to stick around here after my father gets out of prison."

There was a moment of silence.

"Is this true?" Smallstock demanded.

"Ma and me got better things to do," said William.

Smallstock became both avuncular and ironical—"I guess maybe your father will have something to say about what you do."

"I don't care what he says," said William.

"Most young men would be very happy to be the only son of a man who owns a big sugar company and a bank," said Smallstock—"in spite of him having a little trouble right now."

Julia wanted to fling her arms around her tall son, her somewhat befuddled champion. She feared that this exposure of her lack of interest in the future of the Clayton Sugar Company, and the future of Thomas Clayton himself once he was out of prison, might somehow work to her disadvantage. So with a bright smile she said, "I do declare, one can hear tell how women can't stick to the point in any important conversation, and here I am with two accomplished gentlemen trying to settle how to get my husband out of prison and they get themselves sidetracked over what my son's going to do, and he's just going to college if you really want to know. I *did* inquire of you, Mr. Smallstock, how much we have to offer Mr. Van Bibber 'cause I guess he's the main one we got to satisfy."

The lawyer still didn't answer her question. Perhaps he had learned that it is always prudent never to be direct. Or perhaps he just had to talk about what was uppermost in his mind, which was Laura Wilkins. He broke into a nervous sweat simply from remembering her physical proximity and her selection of him as her confidant. She'd sold a painting of herself by some Italian to raise money for Mr. Clayton's release. She'd given some of it to Van Bibber so that he might owe her some consideration along with his obligation to Arthur Wilkins, his regular employer. So Mr. Van Bibber was being rewarded from two directions for his involvement in this affair.

Mr. Smallstock couldn't put out of his mind that Mrs. Wilkins seemed to have settled how she and her Arthur Wilkins could get along. She gave parties on his big steam yacht without her husband being present, and it seemed that Arthur Wilkins went his own way too, although what this way was he couldn't say. The intertwined lives of Arthur Wilkins, Laura Wilkins and Thomas Clayton suggested the working of some supernatural machinery that made ordinary moral strictures irrelevant, just as the ordinary kind of law enforcement was set aside in sending Thomas Clayton off to Georgia instead of just letting Sanford Payne pay damages for what he did in Key Alva and then forgetting the whole thing. "There are folks bent on doing so much with their lives they can't be bothered with the usual way things are done," Smallstock concluded. "It makes a man wonder what life is all about and why regular folks like us live like we do."

Julia was amazed at Mr. Smallstock's train of thought. "What are you getting at?" she demanded.

"Tom's predicament is on my mind day and night," he replied. "It's more than me representing him as his lawyer. There's been a family relationship that goes back I-don't-know-how-far. There was my father Ephraim Smallstock and Tom's father Merion C. Clayton and that poem Merion wrote about my mother so he and my father had to exchange some shots. And after Ephraim Smallstock was wounded in the Wilderness so he was never a whole man again and there were the wild hard years after the War which my mother used to say she couldn't have survived as long as she did were it not for the genteel solicitude of Merion C. Clayton—"

"I know all about this!" Julia cried. Actually, she didn't and she knew she didn't. It crossed her mind that the famous bond between the Claytons and the Smallstocks was more coiled and kinked than she'd ever conceived. Did Edward Smallstock suspect, during emotional stress or in fearful dreams, that Merion C. Clayton might be his real father and that Tom might be his half-brother? If so, did he feel a special responsibility for getting Tom out of prison, or did he harbor a secret envy of Tom's clear-cut parentage? She continued, hypocritically, "I know you are deeply concerned about Tom. But you're getting yourself all upset, Mr. Smallstock, and the best thing you can do, that all of us can do, is be practical and settle on how much we're going to offer Mr. Van Bibber. Just being practical is the best medicine for a fretful mind."

"You been kind of slow in your dealing but nobody doubts you ain't done your best—" Eddy put in.

"I should think not!" Smallstock shot back. Then he mumbled, "I'll settle for as little as I can—maybe less than thirty thousand dollars, no more in any case." With a calculating blink at Julia he went on, "I just guess you're going to be very happy to see an end to all this."

"Yes," she said.

"I'll appreciate it, Mrs. Clayton, if you pay my fee before Tom comes home. He hadn't ought to be bothered by anything related to what shouldn't have occurred in the first place."

"Just send a bill," said Julia. "Address it to Sanford Payne, General Manager, but I'll take care of it."

"Thank you," he grunted.

Julia stifled a cruel laugh. All during Mr. Smallstock's mental torment, which he'd dressed up in a perfervid vision of a prodigious life beyond morals—sanctioned by Smallstocks and Claytons as well as Wilkinses, he'd been anxious about his fee, which was sure to be outrageous. If Lawrence Eddy could get away with money for a house, and if an indifferent wife could use her power of attorney to grab who-knows-what, why should he keep his own snout out of the trough?

Also, didn't he have a special claim?

*

Julia wrote a letter to Thorstein saying that her legal husband would very likely be out of jail very soon and that she and William would be coming to Madison—she couldn't predict exactly when. She was exultant. "Life" was love, and she had to be resigned to her inability—any one person's inability—to repulse the typhoon of peonage in south Florida.

Then the negotiations for Tom's release still lagged. She talked briefly with Smallstock and suspected that he was trying to make a deal with Van Bibber so that he would get a kickback for himself out of the ransom money.

On another Sunday, two weeks after the conversation with Eddy, Smallstock and William, Julia was again under the banyan tree on her way to church. William was not with her. He was eager to collect as many botanical specimens as he could before he and his mother went north.

But there was Lawrence Eddy again, now in a new white suit.

And clinging to his arm, in the pink Sunday-go-to-meeting dress that Julia herself had made, was Caroline—smiling, embarrassed, worried, triumphant.

Why wasn't she at Aurora Academy?

Julia guessed the answer before it came.

But Lawrence, flushing and sweating, was immediately explicit—"Caroline and me, we got ourselves married, Miz Clayton—oh Lord! I didn't want to surprise you like this but we just love each other so much we couldn't wait and there we were up in north Florida and we just walked out of Aurora Academy and went straight to the Reverend Blanding in Olustee because he used to be Caroline's Sunday school teacher and she wouldn't have nobody else tie the knot, and we didn't see why we should have a big ceremony or anything like that, what with Mr. Clayton still being in prison and unable to give her away formal-like..." He gushed a mixture of chronicle and self-justification. He realized that Caroline was only seventeen but she was already a big lady and wanted to be married as much as he did. She was very unhappy at Aurora Academy and wanted a home, which he now gave her since he had a big house empty except for himself and a nice church-going colored woman who was doing the cooking and cleaning just fine. They'd bought a trousseau in St. Vincent—

Caroline spoke for the first time—"Oh Mama, after church can I show you what I got?"

No doubt Caroline remembered some remark that getting married too young was not a good idea and was now rent with anxiety about how her mother would react. Blushing, twisting her hands around a dainty handkerchief, she was trying to excuse herself, she was crying out for compassion and love. Julia's head throbbed. Her big, lovely and thoughtless daughter, who had inherited Tom's physical amplitude and vigor but none of his ruthless enterprise and cruelty, hadn't even been ready to go off alone to Aurora Academy! How much of her lovely innocent's elopement and marriage was just flight from a loneliness she couldn't stand? Or from a futile bookish summons to a mind totally unlike her mother's?

In the same flicker of time in which Julia began to respond to Caroline, she considered Lawrence Eddy as never before. In acquiring Caroline, was he grasping another part of the Clayton property before Tom got out of jail? Or did he truly love Caroline? Was it possible to mix up such contradictory motives? At least, Lawrence was a far cry from Tom…

Julia threw her arms around her trembling daughter, her first baby, now bigger than she was, kissed her, and said, "Of course I shall see what you got yourself in St. Vincent, and see you in your own real home with your husband, and now you are married I'll love you more than ever."

Caroline wept.

Lawrence said, "Oh please don't cry, babydoll. Didn't I tell you your mother would understand, that she'd remember what it is to be in love?"

XXI

Thomas Ewell Clayton was leading an aged and dispirited mule that was dragging a cultivator between rows of turnips. A skinny white man who had murdered his wife was guiding the cultivator. Leading the mule wasn't strenuous, wasn't even really necessary, and Tom was smoking a fine Havana cigar. He knew the day had come for delivery of the money. Leading the mule checked feelings he wasn't ready to let out—yet.

A jaded pony carrying a weary old man who was in for life for a reason everybody had forgotten appeared on the edge of the field. He was the warden's messenger.

To the man who was guiding the cultivator Tom said, "Time has come for me to leave this place."

The messenger was smiling.

"You got news, Sam?"

"Happy to say I have, Mr. Clayton. Good news you been waiting for has come."

Tom drew a cigar from the breast pocket of his shirt and handed it to the messenger, drew another from the pocket, considered a moment, and gave it to the man guiding the cultivator. Then he started directly across the field, stepping over the rows of turnips.

"In Mr. Burlitt's office," called Sam.

Lawrence Eddy was waiting, unarmed of course and wearing an ordinary brown business suit. His smooth face, like a boy's, was rigid with fear that his newly acquired father-in-law would disapprove of the marriage and might fire him from the bank.

"Hello, Lawrence," said Tom, shaking his hand. "Glad to hear about you and Caroline. Life had to go on, I figure, regardless of me being holed up."

Lawrence was so relieved that he almost cried. "Hello—father," he mumbled. "I hope you ain't going to object to me calling you that."

"No, I ain't going to object."

"Everything's all settled here, down in Key Alva too. So you ain't going to be holed up no longer."

"Let's get out of here."

The warden was even more friendly than usual—"There's clothes for you in that room, Mr. Clayton, if you care to put them on."

When Tom came out, wearing a blue suit, it was obvious that his relaxed manner had put both Eddy and Benjamin Burlitt at ease.

"Here's a letter for you, Mr. Clayton," said the warden.

Tom looked at the familiar writing on the envelope, at the St. Vincent postmark, and put the letter in a jacket pocket.

Lawrence handed him a wallet—"There's a hundred dollars in this."

A miserable sum! How much money had there been in his wallet when he was nabbed in Key Alva? A thousand dollars? Two thousand? Did Eddy think that just because he was now son-in-law—

The warden was speaking—"Mr. Clayton, if our paths cross again, I'm going to be making your acquaintance for the first time—like, what I'm saying, two gentlemen just being introduced."

"This has been agreed by everybody concerned," said Lawrence.

"Because of the circumstances, I'm forgetting I've met you," the warden went on.

"Edward Burlitt down in Key Alva ain't never met you either," said Lawrence. "For over a year now you been in a number of localities in connection with the war—that's what we all been saying."

"There's a man whose name we ain't supposed to mention wants it that way," said the warden.

"We don't even need to mention there's a man whose name we won't mention," said Lawrence.

Tom was surprised by Eddy's ironic tone. Life was changing him.

"The country needs a man like you, Mr. Clayton," said the warden. "Thing that makes me the maddest is they didn't just blow up the *Maine* but now they offer to pay for it—as though that would help."

Lawrence glanced at the satchel on the desk which contained what was being paid to Benjamin Burlitt - "Yes - yes." Patriotic steam seemed inappropriate. "There'll be a commission waiting for you, if you want it," he said to Tom.

"That man we ain't supposed to mention," said the warden.

"So we won't!" snapped Lawrence. Had he discovered that he had a temper?

"No, we won't," agreed the warden, holding out his hand.

"You forget," said Tom. "We ain't never met." Without another word, he strode out of the building and stepped into the buggy which his new son-in-law had hired.

Eddy unhitched.

The road to the entrance of the prison farm led through a field where prisoners were working, and a guard hailed them—"Good luck, Mr. Clayton. Sam told me you was to be let out."

Tom waved but did not reply. Already, the prison was passing out of his mind.

While they were riding in the buggy to the livery stable and railroad station, Eddy remarked, "This has cost us over twenty-eight thousand dollars."

"Money ain't nothing." Then Tom made polite inquiries about Caroline, did not mention William, and checked up on his wife. Now that she'd got Sanford Payne to fire Obadiah Giles, was she able all by herself to handle the bookkeeping?

Lawrence assured him she could and did. Bookkeeping was not the problem! He spoke of the sugar company in an apologetic tone even though he wasn't responsible for it—"It's afloat because the market for sugar is good, but I talked with Long Algy and he tells me some of your best men have quit. They feel like it's Mrs. Clayton running the company, not Mr. Payne, and they don't like working for a woman."

"What's Sanford have to say?"

"He don't say nothing. He don't want to talk."

Near the railroad station was a general store, and Tom went in to look at rifles. One of those on display in a locked gun case was a Winchester which had been a new model a few years before. He had one like it at the company.

"Let me see that one," he said to the storekeeper.

He handled it a long time, raising it to his shoulder and sighting at a number of objects out of the window—the eye of a dog, the head of a redbird, the ears of a mule—working the lever back and forth, running his big hands over the barrel and stock.

"I'll take it," he said. He also bought two boxes of shells.

"You want that on the train?" asked Eddy. "I didn't even bring a pistol."

"You go on this train and take care of my bank, and your wife," said Clayton. "I'll get back home in my own way." He slipped seven cartridges into the Winchester and stuffed the boxes in pockets. Then, with the rifle in his right hand, he walked out into the street.

Lawrence Eddy dogged his heels like a child trying to get attention.

Between the store and the railroad station, Clayton stopped to speak— "Reckon you can get your train over there, Lawrence. I'm heading down this way. Much obliged for what you done to get me out of that place." He shook his son-in-law's hand. "One of these days I'll turn up in Fort Harrison."

"What are you going to do?" Eddy blurted. He was confronting a state of mind utterly beyond his understanding.

Clayton skittered his eyes across the anxious face of his young banker, who looked away. "Have the *Bonefish* or the *Laura* at the dock in Fort Harrison," he said. "Don't let either one of my boats go up Lost Man's River. One thing you got to learn, Lawrence, now you're a married man— women get funny notions. And I don't want my wife to have any way of skedaddling away from where she's supposed to be, waiting for me and staying right by my side when I get home. Do you understand me?"

"Yes—why, why yes," said Lawrence, uncertainly.

Tom took the road south, without looking back.

He would never be able to estimate how many days and nights he walked the dusty or muddy roads of Georgia and Florida. He couldn't tell how he spent those days and nights. What he thought might have happened merged with what he wished or feared. Then belief, wish and fear combined with what he dreamed as he slept in a field or on a pallet in some sharecropper's cabin. He traveled by direction, like a migrating bird, never asking the road to any particular town. Sometimes he plunged into creeks and wallowed like a bull.

He realized that he could tolerate encounters only with human beings who had no meaning in his life. Those who did have meaning would not be safe. Even Laura.

He met an old man driving an oxcart with a load of wood—a Florida settler with an old-fashioned long white beard and dressed in cotton pants and shirt full of holes. His eyes, cloudy with age, showed no surprise at the sight of Clayton, wearing his new blue suit and carrying a new rifle. "Howdy," he said.

"Howdy," said Tom.

"If you ain't in a hurry, you can ride."

"Thank you, sir."

After they rode a piece, the old man said, "Reckon we are going to fight Spain."

"Is that so?"

"Well, from what the papers say, that's what I'm inclined to think."

"I don't read the papers much."

The old man looked Tom over. The blue suit was of good quality but stained from his having slept on the ground. "That's a mighty slick rifle you got. Just buy it?"

"Yes."

The old man jerked his head toward the pile of wood behind them—"Only rifle I ever owned is one I used in the War Between the States. Back there in the woodpile wrapped in a piece of canvas."

"Tain't the rifle. It's the man."

The old man took a square of chewing tobacco from his pocket and held it out. "Care to chew?"

Tom bit off a chaw. "Thank you, sir."

The old man lashed out with his whip—"Git! Git!" The oxen didn't move any faster. "You a Florida man?"

"Yes."

"Don't intend to be impolite. I figured you was. A Florida man has a way of talking."

"A Florida man is generally a fighter, if he hasn't caved in."

"Yes, *sir*!" the old man spat. "Back in the year Eighteen Hundred and Sixty-one when that beautiful war got going, I had every reason to hope for a good life. My father owned niggers. I didn't have to drive a cart with oxen."

"Were you in the war?"

"Yes. Yes indeed. I was in the war start to finish. I'm a Southerner to the backbone, yes sir. My name is Langhorne, and my father commanded the Sixth Florida regiment, Confederate States of America."

"Well well..." Tom felt unspeakably weary. The old man's words evoked a mixture of anger and nostalgia that had oppressed him almost from birth. Yet he told the old veteran that his father was Captain Merion C. Clayton of the Fourth Florida Regiment, Confederate States of America, and then bathed reverentially in the forgettable flood of chatter this priceless information released. But all the time he thought: here I am forty years old, and I have no more reason to hope for what this old nobody calls a good life than he has. Owning a bank and a sugar company in some trouble because of a woman who thinks of what-should-be instead of what-is, ain't much for a man who might have run the whole state and maybe more if he'd played his cards right. He cut a pretty poor figure compared to the Yankee magnate Arthur Wilkins.

He imagined Wilkins and his man Van Bibber coming after him on this road, and picking off both of them with his new Winchester. But he had occupied himself in prison with violent fantasies until he was gorged with them. Couldn't he think something new? Something other than lying in bed with Laura, then waking up with his teeth grinding and hearing himself growl?

"You must be the Thomas Clayton who ended the nigger riot near Olustee some years back."

"Yes, I am."

The old man was too polite to ask the obvious next question: what was *that* Thomas Clayton doing alone on a back road, in a suit that had been slept in, walking, and carrying a new rifle?

Clayton got down from the seat of the cart and said, "Thank you, sir. You've given me a rest. I'll walk on ahead."

"You're very welcome, sir," said the old man, disappointed but too proud to say so.

After a plunge in a black creek he drew from the pocket of his jacket the letter from Laura which the warden had handed to him just before he left the prison. He wondered why he had put off reading it but had no explanation for himself.

Dear Tom my sun is this night of my life—

My state of mind is very peculiar—I feel almost as if I were going insane. All day long I talk and talk and people talk and talk to me. There are different kinds of people around me and all the time I talk to them I'm afraid of them all except for Johann Mowrer who plays the organ in my church. Every night I lock my door I look in my closets I look under my bed. I sit very still and listen until my ears ache and my brain does too. I think of us and you are not with me and my legs tremble and my heart thumps and I shiver even though I have more blankets and quilts than I need. It seems like somebody is kneeling on me and choking me. I try to throw off the weight but I can't and I shout Tom Tom. I wake up hearing Tom Tom echo in my big room...

Then the letter became so mixed up he couldn't figure out what Laura wanted to convey. There was some reference to money for his release, but whatever she might want to say about that was late in coming to him, anyway. He figured that his being on the prison farm had driven both Laura and him out of their minds. He had an erection and cursed.

That night, for fifty cents, he slept in a room above a saloon and dreamed. He was in the greenish Tapestry Room of the Alhambra Hotel. Around him were men in evening suits and women in fancy gowns. They bowed to him. Then came Laura in an apple-green robe, her red hair piled in curls on top of her head and crowned with a diamond tiara—as in the picture that Italian fellow painted. She held out a platter with the head of the President of the United States. The head looked at him, comical and meek as Richard the Barber, and winked an eye. He laughed, and Laura laughed, too. Then he was in a gray-green cane field where a Negro man was building a house, hammering nails to apply the siding to a frame. The hammer swung back and forth with a slow and steady power that was unreal and magical, the nails entering the wood to the head under each perfect blow. He tried to give some order to this Negro, but only a toneless cackle, as though from some faraway bush, came from his painfully sore throat. The house grew. He reached for his six-gun, but it wasn't on his hip. The Negro looked at him, his ridged brow shadowing his eyes. He raised his hammer, now a railroader's sledge. The house became a coffin and Tom, he, just Tom, was inside, the boards pressing his arms and chest—

Help! Help!

He awoke saying, "Laura, Laura, if we don't kill Arthur Wilkins, it will be the end for both of us."

The next day a boy about twelve years old, a cigarette in his mouth and an enormous spur strapped to each bare heel, reined up a roan mare and greeted him—"It's a pretty day, ain't it, sir?"

"Reckon so."

"What time is it, sir?"

"Later than I thought." And with a gesture he swept the boy from the saddle and took his horse.

The rest of the day and a good part of the night he galloped that roan mare until with a series of convulsions she collapsed and died.

And on the day after, he reached Fort Harrison.

He was struck by his own transparent reflection in the plate-glass window of his bank. His blue suit, which he'd put on clean and pressed at the prison farm, was stained green and brown, and on the left shoulder was a smear of dried blood. He couldn't remember how he got it. His red hair and beard, bleached a bit, looked hot, like the center of a flame. Both thrust out from his head in tufts that were sticky with sweat, dirt, crushed insects and clinging seeds. On one temple was a purple and green lump from the bite of some semi-poisonous insect which he had scratched and infected. "Howdy, old yellow eye," he said to his image.

Inside, he used the butt of his rifle to push open the gate which separated the public from bank employees, and headed for the door marked *Lawrence Eddy – President.*

The cashier said, "Sir, does Mr. Eddy know you're coming?" and at the same moment pulled a lever which sounded an alarm.

Clayton turned around, and the man went to the floor behind his grill.

The office door opened and Lawrence appeared, a six-gun in his hand.

At the sight of his pale face and quivering chin, Clayton put the butt of his rifle on the floor and leaned on the barrel, waves of rasping laughter erupting from his chest.

After a few seconds Lawrence laughed too, deferentially. "That's all right, Gerald," he said to the cashier. "This is Mr. Clayton, who owns this bank."

Whereupon Tom pushed into the cage with the cashier, opened his drawers, plunged his fist into a nest of twenty-dollar bills, and put some in his pocket.

"Why, Mr. Clayton—" began the cashier.

Lawrence interrupted—"Say, father, that's going to make keeping accounts kind of hard."

"What's hard about it?"

"Gerald here won't know how much you took."

Clayton addressed Gerald—"You know how much you had?"

"Yes, sir."

"You can count money?"

"Yes, sir."

"You can subtract?"

"Yes, sir."

Lawrence objected—"There's Miz Wilkins and the other stockholders."

"Let's see. They own forty-five percent?"

"That's right."

Clayton peeled the bills in his fist, counting them. He'd taken five hundred and forty dollars. "Gerald!" he snapped.

"Yes, sir."

"How much is forty-five percent of five hundred and forty?"

"Two hundred and forty-three."

Could the fellow really figure that fast? The majority stockholder gave the cashier a look that sent him reeling back against his counter. Then he counted off two hundred and forty and handed Gerald another twenty-dollar bill. "You'll have to give me change for this."

After Gerald handed him the change, he added three dollars to the two hundred and forty and handed the pile of bills to Lawrence. "Forward this to Miz Wilkins, Jeb Brown and Lewis Butler in the right proportion. Tell them I decided it was high time we took some profit out of this enterprise."

There were shouts outside. The alarm bell had attracted attention.

Clayton stuffed his own profits in a pocket and went to the door. "Well well well—" He opened the door, raised the Winchester, and fired. Bullets furrowed the road beside two constables. "Stay where you are, drop your guns, and put your hands up!" he bellowed.

He bracketed them again to make sure they did as they were told.

When the guns of both of them were on the ground, he said, "Now you, Harry, I want to ask you an honest question—are you thirsty?"

"Hain't give the question no thought." The constable didn't recognize Clayton's voice and was just confounded.

"Well, Harry, this is Thomas Ewell Clayton talking. We're closing up this bank for the day, and I'm taking everybody here and you and all your boys to Sweeney's tavern for a drink."

*

A sweltering afternoon.

On the fish wharf in Chokoloske, Long Algy was trying to convince four black men they'd be in the worst kind of trouble if they didn't go back to work up Lost Man's River. The big boss Mr. Clayton was in Fort Harrison, he'd soon be going back up the river, and he wasn't going to tolerate niggers leaving the Clayton Sugar Company while owing money for victuals. Long Algy was uncertain whether he should try to persuade these four black men or just draw his gun and order them into the launch *Laura*, which he'd been able to borrow for this expedition. He knew that the company was coming apart because peons ran away and bosses quit, but the relationships of those who ran the company baffled him. Why did Mrs. Clayton go out of her way to keep bosses from doing what had to be done so the company could make money? Why did General Manager Sanford Payne lie down on his job? Why did Mr. Clayton order him, when he borrowed the *Laura*, not to let Mrs. Clayton use the launch in order to bring herself and her son down the river to Fort Harrison?

But Mr. Clayton seemed happy he was determined to get back workers who'd run off, maybe Mr. Clayton might get mad at Sanford Payne and fire him, and maybe he, Long Algy, might become General Manager of the Clayton Sugar Company.

"I remember you, boy," Long Algy said to one of the four blacks. "What's your name?"

"I done lost my name when I was cutting cane, and I can't find it again."

"It's dollars to doughnuts you owe money—"

"I's right satisfied fishing."

"How much money you get now?"

"Enough for chick peas and chitlins."

"You get paid by the day?"

"I gets a share when we sell the fish."

"How much—"

"I can't rightly say, boss. I never learned sums."

"Who your boss man?"

"He sitting right here."

Long Algy looked at a fifth black man he'd never seen up Lost Man's River. This man had a neat mustache clipped in the Spanish style, he was wearing a clean shirt and jeans, and he had around his head a red bandanna in which fish hooks were stuck.

"How much you pay this nigger?" Long Algy asked him.

The man shrugged, smiling, but did not speak.

Long Algy scowled. This could go just too far.

"Boss, it like the coon and the dog," said the man who didn't know sums. "Coon say to dog, 'Why you so fat and I so poor?' Dog say, 'I lay round master's house and let him kick me. Then he give me bread and lard.' Coon say, 'Better I stay poor.' Boss, I's like the coon."

Long Algy argued, increasingly frustrated and angry. Any man he had to shoot wouldn't cut cane! But at last his right hand shivered toward the butt of his gun.

Red Bandanna was in a shed on the wharf, and at that moment he came out with a rifle, an old Sharps.

The fisherman said, "Mark, is that there the rifle you used for shooting the pantercat through the eye?"

Without another word, Long Algy strode back to the launch *Laura*.

Laughter—"Kyar kyar kyar!"

A man said, "Mr. Thomas Clayton he have to come hisself. Boss men ain't got no stomach for doing what he don't do."

The sugar company boss who came and went in the company's fancy launch put the men on the fish wharf in a good mood for just sitting and talking. Besides, it was too hot to do anything else.

Mark Richardson said, "Joshua Dale he aims to go for Mr. Clayton on account of him killing a white man named McLevy."

"McLevy?"

"Him folks call sailor come home from the sea."

A man who had worked a long time at the sugar company said, "I was dragging out stumps. There were a black cat big as a panther looked at me and asked me to follow. So I did. I seed McLevy's cabin. The sawgrass was high as my head right to the door, which was hanging loose. I looked inside and there were an old man in a rocking chair. 'Who're you?' I say. And he say, 'Nigger, address me Mr. McLevy.' 'Mr. McLevy dead and buried,' I say. And he say, 'Nigger, Mr. McLevy died out of Christ—you tell folks that. So I sitting in my home until it rots.' That were the ghost of Mr. McLevy and to this day it bothers me so I can't sleep."

Mark said, "Joshua Dale he figures there a law against killing McLevy 'cause he were a white man. And so he might get hisself made a deputy and go after Mr. Clayton."

The fisherman laughed—"Law am a ghost."

With Thomas Clayton back in Fort Harrison, it was not possible to talk about anything without having in part of one's mind either Mr. Clayton or his troubled company.

Mark Richardson told a long story about meeting up with the biggest old bear he'd ever seen, going after fish in a creek. Mark's rifle had been set against a stump while Mark fished too, and the bear was right next to it. So Mark told about his long talk with the bear, which had to do with his family and the bear's. Finally the bear walked off—"like a preacher in new pants too tight for him he was that dignified." Mark got his rifle again, and he reported what he said at the time—"Old bear, I ain't got no hankering for your brown coat that is too thin in summer anyhow, or for your juicy flesh. I got hog meat in the smokehouse. Live, old bear. You ain't Mr. Thomas Clayton."

*

Fort Harrison had changed during the year Thomas Clayton was away—not in prison, as some malicious people claimed but in Washington and elsewhere doing confidential work for the Federal government. Captain Grotius Van Bibber, vice-president in charge of protection services for the Pamlico and Gulf Railroad; Mr. Clayton's lawyer Edward Smallstock; Sheriff Edward Burlitt in Key Alva; and Mr. Clayton's banker and son-in-law Lawrence Eddy all said Mr. Clayton was doing this confidential work.

On a bulletin board before the office and printing shop of *The Fort Harrison Gazette* was a cartoon which showed three swarthy men around a nude white woman. "Spaniards Search Women on American Steamers!" At eight in the morning, a band consisting of one trumpet, two trombones, a bass horn, two fifes, a bass drum and three snare drums tootled *Dixie* from the schoolhouse to the square in front of Sweeney's tavern. There they played martial selections for about fifteen minutes while the Fort Harrison volunteers joined ranks for their daily parade to the Fair Grounds. This was a broad sun-baked pasture with a half-mile race track and pens for the exhibition of cattle, for it had been discovered that savannahs northeast of the city were rich in grasses that fattened certain tropical breeds of beef critters. Near these pens was a pleasant grove of live oaks beneath which the ladies' auxiliaries of three churches and two lodges served luncheons on trestle tables of rough boards.

The spectacle of Southern manhood rallying to the flag which a generation before had deprived them of property, with well-dressed gentlemen marching beside workmen in tattered undershirts and shoes laced up with string, prompted Clayton to say, at his daughter's supper table, "Seems like some fellers got to have a dirty picture and a brass band and got to feel low-down and uncomfortable, got to march back and forwards in the hot sun—saw a couple of them faint away out there this afternoon—go through all kinds of rigmarole before they can get up the nerve to shoot a few dark-skinned foreigners."

Lawrence Eddy laughed. He was showing Caroline how much he appreciated and admired her father.

Tom talked to his daughter about the responsibilities of being a wife. Could she speak to her mother about how much her husband needed her in view of the injustice just done to him? Hadn't she promised she'd stick by him when they got married? He didn't like to keep his wife and William, too, up Lost Man's River against their will, but if Julia was going to have giddy notions about running away what could he do? Now that Caroline was a married woman herself, maybe she could get her mother to see what her duty was.

Plainly, Caroline was not going to talk in this vein to her mother.

But Tom saw that his authority, and the fact that he was accepted by all as an important citizen in Fort Harrison, confused Caroline. He hoped she'd become at least a little critical of her mother and become loyal to him because of Lawrence's position at his bank. She seemed not a very smart but sensible girl. But he couldn't be much concerned with Caroline.

He had to act fast, to do for Arthur Wilkins before he changed his will, cutting off Laura. Putting the sugar company back in shape would have to wait.

It was important that Arthur Wilkins, and those around Arthur Wilkins, should believe that he was sticking by the agreement made as a condition of his release from the prison farm. He recalled Joseph Rourke and thought that in like manner he should never appear to be responsible for what was going to happen to Arthur Wilkins. With this in mind, he met Van Bibber in an upstairs room over Sweeney's tavern which had become a kind of officers' club.

"Good afternoon, Tom." Van Bibber extended a square and blunt hand.

"Howdy, Grotius. Glad to see you."

"It has been many years—yes?"

This remark was a test. Would Clayton appear to forget, as had been agreed, that Van Bibber, acting of course for Wilkins, had been present during the fracas and arrest in Key Alva? To say nothing of his role in the subsequent negotiations!

Tom replied, "Years—yes—since we had that nigger trouble finishing the main line to Payhokee."

Grotius smiled and became very cordial—"Arthur Wilkins and the rest of us have never forgotten that."

"How's the railroad doing?"

"It is difficult to supply the transports at Payhokee over a single track."

Others in the room above Sweeney's tavern had a sense that this conversation between the vice-president of the Pamlico and Gulf Railroad and the local banker and owner of a sugar company was important, and they listened.

"Then the Pamlico and Gulf is doing well," said Tom, approvingly.

"I do not complain."

Sober nods. Someone chuckled.

"Have a julep with me, Grotius."

"Thank you, Tom."

They swapped bloodthirsty and conventional remarks about the patriotic duty to slaughter Spaniards until an aged black man went downstairs to order their juleps and then came back to serve them.

"The Governor would like to have you take command of a regiment, Tom."

This was part of the agreement, but Tom pretended delight and astonishment—"You don't say so, Grotius!"

"I do say so, Tom. I talked with the Governor last week."

"Mighty kind of the Governor, I must say."

"Not at all. He knows ability when he sees it."

"I never been a professional army man."

"The professional army men haven't fought since Eighteen Sixty-five and they're all too old."

"Well, Cuba is no place for a man in questionable health, it's true."

"The Governor said to me that what you did in Olustee showed you can run a complicated operation. That was the closest thing to a war in this country since the War Between the States."

"There's anarchy kind of like that in Cuba now, and I don't like it. I lost a good business in Cuba because of this anarchy."

"I know."

"You do?"

"You were up and coming in Cuba until this anarchy set in. Now that your operation up Lost Man's River is in trouble—"

"Who says it's in trouble?" Tom almost lost his temper and permitted a glimpse of his hatred—for just a second he forgot his determination to make Van Bibber believe he was keeping the agreement made as a condition of his release from prison, and even that he would probably be amenable to whatever Arthur Wilkins dictated. It was true the company was in trouble, but he raged inside at Van Bibber's complacency in knowing about it and saying so.

Luckily, the vice-president for protection services interpreted the little outburst as simple-minded pride—"All I'm saying, Tom, is you're going to have a lot better opportunity in Cuba after the Spaniards are driven out."

Tom controlled himself—"Maybe so."

"Have a great future, Tom—in Cuba."

The conversation with Van Bibber made him impatient. He went to the bank, got stationery and a pen, and wrote a brief note to Laura. He told her to do nothing, not even write to him again, until he did for Arthur Wilkins. After that, they'd be free.

But he never mailed the note.

A customer of the bank who knew Lawrence gave them news—the big yacht of the magnate Arthur Wilkins had just come in and was anchored in the harbor.

XXII

Julia was sitting on the screened verandah of the big house, mending one of William's shirts. She no longer went to the office. Long Algy and the silent Greek who ran the launch had shown that they now took orders from Tom by refusing to take her and William down the river. But she expected the schooner *Bonefish*, which she hoped would take her as far as Payhokee and the railroad. She'd replaced the former captain of the *Bonefish* with her own choice, a man named Michael Kennedy who knew how to sail and kept the steam auxiliary engine polished. Kennedy had never even met Tom.

She was eager to finish mending all her own clothes and William's too — it seemed untidy to put torn clothes in trunks.

She'd written a long letter to Thorstein but couldn't mail it until she was able to go to Chokoloske or Fort Harrison. In the last letter she had been able to mail, she'd told Thorstein that Tom was about to come out of prison and that she'd soon be with him in Madison. Not hearing from her would make Thorstein worry.

Sarah came up the walk from the dock. The morose cook had become quite friendly after learning that Julia was going into the outside world. Probably she hoped that Julia would forget her hostility and take her along — where could Julia find as good a cook? "Miz Clayton, there a ship in the river," she called.

"A ship? Is the *Bonefish* back?"

"Oh no ma'am. I mean a different ship."

Julia stood up so that she could see past a clump of oleanders. Sure enough, there was a gleaming white ship with a tiny ripple in the jet water under its clipper bow, a whiff of smoke from its one raked funnel, and the gilded name *Empress* glittering. A chain rattled and the anchor dropped.

Whoever was navigating the ship must have decided against going into the shallow water next to the dock.

Julia had read in *The St. Vincent Chronicle* about the *Empress*, the luxurious yacht built for Arthur Wilkins. Had the magnate and Tom resolved their differences and become friendly again? Was the Wilkins marriage intact after all? Was Wilkins coming to look over the sugar company, with some thought of buying it? Was Tom on his way back to the respectability and promise of earlier days, when he'd been Wilkins's protege and had been singled out by the President of the United States as a token guarantor of Florida's glorious future? Why not? Perhaps Tom's usefulness to the magnate outweighed past crimes and ugly emotions.

She seized her reticule, which contained her revolver, and hurried toward the dock. A whistle blasted so that all sorts of birds, cackling and whistling, wheeled from the trees and water. Sailors in blue uniforms moved about the deck. A white dinghy was lowered from davits. Down a narrow stairway at the side of the yacht came Tom. He was wearing a white suit and his red hair glistened like a copper helmet. He sat in the rear of the dinghy. A sailor stowed suitcases and took the oars.

Then, as the dinghy approached the dock, Sanford Payne came, followed by Richard the Barber. She was comforted by Sanford's presence and then felt the absurdity of her own position in being protected from Tom by this notorious gunman. Her special motherly sort of relationship with the Gray Man, which she'd cultivated in order to have as much influence as she could get in the sugar company, might now be useful for this additional reason.

Tom spoke first to his so-called general manager—"You ain't wearing your gun, Sanford. You got matters in hand so you don't need it?"

"I don't need it coming to meet you, Tom." Sanford was aware of the suggestion of criticism in Tom's question, and his matter-of-fact tone hinted that he *might* need his gun while meeting Tom.

Julia liked Sanford's tone. Would Gray Man at long last overcome his strange dependence on Tom?

Tom looked at her—"Well, you're here to welcome me, just like a wedded wife should. I can see by the color in your face you been out in the sun where you hadn't ought to be, but it does set you up—"

Julia interrupted—"I realize I no longer have power of attorney here. So there's no reason for me and William to stay. Keeping me from using a boat is foolish and you're making trouble for yourself as well as me. I'll find some way to leave."

Plainly, Tom was puzzled. He really didn't, couldn't, understand her.

Before he could make up his mind what to say, Sanford Payne asked, "Is Mr. Wilkins coming in?"

Tom turned away, toward the house. "What makes you think Arthur Wilkins is here?"

The dinghy had gone back to the *Empress* where Caroline and Lawrence waited at the rail.

Julia waved, and they waved back.

Richard the Barber followed Tom with suitcases.

Sanford stood by her side, hesitating to walk away from her in order to follow Tom. His need to attach himself to some decisive authority was mean and pathetic, and he was torn between reliance upon Tom's brutal certainties and her own nurturing concern for him, which was sincere to a degree. His growing indifference about the condition of the company made her hope that she was changing him. Would he ever be able to face whatever it was in his background and nature that tormented and shamed him, so that he had to conceal what he actually was by becoming Gray Man?

"Well, Sanford, you can see for yourself why I can't stay here any more," she said. "Tom and I have scarcely a civil word for each other. Life hereabouts won't be happy from now on, and I just hope you can look after yourself and do what's proper."

"Aw Miz Clayton, I don't know what I'm going to do," he said.

Then he followed Tom and Richard.

Caroline was wearing a new pink and white dress. She made a comedy out of managing the long skirt as she descended the narrow stair down the side of the yacht and stepped into the teetering dinghy. She squealed. Lawrence fondled her and patted her into a secure perch on his lap. She kissed him and pressed his arm more firmly around her waist. She hailed Julia as they floated near the dock—"Oh Mama, Miz Wilkins invited me and Lawrence on her big yacht, and I never did see anything so grand!"

Caroline's elation was partly pretense, obviously. She couldn't avoid the father who had treated her mother brutally and left her for another woman. Now Caroline felt guilty because she was getting along with her pleasant and frightening father.

Julia put out her hand to help her daughter out of the dinghy.

But Caroline ignored it and bounced to the dock in one powerful spring, almost dumping Lawrence and the sailor in Lost Man's River. "Oh Mama Mama Mama, everything has been so scrumptious!"

Julia embraced her and said, soberly, "I'm grateful to Miz Wilkins for bringing you here—and your handsome husband—hello, Lawrence. William and I are almost packed to go north, and I've been worried about being so far from you. . ."

They began to stroll toward the big house. Caroline chattered about the dramatic arrival of Laura Wilkins and friends in Fort Harrison, and about the elegant way they talked, like nothing Caroline had ever heard. Couldn't Mama forget the bad things Daddy had done, he wasn't doing them any more, and be nice to Daddy just this once? Caroline stopped walking because she had something to say to her mother. Now that she herself was married and so happy she could hardly breathe, she was at the same time so sad she couldn't bear it that her mother and father didn't get along the way she and Lawrence did. She knew she couldn't stop her father from "going with" Laura Wilkins, or her mother from "going with" Thorstein Brach. But for this once, couldn't Mama at least *act* as though she were a real wife and be friendly to all the people on the yacht? Everybody in Fort Harrison thought the world of daddy. Caroline and Lawrence didn't tell anybody about his being in prison because that crooked sheriff in Key Alva and his brother in Georgia had schemed to rob Daddy. Everybody thought Daddy was busy helping his country to prepare for war in Cuba, and Caroline was happy to let them believe that because it was partly true anyway since Daddy expected his commission as colonel, or at least lieutenant-colonel, any day now.

Julia cringed. Was the fairy-tale quality with which she'd misrepresented Tom during Caroline's infancy coming back to haunt her? Was this quality resurrected by the exotic luxury of the Wilkins yacht? She said, "For heaven's sake stop, Caroline."

But Caroline was wound up—"There are chairs enough for everybody in the big dining room and you'll sit at one end of the table with Daddy at the other end and you'll be hostess." *Hostess*—had Caroline ever used this word before? "Mama, please, it's going to be just nifty." *Nifty*! Another new word?

"You must believe me, Caroline," said Julia. "Your father doesn't have any expectations one way or the other about my sitting down with all these people. They're Miz Wilkins's company, not mine." She nodded toward the young banker and husband, who had been silent and glum during Caroline's effusion, and went on—"Lawrence understands how it is with me and your father, and I know what's best for all of us. I'll just stay in my bedroom while the company is here, or in my office."

Caroline pouted—"Oh Mama—"

But then William came, grinning.

"Will!" screamed Caroline, and rushed to give him a hug.

Lawrence and Julia were alone together for a few seconds, and he said, "There's nothing right about Miz Wilkins coming here on her husband's yacht. I don't know how she got hold of it, and I don't know what her and Mr. Clayton have in mind. I don't like it and I wish Caroline and me had nothing to do with it—"

Julia nodded to show that she understood—or that she understood his lack of understanding, which matched her own.

She found that Tom had already given Sarah his orders about dinner, and the cook was frantic.

Julia put off making an arrangement for William's supper and went to her bedroom. From her window she could see the dock and the *Empress*. In addition to Caroline and Lawrence, two women and three men were waiting on the dock for the dinghy, which was now bringing Laura Wilkins. Probably because she didn't wish to crush her elaborate gown in the low seat, she stood, holding ropes from the little tiller for support, while the sailor rowed. Evening was coming on, and in the low sunlight filtering through the jungle on the far river bank, she seemed to be dressed in a frothy white and golden cloud above which her auburn hair glistened with violet in the sunset's yellow glow. There were bows of white ribbon on her shoulders and a mist of lace about her breasts. Her round white arms were bare. This beauty in her dramatic gown seen against the jet water and the shack of the rum maker Wheeler and moss-covered cypresses and oaks and palms on the opposite bank was startling, to say the least.

One man on the dock separated himself from the group, ran back and forth, evinced his ecstasy by screaming in some foreign language, lay flat and beat his palms against the planks in frustration with the inadequacy of what he aspired to express, and ended simply by giving Mrs. Wilkins his hand to help her out of the dinghy.

Julia left the window and took up a pen to write Thorstein about this latest event. But she wondered whether she would be able to go to Madison as fast as any letter.

*

Lawrence Eddy had become used to the admiration and respect of almost everybody in Fort Harrison because he was president of the town's only bank—and so young too! He was aware of two essential aptitudes. He'd mastered the skills, demeanor and outlook required for successful bank management, in dealing with both employees and customers. And he'd been artful during his rise in showing his employers appropriate acknowledgment of their authority and presumptive wisdom, first to his uncle in St. Vincent and then to Thomas Clayton. During the halcyon interlude while Thomas Clayton was in prison, he'd had the heady experience of operating without oversight of any authority, and the bank had prospered. Partly luck. There was a boom in Fort Harrison. The northern well-to-do were building winter homes. It was easy to arrange safe and profitable mortgages.

With the rampageous reappearance of Thomas Clayton, and a week later with the disrupting arrival of the Wilkins yacht, Lawrence's identity had been recast. Engulfed in the Laura Wilkins circle, he'd become simply the handsome young schemer who'd seduced and married Thomas Clayton's daughter, thereby becoming heir to what his bold and violently enterprising father-in-law might acquire. Of course, inheritance was iffy. Thomas Clayton was in splendid health and anyway not *that* much older than his son-in-law.

At first, Lawrence resented the niche assigned to him in frequent interruptions of his speech, in eyes that never met his, in attention directed elsewhere no matter what he said or did—in short, in endless intimations that he wasn't much.

But it didn't take long for him to become more than a match for these put-downs. His self-regard was especially overpowering at this time. He'd just found sex beyond the most lascivious dreams of his starved bachelorhood. None of these folks on the yacht had what he and Caroline had in bed, sometimes on the parlor floor, and twice, behind a locked door, on his desk at the bank. Along with his new carnal and emotional aplomb he felt that he had more and more ability, as a cool and experienced banker, in appraising people's capabilities and motives.

There was a young Argentinian whose father apparently preferred supporting him on a world tour to keeping him under foot on the ranch. There was a French mademoiselle who wore a conspicuous cross on her breast and showed signs of hoping for religious solemnization of her relationship with the Argentinian. There was a philosophy professor from Columbia University in New York and his German-born wife; these two probably regarded time spent on the Wilkins yacht as an extra dividend on a Florida vacation. A very excitable French artist might at one time have been attached to the mademoiselle, or vice-versa. An organist from Mrs. Wilkins's church in St. Vincent was unhappy most of the time. He didn't like being away from his instrument, and he was probably even more harshly judgmental than Lawrence about the people he was with, and certainly more afflicted by the absurdities to which he was subjected because of his dependence on Laura Wilkins.

The owner of the sugar company took the whole group on a tour to see the refinery, the warehouse and the narrow-gauge railway train. After his long absence, he himself was probably eager to look things over.

Lawrence and Caroline were by themselves for the first time that day. In a hammock on the screened porch facing the river, Caroline unbuttoned her dress so that he could nibble her breasts. Then there was a new arrival in a skiff at the dock. It was Wheeler, the rum maker.

"Oh piffle," said Caroline, buttoning her dress.

Lawrence was disgruntled too. An erection was coming on.

The rum maker bent over to tie up his skiff, and two enormous buttocks heaved up to conceal the rest of him.

"Over yonder on a clear day you can see Breadloaf Mountain," said Lawrence.

Caroline whooped and gave him a hug.

Wheeler approached, carrying a jug. "Who's it sitting here?" he asked. "I can't make out through this mosquito screening."

"Caroline Eddy who used to be Caroline Clayton and Lawrence Eddy."

"Feller runs the bank in Fort Harrison?"

"The same."

"Well, I'm please to meet you, Mr. Eddy—and Mrs. Eddy."

"Likewise."

"I see Mr. Clayton's come home and he's brung some folks with him. Is that his boat out in the river?"

"No, that belongs to Mr. Wilkins the railroad man."

"Do tell. What I come for Mr. Clayton always appreciated my rum. I make rum that's what I do."

"I'm thinking that jug has some of your rum."

"It does. This here's the best rum I ever made count of how the skiminings from the mill gets richer with time."

"Do you want to give Mr. Clayton this rum?"

"That's my intention."

"Are you making a present of this rum to Mr. Clayton or are you selling it?"

"I'd be happy to give Mr. Clayton a present but I know he won't have none of that. I'm a poor man compared to Mr. Clayton, and all I can do to earn my own keep is make rum."

Lawrence bought the jug and said, "I sure would like it if you could bring me two more jugs before suppertime."

Wheeler would have to row across the river again, but he agreed to do it.

After he waddled away Caroline gurgled, "What will we do with three gallons of that old feller's rum?"

"Become very entertaining, I hope." He unbuttoned her dress.

Again, he and Caroline were interrupted. The party returned from looking over some of the assets of the Clayton Sugar Company. The owner addressed his daughter—"Seeing as how your mother won't have anything to do with getting us some supper, it's up to you to go out in the kitchen and take charge. Sarah's a good cook but slow as a snake shedding its skin and lacking in style."

Caroline trotted away, the others drifted off, and Lawrence stretched out on the hammock. Lying on his side, he looked across the lawn to Lost Man's River where the *Empress*, a recondite visitation, floated at anchor. Giant cumuli surged from the north as on every afternoon at this time of year, loosening dry thunderbolts back in the swamps. To the grandeur of the sky the spectral *Empress* added a dread that things were not what they seemed. The persistence of the apparition assured its reality. Hallowed habits and ordinary values became questionable.

Lawrence slept and had a disturbing dream he couldn't remember. He was awakened by Caroline on her knees beside the hammock and giving him a long kiss—"Supper, sweetykins!"

It was dark and lamps had been lit. Startled, Lawrence looked at his watch. Three hours had passed.

Caroline laughed — "I wouldn't let anyone disturb you, not a soul!"

At the door to the large parlor, where the others were sitting, an enormous black man bellowed, "Supper served!"

"I taught him to say that and I made him put on that old suit of daddy's," said Caroline. She was aiming at style, pleasing her father.

The black man was an arresting sight. The suit, which fit quite well, was of close-woven brown flannel in which a long slit down the back had been mended. But his feet were bare. Nobody's cast-off shoes were going to fit those feet. There were great toes thick as wrists with red nails curling over the ends like cats' claws. Calluses from a lifetime of going barefoot provided gray pads for his soles.

"Answers to the name of Hot Ash," said Caroline.

The dining room glittered with candlelight, china and cut glass.

Caroline was acclaimed. Such a nice supper, and arranged with scarcely any notice! It went without saying that the loyalty of daughter, in view of the narrow-minded jealousy and withdrawal in a funk of Mrs. Clayton, was touching and deserving of warm-hearted appreciation.

Laura Wilkins placed a kiss on her own soft palm and then planted it on Caroline's soft cheek.

Lawrence flinched. What might be the consequences of his Caroline being taken in by Laura Wilkins and her pack? He'd encountered the power of Arthur Wilkins behind those involved in the ransom negotiations, and the total disregard of Arthur Wilkins in this company suggested a childish make-believe.

Mr. Clayton went to the head of the table and seated Mrs. Wilkins on his right. Then everybody sat, pell-mell: the Argentinian, the mademoiselle, and the artist on Laura's side of the table; the philosopher and his wife, Sanford Payne, the organist and Lawrence on the other side; Caroline at the foot — hostess.

Sarah entered with Hot Ash, who was useful as a kind of sideboard. He held an enormous tray from which Sarah took serving dishes, which she held for each guest. And as each person drank the julep concocted mostly from Wheeler's rum and became exalted with the odors and tastes of ham and turkey and sweet potatoes and turnip and field peas, almost all talked, generally at the same time.

The organist gulped his first julep and with eyes at first as indifferent as a snake's glanced at Hot Ash, whose tray held along with everything else a pitcher of julep in which ice rattled. Suddenly grinning, warming up, he winked at Hot Ash, crooked his finger, and said, "Here!"

"That's all right, Hot Ash," said Caroline. "Take the tray so the gentleman can help himself."

Then almost everyone wanted another julep.

"You are charming," the artist said to Caroline. "Who would expect in this wilderness to find young lady so, so, so—oh, how I should do portrait—yellow hair, amorous eyes, rosy bosom, form *sensuelle*—*La Vierge Americaine*—I do not mean to doubt your powers, Mr. Eddy—" and to the organist—"ah, Johann, console yourself with this excellent rum of the region while I tell this most lovely one what is in my heart!" Then the man murmured slow and languid phrases in French.

Since Lawrence wasn't defending his wife's respectability and perhaps honor, the Gray Man said, "Sir, I ain't sure I understand your remarks to Mrs. Eddy. Would you like to repeat them in a language I can understand and so's to make your intentions clear—*sir*?"

The artist gave the nominal manager of the Clayton Sugar Company a glance expressive of great confusion and then looked to Lawrence and Caroline for assistance.

Caroline pleaded with Payne, "Please don't be upset. This gentleman is a foreigner and has a different kind of manners. He don't mean no harm—"

Lawrence felt mean and inclined to provoke a quarrel, as long as he himself could not be held responsible. So he added, grimly, "Probably not!"

The organist Johann leaned toward Payne and muttered with melodramatic intensity, "Keep an eye on that Frenchy!" Then he leaned his bald head on his fist and howled.

Payne grunted.

The Argentinian and mademoiselle talked with Sanford in a sincere and friendly way. They were finding him an interesting experience. Payne told the Argentinian he'd like to take him out West and show him around. Was he keeping to himself a yen to leave the Clayton Sugar Company?

"Thank all the gods for appetite and taste!" exclaimed the artist. He dabbled a red and tender piece of ham, which had a little trace of baked sugar and clove along one edge, into a sauce so rich and hot it seemed alcoholic even though it wasn't, waved it ecstatically before his eyes, sniffed it, slipped it ever so slowly into his mouth, masticated it with a rolling motion of his jaw and in-and-out slurpings of his rather full wet lips, meanwhile ogling Caroline with such a soulful expression that Sanford leaned forward and said, "Here, sir!" But the general noise was such that the artist didn't hear him. Closing his eyes as though the swallowing of this single tidbit of sugared, cloved, and hot-sauced ham was inducing a blissful slumber, he said, "My dear young lady, you are the one who now gives me one of the most sublime moments of my life. I swear that never until this moment have I known true rapture. Never have I been borne away—"

Caroline interrupted—"But it's not me, sir—" At this moment Sarah was serving buttered and peppered turnip off the tray held by Hot Ash. "It's Sarah who cooked all this," Caroline went on, rather desperately. "You're right, sir. Nobody can cook like Sarah."

The artist regarded Sarah with a wildly intoxicated gaze, stumbled to his feet, held aloft his julep with rapturous abandon, spilling a little, and cried, "Sarah—ah, this is Sarah, yes? *A votre sante*, Sarah. Drink, *mes amis*, drink drink, drink—ah, Sarah—"

All except Payne responded, some with enthusiasm or like Laura Wilkins and Thomas Clayton with indifference. Gray Man remained seated. Was he disappointed? He couldn't throw out or beat or shoot a fellow who was obviously crazy.

"Mr. Payne," Laura Wilkins called, sharply, "I understand you managed this little empire during Mr. Clayton's absence. I do admire a man who can take hold when there's an emergency."

"Oh ma'am, 'twarn't nothing at all," Payne muttered.

"Don't tell *me* 'twarn't nothing at all'!" Laura commanded. "I want to know what you've been doing!"

So do I, thought Lawrence.

Plainly, Payne did not regard Mrs. Wilkins's question as a probe into his incapacity. Rather, he looked upon it as a genteel invitation, as an opportunity to display his qualities, and he replied, "I been sitting tight like Tom always did and thinking about keeping the bosses up to scratch and dealing with Mr. Sheriff Edward Burlitt if he comes up the river. I left the bookkeeping and such to Miz Clayton."

"What would the good sheriff come up the river for?"

"Don't matter what he'd come up the river for. He's out to ruin. Bosses we got here ain't no positive gents but they know how to make niggers dig ditches and cut cane. Can't have Burlitt take none of them away."

"Did Burlitt come?"

"Not while Tom was away. He come once while Tom was here."

"I wish I'd been here then!"

"It were something to see the reception Tom give that sheriff. He come here thinking to take Tom—'Boys, I got to take that man,' he was saying, and he had two deputies with him in his boat and Tom raises his Winchester—*poom!*—must've been fifty yards, and there was a hole in Mr. Sheriff Burlitt's hat. A feller fishing found it."

Sanford Payne burst into a fit of laughter that cracked and contorted the sheath of white gristle around his features. It was terrifying.

Lawrence had never heard of this incident. So Edward Burlitt had his own reason, as well as suggestion or orders from Arthur Wilkins, to put Tom away!

At last everyone at this tumultuous supper party was listening to one person, and Sanford made the most of it. At length, with many digressions of mysterious significance, he told a confused and savage chronicle. He'd witnessed Tom's shooting of Burlitt's hat—he'd been waiting with his forty-five, and if Burlitt and his boys came closer he would have shot them, but they were far off for a revolver and he hadn't had time to get his rifle. He talked on and on about all kinds of circumstances for shooting: close up, *poom!*—from ambush, *poom!*—from a horse, *poom*! He finally became so technical he was boring. Laura Wilkins leaned her head against Tom's shoulder. The Argentinian and the artist both pawed mademoiselle.

The Germanic wife of the philosophy professor spoke for the first time in many minutes, her accent thickened with drink—"The bull vent ofer the cow, and *poom!*"

Hilarity.

Others elaborated:

The rooster over the hen—*poom!*

The shepherd over the sheep—*poom!*

The priest over the nun—*poom!*

Lawrence had remained sober. It had been his intention when he bought Wheeler's rum. He didn't like it that Caroline had to hear the kind of jokes that might be bandied about in saloons. Especially since in spite of his cautions Caroline had drunk too much and was giggling.

Payne wasn't laughing. He looked frozen while everyone else was sweating from the heat, humidity and drink. The jokes mocked his jibber-jabber about guns, about the *poom* of shooting Burlitt's hat and so on, but did he comprehend this?

Then he noticed that Sarah was carrying the heavy tray and was having trouble with it on account of its size and weight. "Where's that man Hot Ash was helping you?" he asked.

"He gone, Mr. Eddy. He just lit out."

"Lit out where?"

"He never told *me*. He just gone, and he wearing Mr. Clayton's suit."

"Oh dear," said Caroline, "can you manage without him, Sarah?"

"Yes ma'am—"

"It's all right, darling," Lawrence said to Caroline, and in a way to Sarah as well—"it's a mighty fine supper and it's a downright shame some of these folks are beyond appreciating it."

Mademoiselle stood, leaned across the table, most of a breast surging out of her skimpy and mussed-up gown, and grinning witch-like at the stupefied Gray Man she purred, "Adorable Mr. Payne is over the charming little black man, and *poom!*"

Sanford Payne lurched up, tipping over his chair. There were small red splotches on his cheeks, and his slab-like features quivered. He was like a specter in a nightmare.

Mademoiselle collapsed back in her chair, aghast and appalled.

"My God the man is crying," Lawrence muttered to Caroline.

Her blue eyes brimmed—"Oh poor Mr. Payne."

The Gray Man was like a post, his body rigid while his mouth and chin shook with silent sobs. He was oblivious to how he looked to all these alien and frenzied people. His eyes were glazed as though he were dead. Lawrence had the passing but very disturbing thought that some higher power—God?—was making him witness for his edification the torment of a soul in Hell. He had to pay for the incredible joy of his marriage.

How could this gang ignore Payne? Yet, most of them obviously did. The philosopher's wife was shouting above the rest about the affair of a Columbia professor with an instructor's young wife. The humor was in the bizarre settings—a furnace room, a library stack for Japanese history and literature—"Who vent there? They could fornicate in private, ja? Until the ins*tructor*, who vas vorking on doc*tor*al thesis, found note about samurai. Who *vas* samurai?…"

Suddenly, Payne's ramrod body seemed to melt, and Lawrence sprang up to keep him from falling. He said to Caroline, "Come, let's get this poor feller out of here." He was making an excuse to take Caroline out, too.

"Please, you all go on having a good time—please," said Caroline, standing.

Who heard her?

Then Laura Wilkins was taking Payne's limp left hand.

The Gray Man recovered enough to say, "I'm sorry, Miz Wilkins. I got a million devils in me—"

She interrupted—"Sanford, what you said about helping Tom, about being ready to protect him when that sheriff came—well, I want you to know that *I* think you were superb!"

"Oh Miz Wilkins—"

Along with the reek of rum from Payne, Lawrence took in—or did he imagine?—a fragrance from Laura Wilkins as of no particular flower but as of all flowers. Her voice was a musical instrument but no particular musical instrument—"*Dear* Sanford, you mustn't mind Germaine Dupois or anyone else I brought with me on the yacht. I have a good time with them and I want you to have a good time, too. Please have a good time, Sanford. You don't mind if I call you Sanford, I hope, and you must call me Laura." She smiled, making a kind of game—"Repeat after me: I shall call you Laura. Go ahead. Say it!"

The Gray Man couldn't return her smile, but he did mumble, "I shall call you Laura."

"Germaine!" Laura shouted across the table. "You've offended Mr. Payne with your stupid joke. Maybe he has feelings even though he does know how to use a gun. Maybe he has *more* feelings on that account. Maybe he has more feelings than you have, you cow! Just because you come from gay Paree don't mean you've got a monopoly on sensitivity. Jesuchristus! I can't imagine what got into you!"

Mademoiselle clasped her hands in a begging posture and shrilled, "I love you, Mr. Payne!"

"Oh you vulgar bitch!" exclaimed Laura, without heat, and turned back to Payne—"We must put you to bed, Sanford. And you must think of pleasant things. Think of me, of what I say—"

But it was obvious that Payne couldn't really think of anything. He slumped against Lawrence, who had to grab him under both armpits to keep him from falling.

"Johann!" Laura shouted, "come and help Mr. Payne—and help Mr. Eddy!"

The organist, the only one at the table who had become silent and self-absorbed, turned his hawk's eyes on his benefactress. He seemed to ignore her words and simply study her.

"Snap out of it, Johann!" she cried.

Tom Clayton, still at the table, was laughing.

Johann Mowrer moved as one aware that he had drunk too much but by strength of will would control the effect. He rose up, placed his folded napkin over the back of his chair, and came to put his arm around Payne so that with Lawrence they could ease the half-conscious Gray Man toward the arched opening to the hall and stairs.

Caroline hurried ahead to turn up the wick of a lamp.

"This fellow stinks," said Mowrer.

"I'm glad somebody besides me is able to notice that," said Lawrence. He was irritated. The evening was no longer fun, no longer an adventure.

Payne seemed to recover a little. Lawrence and Johann Mowrer did not have to support his weight, but they did steady him.

Laura halted their progress. She stood before the Gray Man, held his face in her hands, and forced him to look into her large eyes—"Oh Sanford, you dear reckless man, you've had too many juleps—"she laughed lightly—"perhaps I have, too. But you and I can do whatever we want to do, can't we? Shooting, doing with our bodies—having pleasure—oh, no shame, Sanford, no shame for anything—do you hear me? There's a glorious destiny for Tom and me, and you're going to share it, Sanford."

Payne gave an incoherent sigh.

She laughed again—"There's a *time* for drinking, a *time* for shooting, a *time* for—" she hesitated and glanced at Lawrence.

He knew that she had been about to become explicit concerning Payne's time, and how it might be used to elevate the destinies of Laura Wilkins, Thomas Clayton and Sanford Payne. But she wouldn't do it while he was present. What did she and Tom have in mind? Laura's commandeering of the Wilkins yacht was such open defiance that Wilkins was sure to strike back in some way. Whatever Tom and Laura had in mind, they would have to act fast. On the other hand, was it possible that Tom and Laura had no plans at all, that just being together even once was worth more than any possible and calculated future?

Payne was muttering something incomprehensible.

"A *time* for doing what I must do, for doing what you must do," Laura concluded.

Payne nodded—yes.

It was a bizarre exhibition of hypnosis. How could Payne become affirmative, even in his alcoholic haze, when it was impossible to know what Laura Wilkins was talking about?

"Oh la la la," she said, daintily. Standing on tiptoes, she gave him a light kiss on his pale cheek.

It was almost at that very moment, as though the kiss exploded, that a rifle banged outside in the dark night. The sound came from quite nearby, perhaps from near the refinery.

All except Tom Clayton came to a standstill. He was up from the table and pushing past the others toward and up the stairs, and as he passed he said to Payne, "Sleep it off, Sanford. Time I take charge here, personally."

Payne's small black servant Richard the Barber had been sitting on the stairs and eating a piece of pie and listening to the goings-on in the dining room. He scuttled out of Tom's way in such frantic haste that he dropped and smashed his plate.

Caroline said, "I'll get Sarah—"

The rifle banged again.

Richard the Barber and the smashed plate, not the bang of the rifle, seemed to revivify Payne. "Pig!" he snarled.

The little servant's eyes glittered behind his spectacles. "Please don't hit me, Mr. Sanford—" He twisted toward Caroline—"I'll clean it up, Mrs. Eddy—please, Sarah don't have to come. I'll get a dustpan." He scampered toward the hall's rear door to the kitchen, bumped into something in the dim light, and gave a soft cry of pain.

Johann Mowrer went to the stairs. Had Caroline assigned sleeping accommodations? Three steps up the organist turned—"Thank you for an enchanting evening, Laura." For him, the queen was hostess, not Caroline. "If you didn't have the soul of a musician, *appassionato* and when you're drunk *sentimento*, I'd tell you to go to hell."

"You dirty snake," said Laura, laughing.

Mowrer had to press his back against the wall to make room for Clayton, who was coming downstairs with a rifle. He glanced at Laura but didn't speak as he hurried out, the screen door of the porch banging behind him.

"There ain't much he can do while it's so dark out there," Lawrence said to Laura. He guessed there was probably a breakout from the Clayton

Sugar Company—an effect of Julia's steady on attack on the brutality of the bosses combined with desperation because of the yacht and the return of the ruthless king. The blacks must realize that whipping and shooting would be condoned again, probably encouraged.

"There's *always* something Tom can do!" exclaimed Laura.

"Well, I don't know," said Lawrence. "What's he going to accomplish with bullets flying around while you can't see your hand in front of your face?"

Richard the Barber was creeping with a dustpan, and Payne, fairly steady now, kicked a piece of broken china toward him—"Leave off that and get me my gun, the one with the pearl butt. *Quick*, fat ass!"

But Richard couldn't go upstairs immediately because Julia was coming down. She was wearing her usual plain white shirtwaist, blue skirt, and also a wide-brimmed straw hat with mosquito net over it and veiling her face. She was carrying a lighted lantern and her reticule.

No one else moved. Conversation in the dining room was muted.

"Don't go out, Miz Julia," said Lawrence. "What's going on out there ain't nothing you can do about."

She might have glanced at him but because of the mosquito net he couldn't be sure.

She hesitated before Gray Man—"This is not your responsibility, Sanford." And - seeing Caroline - "I'm glad you never wanted to stay in this place." Then she was out through the screen door, closing it quietly.

Sanford said nothing, but Richard seemed to know what was in his mind and went back to his chore with the dustpan, forgetting the command to get his master's gun.

Caroline went to the screen door and looked out. Her mother's lantern was bobbing off toward the refinery.

Lawrence realized that his mother-in-law hadn't spoken to him because he couldn't help her, and he was ashamed. Somehow his exclusive preoccupation with the Clayton Sugar Company's banking and money made him less than a man.

Then he was aware that Laura Wilkins's face blazed. Julia hadn't even looked at her, had been completely indifferent to her presence.

William bounded down the stairs, one hand clutching a rifle and the other fumbling with the sleeve of his shirt, which was only half on. "Did ma go out?" he asked his sister.

Caroline nodded—"Toward the refinery."

With a slam of the screen door William was gone, too.
Gunfire again.

*

In the dark, Mark Richardson rowed his skiff past the ship, silent, at anchor near the dock of the Clayton Sugar Company. Red, green and white lights sparkled. Back among shadowy trees some windows in the big house glowed, and he could hear a woman's high-pitched laugh. He rowed hard to go past where he might be seen, to leave mosquitoes behind, and to take the edge off his anxieties. Had the man who'd come to Chokoloske, dirty and covered with sores, weak and starving after a week in the swamps, been exact in telling him just how he could find Amos Peters? What if even one direction the man had given him was wrong? In the miles of cane fields beyond the looming refinery and warehouse he couldn't hope to find Amos.

He followed the main channel past the warehouse, as he'd been advised, and then into a more narrow channel to his right.

About a mile up this more narrow channel he came upon a platform on posts overlooking the water. Just what he'd been told to expect! A cloud drifted past the moon, and he could see better. The platform rose above a tangle of growth, with a rocking chair on top, out of place and foolish. The man who'd escaped from the Clayton Sugar Company had explained: one of the bosses had ordered his crew to build this platform because it pleased him to sit in the rocking chair with a jug handy and a rifle for shooting at alligators, flamingos, or any other reptiles, birds or beasts that moved.

Mark pulled up his skiff under the platform and followed a clear path not more than five stones' throws to Barracks Four. The mosquitoes were fierce.

The man who knew the whereabouts of Amos had not told Mark about the smell of Barracks Four — rancid pork fat, sweat and shit — or about how folks lived there. Smoke curled out the doors at the ends and out of vents under the eaves. The place looked on fire but it wasn't. Standing in the doorway, Mark saw that smudges had been made on the dirt floor at each end of the long shed for keeping out mosquitoes. In the flicker from the smudges he could make out folks sitting or lying in bunks against the walls, some near the floor where the mosquitoes could get at them and others near the rafters where they choked on the smoke. Most of them weren't stirring much. The ones he could see clearly, on the ground around the smudges—young and old, male and female—looked shrunken and gray in the dirty yellow light. There wasn't much talk, but the sudden scream of a woman in a dark corner made the hairs on Mark's neck prickle. Nobody else seemed to notice. He'd seen a lot of people, both colored and white, who lived in misery, but nothing as bad as this.

He strode to the nearer smudge, showing himself, and said in a loud voice, "I's looking for Amos Peters."

His appearance and words were like a thunderclap. The thin gray folks near him were on their feet, shivering, several talking at once. Somebody said, "It's a nigger with a gun!"

The stirring of bodies and hum of talk were like a sudden wind.

"Mark!" It was the voice of Amos. "Mark—Mark—I's here!"

He thrust himself among several people to an upper bunk, his head swimming with fumes from the smudge, his heart leaping. One worry was over—the man who's escaped to Chokoloske had been exact! Now—to get Amos out of this hellhole! A hand touched his face—"Mark—Mark—"

He couldn't see into the dark bunk, but he stroked along the arm beyond the hand, found and hugged the body. Were these scrawny shoulders Amos?

"Mark—Mark, I always knowed you going to come." The words were almost a howl. But yes, it was Amos's voice.

Mark's own voice was hoarse—"I's taking you home."

"I knowed—" Amos began but choked on a sob.

"What you knowed is come."

"Yeah, I knowed," Amos said, firmly now.

Mark could feel him slide down from his bunk.

Then Amos cried out with pain but said right off, matter-of-fact, "I has sore feet."

"Sore feet?"

"I was in water digging and my feet is all solid sores."

"Can you walk?" Mark didn't want to say how far Amos would have to walk. He didn't want to say where the skiff was pulled up. One or more of the gray shapes around him might be inclined to fight for the skiff.

Amos went on, "A boss man stabbed my risings to see the matter pop out."

"Iffen you can't walk I can carry you."

"I can walk."

Mark could see him as he limped past the smudge. He was favoring his left foot. Mark followed.

At that moment, just before Amos reached the door opening, there was the bang of a rifle—Mark guessed about a quarter of a mile away.

The fear in Barracks Four could be sucked in the nose and mouth, as actual as the smoke. For an instant there was no talk and only the rustle of shadowy bodies in a rush toward bunks, like a stir of birds when a snake comes. Folks had to show they had no part in whatever caused the shooting.

Amos stopped hobbling and turned. He'd learned to head for his bunk when others did.

Mark pushed his shoulder—"Go on."

There was another shot, this time much farther away.

They walked out of Barracks Four and stood without moving for a little while, listening, silent, Mark with his rifle ready. Finally Amos looked up, smiling, his mouth open to take in the clean air, to suck in the bright new moon. The only sound came from mosquitoes.

"I has the skiff at the river," Mark whispered and began to walk ahead.

Amos staggered and nearly fell into the cane beside the path.

Mark turned back. He was holding his rifle with his left hand, and he threw his right arm around Amos to take some of the weight off his sore feet. "Easy," he said. There seemed to be no reason for hurrying.

Amos said, "It were a devil on earth that stabbed my feet—yeah, a devil on earth spreading iniquity."

"You talking like your grandpa Azri."

"I ain't never going to forget grandpa Azri. I was little when he was whupped and killed, but I remember."

"Can you go faster?"

"Almost I can fly."

The fact was Amos was no way near flying. He was deadweight on the shoulder of Mark, who laughed—"You flying like a log." He thought of how it would be when they were home in Chokoloske, and he added, "Oh Lord, Bina's going to be happy. She *worried, that* worried—"

The path through the cane was narrow, they couldn't go side by side, and Mark pushed ahead, hunching forward step by step and almost dragging Amos, who touched the ground as gingerly as he could with his wounded feet. Mark was thinking that being a slave in the Clayton Sugar Company had changed Amos. It didn't seem possible that he could remember any words from his Grandfather Azri's sermons. *A devil on earth spreading iniquity*! He'd never showed before that he remembered such words, and now he did.

They were near the end of the cane and the beginning of the thick growth on the edge of the water. The mosquitoes were thicker. Mark had a folded net in the skiff, and he thought that he'd have Amos lie under the net while he rowed as hard as he could. He had in mind a backwater about a mile below the sugar company's dock. They could hide there, the skiff in sawgrass and both of them under the net—then continue down the river in daylight, when the mosquitoes would be tolerable.

The shout came like a sudden pain—"Hey! That you, Gus?"

Looking back, past Amos's arm across his own shoulders, Mark could make out a man next to the corner of Barracks Four, plain in the moonlight, the head very large and ghostly under a wide-brimmed hat draped with mosquito net. Instantly, he had in mind a choice: he might flop down with Amos and fire a shot near the man to make him keep his distance; or he might just keep going. The jungle by the river was only a couple of dozen hunching steps away. He was silent and kept going.

Amos let him go and staggered by himself, so that they both could go faster.

"Iffen that's you, Gus, answer me cause iffen it ain't you I'm going to shoot!"

It was said in Chokoloske that any peon trying to run from the Clayton Sugar Company could be shot, but there was always some disbelief. Why shot? A person who was shot couldn't cut cane. Why not just whipped?

No, the man wouldn't shoot. Even if he did, in the moonlight, as far away as he was, he wouldn't aim right nohow.

The deep black under the trees by the water was close.

Mark trotted three or four steps and looked back—"Run if you can."

Then he felt his neck and chin streaming with blood and heard the explosion. "Oh Lord, I's dead" he thought—might have said.

Amos was lying in the cane next to the path.

Mark put a hand to his neck and knew the blood came from Amos, not from himself. On the ground, he found the arm of Amos and knew the meaning of its lifeless weight—he didn't need to see where the face had been, speaking, hoping—

Mark stopped thinking.

A bullet from the Sharps twitched the mosquito net hanging from the broad-brimmed hat. The man fell against Barracks Four and lay there.

*

Laura was naked, too. She was standing by the open and screened window in bright moonlight. The shifting of soft shadows on her breasts, belly and pubis gave him a new vision of her, an incitement to desire that became an irrelevance, an encumbrance, at this time. He knew that now, at last, he understood her mixed feelings about her own beauty. She made good use of her beauty as a ticket to power. At the same time, as the object of a perpetual male yearning just to rut, she became impersonal flesh, a human being without character, an outcast from ordinary give-and-take. She was forced to live intimately inside herself. No wonder she was a little crazy! He strode to her, embraced her more tenderly than he ever had, and as she took his hard penis in her hand, he just said, quietly, "Ah, Laura—" He had no words for what he felt.

That afternoon, while the *Empress* floated cautiously up the unmarked channel of Lost Man's River, they'd wrestled and joined with a savagery like combat in the master stateroom. She'd mashed his penis against her clitoris and all over herself, kneading and pulling him. He was still sore.

She too, perhaps.

There seemed to be thorns inside his body, piercing outward rather than inward. His jaded flesh remained hot and awake.

They reached a peak quickly and then were quiet, side by side on the big bed.

"You must tell me exactly how you're going to do it," she said. This was what she had been thinking!

"Toward the end of every month Arthur takes his fancy train to Payhokee."

"I know. It's given me a little peace."

"He has to be in the middle of the army getting ready for Cuba."

"Oh yes—" and then, contemptuously—"he was going to follow the navy in the *Empress*—" she laughed—"but I had a better use for it."

He was bitter about her reckless appropriation of the big yacht. Van Bibber was in Fort Harrison, and no doubt Wilkins already knew that he and Laura were seeing each other. Wilkins was sure to retaliate immediately.

Here, up Lost Man's River, with his armed bosses and Sanford Payne, he was safe from whatever Wilkins could manage. But Laura was making him feel pressured to act fast, without enough care for an unfathomable means of killing Arthur Wilkins. If only he'd been able to get in touch with Laura *before* she bribed a number of people and took the *Empress*! She should have done nothing for two or three weeks, even a month. It should never appear that he had a reason to kill Arthur Wilkins. He thought of his success in being found innocent at his trial for the murder of Joseph Rourke. But killing Arthur Wilkins was another matter. Nobody would ask whether the deceased should have departed! He didn't like his own plan, which Laura was asking him about. "I know that line to Payhokee the way I know you," he said.

"You still have a lot to learn about me!"

With emotion, he made a kind of avowal he'd never made before—"Learning about you is the best thing I ever done!"

They were both silent for a time. Then she asked, all practicality, "How will you know when Arthur's going to take his next little jaunt?"

"He has fresh fish took on his train just before he starts out."

She imitated his way of speaking—"How will you know when he has fresh fish took on?"

"Sanford's little nigger servant will see it took on."

"Sanford's nigger servant?"

"Maybe you saw him around tonight and maybe you didn't. Fat little nigger we call Richard the Barber because he knows how to cut hair an' trim beards."

"I saw him—just before you went out with your gun."

"That little nigger's been with Sanford for years. Once we made him behave in a way that's contrary to his own nature, but I don't need to go into that now. All he has to do now is keep his eyes open and send a wire as soon as the fish is took on. Sanford and me will be waiting at a boarding house in Olustee, just like we're enjoying a little hunting together where we know the country."

"And then?"

"You got to know *every*thing?"

"Oh Tom—" she stroked his face, beard and neck. "You don't realize how I've suffered under the thumb of that man."

If she needs comfort for her hatred, she must have it, he thought. "All right—it's a simple matter. Sanford and me will rip up a rail so the train is stopped, maybe wrecked. Then Sanford will do it."

"His engineer? His cook?"

"Clean job. Engineer, cook, anybody else not important. I hope Van Bibber is aboard."

"Where will you be?"

"By the time Sanford is doing it, I'll be with my regiment. Some of my men got malaria and need looking after."

"The whole nation will be shocked."

"It'll be the kind of shock that makes folks foolish. The newspapers will go on about the assassination of Garfield and the attempt to kill Frick, and like pulling a rabbit out of a hat some lawman will find an anarchist."

"It's possible—likely, I guess."

"There'll be a big to-do, and I'll be in Cuba getting back our property that was burned." Mildly ironical, he went on, "I'll be serving my country, and just to think—it was Arthur Wilkins who arranged for my commission!"

XXIII

Early in the morning, before the guests from the *Empress* stirred, Julia met Tom at the foot of the stairs.

Already, he'd been out. He was wearing a Panama hat, white shirt and pants, high boots which were muddy, and revolver on his hip. There was a swollen mosquito bite beside his nose, and he glowered, the yellow in his eyes glinting.

Julia, terrified, put her right hand inside her reticule and clasped the big revolver but did not take it out. They hadn't been alone together since he'd raped her. There was a whining from strange and unendurable emotions in her ears, but she knew that if he approached her physically she would shoot him. She hoped to walk past him without speaking and go to the kitchen for breakfast.

He anticipated what she had in mind. He stood before the passage to the kitchen and stated, "One of my men was shot last night."

Forced to confront him, she asked, "Who was it?"

He disregarded her question and said, "Men I got working for me been safe here before—"

"Whoever it was, is he hurt bad?"

"Dead. Big caliber bullet right through his head."

"Who was it?" she asked again, quietly.

Again, he ignored her question and asked, "When did you last see Joshua Dale?"

"Joshua Dale?"

"Yes, Joshua Dale. You've met him, I presume. Joshua Dale, the Yankee storekeeper who used to be such a good friend to you, him and his wife Joanna, years ago in Olustee. Do you go see them in Chokoloske?"

She was focused upon protecting herself and couldn't respond immediately. Then, since it was clear he was not about to attack her, she could think about and deal with his suspicions. He was assuming that Joshua Dale had shot one of his bosses and that she had something to do with it, had perhaps put him up to it. She said, "Joshua Dale's much too old for creeping hereabouts at night."

He studied her a moment and said, "You can take your hand out of that purse. Shooting ain't your nature, Julia."

She did not release her grip on the big revolver and take her hand out of her reticule, but he did seem so calm and reasonable that she answered in kind, but with resolution—"It was wrong for you and me to be married, Tom. I know it and you know it. When the *Bonefish* comes back and goes out again, William and I will be leaving on it, and we'll never see each other again."

"You forget—" he said, "William is my son."

"No!" She could scarcely believe what she was hearing. Tom hadn't even seen his son since she'd been raped and William had thrown heavy spikes at him. Then she thought of Caroline's wretched and unthinkable hope that she'd be hostess at a supper for Laura Wilkins and her crew, and for Tom himself. She'd never expected that she would have to protect Caroline and William from Tom—from his influence, especially from skewed and dishonest human relationships, or from a suddenly awakened desire simply to possess.

"You belong here, too," he went on. Then he turned toward the kitchen with a shout—"Sarah, you got any of that rum Wheeler brought over?"

Julia went upstairs again to her own room for the note which she'd written to Thorstein, and she then rapped on the door of the guest room occupied by Caroline and Lawrence—"It's mother, Caroline."

She heard Caroline's murmur, and after a few seconds Caroline opened. She was wearing a plain nightie, and Lawrence remained in the bed, pulling a sheet up and over his shoulders and neck.

"I'm sorry to intrude, Lawrence," Julia said. "But I must have a chance to talk to Caroline and you, in private and before you leave."

"Oh Ma—" said Caroline, distressed. A serious conversation with her mother could only exacerbate conflicts she preferred to ignore.

But Lawrence nodded—"Yes, I have something to say, too."

Julia was simple and direct. She was never going to live with her legal husband, Caroline's father. She was going to live with, or near—depending on unforeseeable circumstances, Thorstein Brach. She would probably manage some business, but that was unforeseeable, too. She might teach

Latin. William would be going to the University of Wisconsin. That's what he wanted. Whatever she did, she'd come to Fort Harrison to be near them when she could. But she hoped she'd never have to see Thomas Clayton. Finally, she told them about Tom's determination to keep her and William where they were, but said she was confident they would leave on the *Bonefish*, when it came back to load up and go out again. She herself had hired the new captain of the *Bonefish*.

She handed Caroline her note for Thorstein—"Please mail this as soon as you're back in Fort Harrison. I've explained why William and I are delayed."

Caroline promised to mail the note. Did this mean that she comprehended her mother's state of mind and heart, that she could put herself in her mother's place? Not really, Julia thought, and no doubt it was just as well. Why should her happiness with Lawrence be tarnished by what her mother was going through?

As she went toward the door of the bedroom, intending to leave, Lawrence said, "Wait, mother, I got something to tell you—warn you maybe—I don't know."

Julia wondered if Lawrence would ever call her ma, as Caroline and William did. "Mother" sounded honorific, befitting her position in the Clayton Sugar Company and her collusion regarding his theft of Laura Wilkins's money and the dragged-out ransom negotiations. She felt that Caroline's husband liked her but also that he was somewhat put off by how hard she'd become. "Yes, Lawrence, what is it?" she asked.

Then Lawrence had a lot of trouble explaining what he had in mind—all he had was hunches there was going to be a lot of trouble and he hoped mother would be able to stay out of it. Mr. Clayton wasn't right in the head—he'd shown that by the way he came back to Fort Harrison from Georgia. And Mrs. Wilkins ought not to be using her husband's yacht, without her husband but with the kind of people who'd never get a loan from *his* bank! Just not sensible, neither Mr. Clayton nor Mrs. Wilkins! Mr. Wilkins wasn't going to like it that his wife got together with Mr. Clayton again, in a way that everybody could see, and especially since he'd arranged for Mr. Clayton to be made a colonel and go to Cuba. But *what* would Mr. Wilkins *do*? No telling! Mr. Clayton and Mrs. Wilkins must know Mr. Wilkins would do *something*. So what did *they* intend to do?

Lawrence was very serious. The reckless behavior of Mr. Clayton and Mrs. Wilkins was no longer a joyous adventure, as he seemed to regard it when Julia first met him. He was glad the Pelican Bank no longer depended for its business only on the Clayton Sugar Company.

Julia was impressed by Lawrence's apparent independence and by the fact that he referred to his father-in-law as Mr. Clayton, in an impersonal and even judgmental tone. She said, "If for any reason William and I can't come down the river on the *Bonefish*, I hope you'll hire and send some boat for us from Fort Harrison."

Lawrence hadn't expected this. "Yes—certainly," he said, after a moment. But he became pale. The mere idea of acting openly against the wishes of Thomas Clayton obviously terrified him.

Julia hugged Caroline—"William and I will spend a day with you before going north..." She spoke as though her plans could be taken for granted. But she felt she couldn't depend on either Lawrence or Caroline to send a boat, if it turned out that she needed one.

Just before noon, the *Empress* steamed down the river, Tom, Sanford Payne and Richard the Barber on board with Caroline, Lawrence, Laura Wilkins and her guests. Julia remembered the man who had so dramatically displayed his ecstasy at the arrival of Laura Wilkins in her frothy dress, a vision on Lost Man's River. He now blew kisses for farewell to the Clayton Sugar Company, to the faintly-heard hilarity of the party.

*

A week after the *Empress* left, Julia and William were in the office when the *Laura* came up the river, followed by the *Bonefish*. On her way out the door Julia said, "Find out if Tom has come back and then come and tell me."

William nodded. He knew his mother was going to her room in the big house to get her reticule and revolver. He had his hunting rifle in the office. There was a stack of fresh-cut lumber nearby, and William sat on it, the rifle across his knees, and waited. He was as eager as his mother to leave. He'd had a lonely and grim time at the sugar company. He'd left friends in Olustee, black folks at home and white folks about his own age in school. Would he ever see them again? Would he have new friends way up north in Madison, Wisconsin? If his mother couldn't persuade Mr. Kennedy to take them down the river on the *Bonefish*, he thought of threatening the man with his rifle. He knew he wouldn't do that—there were too many risks—his father, the Gray Man, Mr. Kennedy himself. But he thought of it.

He just watched, as his mother told him, as with much maneuvering and screaming of birds and shouts of two black deckhands on the *Bonefish* and a black worker from the refinery who came to catch ropes, the *Laura* was tied up on one side of the dock and the *Bonefish* on the other.

His father and Sanford Payne came off the *Laura*; Richard the Barber off the *Bonefish*. Sanford and Richard headed for the house. Sanford, besides wearing two revolvers, carried a rifle and a shotgun. Richard had two large satchels.

Thomas Clayton crossed the dock and went aboard the *Bonefish*. Even at a little distance, William could see that his face was mottled and sweating, his beard was unkempt, and his white pants and shirt were dirty. He gave some quiet order to Kennedy.

The "captain" of the *Bonefish* was squirting oil from a large can on moving parts of the auxiliary steam engine. He now put the can on the deck, went into his cabin, and came out again with a shaving mug and a razor. He drew some hot water from a petcock on the engine and mixed a lather in the mug, which he placed on a small shelf next to a little mirror on the cabin wall. Then he gave the razor to Thomas Clayton, who proceeded to shave around the edges of his red beard.

The return of the owner of the Clayton Sugar Company actuated two automatic but very different responses. Long Algy appeared, and without any need for words, workers were rolling barrels of sugar from the warehouse. The deckhands were removing a hatch cover. And meanwhile, Wheeler had rowed across the river.

"Will Wheeler!" Thomas Clayton bellowed. He put the razor down, gave the rum maker a hand, and hauled him violently from his skiff to the deck.

Wheeler had a jug in his free hand, and he raised it to his own lips. Tom tilted it further—"Drink! It's your own poison! You're fat enough to finish it in a couple of swallers!"

Wheeler spluttered and choked.

Tom yanked the jug away and put it to his own lips.

The rum maker staggered, blinded with tears. His groping hand caught the sling holding a barrel as it swung toward the hatch. The power of the winch sent Wheeler sprawling, and the barrel, dislodged, fell with a crash in the hold.

There was a shout from below deck—"Hey!" Then a black worker thrust his head out of the hatch. It seemed he wasn't hurt.

"You good-for-nothing son of a stinking polecat," Tom said to the worker, casually. He was shaving his neck below his beard.

"It wasn't me knocked the barrel loose, Mr. Clayton," said the man.

"You black nigger bastard!" bellowed Wheeler. He heaved himself so that he was on his hands and knees, and he went on, nicely, "Now, just rest yourself, Mr. Clayton. You been away a long time and it ain't right for you needing to stir yourself soon's you back.

The black man went below again.

"I do appreciate your friendly feeling," said Tom.

Wheeler, still on hands and knees, poked his head into the hatch and roared, "You ignorant black shit you—"

The loose sling whipped out of the hold and barely missed Wheeler's head.

He screamed obscenities.

Tom seemed totally indifferent to Wheeler and the worker in the hold of the *Bonefish*. He said something to Kennedy which William couldn't hear, and Kennedy responded by getting a strap from his cabin, hanging it from a nail on the cabin wall, and stropping the razor. Tom must have complained that it was dull.

William took a few steps toward the dock. It seemed incredible that the rum maker could shriek so at a colored man and not ease his feelings by drawing blood. William was thinking that he might shoot in the air just to attract attention and maybe cool things down.

Wheeler, with considerable effort, was on his feet again.

Kennedy handed over the razor again—"All stropped as keen as it will get, Mr. Clayton."

Tom strode to Wheeler, plunged his left hand into the fat flesh of the rum maker's chest, and went for his throat with the razor.

Wheeler caught Tom's wrist. "Help! Help me!" he screamed. "He's crazy! Kennedy!"

The worker poked his head up through the cargo hatch and silently watched.

Wheeler's feet caught in a coil of rope so that he sprawled, Tom on top of him. The razor wavered close to Wheeler's throat. He gave choked screams but managed to say, over and over, "Kennedy, help! Help me!"

Long Algy was on his way back toward the refinery, and he stopped to observe. It was clear he wasn't going to say or do anything.

Kennedy danced about as they writhed on the deck and said, "What's it matter, Mr. Clayton? Just cause he sounds like a yapping dog ain't no reason to go and cut his throat. Aw, Mr. Clayton, it ain't worth the trouble."

William fired his rifle in the air.

Thomas Clayton released his hold on Wheeler, sat up, saw William, and laughed. Then he stood up and folded the blade of the razor into its handle. "Reckon you're right, Kennedy. Here's your razor. Thank you very much."

Wheeler was prone, his chest and belly heaving, getting back his breath.

"Get up," commanded Tom. "That's my son there had to shoot off his little rifle to remind you how disgusting you're behaving. It's time you started acting like a gentleman — clean yourself up, put shoes on your feet, and come have some dinner."

"I don't feel like eating," groaned Wheeler. He was still flat on his back, exhausted, his fat torso heaving. His shirt had been ripped away from his chest, which was already black and blue. "I knew you was only fooling."

Tom grunted.

"I'm all sweated up now."

"Are you turning down my invitation? Thunderation! Can't folks live in honor and courtesy?"

"It ain't that — so help me, Mr. Clayton —"

"Kennedy, give me your razor again!"

"No, Mr. Clayton, Wheeler can't stand no more of this."

Wheeler sat up — "Oh, all right, Mr. Clayton. I ain't hungry the least bit but I'll come to dinner for the company and the honor, with you inviting me and all, but I got to get me clean clothes and like you say put shoes on my feet..."

William went to tell his mother that Thomas Clayton was back. He would describe what had happened, but he wouldn't make any attempt to explain the state of mind or intentions of the man who was his father. William couldn't understand his own state of mind — why he seemed unable to breathe, why his eyes were hot with tears that wouldn't come.

*

The architect of the big house up Lost Man's River, under the influence of Laura Wilkins, had planned for gracious living. So there was a butler's pantry between the kitchen and the large dining room, even though there was no butler.

Julia sat in the butler's pantry, in the dark, remaining unseen as she observed Tom's back at the head of the table in the brightly lit dining room, Wheeler seated to his left and Kennedy to his right. Her reticule, with her revolver, was on a shelf near her right hand; and a plate of Sarah's fried chicken, with mashed turnip, remained untouched near her left hand.

She was waiting for Kennedy to leave the table and go to the room provided for him while the *Bonefish* was at the company's dock, so that he could have a good night's sleep in a real bed and freshen up in a real bathroom with running water. She wanted to speak to him, without Tom being present, to make arrangements for going down the river and being let off at Fort Harrison.

Tom was liquored up and talkative — "Cuba is one godforsaken place — hills weighing on your chest while you sleep, burying a man, and niggers running all over with machetes. But a man ain't yellow can go with a rifle and add to hisself as a man, add to his juice..." At considerable length, he was urging Wheeler to go with the Fort Harrison regiment to Cuba and make rum.

Sanford Payne came in the dining room. He was wearing his customary gray jacket in spite of the heat, and his pale face was expressionless. He hadn't taken off his gun belt before coming to supper.

"Come and shake my hand, Sanford," Tom said, not stirring from his chair. "You and me, Sanford, we ain't going to be put down just because Arthur Wilkins takes it into his head to go to New York instead of Payhokee. Selling stock — shit!"

"It ain't only that, Tom," said Sanford, not moving.

"Dammit, man, come take my hand!"

"Sure, Tom." And Sanford moved to do so.

Julia thought of Lawrence Eddy's speculations about what Wilkins was going to do, and what Tom was going to do. Had Tom planned to meet the magnate in Payhokee? If so, what could he possibly have to say? Had he planned to murder Wilkins?

Tom held Sanford's hand for a few seconds—"Sure seems good to see a man with the habit of wearing his gun just as natural as a hat on a sunny day. Sit down and eat, Sanford." He shouted, "Sarah!" Then, in what might have been oblique reference to Payne's incompetence as general manager, he went on in an ordinary tone, "By the Lord, since I been away nobody humps to it any more around here."

Sarah passed Julia in the butler's pantry and went into the dining room.

"Goddamnit, woman, when I speak, jump!"

"Yes sir, Mr. Clayton."

"If there ain't enough chicken for Mr. Payne, Mr. Wheeler and Captain Kennedy, go out and kill six or seven."

Kennedy spoke for the first time—"I had enough." He'd been silent and wary. In view of the fracas on the dock, which William had described, Julia thought she knew why.

Tom glanced at Kennedy but didn't speak to him. Julia wondered if the "captain" of the *Bonefish* would now take orders only from Tom, or would he do as she asked, since she had hired him? She knew she couldn't depend on the Greek immigrant who ran the *Laura*.

Tom went on—"Sanford, maybe you can make Wheeler do what he ought. Don't know why it is he can't see his way clear to act in his own benefit, and what benefit has he got but putting rum in his fellow man's gut? Wheeler, wake up!"

"He makes good rum. Ain't no denying that," remarked Sanford.

Wheeler stirred and drank. There was a jug on the table, and Wheeler from time to time touched another jug on the floor beside his chair, as though worried it might go away.

Payne unbuckled his gun belt and draped it over the back of his chair.

"That's right, Sanford. Make yourself comfortable. I been thinking about it, Sanford. You ought to go with me to Cuba too, soon's we take care of business near Payhokee—"

"Like I been telling you, Tom, I don't know about Payhokee—"

Apparently there had been an unprecedented disagreement with the right-hand man, but Tom didn't want to press whatever he had in mind about Payhokee at this time. He went on about Sanford's talents and about Cuba—"Sanford, you ain't got no more head for business than a baboon, but you're the damnedest man with a gun I ever see. And Cuba's the place for a damnedest man with a gun! By God you and me can have ourselves a jamboree in Cuba and make six fortunes…" Tom continued about the attractions of Cuba for some time — idleness, cigars, Wheeler's rum, and occasional exercise with a gun.

Wheeler's head dropped forward on the table.

Tom gave him a rough shove on the shoulder so that he fell out of his chair with a dead weight that jarred the floor. Then he stirred and muttered some curses.

"Can't stand up to his own liquor," remarked Tom.

There was a confused conversation in which Sanford showed that he no longer knew just where he stood in relation to Tom.

Was Tom's recommendation of Cuba a way of demoting him from his position as general manager of the company's Florida operation? Julia heard Sanford say, "I couldn't do nothing with a pious woman on my neck" — and then listened to Tom express sympathy with Sanford's difficulties through a long disquisition to the effect that the flight of workers from the company was an aspect of a national sickness — "The country's going soft and niggers are pushing folks off the sidewalks in Baltimore I heard."

Sanford was not reassured. Was removal to Cuba a punishment because what Sanford did in Key Alva had landed Tom in prison? Sanford felt terrible about what he'd done but it was Tom who kept putting him in unbefitting situations. He didn't *want* to go to that place in Key Alva. He didn't *want* to manage the sugar company. Years ago, he didn't really *want* to stir up all the scum for the Myrtle riot, an act which lost him the wife with whom he might have lived like other men — "When I come home from Myrtle — you got me into that, Tom — she found this little old nigger's hand in my jacket pocket. I swear to God I don't know how it got there. Isabel was carrying at the time and the baby came that night. It had a black foot." Sanford moaned.

Tom told him it wasn't becoming to carry on so and he had a lot to be proud of — "Never would've got started at all, never would've made the Clayton Sugar Company if it hadn't been for you and Miz Wilkins — you fixing it so I got my plantation back and Laura Wilkins backing me with her own money."

Julia had become so used to her intuition that Sanford was somehow involved in the murder of Joseph Rourke that she wasn't surprised at a direct statement to this effect. She wasn't even surprised at this newly revealed horror that connected the Myrtle riot with Sanford's once-upon-a-time marriage. She was aware of a cold and self-confident hatred that could be expressed only in the most expedient actions, with no wasteful misgivings. She assessed all that was going on in the dining room, and she wondered at the effect of this conversation upon Kennedy, a stranger to what Tom and Sanford were talking about. Kennedy was mute, solemnly nibbling his chicken and turnip, and in moderation sipping Wheeler's rum.

Tom continued to be insistent about Cuba. It was reward for what Sanford might do near Payhokee, since it was a sure thing that Arthur Wilkins would eventually take his private train to Payhokee, not to New York. "Christ, Sanford! Didn't you hear what Laura Wilkins herself told you, right here in this room? She has a way of putting things, and she said you're going to have a glorious destiny."

And meanwhile, Tom tried to make clear, Sanford could still be a great help in putting the Florida operation on a sound footing again—"There's niggers in Chokoloske scare Long Algy and maybe some others, but they don't scare you and me, do they, Sanford? Time we round them up and bring them back where they belong." Tom went on for several minutes about Joshua Dale, who had been against him years ago in Olustee, was against him all the time since moving to Chokoloske, and was no friend to Sanford Payne! "Ain't you up to whipping him, Sanford, or maybe doing for him entirely?"

Wheeler lurched to his feet.

Tom laughed and said, "You come to just in time, Wheeler," and raised his goblet to drink. But it was empty.

"'S'all right, Mr. Clayton," said Wheeler. He took the jug from the floor, uncorked it, and filled Tom's goblet. Then he put that jug back on the floor.

"To Cuba," said Tom. Payne and Wheeler emptied their goblets with him.

Kennedy drank only a little and said, "I'm leaving you gentlemen to enjoy yourselves. I'm heading for bed. Thanks for the supper, Mr. Clayton."

Julia rose from her chair and headed for the kitchen and the hall passage. She caught Kennedy at the foot of the stairs. Tom could see them from where he sat in the dining room.

"Captain Kennedy," she said, "I shall want to leave with you, tomorrow, after the *Bonefish* is loaded. William will come, too, and we'll both have trunks." She was trying to make this statement sound ordinary.

Kennedy took his time replying. He looked through the arched opening toward the dining room, and Julia could see in a sudden freezing of his features that his eyes had met Tom's. Had Tom already ordered him not to take her and William down the river?

Speaking very low so that Tom wouldn't be able to hear him, he said at last, "I don't know what to say, Mrs. Clayton. Now that Mr. Clayton's back, I reckon I got to take my orders from him—long as I keep this job. What him and Mr. Payne were talking about, Payhokee and Mr. Wilkins and all, warn't clear to me and I reckon it's none of my business. But to tell you the truth, Mrs. Clayton, they scare me."

Julia thought that if Tom for any reason were not on the dock when the *Bonefish* left, she could probably persuade Kennedy to do as she asked. So she said, "Well, we'll talk tomorrow."

"Yes, let's do that, Mrs. Clayton—" and Kennedy went upstairs.

She got a plate of chicken and turnip from Sarah and took it to William in the office. He was going to sleep there on a pile of sugar sacks while his father was in the big house. Then she went upstairs to her own room. She latched the door, turned the wick in her lamp low but did not blow it out, and kept her revolver next to the pillow on her bed.

She heard Tom stumble on the stairs. He was probably drunk.

Perhaps she slept, perhaps not.

Then the scream—Tom's—"Julia! Julia! I've been poisoned!"

She turned up the wick of her lamp, unlatched her door, and rushed out, her revolver in her right hand. The scream might be a trick, so that she would open her door!

But in the hall his great reddish body was stretched out on the floor, naked and with blue and green splotches on his belly, which was terribly swollen, and froth spluttered from his lips.

"Julia," he moaned, seeing her.

It was a genuine appeal for help, and she could only feel that it was strange, utterly beyond comprehension, that he should beseech *her* after all their contrary lives had been, and that there was in Tom a special certitude that all human beings would do as he required, regardless of other inclinations and past circumstances. For only a second she leaned to put the revolver on the floor in order to do something—just what she didn't know—to help him. Then she straightened and just looked at him.

Captain Kennedy came from his guest room, tucking shirttails into pants—"Godamighty, what's going on?"

"Mr. Clayton says he's poisoned—"

Sarah came from the kitchen to the foot of the stairs.

"Git some mustard and water!" the captain ordered. Already he was dragging Tom to the head of the stairs so that his head could be dropped lower than the rest of him. He forced his fingers down Tom's throat.

Tom moaned and gagged. Probably he realized that Kennedy was trying to make him throw up.

Sanford Payne came from his room, and Richard the Barber peered from the stairs that led to the attic.

Julia said to Sanford what she'd already said to Kennedy—"Mr. Clayton says he's poisoned." She knew she sounded very matter-of-fact.

Kennedy was holding Tom's head under his arm as though he were wrestling, and Tom was vomiting a greenish metallic-looking slime. Over and over Kennedy forced his fingers down Tom's gullet. Over and over Tom retched.

Sarah came with the mustard and water.

Kennedy snapped at her, "Fill a wash boiler in the kitchen, biggest one you got. Fill it with hot water, very hot water. We got to sweat him. Give that mustard and water to Mrs. Clayton."

Sarah did so and rushed off.

Kennedy twisted Tom over, controlling the violence of the writhing and twisting body. He seemed to know just what to do. "I got to hold his jaws open," he said to Julia. "You pour in the mustard and water."

Julia handed the glass to Sanford—"You do it, Sanford."

Sanford did, his pale face stony.

Kennedy heaved up Tom's heavy torso so the mustard and water went down. Greenish vomit was smearing him, and some got on Sanford's gray suit. He hadn't undressed for bed, and he was still wearing one of his guns.

The captain assaulted Tom's gullet yet again, and he brought up more vomiting. The chicken came up, with much more slime.

"Got that water ready?" bellowed Kennedy.

"Some is ready! More coming!" screamed Sarah, from the kitchen.

"Take his head and shoulders," the captain ordered Sanford.

They carried him downstairs.

Julia followed.

Sarah had dragged a big galvanized iron tub which was ordinarily used for butchering hogs into the kitchen. It was half full of steaming water.

"Put him on the floor," gasped Kennedy. Working over Tom had exhausted him.

Sarah seized a five-gallon kettle from the stove and dumped more water into the tub.

Kennedy put his hand in to test it—"We can cool it just a little bit but not much."

Tom was lying flat on his back, drawing his legs up and thrusting them out again, in recurring spasms. The blue and green of the skin over his swollen belly had faded for a time after he vomited. Now the color was deepening again. He groaned constantly.

"Wheeler," Tom muttered.

Payne leaned over him—"Wheeler do the poisoning?"

Tom couldn't reply, and no one else spoke.

Payne seized Tom by the shoulders again, Kennedy by the feet, and together they heaved him into the steaming tub.

He bellowed with pain. The strength of this bellow was the first clear sign that he might live.

"You got to stand it, Mr. Clayton," said Kennedy.

But the shock gave Tom a spasm which pushed the captain away.

"You *got* to stay in this tub," said Kennedy, and he threw himself violently on Tom. "Help me!" he cried to Payne, and the Gray Man did, so that together they kept the swollen belly under the surface, while Tom howled with the agony of the poison and the heat.

"This is for your own good, Tom," said Payne, with instinctive faith in such painful treatment. Richard the Barber had somehow wedged himself into the kitchen, and Payne growled at him, "Fetch some wood and stir up that fire."

Captain Kennedy said, looking at Julia, "We need some blankets."

"You know where they are, Sarah," Julia said. She would observe what was going on, but she wouldn't help revive Tom.

Kennedy gave her a glance that seemed to express surprise before turning back to his patient.

Tom was lying back in the tub, groaning, the calves of his legs sticking over the edge, swollen and with veins a heavy blue-green. Kennedy forced him to vomit again, and the metallic green slime puddled on the kitchen floor. Richard found a rag and cleaned it up, ducking around Kennedy and Payne, who were paddling the hot water over exposed parts of Tom's body. Kennedy took a roller towel, dipped it in the hot water, and wound it like a turban around Tom's head.

"God damn, God damn Wheeler. I'll skin that bastard's ass," said Tom, weakly. But he was coherent.

"Hey, we're licking this poison," said Kennedy.

"If you're all right, Tom, I'm going out and get that Wheeler," said Payne.

Sarah came in with an armful of blankets.

"Make a pallet," said Kennedy. "Do you think you can get over on the blankets, Mr. Clayton? We got to wrap you and sweat it out some more."

Tom put his hands and arms on the edge of the tub and made an effort to lift himself. But he had no strength. He gave a sudden frightened look around the room.

"Easy, Mr. Clayton," said Kennedy. He and Sanford heaved him on the pallet and covered him.

"Sweat's in my eyes," grumbled Tom.

Sarah found a towel and wiped him.

Payne gave his gun belt a hitch and went out through the passage toward the front door.

Richard the Barber was unloading an armful of wood, putting a few split hunks in the stove.

The captain of the *Bonefish* ruminated—"If that blue and green reached his heart, Mr. Clayton would've gone, quick as a puff of smoke. Now that coloring is going away. Give him a night's sleep and he'll be good as new."

Richard said, "I sure is glad Mr. Clayton going to be hisself again. Mr. Payne he just couldn't stand it withouten Mr. Clayton. Now everything going to be all honey-like—just like it used to be." He gave Julia an openly hostile look.

She realized that he hated her because she had acquired strong influence over his master, and perhaps because her constant efforts to prevent cruelty to field hands in some weird way derogated his special status. She sprang on him like a cat and seized his shirt in her fist—"You killed Joseph Rourke! I know you did it!"

For just an instant his terrified face acknowledged the truth of what she was saying. He dropped the firewood he was carrying and hurried out the back door.

"What on earth you mean by that, Mrs. Clayton?" asked Kennedy. "What's that nigger done? Who's Joseph Rourke?"

Tom laughed. The sound was unearthly, a weak cackle.

"For God's sake, Mr. Clayton—" Kennedy began.

"Take him upstairs and put him to bed," said Julia. "Get him out of my sight."

But she herself put him out of her sight by rushing from the house. She had in mind speaking to Sanford Payne. Richard the Barber's effective admission of his guilt made her more than ever ashamed of her years of failure to acknowledge what was true. Esther and Joshua Dale had instinctively been sure of Tom's responsibility for the murder of Joseph. She felt that her own muddled mind shared in the evil. But she now conceived clearly the brutish give-and-take behind the murder—Tom's fraudulent but serviceable power and authority, Sanford's diseased and worshipful truckling, Richard's willingness to do anything rather than endure the lot of other black men. That such relationships were possible could drown one in a sea of horror and despair for humanity. She felt certain that Tom and Sanford were plotting the murder of Arthur Wilkins, and with much more passion she recognized that they intended to restore the brutal regime in the cane fields of the time before she came up Lost Man's River. She would not despair. She'd persuade Sanford not to help Tom in whatever he planned to do.

The night was clear, there was moonlight, a wind across Lost Man's River and the open lawn blew away most of the mosquitoes, and she could see where she was going without a lantern. She almost tripped over Sanford Payne, in a shadow and prone in her path. In spite of her certainty about his part in the murder of Joseph, she reasserted her anomalous affiliation with him. Her purpose was far stronger than her revulsion. "Sanford?" she said, gently, bending over him.

For a moment he didn't stir.

She repeated his name, twice.

At last he turned up his face and spoke quite calmly—"It's all right, Miz Clayton. Don't you upset yourself. I had in mind getting that Will Wheeler for what he done to Tom, but I stumbled and before I could get myself up I got to thinking there ain't no way of crossing the river but taking the dinghy from the *Bonefish* and I don't know if I can unhitch it and find my way in the dark—"

She interrupted—"Sanford, please, Tom's recovered anyway. Leave Wheeler to the justice and mercy of God—" and then, thinking there would be no absurdity for Sanford in what she was about to say, she added—"or to the justice and mercy of Tom himself."

He stood, facing her—"You're so good, Miz Clayton."

She made a sound, neither a snort nor a laugh, that dismissed his statement. "You must look after yourself, Sanford, and not worry about Tom…"

How could she sit on the lumber pile and talk for more than an hour with the man who at Tom's command had managed the murder of Joseph? How could she stand his face frigid and pale as that of a corpse in the moonlight, his breath sickly sweet from Wheeler's rum, his nerves on hold for a new killing time, his soul which out of deranged aspiration to have the approval of Thomas Ewell Clayton had arranged the bushwhacking of the man who brought new life to Esther, who observed and understood perhaps even earlier than Esther her own dedicated love with Thorstein? How could she continue to speak, putting out of her mind the nine little notches on the gun which drooped from his hip? Which of those notches had been filed after Myrtle? Which ones at the sugar company, before her own arrival?

She mentioned Payhokee, and perhaps Sanford thought she knew more than she really did know. If so, was he all the more impressed by what she was saying?

She mentioned Chokoloske, and Sanford said it was a very dangerous place. Tom shouldn't go there alone.

"*You* should *never* go there, Sanford!" she exclaimed, and then went on with what she only half believed but expressed with all the more passion on that account—"You can stand on your own feet regardless of what Tom plans, regardless of what happens to Tom. You said I'm good, Sanford, and I don't know about that. But I'm sure there is good in you…

XXIV

Fort Harrison was a growing commercial center and since the battleship *Maine* had been blown up in Havana harbor and all the hotheads got together on the fairgrounds, the community had become ardent in commitment to the manifest destiny of the nation. It regarded Thomas Ewell Clayton, the owner of the Pelican Bank, as a genuine patriot, well deserving of the commission as lieutenant colonel or maybe even colonel he was about to get. Hadn't Mr. Clayton let his sugar company go to the dogs for more than a year so that he could serve in Washington and, as Mr. Eddy at the bank hinted, on a secret and dangerous mission to Cuba? The general manager left in charge was handier with a gun than with business matters, and the wife entrusted with the bookkeeping had meddled.

A few peons left the sugar company, all on their own. A big black man who went by the name of Hot Ash, wearing a brown suit that had once belonged to Thomas Clayton himself, came to Chokoloske with five other men, three women, and two children who had all been peons at the company. They were half-starved, scratched, lacerated, bruised, stung by mosquitoes and other insects, and one man was sick from being bitten by a water moccasin. For six days their survival had been made possible mainly by Hot Ash, who had an ax, knives and matches taken from the big house at the sugar company. They'd followed or hacked trails across hammocks, waded through sawgrass, floundered in swamps, and crossed waterways on logs or on the broad back of Hot Ash, who in addition to other abilities knew how to swim. The achievement was awesome. The brown suit worn by Hot Ash was so muddy and ripped when he first appeared that it could hardly be seen that it was a suit and not just some tied-together rags. It was Joanna Dale who washed it so that it shrank only a little, mended it, and pressed it with a hot iron so that the big black man who led peons out of the Clayton Sugar Company, as Moses led the Children of Israel out of Egypt, went around Chokoloske wearing what was known to have been worn by Mr. Thomas Clayton, and which therefore provided a perpetual reminder of liberation from peonage, and of how low the Clayton Sugar Company could fall unless Mr. Clayton did something about it.

In general, the people of Chokoloske, unlike the people in Fort Harrison, did not think about Thomas Clayton's presumptive patriotism, or anybody's patriotism for that matter. Chokoloske was still frontier. Its people included Florida blacks, Greek divers for sponges, fishermen from foreign parts, a few guides for hunting parties, miscellaneous outcasts, and a minority of women, black and white, who bore children, cooked and glued together the motley population so that the town acquired a civic character of its own — as far as Thomas Clayton was concerned, more interested in steering clear of his sugar company than in his patriotism.

Chokoloske had no school and no church. It had *Joshua Washington Dale — General Merchandise* and the dock where goods came in and alligator hides, egret feathers, shells and sponges went out. There was a lot more than the usual comings and goings to the Dales' store after the sheriff and the judge came from Key Alva to swear in Joshua Dale as a deputy sheriff. Years before, after Thomas Clayton shot off Sheriff Edward Burlitt's hat, thereby signifying that what went on up Lost Man's River was beyond any law coming out of Key Alva, and Joshua Dale had *asked* to be made a deputy because he wanted to do something about the disappearance of McLevy, the sailor who came home from the sea, the sheriff wouldn't have anything to do with the Chokoloske storekeeper — he'd *never* take as deputy a man who'd been with Sherman's army during the War Between the States! So what had changed Edward Burlitt's mind? Since Key Alva was Arthur Wilkins's town, and since Arthur Wilkins's yacht had been seen up Lost Man's River, it seemed likely that Arthur Wilkins had made some kind of suggestion to the sheriff. But the appointment showed the contempt of the sheriff and judge for Chokololske. Why should they appoint a man who was getting along in years and had just recovered from the stroke? What could *he* do about Thomas Clayton?

Thirteen days after the Wilkins yacht came down Lost Man's River and steamed away, Joshua Dale was sitting on the porch of his store and reading a week-old *St. Vincent Chronicle*. Joanna was inside. "Come out and rest a while," he called.

He could hear her dragging something about.

"It seems the navy's scared the Germans away from the Philippines," he went on, in a loud voice so she could hear. "The *Chronicle* says we acknowledge no overlord to tell us how far we may profit by the excellence of our gunnery and the valor of our troops."

The dragging continued.

"It's like the fox who kills and eats the hen to save her from the hawk."

Joanna came to the screen door.

"Damn it! I wish there was somebody I could talk to," he scolded. "It ain't comfortable being the only human being around who can see the country's going crazy. The soldier boys over in Fort Harrison are dying dirty deaths from malaria or yellow fever, maybe thinking about nice clean heroes' deaths in Cuba or Puerto Rico. Soft in the head! Bought the imperial destiny bill of goods."

"Some men will do anything just to feel important," said Joanna.

Her words struck him as very sensible. He repeated his invitation, coaxing—"Come and sit, Joanna."

"I'm bringing this rug out for a beating."

"Oh damn the rug," he said, wearily. But he rose, went inside the store, bent, picked up an edge of the rug—his back twinged—and gave it an impatient yank. "Hold the door open," he ordered.

"I ain't asking you to help," she said. "With your back this ain't the kind of thing you ought to be doing."

"What *can* I do if you won't sit and talk?"

She held the door, and he pulled half the rug through it. An edge jammed under the open door.

"Just wait," she said, crisply, and kicked it free.

He pulled the rug the rest of the way out the door so that it lay over the porch, the porch step, and a little of the sandy path before the store. He let go, wavered as he stood straight, closed his eyes, and took deep breaths.

"Let it be for now," she said. "I'll get some customer to help put it over the clothesline so we can beat it. I wouldn't bother but everybody comes in the store brings a cupful of sand."

"I haven't had the kind of conversation I'd like to have since Joseph Rourke was shot," he said. Then he was sorry he'd said it. He wouldn't want Joanna to think he didn't like talking with her. The words popped out because Thomas Clayton was on his mind—in going after Clayton because of McLevy, which was a good enough reason for the sheriff and judge from Key Alva, he was *personally* going after Clayton because he would never forget Joseph Rourke. And because of Myrtle, because of Amos Peters, because the liberation of black people that he'd fought for when he was young and strong hadn't stuck. "Now—now, Joanna, please," he said, "just rest and sit."

She did, but then they had little to say. They both knew that Joshua was made a deputy because Wilkins wanted Clayton brought to justice again and because Edward Burlitt was afraid of going after him. They both knew that Clayton would come to Chokoloske for the peons who'd run away—and to do something about Will Wheeler, now hiding out with a Chokoloske woman no better than she should be, and telling several different tales about almost killing Thomas Clayton.

The one good thing about Joshua's appointment as deputy was that he wouldn't have to go up Lost Man's River. The man he was supposed to arrest would come to him. His authority was damaged by peons running loose in Chokoloske, and by a fat slob like Wheeler getting away with an attempt to kill him. Both Joshua and Joanna felt that they knew his nature—he was sure to come.

Joshua passed each day as though he was sleepwalking. Joanna too, it seemed.

In the middle of the afternoon on the day the rug was put over the clothesline and beaten, Mark Richardson came in the store with his Sharps, which was polished so that it shone like jewelry. "The launch from the Clayton Sugar Company is coming," he said. He showed no emotion beyond special sobriety.

Joanna responded in kind—"We've waited enough, and I'm glad we don't have to wait another day."

Joshua just nodded. She followed him through the back of the store, across the small porch between the store and their living quarters, and into the kitchen to the shelfless, glass-doored bookcase where they kept their guns. He took his Enfield and Joanna took the shotgun.

"You won't be needing that," he said, knowing that this probably wasn't true but just showed care for her.

"I hope not," she said.

"Well, leave it here, then."

She busied herself putting in shells—buckshot. "I never favored talking with Tom Clayton. I figure he nor nobody on his place ever talked with Amos Peters. I favor shooting first and talking later, if there be anything to talk about."

"I won't have you coming with Mark and me."

"I accept what you say. You're the soldier. But if Tom Clayton or his Gray Man Sanford Payne or any other boss from his company get by you, there's one or two won't get by me. I won't talk. I'll hide in the store, and when they come in like everybody does come in sooner or later I will shoot. Then—if you're still alive, you can talk all you's so minded."

He put his hand on her shoulder for a moment and walked out.

Mark followed him toward the dock. "Bina told me," he said. "She's been watching the river every day—never takes her eyes off it. She say the launch coming slow, but it coming, and toward here, sure enough." Mark was wearing only some old pants and his usual red bandanna around his head for keeping the sweat out of his eyes. Joshua remembered for the first time in a few years that the fish hooks stuck in this red bandanna had been picked out of the ashes of his mother's cabin in Myrtle. During the countless times he'd fished in the Gulf, there must have been occasions when it would have been convenient to use at least one of those hooks, but he never had.

As they walked toward the dock they could see the launch, still about a mile off.

Will Wheeler caught up with them. He was sweaty, panting and very dirty. In Chokoloske he hadn't been able to take care of himself as he might have done in his own cabin. "Is Tom Clayton coming?" he demanded.

"Seems likely," said Joshua.

Wheeler became shrill—"I never had nothing to do with poisoning Tom. It's all a lie. I don't know how anybody can be so downright slandering and low-down to spread that lie about me. If you're going to talk to Tom, I wish you'd tell him that cause I don't want him looking for me while he's got wrong ideas. It must've been his nigger cook poisoned Tom."

"That ain't what you been saying," said Joshua.

"You ain't heard me right!" Wheeler cried. "I just ain't going to take no sides in any argument with Tom Clayton."

"You do as you choose," said Mark.

"I damn will do as I choose!" Wheeler exclaimed.

Joshua laughed—and was pleased with himself that he could laugh. Wheeler wasn't taking kindly to instruction from a black man. But what could he do about it? Mark in his own easygoing way was just as frightening as Tom Clayton. With his mild expression and thin mustache clipped in the Spanish style, he looked careless and somehow elegant, even though he was barefoot and wore only old pants and no shirt at all.

The old Sharps rifle, bright as a new silver dollar, swung as though it pulled him along.

"Haven't you learned there ain't no civilization here in Chokoloske to keep a colored man from speaking his mind?" Joshua asked Wheeler, not expecting an answer.

They had come to the dock and could see plainly the sugar company launch, the *Laura*, coming in very slow, following the stakes for the channel.

Suddenly, Wheeler was gone.

Joshua cupped his mouth with his free hand and bellowed, "Clayton!"

The launch was near enough so that a man was visible, near the prow at the steering wheel. But the sun was behind him and he was just a shape. Whoever he was, he didn't reply. The piston of the steam engine made a thump-thump, and perhaps he didn't hear Joshua.

A tall and thin woman was casting for shrimp at the end of the dock. She became aware of what was up, gathered in her net, and ran past them on legs like deers'.

Joshua stood on the beach next to the dock—it was as good a place as any for meeting Tom Clayton—and Mark was next to him. "Clayton!" he bellowed again. Joanna said that when he shouted he squawked like a bird with a broken wing.

The thump-thump of the engine started an echo from back of the town, and at the same time there came a reply in Clayton's unmistakable bass voice—"I hear you, Dale."

Some children were about, excited by the guns and the shouting.

Joshua snapped, "You kids, get away! This ain't for you!" Then he faced the water again—"Come in to the dock, Clayton!"

There was no reply, but the thump-thump of the engine slowed down.

The big man named Hot Ash was strolling toward them, as easy in his walk as though he were going to church. Tom Clayton's cast-off brown suit had shrunk so that it didn't cover his broad bare chest, and the cuffs of his pants were several inches above his enormous bare feet.

"You ain't armed," Mark said to him, "and you better get ready to skedaddle if Clayton comes ashore."

This was the first suggestion from Mark that he and Joshua might not survive what was about to happen, since Clayton wasn't going to come ashore if they were able to deal with him.

Hot Ash nodded and sauntered away, slowly, keeping his dignity. His composure somehow suggested that he was delegating a responsibility to Mark and Joshua, who had guns, so that he wouldn't have to skedaddle.

"Your eyes are better than mine," Joshua said to Mark. "Do you see the Gray Man?"

"No, but maybe he's squinching down out of sight."

"Maybe," Joshua repeated.

They had agreed that if both Clayton and Payne came to them, Mark would try to shoot Payne, and Joshua would try to shoot Clayton. *If* Mark shot Payne before Payne shot him, he'd load his old Sharps again and shoot Clayton too. It seemed likely that Clayton would probably shoot Joshua if Mark had to deal with Payne.

The thought leaped in Joshua that the accomplished killer Sanford Payne might not be in the launch and that Clayton might, just might, be fool enough to come without him. Or perhaps not fool—perhaps just a man who didn't want to live, perhaps a man who'd had enough of lonely and bloody striving.

"You got anything to say, Clayton?" Joshua shouted. To Mark, he said, "That man's life has been one big long fever."

He felt right off this was a stupid thing to say under the circumstances—Mark's silence for a couple of seconds showed how puzzled he was.

Mark reaffirmed what they'd already decided—"I will shoot Sanford Payne if he shows hisself, and you will have to shoot Clayton, Joshua."

"Yes," said Joshua.

Mark turned and shouted angrily at one of his own children—"Peachbud, you go over there behind those trees. You hear me? You do as I say!"

"I can make out only one man," said Joshua.

"I see good enough now," said Mark. "There is only one man—Clayton hisself. But we can't know what is hiding in the bottom of the boat, or behind the engine."

Somewhere, a door slammed and voices chattered. The town had become aware. The carpenter who had built the dock had a pistol in his hand but remained at his house.

Clayton, or somebody, shut down the engine so that the launch rode on its own momentum toward the beach. Clayton wasn't going to tie up at the dock, or try to. The sun was behind him, but his face was plain under the brim of a Panama hat. He was thinner than Joshua remembered.

The launch scritched on the beach, and Mark put one bare foot on its prow as though he was going to shove it off again, rested the muzzle of his rifle on the stem between his big toe and the toe next to it, and balanced it there with his right hand on the butt.

"This man facing you is Mark Richardson," said Joshua. "Mark ain't putting down his gun. You might say I'm talking to you as deputy sheriff, just appointed, and Mark is my gun, so to speak. The fact is I don't want any shooting here in Chokoloske, now or ever. But if you make it come to that, Mark is facing up to it."

Clayton looked at Mark but spoke to Joshua — "First time I ever heard of a white man hiding behind a nigger."

"Ain't hiding no place," said Joshua. "I'm taking you to Key Alva to answer charges about a man named McLevy, who used to live where you now got your sugar cane. It's according to law."

"Law!" exclaimed Clayton.

"Handy, but not so handy as Mark here," said Joshua.

"Only law up Lost Man's River is the Clayton Sugar Company."

Useless boast, thought Joshua. Would Payne come from behind the engine? But Joshua seriously considered, for the first time, the possibility of survival, with some kind of hearing, or perhaps even a trial in Key Alva, with witnesses, and he spoke loud enough so that the carpenter and others could hear — "That ain't how I see it. I'm taking you in —"

"Big talk!"

"A man my age gets tire of talking."

"Dale, you know a man don't try anything like this with me and live."

"I've known some who didn't live. How old was Amos Peters, Mark, when he died at the Clayton Sugar Company?"

Mark didn't answer, and Joshua saw that he wasn't able to speak. He had an extra shell in his teeth, for fast reloading if he had to fire his Sharps.

"I'll tell you, Clayton," said Joshua. "Amos Peters was sixteen. I know you didn't kill Amos Peters, not you yourself. You just fixed it so it happened, like that big riot in Myrtle years back, and the bushwhacking of Joseph Rourke. You're a low murdering scorpion has to be stomped. I know it and you know I know it. You got any sting left?"

There was an indeterminate time of silence. A slight breeze lapped ripples on the beach and against the stern of the launch. Clayton did not speak. Joshua knew his time had come. The owner of the Clayton Sugar Company stood by the wheel of his launch, planted there it seemed, and Joshua sensed the gathering of sinews in the heavy muscular body under the white shirt...the man's face was in shadow under the wide-brimmed Panama hat, and a glint of sun made his red beard shine.

Clayton reached for his gun.

Mark's rifle whirled level and fired.

The heavy bullet tore into Clayton's chest, passed out his back, and splashed a hundred yards out in the channel.

Clayton's right hand was closed on the butt of his revolver, which was only half out of its holster.

Somewhere a woman screamed.

Mark was running out on the dock. Already he had reloaded.

Where was the Gray Man?

From the dock, Mark could look down into the launch. He lowered his rifle. He wouldn't have to shoot down at Sanford Payne or anyone else.

Clayton had propped himself so that he was still standing even after Mark's bullet passed through him.

Joshua shot him with his Enfield. Couldn't have it said that Clayton was shot only by a black man.

Clayton fell.

As sharks go after any bloody organism, men came from the town in a rush, with guns, to join in shooting the body of Clayton. The carpenter came. Will Wheeler had somehow got himself a large revolver, and he came.

Joshua found himself on the dock beside Mark—"I don't know why I can't keep back tears, Mark. I'm old enough so I don't have too long anyhow." But in his elation at being alive he couldn't think any more about the Gray Man, whose presence in the launch might have meant he would now be dead. He couldn't soil his feelings by thinking about Sanford Payne any more, by wondering why he hadn't come. He noticed Wheeler emptying his revolver in the body of Clayton and said, "What has to be done can have consequences that make a man ashamed."

It happened there was a Seminole on the beach, an unarmed man who took no part in the shooting. He made a remark.

"Chitkolalayoke," repeated Joshua, and translated—"Rattlesnake. If you gentlemen agree," he said to those viewing the body, "I propose we take old Rattlesnake over to Rattlesnake Key and bury him."

Mark and some others towed the sharpie next to the launch *Laura*, and the body was put on a stained part of the deck where fish were cleaned.

The men who went to Rattlesnake Key made only a few comments. One tied a piece of rope around the neck of the corpse—"He warn't good enough for shooting." The carpenter said, "Now I can go as I please without fear of getting my throat cut." A fisherman who often worked with Mark said, "Us colored people can breathe again."

Rattlesnake Key was a desolate sandbar with one small clump of twisted mangroves, palmettos and tough grasses. On the lee side, the channel was so still that the sharpie could be eased aground in two feet of water. A couple of men heaved the body over the side, and a couple more grabbed the feet and dragged it on shore.

It was a quick matter to dig a deep hold in the sand, which immediately began to fill with salt water. When the body was dumped into this hole, when rocks from the ballast of the sharpie were chunked down on top of it, and when the sand over the spot was brushed smooth, somebody said, "Now—I reckon he won't get up again."

XXV

At ten minutes before twelve, as Julia was adjusting her widow's veil before the mirror in the guest room of her daughter and son-in-law's house in Fort Harrison, there was a knock on the door. "I'm all ready," she said.

The door opened and Caroline came in. She was dressed in black and her eyes were red. "The carriage is here," she announced and then, looking at her mother's face, went on, "You ought to cry too, Ma. You'd feel better."

"For many years, while Tom was alive, I stopped lying to him. It would be a foolish thing to lie now, to you or anyone, now that he's dead."

Her blunt inference that she was not saddened by Tom's death, and that she freely acknowledged this state of her feelings, made Caroline cry again. Julia regretted that she'd spoken so bluntly, and she continued, "I've already cried, many times, for the true father you never had, Caroline. I can understand if you do your crying now."

As Lawrence handed her into the carriage, she felt that he resented her composure. He said, "This has been done for you, mother, and for Caroline of course."

With Lawrence she felt she could be brutal—"For Caroline, yes. For yourself, too. For your connections here in Fort Harrison. This funeral is like most funerals. It's for the living, not for the dead, or even for anyone who's died a little with the dead."

For a few minutes they rode toward the church in silence. William was in his Sunday suit. He'd refused to wear a mourning band and had quarreled with Caroline about it.

As president of the Pelican Bank, Lawrence Eddy could not permit the body of his father-in-law, and a man about to be made lieutenant colonel of the volunteers, to be treated like carrion. Three days after the shooting, the schooner *Bonefish*, which had already brought the widow and her son to town, went to Rattlesnake Key. On board were an undertaker, two laborers with shovels, Lawrence Eddy, Captain Kennedy, a deckhand, and a lone wanderer who happened to be in Chokoloske at the time of the shooting. This man was paid five dollars for guiding them to the site of the burial. After the *Bonefish* returned to Fort Harrison with the exhumed body, he was never seen again in that part of Florida.

There were two letters from Thorstein in the company box at the Fort Harrison post office. In the most recent one he wrote that he was worried sick. He apparently hadn't received the letter she had given Caroline for mailing, and he knew only that Tom was out of prison. There was no telegraph in Fort Harrison. So she gave Kennedy a telegram to dispatch from Payhokee where he was going in the *Bonefish* with sugar and molasses— *Am well. Tom killed. Letter will follow. Love. Julia.* She couldn't feel any satisfaction in Tom's death removing the need for divorce. She just felt excluded from any meaning in the observance of form and customs, and a need for Thorstein that transcended any of the world's conventions. But Tom's death freed feelings she could now indulge. She could delight in William's eagerness to begin a new life as a university student. As a kind of protégé of Thorstein Brach, did William know that he was in some sense acquiring a father? Julia had taught William the Latin words that best described Thorstein. She smiled and broke the dismal silence by quoting them as they rode in the carriage.

William translated for Caroline and Lawrence—"He is happy who is able to learn the causes of things. He stomps under his foot all fear and inexorable fate, and the big racket of greedy Hell."

"Well, that's a fine thought!" exclaimed Lawrence. His enthusiasm was probably a little false because he didn't know what William was talking about, but he was eager to cut short the gloom.

William gave Julia his arm as she got out of the carriage.

She knew by name some of the people standing about, but she avoided their eyes. She was aware of a group of colored people at a little distance from the door to the church. Richard the Barber, in a new blue suit with a black band of mourning on the sleeve, was holding forth. What was he saying about his own role in the life and death of Mr. Thomas Ewell Clayton? His master must be somewhere about, probably in the church.

She could feel William's arm tremble when he saw the silvered casket. She took his hand as they walked along with Caroline and Lawrence, behind an usher, to take the front pew.

The organ began to whine in a soft and sentimental tremolo which in the tradition of ecclesiastical showmanship was calculated to torment the exacerbated nerves of the mourners.

Caroline sobbed.

After a few moments of this barbarism, the officiating minister entered the front of the church by an inconspicuous door in the varnished paneling and strode to the pulpit, his black muslin gown billowing behind him. This minister, a Mr. Ronald Maddox, was a recent and promising graduate of a theological school in South Carolina, and he took his duties earnestly. He was a man above average height, with sparkling black eyes which he employed in a somewhat theatrical fashion, a neatly trimmed bush of curly dark brown hair, and a ruddy lean face.

Julia knew that Lawrence had talked to him about the need for special delicacy and tact.

Once the organ ended its outrage, the minister fixed his dark eyes upon Caroline, whose sobs had attracted his attention, and began—"My beloved, peace be unto you."

Caroline repressed her sobs, and the minister allowed silence to deepen while he looked about at his congregation, which consisted of about a hundred people on the floor of the church and three colored people in the balcony, Richard the Barber and the two servants of the Eddys.

The Reverend Maddox read from an open Bible: "In the end of the Sabbath, as it began to dawn toward the first day of the week, came Mary Magdalene and the other Mary to see the sepulchre..."

Having attended funerals before, Julia realized that the minister was going to talk about immortality of the soul. It occurred to her that Thorstein had no religion—he was too busy learning causes and stomping inexorable fate. She wondered about the effect of what had happened on her own religious beliefs. Immortality? She couldn't bear the thought of meeting Tom in another world. Her soul and his could never exist in the same spiritual sphere. The avowal of marriage as a compact made in Heaven, lasting to eternity, beyond death, seemed an outrageous affliction related to her past confusions and errors. She didn't know what she believed.

She listened to the minister.

He plunged into a complicated theological proof that the soul was immortal. The ingenuity of his explanations provided newspaper copy and conversation for the devout. "It is natural for mankind to have one world at a time," he said. "However, two worlds are ours: this world of material shadows, of strange and unsubstantial forms which often seem the only reality, so frail is human knowledge; and, on the other hand, there is that other world, unseen but not unreal, untouched but not unknown, the world of thought, the world of our deepest spiritual emotions, the world of our everlasting souls..."

For a time, as Julia sat with bowed head to shut out the sight of the casket, so that only the overpowering scent of flowers and the minister's numbing assurances could penetrate her senses, it did indeed seem painfully desirable to attain a sleepwalking state in which the unseen world of everlasting souls was the only reality. The world of the Clayton Sugar Company, with its bestiality and beatings and shootings, of the almost playfully schemed and unpunished murder of Joseph Rourke, of the complacently approved slaughter in Myrtle, of the bloodthirsty craze for war staged every day on the parade ground in Fort Harrison—the world in which she herself had been chained to a tyrant and a killer—still chained by her very presence at this ceremony—was this a mere world of shadows?

Julia became impatient. Shadows? Unsubstantial forms? Hardly! To claim so was to scorn her life.

The Reverend Maddox finally arrived at that part of his funeral sermon which bore specifically upon the deceased—"Never was there a man whose energy and initiative provided better evidence here on Earth of God's gift of immortality of the soul. The achievements of Thomas Ewell Clayton will be visible for a long time, and that will remind us of mankind's resolve to copy that permanence which in a true sense will be achieved only in Heaven. There are steel rails linking the Atlantic and the Gulf. There are countless spurs tapping the timber reserves of yellow pine and cypress. There are trackless morasses of our fair state now made productive..."

Julia had taken it for granted that the minister would have something to say about Tom, and in spite of Lawrence talking to him about delicacy and tact that he might not entirely ignore Tom's crimes. She felt ready to face publicly her own guilt by association with him. But this fatuous whitewash job in the pulpit was an attack on the dignity and meaning of the church. He concluded by pointing out that the Clayton Sugar Company and the Pelican Bank had opened up this part of Florida to other enterprises. Fort Harrison had boomed. Cattle ranches and the fishing industry thrived. The dear departed one was an intrepid pioneer, one of the last in a country that was rapidly destroying its last frontiers, to whom the community, the church, the state, and the whole nation owed a debt of gratitude. "When any tourist comes to Florida, or when at any breakfast table a man, a woman, or a child takes a spoonful of sugar, may he think of Thomas Ewell Clayton and his achievements!"

It occurred to Julia that this ambitious minister wasn't the only person overwhelmed by Tom. At one time the President of the United States. Arthur Wilkins. Pamlico and Gulf employees and bosses at the sugar company. Sanford Payne. Lawrence Eddy. The lawyer Smallstock. Even Caroline, in her confused and hurt way. And more than anyone else, probably, Laura Wilkins.

At the final moments of the service, Julia couldn't help trembling, and she had the bitter thought that her disgust and anger might be taken for grief. William put his arm around her.

"Oh Lord, bless the wife this man has left behind and sustain her...forever and ever. Amen."

The ordeal was over—almost. Condolences.

Sanford Payne came, confident of mutual understanding, a wide mourning band on the sleeve of his gray suit—"If there's anything I can do, Miz Clayton—"

She said, coldly, "No, there's nothing."

He had to unburden himself of self-reproach because he hadn't been with Tom on the fatal trip to Chokoloske—there was nobody like Tom and now Sanford felt like an old bottle being thrown away and maybe it would have been better if he had died in Chokoloske, too.

Julia couldn't bring herself to sympathize with him, but she did ask what he was going to do, now that there was no longer a place for him in the Clayton Sugar Company.

He brightened a bit and said that the "Dutch feller" who worked for Mr. Wilkins had found a spot for him in the Pamlico and Gulf, which was going ahead with railroad trestles across the keys.

Now, this was an appropriate absurdity after an absurd ceremony which concluded a number of absurd relationships, including one of her own! So Sanford was going to work for the man whom he and Tom had plotted to murder!

Six soldiers from among the parade ground volunteers were bringing the casket out of the church and bearing it toward the hearse.

"There's something you can do for me, after all, Sanford," she said.

"Just anything at all, Miz Clayton."

"I do not wish to go to the cemetery. It will take a load off my mind if you sort of represent me at the cemetery. Not that I'm expected to say anything, or that you'll be expected to say anything. But if anybody asks about me, and I don't expect anybody will, you'll be there to say I just don't feel like going to the cemetery. I don't feel it's necessary for me to see Tom being put in the ground, this time for keeps."

William convinced Caroline that there was no need for her to go to the cemetery, either. In the carriage, on the way back to the big house acquired with the money of Laura Wilkins, Caroline seemed quite recovered.

And there—sitting on the steps to the front porch, a suitcase next to him with a rumpled jacket tossed over it, in shirtsleeves because of heat, sweaty and dirty from three days of constant travel on trains and the final steamer trip from Payhokee—was Thorstein Brach. As he'd said in his last letter, he'd been worried.

*

When Laura arrived in New York on the *Empress*, her husband greeted her, alive and aggressively cheerful, anticipating a divorce negotiated with less hostility than he'd faced in the recent acquisition of an oil company near bankruptcy.

For a number of pettifogging business reasons Arthur had deviated from recent routine. He had not taken his private train across Florida when he was expected to do so. Thus, he had avoided what she and Tom had planned for him.

Nothing for Laura to do but go back to Florida on the private train that was supposed to be wrecked—with Arthur! And to the Alhambra Hotel in St. Vincent. The marble palace which Arthur was building further south was not yet ready for occupancy. By wonderful good luck, the lawyer Claude Lyman had become ill during his days at sea on the *Empress*. So Arthur still hadn't changed his will.

On a morning that began like any other, she came across a front-page item in *The St. Vincent Chronicle*:

Fort Harrison, July 27 — Thomas Ewell Clayton, President of the Clayton Sugar Company and pioneer in south Florida development, was killed by gunfire of unknown persons in Chokoloske at about one-thirty in the afternoon of July 25…In Chokoloske, residents were unwilling to talk to reporters, but…Mr. Clayton was preparing to go to Cuba with…Funeral services…

Laura never read the whole item. She threw herself screaming on the floor and was only kept from hurting herself by first a maid, then by nurses.

Arthur came to see her while she lay in bed, cold and stiff. Her physical breakdown didn't keep her from understanding Arthur's mood — how Tom's death and her own collapse gave him an opportunity for self-aggrandizement. He was nauseating in his magnanimity. Now that the divorce was imminent, he could acknowledge that she'd contributed to his peerless life, had kept him fired up, had put juice in his old balls. Now the silly fool thought he was going on to something better and so was gently condescending in his inquiries about how she felt. His rotten conceit galled her, but she lay without moving and said nothing.

He assured her with an appearance of kindness that the news was true — Tom Clayton was dead. Divinely beyond jealousy, he paid tribute to his wife's former lover. It was more significant that the man was his own erstwhile protégé. Neither Claude Lyman nor Grotius Van Bibber nor any of the younger men, especially his own son, seemed from the perspective of nearly threescore years and ten to have given him the gratification in work and achievement he'd shared with Tom Clayton. "What nerve the man had!" he declared. "Lined up those railroad bosses and Van Bibber's crew like he was fixing up a shooting match with clay ducks. And then by George he put the main line through to Payhokee in jig time. But he was cruel. Always lived among violent people. Just the same I wish he was still around and working for me. He wouldn't balk at putting that railroad across the keys. He wouldn't be fazed if a man fell off piling and fed the sharks. Not him! I'm being honest with you, Laura. I don't care any more about you and him. I wish this hadn't happened…"

XXVI

After an insensate summer, after the divorce, Laura was retired to a fifteen-room hunting lodge in the Adirondacks with an annuity of twenty-five thousand dollars a year. Arthur owed that much and more to his own reputation as a Christian gentleman. The lodge was furnished with a pipe organ, and her rustication was assuaged by friends, most often by the musician Johann Mowrer.

When the world of sound flooded through the open windows out among the pines where in summer Laura took her afternoon tea, she could dream of the past, or simply dream dreams, the real past and real dreams fusing to form new expectations. She could in the same fantasy alight from the yacht *Empress*, ride a carriage in triumphant procession after the conquest of Cuba, and be saved from the raging Atlantic by the strong arm of her red-locked lover.

Often it seemed that Tom was still alive.

Once, when Ouija repeatedly spelled *red*, she smashed the board and went to bed.

A year after Tom's death, she began to write letters to the Czar of Russia, addressing her missives to the Hermitage in St. Petersburg and putting a dollar's worth of stamps on the envelopes:

> Dear Alexander,
>
> You will at first be surprised by this letter. It comes from one you do not know at present, although you are destined to know her better than anyone else in the world. Do not ask me how I know this...our lives are entwined by mysterious powers that defy human intelligence.
>
> I am at present held prisoner by a vicious American millionaire...Oh my dear Alexander, it has come to me in a dream that I shall bear you a child, a great hero, who will

continue the name of Romanoff forever and ever, to all eternity...

She wrote many letters in this vein. When Czar Alexander did not reply, she wrote similar sentiments to the Kaiser of the German Empire. She signed herself *Laura Regina*.

The intensity of her life of the imagination seemed reflected in her physical well-being. Magnificent in beauty, she sat in the great central room of her lodge and conversed with animation or listened to Johann Mowrer's music, hearing the sound of the sea, the magic language of power, the unutterable inner melodies of desire.

*

Julia and Thorstein lived as wife and husband in an unpretentious seven-room house in Madison but never acquired documents attesting the legality and presumably the sanctity of their union. The problem was property. The disposal of Richmond Plantation, through Tom's husbandly authority, was a painful memory, and Julia was determined that nothing like that would ever happen again. She consulted the lawyer Smallstock about the sugar company and the majority shares in the Pelican Bank which she'd inherited. He hemmed and hawed for several hours, but the upshot was that the law in almost all and perhaps all states confirmed property rights of single women much better than those of married women. She felt that she alone was responsible for the sugar company and the bank, and that she wouldn't water down this responsibility through marriage. Happily, Thorstein didn't want the responsibility anyway. For both of them the law was a pig, especially regarding marriage. But from the perspective of its muddy sty, Julia, as the single widow of the enterprising Thomas Ewell Clayton, could sell property, buy property and manage property as she chose—thank you!

Everything up Lost Man's River was sold to a company in which Arthur Wilkins was a silent partner. After meeting the new management, Julia believed that life up Lost Man's River was going to be as humane as possible under prevailing conditions.

She bought a dairy farm.

She remained the majority stockholder of the Pelican Bank in Fort Harrison, traveled there every winter, with Thorstein, to see her daughter and five grandchildren, and to audit the books of the bank so that her son-in-law wouldn't be able to steal.

William liked study, became a Latin professor at Amherst College in Massachusetts, and wrote a book on Roman farming as revealed in Virgil's *Georgics*. He married, and he and his wife had one child.

Thorstein, always absorbed with the causes of things, thought he knew why he remained faithful to Julia. Property, owned or simply desired, made people too restless and anxious for love. Whether they had property or didn't have it, the frustrated desire for it, or for more of it, constantly reminded them of their shortcomings so that they felt like worms. Thus, the relationship with property destroyed any possible confidence in emotional power, and people salved their injured egos with the cynical conviction that any person's selection and commitment for love was pathetic self-delusion. A loveless person had to believe that everyone else was loveless, too. He himself had once believed this—without ever putting it in so many words. The reason he'd believed this was that he'd been rootless and poor, and so couldn't know what he was capable of. He'd been more infected by the tumefaction of property than he'd realized!

Julia thought there was nothing more noble than seeking the causes of things—even the austere buildings of the University of Wisconsin must admire Thorstein! During their first month together she worried that her life had made her hard, unworthy. Then, with the daily play of her mind, and his, and with the daily touching, she stopped worrying. Was it possible that the wild beat of rages in her blood had braced her for a new journey? Was she now able to sing the fall leaves off the trees in her new northern land? Was her body warmer while the powdered snow was deep? Did her spirit come up and blossom in the thawing earth of spring?

What had she become after so many throes and convulsions? What a mystery!

About the Author

John Ashworth, novelist, journalist and playwright, was educated at Harvard and taught writing at Columbia University for twenty years. Included among his works is the O. Henry prize short story, *High Diver*, that was made into a film by Universal Studios. Eudora Welty commented on "the vitality in its grim symbolism and its bone-crushing action . . . a firm piece of work, wasting not a word or a moment."

As a journalist, he analyzed foreign news reports for the Office of War Information in World War II, and did a stint as foreign correspondent for the *Hindustan Times*. He wrote for the Boston *Transcript* and major national magazines such as *Harper's* and the *Atlantic Monthly*. As playwright, he wrote *Canterbury*, based on Chaucer's *Canterbury Tales*, and *Burning Bright*, a play about the sedition trial of the English poet, William Blake.

When he died in 1993, Ashworth had just completed this novel, based on research done while living in Florida in the 1950s. Using a wire recorder, he had interviewed survivors of the infamous race riot and massacre at Rosewood in 1923, in which the African American town was wiped out. Years later, the survivors and descendants sued the state of Florida and won, in 1994, a small but historic settlement. The incident is an integral part of the novel, set in Florida in the 1890s, when Northern big business collided with old plantations, the frontier, and a legacy of racial antagonisms.

The Florida Historical Society

Celebrating over 150 years of service to the people of Florida

The Florida Historical Society, founded in 1856, is the only statewide historical society in Florida. The Society is a 501(c)(3) not for profit organization as recognized by the Internal Revenue Service. The primary mission of the Society is to collect, preserve and publish documents and other materials relating to the history of Florida and its peoples.

Membership Benefits Include:
* A complimentary annual subscription to all Society publications:
  The Florida Historical Quarterly (4 issues) and the Society Report (4 issues).
* A 10% discount on all items in the The Print Shoppe.
* Free admission to the Library and Archives as well as the Saturday Lecture Series.
* Invitations to all events and functions sponsored by the Florida Historical Society.

For Membership Information:
  Call: (321) 690 - 1971
  Fax: (321) 690 - 4388
  e-mail: membership@flahistory.net
  website: www.florida-historical-soc.org